WATER BOY

A NOVEL

GARY REISWIG

SIMON & SCHUSTER
NEW YORK LONDON TORONTO SYDNEY TOKYO SINGAPORE

SIMON & SCHUSTER
Simon & Schuster Building
Rockefeller Center
1230 Avenue of the Americas
New York, New York 10020

SIMON & SCHUSTER and colophon are registered trademarks
of Simon & Schuster Inc.

Designed by Hyun Joo Kim
Manufactured in the United States of America

1 3 5 7 9 10 8 6 4 2

Library of Congress Cataloging in Publication Data
Reiswig, Gary
Water boy: a novel / Gary Reiswig
p.   cm.
1.City and town life—United States—Fiction. 2.Fundamentalism—
Fiction. 3.Football—Fiction. I.Title.
PS3568.E523W38   1993   93-2218
813'.54—dc20   CIP
ISBN 0-671-79506-6

To my father, Fred, my mother, Della, and other people on the Great Plains who taught me—never say die.

AFTER THE GLORY

PART I

CHAPTER 1

H is was the first funeral my parents ever took me to, and I wanted to stare and stare and keep staring. My father, over my mother's objection, had allowed me to stand up in the church pew so I could see Jimmy Lee Watson floating inside his casket.

I can still smell the gladioli and perfume and soap, smells I have since always associated with funerals, and I can still hear the preacher comforting the family, was the will of God, he said, which brought the death of such a young boy, blessed be the name of the Lord, and the people shouted "amen" and "praise him."

When my eyes got tired from looking at Jimmy Lee, I entertained myself by watching another family who sat one row in front of us. They had a boy the age of Jimmy Lee and me named Danny. My mother thought the boy's name was odd because their last name was Boone and Daniel Boone was a historical person. For some reason she disliked the Boones although they were members of our church, the First Baptist Church of Cimarron, but I can still see revulsion on my mother's face that day when they sat down near us. My father liked the Boone family. He planned to write a story in his newspaper about them. Even I could see there was something extraordinary about the Boones.

Arved, the father, never walked anywhere without holding on to either his wife or son. The mother, Thelma, who was a blond, large-boned woman, conveyed a sureness that neither the man nor the boy questioned. Danny seemed sad, mature beyond his age.

Danny used to play with Jimmy Lee. They were close neighbors, and the Watsons had tried to convert Danny's family to the Pentecostal way, but the Boones liked our church because our pastor was known as a hard worker who helped out any church member who came up short-handed in harvest.

During the service, Danny Boone turned around to look at me. When I caught his eye, I made a face. He ducked, hiding behind his father. In a minute or two, he peeked out and made a face back. This game went back and forth distracting me from thinking about how Jimmy Lee had died. It was also the beginning of my friendship with Daniel Boone, a friendship that changed my life.

I had not been a good friend of Jimmy Lee, the dead boy, because we were of different churches. We were, however, born the same night in Doc McGrath's little hospital, and our mothers were roommates, because there was only one room in the maternity ward. The day before Jimmy Lee passed away, my mother and Mrs. Watson bumped into each other on Main Street. While they reminisced about their stay in the hospital, Jimmy Lee showed me the marbles he had with him. I had a few of my own marbles, although Mother never allowed me to take them out of the house, insisting I'd lose them, and Mother did not like anything to be lost. But I had already begun to disobey her, had already begun to sneak. Jimmy Lee and I slipped away, squatted down next to Old Man Goggin's store, and began a game, his cat eyes against my clears, for keeps. I was a deadeye shooter, my father had taught me, and I had won half a dozen of Jimmy Lee's marbles before our mothers stopped us.

Both of us cried. I cried because Mother scolded me for disobeying her, and he cried because he wanted his marbles back. But both of us knew better than to tell we had been playing for keeps. Keeps is gambling and gambling's a sin, but we begged them to please let us play together. They promised, the very next day, they said.

By the next morning, Mother had changed her mind. She'd had a dream, she told my father at breakfast. She had been warned by our Lord there was danger out at the Watson farm. Besides, she was suspicious that the Watsons might indoctrinate me with their crazy Pentecostal ideas.

"Emma," my father said, as he looked down at his feet, "why, why do you . . ." and then he didn't finish. He stood up and grabbed me by the wrist. "I'm taking Sonny out to the Watsons' farm so he can play with that little boy. He has no friends, Emma. It's time our son had a friend."

We headed to the car. He was dragging me by the arm. I looked over my shoulder, I could hardly keep my feet. My mother was standing in the doorway. "Sonny, be very careful," she called. She covered her eyes with her hands.

The Watsons lived in a square, unpainted farmhouse. My father told Mrs. Watson he'd pick me up that evening before supper, and drove off.

"Let's play marbles," I suggested. Jimmy Lee refused. "Let's make a playhouse," he said. I refused. I took out the marbles I had brought with me, the ones I had won from him yesterday, and a few of my own that I had hidden in my overall pockets. I made a circle for the game. When Jimmy Lee saw his marbles in the circle, he stomped away.

He went into the hayfield that his father had raked the day before and began constructing a playhouse in a hay windrow near the center of the field. I was determined not to make a dumb playhouse, but I played where I could watch him. The wind blew the

11

scent of sweet grass and whipped little pieces of straw into the air. When he finished, he had a cave in the hay big enough for the two of us. When he crawled inside, it was almost dark. I must not quit my game of solitary marbles to join him in his straw playhouse. My mother had warned me, there's something wrong with this kid.

Mr. Watson hummed, one foot on the tractor's fender, making sure the windrow was pulled straight in so the baler wouldn't clog. Around and around the hayfield he circled, the tractor popping and shivering, the tines of the baler fluffing up the hay before it entered the packing chamber. Each round, the rig came closer to the clump near the middle. I had hit twelve shots in a row when I looked up and saw the baler heading toward the playhouse.

I knew how to cup my hands and shout through them. "Jimmy Lee's in the playhouse!" But Mr. Watson was a good long ways away, and the baler was noisy. I ran inside the house. "Jimmy Lee's in the playhouse," I told Mrs. Watson. Hers was the sweetest smile, and she said later I had been so calm, so polite, she hadn't the faintest idea what I was trying to tell her.

"Yes, I know honey, you should go play with him," she answered.

Tooter Watson admitted he saw the hump in the windrow, and geared down the tractor so the baler wouldn't slug. But his old sidewinder rake often made bunches. He saw nothing unusual enough to make him stop. The wind, the monotony of the tractor's motor, the noise of the baler, and the boredom of waiting for a friend who wasn't coming, must have lulled Jimmy Lee to sleep. Before his mother could get to him, he was packed, bound in baling wire, and spit out the baler's back side.

It was then I began to worry, after I smelled the flowers and looked into Jimmy Lee's face, which lay, stitched together as best they could, within the shiny pale casket. Gone was any sense of childhood safety. I was left shaking with new knowledge, the possibility of horrendous death, and in awe of my mother's vision.

At graveside, Danny Boone stood near me while I stood near my mother. I had on a blue suit, with short pants. My black and white saddle oxfords were nearly new, my father had polished them before the service. I edged my foot over near Danny's so I could see if my foot was larger than his. Mother kept pulling me away, but my wish to be near him was unquenchable, as if our closeness might erase how I felt about Jimmy Lee dying. I stared first at Danny, then up at Arved, his father, who towered over us, taller even than my father. I was drawn to this farmer's sunburned face, to whatever made him different. Arved stood with a sober self-control as if he were listening to some inner voice. My father was a busy, kinetic man, his eyes were always scanning, his hands reaching into the pockets of his tailored suit for scraps of paper on which he wrote notes to remind himself of everything, and he was forever bending down to flick dust off his shoes. Danny's father stood like a rock.

Mother jerked my arm, and bent down to whisper in my ear. "Will you stop staring at that man? It's not polite, the man is blind. Can't you see that?"

My mouth felt dry. There was a hot wind. I licked my lips, they were cracking. In front of us was the preacher, and beyond the preacher was the small mound of fresh earth, the gravestones, the barbed wire fence around the graveyard, and eventually the horizon. That was all, except the flat monotony of the country.

When the service ended, Danny's mother, as if it were prearranged with my father, invited me to go home with them. My mother refused, but my father interrupted her.

"Everything will be fine, Emma, let the boys play." He clipped his words in a tone of finality he rarely used. As if he had anticipated the moment, he stepped to the car, opened the trunk, and lifted out a brand-new football. "It's a present," he said, "you boys play ball." Then he added, speaking to my mother, "That's what Jesus wants boys to do, have a little fun. God knows there's little enough of that around here."

G A R Y   R E I S W I G

Danny and I skipped off, tossing the football between us. Danny missed a catch and the ball bounced among the tombstones and we chased it, oblivious to the sacrilege of tromping over graves. Arved Boone walked with his arm tucked through the crook of his wife's elbow. Mother's words came back. "The man is blind. Can't you see that?" Being near a blind man seemed so dangerous. Suddenly, I remembered the disaster that had taken Jimmy Lee to heaven. The happiness I felt about my new friend sank into my stomach. I knew I had done wrong with Jimmy Lee. I never should have played for keeps; Mother had warned me, it was wrong. I turned back to look. The pupils of Mother's eyes were small dots against her eyeballs, her mouth was open as if she were screaming, but there was no sound. Before I could run to her, Danny pulled me into the back seat of the Boones' car.

After that, my father, afraid my mother was making me into a sissy, sent me home with Danny after church almost every Sunday. Football was the only game Danny liked to play except cowboys and Indians, which we played in the pastures and draws. Whatever we played, I played with great intensity in order to distract myself. I seemed to face death each moment I was away from my mother. I have been unable to shake that feeling no matter how far I have lived from Cimarron.

14

CHAPTER 2

J ust before the road from Texas makes a slight bend and you can see the heat waves rise off the low asphalt roofs of town, there is a large road sign with words painted in night-glow letters: JESUS DIED FOR OUR SINS. HE IS LORD IN CIMARRON. In Cimarron, the only faith is the simple Protestant Faith, the only source of faith is the Bible. In Cimarron, there are no theologians, no priests, no religious statues. The ministry is not a career to be selected; Cimarron's pastors have been called, not hired, and when they preach, they speak not merely the "word of God," they speak "the *words* of God."

To put it plainly, one message holds out hope in Cimarron. JESUS IS COMING SOON! This longing is apocalyptic, hoped for, prayed for.

My mother's family belonged to the Church of England. She came to Cimarron when she was four with my grandfather Raleigh after my grandmother died. To handle his grief, Granddad sold the estate that had come to him from his dead wife's family, came to Oklahoma, and purchased a five thousand acre ranch in Cimarron County. He found the land was vast and almost inviolable, not as pure, as chaste, as willing as he had hoped. He found ranching in the Panhandle had no similarity to raising Herefords in England. He lost his cattle in blizzards and to the lightning, then he sold the land, section by section, to pay his bills.

Through those years as he was losing the ranch, he doted on his daughter, buying expensive gifts he could not afford, and imprisoning her in the ranch house. Not that he locked her up, it was his generosity, his gentleness, his vulnerability, the same qualities that had made him easy prey to the unforgiving prairie, that kept my mother bound to him at home. They lived in the ranch house, decorated with the memorabilia of their English family, almost as if they were husband and wife. My mother's only contact with the outside world, except the one-room school she attended, was the small nondenominational church down the road from the ranch. She walked there every Sunday. The pastor, a nearby farmer, baptized her when she was eleven, and by thirteen she taught a Sunday school class of children who were nearly her own age. She never attended high school, had no dates, and belonged to no clubs. She stayed home to keep house for her father.

In her dreams, Mother intended to marry a refined gentleman like her father. She saw her husband sitting with her beside the fire while she knitted sweaters, hats, and mittens for her daughter, who practiced the piano, playing simple Brahms and Mozart, whom she had learned about from books brought with them from England. She imagined this fireside scene despite the fact there were no trees for firewood, and no fireplaces. She waited through her teens as creditors hounded her father, and the land shrank until they owned a piece of ground no larger than a city lot. Through her twenties she took care of her father, waiting long past the time women got married.

On one of the rare occasions she ventured away from my grandfather, she met my father at a box supper social given to support the Sunday school where she taught. Granddad objected to her plan to go out, and became ill the moment it was time for her to leave. She went to the box supper anyhow. She asked a neighbor to look in on her father until she returned. When she came home, the woman said her father was fine, and what she needed was a husband, that it was God's will for women to marry and have children, and that it was time. My mother knew the man she wanted. She had met him at the box supper.

My father was an experienced man, already in his early thirties, and had an established business. He had worked for a printer in Guthrie for twelve years, and had saved enough money to buy the defunct *Times-Democrat* in Cimarron. He was a natural salesman, and became successful almost immediately, applying the skills he had learned both in Guthrie and in the print shop of the Kiamichi Baptist Orphanage where he had grown up. With money coming in, he became a snappy dresser, and courted many eligible women, but by the time my mother met him, he was ready to settle down. Emma Raleigh was the most refined woman he had ever met, and the Raleighs still gave the appearance of being more affluent than they were.

William Schultz was the most gorgeous man my mother had ever seen. But she knew nothing about his family, which worried granddad Raleigh. When Mother tried to introduce her dashing newspaperman, her father refused to extend the common courtesy of a handshake. Despite her father's objections, they proceeded with wedding plans. Emma Raleigh believed William Schultz, with or without pedigree, was her first and last chance to have a husband. They were married only four weeks after they first met.

William moved into the Raleigh home with Emma and her father. Three months later, the bank foreclosed on the house. My father mortgaged the newspaper, and purchased a house in town. At the insistence of my father, granddad Raleigh was moved to the old folks home. It was like ripping an infant out of her crying father's arms. Mother never forgave him for banning her father from their house.

By that time, I was already on the way. After I was born, my father spent most evenings at the office working with his presses, and the cafe booth rumors whispered he was also playing with the ladies.

Instead of the daughter she longed for, my mother gave birth to me. My oversized head ripped her apart on the way out. She described her days after my birth as "her descent into hell," and it was not until the new, young Pastor Toon helped her find "the real Jesus" that she came out of her depression.

When I was old enough to behave properly, my mother took me with her to visit my grandfather on Sundays. Every Sunday, he'd ask the same questions.

"How's your husband?"

"Fine," my mother answered.

"Has he bought any land yet?"

"No, not yet."

"Man's not much good without land," he'd say.

"Well, Bill's too busy to worry about land and livestock, he is making us a good living with the paper."

Granddad would turn his head, and look at her skeptically. Then we knew it was time to go, and we'd leave.

"Is he in heaven?" I asked when he died.

"I don't know," Mother said. "I just don't know. He was sprinkled as a baby, but never baptized in the true way." She began to weep.

When we buried my grandfather, my father said to my mother, "Well, your dad finally got himself a piece of land he can't lose." My mother's body stiffened as if she had been stabbed.

Mother comforted herself by retreating more deeply into her faith. "God speaks to me in my dreams," she told me. "God has a plan for you, Sonny. God gave us a sign when you were born."

My mother had nursed me until the day of my third birthday when my father gave her an ultimatum and left the house to stay in the tiny sleeping room he had arranged at the newspaper office. What was the sign that had made her allow me to suckle long past the time I could ask to nurse with a complete sentence? Whatever it was, after three days of humiliation caused by my father's absence, she capitulated and took away her breast. But by then Mother and I shared an intimacy that fed both of us in ways even a mother's milk cannot, no touch off limits, no comfort spared.

Imprinted on the screen that hangs behind my prying eyes are vivid, yet wavering, images of those early years, when I slept in Mother's room, watching my father's angry face as he headed for his own bedroom; then I heard my mother pray that I claim my place in God's plan, and be a great preacher. I imitated her breathing as it became deep and regular, my head out of the covers so I could see the sheet hugging her curvaceous figure in the dim night light.

I was eight, it was just after Jimmy Lee died and I had met Danny, when my father finally forced Mother to move me from her room onto the friendship bunk beds he had purchased for my own room. When she gave in, she sent me into a room of spinning terror. It was then the Lord appeared to me. It was a few days after my father had brought me a package of metal soldiers, twelve Union and eleven Confederates, that he had found in a junk shop. My mother had thrown away my marbles.

We had planned to have a picnic on Clear Creek that weekend. My father had promised we'd play catch, so the football was packed with the lunch in the picnic hamper and I was helping Mother carry it. Mother had insisted that I not take the soldiers because she was afraid I might lose them and she knew how much they cost. But I had sneaked one into my pocket, a Union rifleman down on one knee. We stood in our front yard while my father brought the car around. A small cloud hovered overhead but it didn't look stormy. One hand was wrapped around the metal soldier inside my pocket, the other was on the basket handle. A prickling sensation ran up my spine, and Mother's hair stood straight out for a few seconds before it frizzed up into tight little curls, and there was a crackling noise, like paper being crumpled or bacon frying. In a blue screaming streak, lightning struck our crab apple tree.

My father careened around the corner, having heard the bolt of lightning and the clap of thunder. I was screaming hysterically, but Mother was calm. "Look at that, Bill, God split that barren little tree right down the middle. It's a warning from our Lord."

"A warning about what?" My father laughed, as if he saw something funny about how we had nearly been hit by lightning.

"About being frivolous, we're going down to the church," and she grabbed my hand, jerking it out of my pocket. I had no choice but to hide the soldier in my clenched fist as best I could, and to go with her, sobbing.

When we returned from the church in the late afternoon, I investigated the doomed tree exercising both caution and curiosity, for I had heard Mother say lightning never strikes twice in the same place. A rock had been heaved up at the base of the tree where the trunk had split and expanded. I took the rock into the house with me. It was smooth, oblong, and had some interesting glittery specks in it.

That evening, I was in the bathroom preparing for bed. Mother had filled my tub, and left me alone for a few minutes. I had sneaked some toys into the tub. The Confederate fort came under attack from the Union. The battle raged, became violent, there was some splashing. Suddenly, Jesus walked in, closing the door behind him.

He looked almost like I expected him to, maybe a little more bald in front, but otherwise the same. He wore long hair like in the pictures I'd seen, but no beard. His eyes were steel gray, and he was almost as tall as the door. He didn't say anything, he just stood there

20

looking at me with a gentle expression. I didn't say anything either because I knew it wasn't respectful. Then he reached into his clothes and brought out a stone. The stone was polished, mostly brown with some white alabaster running through it, and the light reflected off some glittery specks. It was the same stone I had found beneath the tree. He dropped it in the tub, and it made a shell-sized chip in the white enamel. Then, Jesus smiled and walked out. He didn't bother to open the door, he went right through the wall.

I scampered out of the tub, splashing water. Hearing the commotion, Mother hurried in. She had been pushing down the bread she had stirred up, and her hands were coated with flour.

"Jesus was here," I told her. "He gave me this." I reached into the bathtub and handed her the rock.

My mother kneeled down and embraced me, tenderly. Her hands with the flour on them stuck to my wet skin.

"I saw that rock beneath the tree," she said. "This is confirmation. You've been called, Sonny, you're a special boy, a very special boy." She dried me, put me in my pajamas, and we waited for my father.

At first, she didn't tell him anything. To wash, he went upstairs to the bathroom, and he came stomping back downstairs, furious. "Who put that chip in the bathtub?" he bellowed, glaring at me.

I was terrified. But Mother reported, as if the events were nothing more than a good day at school, "Our son saw the Lord."

"The hell he did," my father bellowed, "and I suppose the Lord chipped the tub?"

"That's not important," my mother replied. "It's the fulfillment of the sign, it's what the lightning was about. Jesus said, 'Upon this rock I will build my church.' " She retrieved the stone from where she had hidden it, and held it up in front of my father's face.

My father's fury began to abate. "Emma, don't get started like this."

She pushed him, shoving the rock in his chest until he sat down in the recliner she had given him for his birthday. She brought him his dinner as if nothing had happened.

The next day, the church service began with the baptism of a young woman who had been converted recently. The pastor led her into the baptistery, which was elevated so the congregation could see converts buried in the water. As he lifted her up, having dipped her, I could hear her breath. There was a rushing noise, the swell of music from the organ, and the water running from the woman's hair, and the faint pinkness of the woman's flesh under the white baptismal robe. It seemed there was a holy power in the church. My lying, my sneaking stood in stark contrast to the purity of the young woman who had been baptized.

When the invitation to come forward was sung that day,

> "Are you washed in the blood,
> In the soul-cleansing blood of the lamb?"

I slipped off the pew, walked right in front of my shocked father, and sprinted up the aisle. Our pastor squatted down, and whispered, "Sonny, go back to your parents."

I shook my head. "I want to be a preacher," I said loudly, "and I want to baptize people," I added. The congregation twittered, denim and gabardine rustling.

The pastor said, "Sonny, that's wonderful, but you're too young to decide such important things." Then my mother was beside me.

"You don't understand," she said in a shrill voice. "God put a sign on him, he's been called."

"Even so, he'll have to wait until he's accountable," the pastor said. "Age twelve, thirteen, certainly not before eleven. And Emma, you be careful you're not listening to the devil."

Afterward, people came up to me. "You stay with it, Sonny," Pomp Reed said, "you show them. You'll be a fine preacher, and put the old devil on the run." They all avoided my mother, except Mrs. Shuler and Elberta Munion.

"You know what you're doing," Mrs. Shuler said. "Don't let that preacher scare you."

Elberta said, "Emma, if you ever need to go anywhere, let Sonny stay with me. I'll be happy to keep him." She winked at me, and, with a hand so fat you'd think she couldn't close it, pinched me hard on the cheek.

At bedtime, I slipped my toy soldiers and the kitchen flashlight into my bed. After Mother had tucked me and we had said our prayers, I pulled the covers over my head, turned on the flashlight, then arranged my two armies to do battle on the lumpy terrain of my mattress. They were evenly matched, eleven on each side, because I had selected the rifleman down on one knee, the one that had been hidden in my hand when the lightning struck, to be set apart, to watch.

It was only a few weeks later when my mother decided to be rebaptized. "Not in the church baptistery," she told Pastor Toon, "in the river, like John baptized Jesus. And I want you to wear a brand-new suit," she told him, "not something you've worn to someone's wedding or funeral. A pure, virgin suit. I'll pay for it. Won't we, Bill?" she asked my father. My father spread his hands in weary consent.

"Thank you. I can really use a new suit, even if it gets wet the first time I wear it. And I think this is exactly what you need, Emma, a new baptism, get some old ideas out of your head, get a fresh start with the Lord."

My father and I and a few church members the pastor had called were the witnesses. Mother surprised everyone. She stripped off all her clothes, waded in stark naked. The pastor recovered his poise, said the blessing, and baptized her. She threw her arms around the startled minister, kissed him on his face and neck, pressing her breasts into his wet suit, crying with joy. The water ran out of her hair and down her back. She splashed out of the river, her face serene and radiant, her breasts bobbing, and her pubic hair glistening. The others who had come to witness the baptism had already made a hasty retreat to avoid seeing a naked church member coming out of the river.

She told my father when he asked her why: "I wanted nothing between me and the cleansing waters of holy baptism. But you'll never understand anything holy, will you?"

After that, my parents stopped getting together. Although they had slept in separate rooms since my birth, she sometimes had sneaked in to see him and I could hear him teasing her and her laughing. After her baptism in the river, the house became even more somber than before, and my father stayed at his office later and later.

CHAPTER 3

On the same road where the sign stands that says Jesus is Lord in Cimarron, there's another sign closer to town that proclaims in eye-catching black and gold letters, THIS IS DEVIL COUNTRY. SUPPORT THE CIMARRON DUSTDEVILS.

There are two kinds of boys who grow up in Cimarron, those who play football for the Dustdevils and those who don't. I don't mean football like it's played in the East, a few fans in rickety bleachers—I mean Oklahoma high school football where the Friday night lights ignite stadiums built out of concrete and steel, with fields where the grass is clipped and watered and paid for by public bond issues—I mean stadiums crammed with fans whose lives are dulled with a sameness broken only when the lights flare and the battle begins. In Cimarron, people will die for the Dustdevils.

Danny Boone and I were the closest of friends and when we reached high school age, this was the one difference that set us apart from each other. A few months before we entered high school, I decided not to play football for the Dustdevils.

I will not claim I was as good a football player as Danny. He became a high school all-American. I doubt I had that kind of potential, but the football games we played in childhood were usually close, and the outcome was not predetermined. On the day I stopped playing football for good, he was at my house, and we were playing in the street. I had just tied the score. Danny made a move to run around me, but did not protect the ball. I knocked it out of his hand. It bounced off the hard road right into my hands; I started to run. It seemed like my body exploded. I landed on the side of the road, in the worst patch of sandburrs on our street. I couldn't see, except black, with thousands of pinhole lights twinkling. My head rang. I couldn't breathe. I thought I was dead. Somehow I made it into the house.

My parents were in the living room. By the time I made it inside, I had recovered enough to cry. My shirt was pinned to my skin by the sandburrs. Sandburrs first pierce so easily, but once they're in the flesh, they curl into unforgiving hooks when you try to pull them out. My nose was bleeding, I was sucking in blood and snot and tears. When my father heard my blubbering, his face swelled with disgust.

"Stop bawling," he ordered. "For God's sake, you're nearly fourteen years old! You're too old to cry."

"That's it, Bill," Mother said, "no more football. It's too brutal. I don't want Sonny abused."

"Nonsense," my father said, "it'll help him grow up." Then, he turned to me. His clean-shaven face was confident, his full lips were slightly parted, his green eyes danced. "You have to give it back, hit him as hard as he hits you. Get out there and give it another try." At that moment I swear I hated him. I remembered Jimmy Lee Watson, how Mother had saved me, and how she was the one who had stood beside me when I had gone forward at church. Flooding me were the memories of those warm nights when I slept in her room. I'd show him, the son of a bitch.

I still had the football in my hands, I wasn't a fumbler. I grabbed my mother's scissors and stabbed the ball. The air whistled as it came out, smelling like hot rubber. My mother had her face turned to heaven, her eyes were open but rolled up, the whites were off-color like agates. My father seemed deflated himself. He ran his hands through his hair, took a handkerchief and dusted his shoes, then walked to the laundry chute and shoved it down. He paused to look at me when he went out the door. It was a moment laden with possibility, but I do not blame him for letting it pass.

When school began that fall, Danny went out for the football team. I had aligned myself with my mother. So I hung around the locker room waiting for the others to finish practice.

Our grudge with Brice Miller began that year when we were freshmen. I say "our grudge" because I loathed Brice as much as Danny did, although when the fights started they were always between the two of them. The grudge began the week before the first football game.

Brice was the Dustdevils' star player, but the townspeople, having watched Danny practice his moves as the second-team quarterback, began whispering about him, the future of the team, a glorious future, they sang. Brice did not enjoy having his fans talk about a freshman. He had no interest in sharing the glory.

But Brice was not ignored by any means. The papers had touted him for the all-state team. The *Daily Oklahoman* jumped ahead of my father by calling Brice the "most intimidating football player west of Chickasha."

"Damnit, I only wish I had thought of a phrase like that," my father lamented.

It was true that Brice had the unbridled meanness to be a great football player. He was the best football player the team had developed in years, and was sure to get a college scholarship and go on to play for the glory of the town. However, he lacked a commitment to the work ethic. He didn't train as hard as he should, he sometimes drank beer with the men who hung around the domino parlor and were friends of his father, and sometimes he

smoked and ignored curfew. Brice's lack of commitment to training aggravated Danny, whose dedication to football became more
intense as people hinted of the glory that might be his.

With the help of his Uncle Kirk, Thelma's brother, a star halfback for the Dustdevils in the forties, Danny laid out a course of
old tires that he ran through twice a day. This trained him to lift
his legs high when running, and to develop balance and leg strength
for changing direction in the open field. He believed it was his des-
tiny to be a great Dustdevil player.

Danny complained that Brice was holding the team back with
his lackadaisical attitudes. I told Danny he should talk to Coach
Lipscomb, tell the coach that Brice wasn't keeping the training
rules. But Danny decided to try another tactic. He would show up
Brice Miller for what he really was in practice, in front of the coaches.

That afternoon, Danny, playing defensive halfback, screened
himself behind a linebacker, and when Miller barreled over the defenders at the line of scrimmage, about to break loose for a long
run, Danny knifed in, tackled the big fullback around the ankles,
and smashed him down. Although I knew from playing against
Danny myself that he was a hitter, I thought the explosive ease with
which he had tackled Brice, a senior star fullback, was a fluke, and
I was afraid of what Brice would do to Danny the next time Danny
tried tackling him.

Coach Lipscomb made the offense run the same play, and Danny
did it again. This time, Brice got up very slowly, the wind had been
knocked out of him when he hit the dry turf. I cringed. Danny was
starting something.

Coach was enraged. "Run it again, and do it right this time,
Miller!" For the third straight time, Danny drove Brice Miller, his
training habits, and everything he stood for straight into the snot-
assed ground.

Coach Lipscomb charged onto the field, slapped Danny on the
butt, "Way to hit, Boone." Then he stood up to Brice, inches away,

spitting into the big fullback's face as he shouted, "Miller, you let a fuckin' freshman knock you on your fat ass. That tells me something! Things are going to be different!"

"You're dead," Brice hissed at Danny. Danny glanced toward me and smiled. We made it through practice, but Brice seethed, watching Danny through slitted eyes.

The very next day, I tagged Brice with a nickname. The name was suggested by Cannonball Conner, the assistant football coach, who was head coach of the girls' basketball team.

The girls' coach last year, a blond, twenty-four-year-old man that our superintendent, Egbert, had hired out of Colorado, was fired before the end of his first season because he had a habit of resting his hands on his girls' legs. None of them ever complained, and there was a rumor that the young coach might be seeing one of his girls outside the gymnasium. In the county tournament championship game, the team huddled around the coach, who, while talking girl to girl, stroked their legs, giving them a pep talk, inspiring them. They lost by twenty-five points.

Egbert stomped to the bench, fired the coach, and appointed Cannonball, who was a dwarf, not much bigger than half a man, bug-eyed, webbed fingers on hands no larger than a medium-sized meatball. Egbert figured no Cimarron girl would want Cannonball's hands on her legs.

The day I gave Brice Miller his nickname, I was in the football dressing room. "If you're gonna be around here, Schultz, you might as well be useful," Coach said. So I became the team manager, "the water boy." I didn't mind the job because it gave me a chance to be around Danny and to play tricks. While I repaired equipment, I hid sandburrs in some of the pads. Part of the pleasure was not knowing who might get a pad with a burr in it, a simple pleasure, watching the unlucky one tug at his equipment where the burr poked his skin.

Practice had ended early because it was the day before our first game, and Cannonball bounced around talking about his girls' basketball team as if he were succeeding Henry P. Iba, the legendary coach at A&M. It was Cannonball's first opportunity to coach outside Lipscomb's shadow.

At the opposite end of the dressing room, Brice Miller paraded around naked, flexing to intimidate the younger, less endowed boys, his ego seemingly undiminished by yesterday's humiliation on the practice field. Miller was one of those guys who gets labeled "a stud" in the nakedness of athletic locker rooms. Honking across the room, Cannonball called him over to the old training table that served as the assistant coach's desk.

"Stay away from my basketball girls, Miller," Cannonball bayed, his head only a foot or so above Brice's navel. "Stick that horsedick in one of 'em, she'll never play basketball again. You might even kill 'er."

I tossed a worn knee pad into the pile of discards. "Killer," I shouted, "Killer Miller." The name spread through town like a prairie fire blown by a hot wind. Men in the domino parlor repeated it, nodding and smirking, as they sipped their beverages; women sniggered in the laundry as they whispered to each other explaining why Brice was now called "Killer." From that day, no one except Dovie Lasher ever called Brice Miller by any other name.

Cannonball was concerned because Killer had been dating Dovie, his basketball team's star forward. Dovie had been the girl primarily implicated with the young coach last year, although nothing was ever proven and my father had written an editorial about the right of privacy, and about damage caused to people by unfounded rumors spread by bored busybodies.

Dovie's relationship with Killer was an affair I couldn't figure out, because she could have had any guy in town she wanted. Killer was a bully, and always led the sadistic rites of freshman initiation, taking the boys' pants off, and twisting girls' arms behind their backs, then dousing their chests with cold water to expose which ones wore padded bras. I grant the fact he was handsome, and perhaps his appetite for degrading people gave him a seductive appeal to Dovie.

Dovie Lasher's reputation was not based totally on the rumored affair with the fired coach. First of all, she was the most beautiful girl in town, although she was not fashion-plate beautiful. Freckles dotted the bridge of her nose, and her lips were not thin and Protestant-looking, but full, giving her an exotic look. Her smile made her appear genuine to those who knew her, but taunting, mocking to those who didn't. Her eyes were not properly downcast like women's eyes were supposed to be, but were fully open and soft when they looked at a man.

There was an aura about her, a directness and sweetness that existed alongside of a simple, unadorned power. She flirted with any man she admired and got away with it. It was true some people talked about her, someone was always whispering, but she didn't seem to care, and other people took up for her. She was a Methodist church member in good standing. Yet, she lived under another set of rules, rules not ordained by people inside churches, rules of the community that allowed special girls to flourish outside the usual morals, a girl who is beautiful, a girl who makes the net swish with that sweet sound when the ball goes through.

Over the noon hour on Friday of that week, the day of the first football game, Dovie came to sit with us ninth-grade boys who grouped near the brick wall at the northern end of the school yard. We all waited there while we got old enough to drive, and to drag Main Street. Dovie sat down between Danny and me, leaning so her breast touched Danny's arm. It was obvious, no one could have missed it.

Killer saw Dovie flirting with Danny, so when the bell rang, he caught Danny on the school steps, shoved him against the rail, and ordered: "Stay away from my girl, you little chickenshit, or you'll lose your nuts." The rage on Killer's face would have frightened any normal younger kid, but not Danny. He just crinkled up his eyes in a mocking little grin. As Killer tramped inside, Danny laughed out loud. Like a fool, Killer looked back, and others laughed.

The game that evening against the Shattuck Savages was a near disaster for the Dustdevils, who were expected by the townspeople and the sportswriters to make a run for the state championship. It was a game the Dustdevils should have won easily, but won only by the grace of the Savage kicker who missed an extra point. It was an ineffective game for Killer, the first time in over two seasons he had been held under a hundred yards rushing. If Killer could not improve his performance, future defeat was inevitable because the competition would get stiffer.

When the team was dressed for practice on Monday, Coach pointed toward the traveling bus. "Hop on, boys," he said, "Cannonball has a treat for you all."

I picked up the equipment bag and tossed it on the floorboard of the bus, taking the first seat. Danny sat down beside me. As the bus gathered speed, I looked out the window. Main Street rolled by. From the high seat of the bus we could see behind the neatly painted facades to the unsightly patches, and the flat tar paper roofs. My father was looking out the window when we passed the office of the *Times-Democrat*. Coach Lipscomb, who was driving, shifted to a higher gear. Cannonball, who was sitting behind us, pounded Danny on the shoulder pads.

"Boone, I want to see you do your stuff today, you're in good shape, maybe the only one who is. You're gonna help me get these other guys in shape."

We crossed the river. To the left stretched the sand hills. Each year those ancient hills, which were actually mammoth walking sand dunes, moved with the wind a few feet farther from the river, smothering cottonwood trees in a silent tomb; then, decades later, moving on to expose the blackened trees. I never came to this place, or even passed by it, without getting a chill. Something about the dead trees, how they had been buried alive, then resurrected in form but without life, left me with a spooky, uncertain feeling.

We slowed down, entered the rutted lane that led to Lovers' Roost, the perimeter of the sand hills. Coach drove past the roost, beyond where the road ended, and finally parked near some old cottonwoods that lay in the path of the largest dune. The dune angled toward the sky, a steep mountain of sand, stretching half the length of a football field.

"Okay, boys, sit down, let's have a little talk." We chose a place where there was no sand, and knelt down in the grass, which provided a comfortable bed for lounging.

In his low-cut cleats, Coach shuffled around closer to the slope, making tracks where the sand had drifted. He turned his back to us and looked up, where the wind had left ripples like waves in the great dune. Then he began.

"I know what some of you think. You think football should be fun. It's a game, like any game. You think, you go out for football, you'll be more popular, girls will like you, or your dad wants you to go out. All that's bullshit. Of course, football's fun, but not that kind of fun. Football is not a cute game for namby-pambies who want to impress some giggling girl or for babies who want to make daddy proud. Football is for men; it's war. You go on that field to hit, to hurt, to maim, to win. It's a test of your manhood. It's having balls, and above all, it's preparation for your whole life."

Coach stopped talking and bent over, picking up a branch that had fallen from one of the trees. Holding it between his legs, he snapped off the dead twigs, which left a smooth stick about four feet long, an inch in diameter. With its point he sketched a U.S. flag in the fine sand. I squirmed. My movement made a rustling sound in the dry grass. Cannonball glanced at me. I crouched down, lower.

"You see, that's why I'm a coach. The toughness you need to play football is what you need for life, and that's what builds a strong country. You may hate me today, but someday you'll realize I cared. I wanted you to be men, American men." He finished the flag, dotting in the stars. I had sunk so low I was watching him through the ripening heads of grass.

"Some of you are still boys. I don't mean in size. How much you weigh has nothing to do with being a man. Some of the best men I know are little men. Some of you are small in your souls." He threw the branch away. I pulled a piece of grass and put it in my mouth. My thoughts broke, shattered. Mother was probably setting the table. I recalled the day a few months ago when I had deflated my football, had chosen, not warrior, but water boy. The grass where I lay was prickly. I longed to touch my mother's skin.

"I can only liken the experience of football to going foxhole to foxhole, dodging mortars, picking off yellow snipers, looking out for one another. I fought with some real men. We survived because we fought together. On this team you have friendships that mean more than relatives, and I'll tell you why. Because of the blood. Why were Christ's disciples willing to die for him? Because of the blood. When you play hard, you give your blood. You see it on your jersey, and on your opponent. That's what cements us together as a team, it's the blood you shed."

Lipscomb paused, then turned to look at his senior star fullback, the one player who must lead the team if there was to be a state championship. Killer was surprised, and looked away. Then Lipscomb moved on, his gaze going boy to boy, man to man. If a boy looked away too soon, the coach snorted, jerking his head backward in a short gesture of disdain. He passed over me without even a glance. I looked at Danny. His face was aflame, emboldened by the challenge Coach had thrown out.

"I assume all of you want to win," Coach boomed. "If you don't, get off the team now. To win means to give your all. If you're not prepared to give yourself, go, today. I don't care who you are, or what the newspapers say about how great you are, don't take up my time on the practice field with your wishy-washy attitudes. All right, what are we going to do?" I knew what he wanted, so I shouted with Danny and a few others who caught on.

"Win!"

Coach whirled and crouched in a gunfighter stance, pointing his finger at the lounging boys, sweeping slowly, once again stopping at Killer. "Only a couple of freshmen and the water boy, that's all who want to win? What the hell are we going to do?" he screamed.

"Win!" everyone shouted. "What?" "Win!" "What?" "Win!" "What?" "Win!" Coach let it get quiet.

"Take over, Cannonball," he said to his assistant.

Cannonball lined the team up. "We're gonna get in shape, boys," he wheezed. His heavy glasses clung to the bulbs of his nose, a grin spread over his prematurely aged face. Toward the river, the dead trees resurrected after years beneath the sand reached upward with their skeletal limbs. Lipscomb trudged up the dune, his feet digging out deep gouges in the soft hillside as he headed for the top. It was one of those rare days without much wind. When Coach reached the crown of the dune, he called down.

"Go on three, and start together. Let's see who's got guts on this team. Down . . . set . . . hut one, hut two, hut three."

They were only ten yards from where the sand sloped upward. Danny surged forward, behind Killer, the two of them clearly leading the others. After the first thirty leg pumps, they were barely a quarter of the way up. Their breaths rasped in and out. Then, Danny was more than halfway up and alone in front. Danny made it. Coach slapped him on the butt. Killer finally made it, too, and some others were not far behind. Then the rest straggled to the top. I felt the guilt that a child feels when his friends are being punished for something they've done wrong after he had warned them they better not do it, a guilt associated with foreknowledge.

"Line up, let's go back down," Coach said. The line formed slowly. "I see the easy living has taken its toll," the coach bellowed. "What do you think this is, a picnic? See any tables? Any potato salad? Any lemonade? Run down backward. Listen to me. Relax those arms. Pump your legs high."

They started down backward. The loose sand gave way beneath their cleats, and the holes they had made on the way up became traps for them on the way down. Danny reached the bottom ahead of all the others. Killer was fading.

"Line them up," Coach shouted down to Cannonball. There were still half a dozen boys making their way down the hill. The line formed even more slowly. Cannonball razzed them.

"Looks like Boone's the only man in shape, the rest of you look a little green around the gills." Their mouths were all rimmed white with cottonmouth, which they could not lick off.

Cannonball started them. Killer struggled near the back of the pack. Danny reached the top and stood beside the coach. The others toiled laboriously. Finally, they all made it, and Coach sent them back down.

Ten steps down the hill, Killer fell. It seemed like Coach was waiting for it to happen. A moment of fear, even empathy for Killer, caught in my throat as I cried out a spontaneous warning, "Get up!" But Coach had charged down the loose slope and as Killer struggled to stand, Coach kicked the big fullback in the butt. Killer went down, grabbing his buttocks.

"You pussy, move your ass!" Coach screamed. No one could look away, although none of us liked what was happening, even those who hated Killer. When Killer tried to get up again, Coach kicked him on the other cheek.

Killer rolled onto his back. Coach pounced, straddled him, lifted his head up as far as he could, then he slammed Killer's head down, slapping the earpieces of his helmet. Killer's head rolled, left, right, left.

"You're the captain of this team," Coach screamed. "What kind of example do you think you're setting? This is what messin' with women does. You can't play football with your finger in some girl's cunt! Now get up, and you run. You lead this team. Intimidating? All-state? My ass!"

After that, Killer worked harder in practice, became more intimidating in games, and was, also, more surly toward anyone who happened to be in his way.

Although Killer's training habits changed dramatically, what Coach had said about messing around didn't seem to make any difference. Killer continued to date Dovie, dragging Main Street, Dovie sitting so close it looked as if she had pushed halfway inside him.

With Killer's power running, the team won thirteen games. In the state semifinal, Danny, substituting for the first-string quarterback, who had been knocked unconscious, called an option play, and with brilliant open-field running scored a touchdown, garnering a lot of publicity. "A future leader of a greater team than this one," the newspapers proclaimed.

In the state final, Killer got shut down by a superior defense and the Dustdevils lost. Everyone grieved, no one could get over it. It was like a shroud hung over the whole town. Terrible things happened. Duffy Duncan's brother, who had always seemed a little bit crazy, killed himself. An Elston boy, who had played center on the team three years ago, was thrown from a horse, broke his back, and was paralyzed. "I just wasn't watching," he told his father when the boy was asked how it had happened.

Had not Cannonball and Dovie Lasher led the Devilettes to the county championship and into the third round of the basketball regionals, the town might have been even more depressed. No one thought much about the bad feelings between Danny and Killer.

CHAPTER 4

L ate winter, the grudge heated up again. Dovie had sent Danny a Christmas present, then she sent him a valentine. Both times, Killer found out. She may even have told him. Killer lumbered around school, scowling, muttering. What I had feared from the time Danny first harassed Killer finally happened in the spring.

Danny and I had taken care of my father's office over the noon hour. He often asked us to do this, and was always vague about where he went. While he was out, we unlocked his gun case, hefted his collection of cavalry repeating rifles, six-shooters, and buffalo guns, sticking them out the windows of the print shop, pretending to fight battles as if we were little boys again. Gun collecting was one of my father's passions, and, although none of them were particularly valuable, he had asked me not to handle them, but I saw no harm in it. We had barely locked the case and put away the key when my father returned. He hung up his suit coat, and settled down into his desk chair.

"Thank you, boys, anything happen I should know about?"

"Routine," I said. "Slim placed his ad, and P .O. paid his bill. The check is attached to the invoice."

"How much weight have you gained?" he asked Danny.

"Coach has me on a weight-lifting program," Danny answered.

I watched my father, as I often did, trying to find parts of him that looked like me. I considered my father to be the best-looking man in town.

"We're all looking forward to next year, Danny. Everyone's talking about you." He pulled his green visor down over his eyes.

Danny and I shuffled toward school, scraping our feet on the new concrete walk. The sun was not quite due south, so the shadows from the false storefronts cut across the sidewalk like jagged teeth. Between buildings, a few scrawny elms just starting to leaf out reached above last year's mule tails and thistles, casting spidery images. As we walked by the leather shop, LaFaye Jett looked up from his sewing machine. His window was dirty, but we could see him smile and wave and we waved back. We had walked to town in our shirtsleeves because it felt like spring, but there was a tension in the warm air that hung over the street.

I watched Danny from the corner of my eye, something burning, licking at my insides. His Levi's fit snugly around his hips, and his buttocks were muscular and rounded. He had grown heavier through his chest, like my father had said. His strides were long. I had to walk fast to keep up with him. One pant leg had worked its way into the top of his boot. It gave him a jaunty air as he moved with that natural athletic suppleness he had, full of confidence, almost brash, yet not conceited in an offensive way.

My Wranglers with the zipper fly were cinched around my waist by a thin belt my mother had bought at LaFaye's shop. There was a large fold in the stiff fabric. Mother always seemed to buy my pants a couple of sizes too large.

The poster on the theater advertised a western movie. Killer and his pal, Harley Pugh, were leaning against the billboard. Killer had been offered several football scholarships and had signed to play for the Cowboys of Oklahoma A&M, but he already toted a paunch and slouched with the indifference of someone who senses he won't make it, who feels he has already reached the pinnacle of his life, and now he hangs around town, works at odd jobs, and remembers the year they almost won the state title. The word around town was, Killer is a has-been.

As we approached them, Killer and Harley shelled peanuts, tossed the shells in the gutter, and chewed with their mouths open. "Well, well, look here," Killer said, peanuts spewed out his mouth, "two homos, and one of them's a hotshot." As we passed, Killer gave me a push in the rear with his foot. I whirled, angry.

"Hey, this one wants to fight." Killer laughed, putting up his fists, weaving side to side, mocking me. I looked at Danny. He didn't look back. I calmed myself, backed away, and so we continued our walk toward school. I was seething. It was too late when we heard them.

Feet crunched on gravel, breath hissed through clenched teeth. Killer shouted, "Get the hotshot!" Danny went down, grunting. Sand peppered me. I veered toward the middle of the street, then turned back to watch.

They dragged Danny, kicking and bucking, onto Mrs. Farragut's buffalo grass lawn, then they spread-eagled him. I glanced up at the white clapboard house. Tendrils of song from the old woman's phonograph drifted out her windows. She had heard the scuffle, her milky face loomed behind her lace curtains. She knew us all, Brice Miller, Harley Pugh, Danny, and me. I felt myself drawn with her into the spectacle.

I dropped to one knee, forearm resting across my thigh, wishing for help. But there was no one. The teachers would not feel responsible for conduct this far from school, even if I ran and made it there in time. Just another prank, they'd say, a joke inflicted on young students by older ones. I was helpless unless I chose to get tough.

On the grass, the struggle. They could pin Danny down as long

40

as both of them held on, but when Killer let go to reach for Danny's Levi buttons, Danny always broke free, and Killer had to help pin him again. Through my fear and worry, I detected a faint glimmer of satisfaction, a feeling that justice was being served, not for what Danny had done to Killer, but for what Danny had done to me just by being Danny.

I shook off the contentment and looked around for a weapon, a rock, anything. Nothing in sight, just some small stones, hardly larger than the gravel that had been kicked aside by passing cars. I decided to intervene weaponless, so I stood up, inched closer, then sprang at Killer, hoping to bowl him over, give Danny enough time to get away. But Killer was expecting my move, and landed a savage jab below my ribs. I staggered backward as if plugged by a shotgun blast, the wind knocked out of me. Through bleary eyes I watched the scuffle get more violent.

Killer slapped Danny's face, whap! whap! "Bastard, make things fuckin' hard," Killer brayed, then he bent over Danny, his face inches away. "You might like it. You like to show off."

Danny jerked a leg loose, brought it up with all his strength, and his knee caught Killer's buttock. Killer's head shot forward as Danny's head butted upward and smashed Killer flush in the mouth. Killer's lip split open. The sight of blood made me queasy. Harley stopped grinning.

Blood discolored Killer's teeth, leaked out the corners of his mouth down his lip. He spat, pressed his shirtsleeve to his mouth. A couple of loafers ambled out of the domino parlor to watch.

"Coach won't like this," Harley said, "let's show them the other one. Coach won't mind if it's the water boy." I didn't run. I'd give myself over in Danny's place if that's what they wanted.

"No, hotshot needs a lesson."

They dragged Danny, thrashing and jerking, to Mrs. Farragut's yard gate, opened it, positioned Danny's legs in the path, forced his feet out flat, then closed the gate over Danny's shin bones, pin-

41

ning his legs. But Killer was taking no chances. He reached into his boot and pulled out a hunting knife from a holster he had strapped there. He brandished the blade in front of Danny, then pressed it against the soft skin behind Danny's ear just hard enough to open a cut. A thread of blood trickled through the short hair on Danny's neck and soaked into his collar. There was fear and a sickly ache inside me, that feeling a person gets when someone you love is hurt and you can't take it away. All secret pleasure had evaporated.

"One move from you and you'll be an ear short, pretty boy." Killer spat out bloody spit. Danny lay still. Killer reached down and unbuttoned Danny's Levi's. I watched, down on one knee, with terror and fascination.

"Let's wait a few minutes until they get closer," Killer ordered. I followed his glance. Three girls, all basketball players, huddled with their arms around one another as they strolled up the street toward us. Dovie Lasher moved with powerful, limber strides in the center of them. Their laughter let Danny know they were approaching. He was breathing hard, his eyes were closed.

"Okay, now." Killer opened Danny's Levi's, exposing his underwear. He glanced toward the girls, who were still talking and giggling, then grasped Danny's shorts and pulled them down.

Killer hid the knife so it looked like Danny could have struggled and got away if he wanted to. "Hotshot has something to show you all." Killer looked up at Dovie.

She advanced ahead. The other girls walked slowly, glancing furtively toward Danny as if they didn't want to peek.

Danny's lower belly was sweaty and white where it sloped into the shadowy darkness of new hair. I moved closer. I felt the interest of an acute observer, with a sense of flying over them and seeing the whole scene. Killer was going to wish he had never tried to pull this stunt. He had misunderstood how things were with Danny, and with Dovie.

42

"Let him go," Dovie said.

Killer laughed, a thin, reedy snicker.

"Come on, enjoy yourself. You don't see many without foreskins. Besides, he loves it. He's a hotshot."

The scorn in his voice caused the others to shrink back, but Dovie stood her ground. She looked intently at Danny's face. His eyes were mere slits, but I thought he could see her. She turned toward Killer, her hands on her hips. She appeared relaxed and not much concerned, the corners of her mouth curled in a puckish smile.

"This isn't doing anything but making you look like a fool," she said. She shook her head, as if Killer were a small boy and she was ashamed of him. "You think being naked is bad?"

She reached up, unbuttoned her blouse and let it gap, then held it open with her arms, which were bent at the elbows like wings. She turned a full circle so we could all see her brassiere, which was plain, no wires or supports. She protruded only from her own fullness. She waited a moment. When Killer, who seemed to be shocked, made no gesture to let Danny go, she took off her blouse, brought her hand up her own back, unfastened the bra, and her breasts came free, visible to us as she pulled her bra over her head and tucked it into her skirt pocket. I thought of my mother naked at her baptism. They both seemed, somehow, to be making the same point.

Dovie straddled Danny. She nudged him gently with her toe. She wanted him to see her. He opened his eyes. Killer and Harley both turned him loose, but Danny didn't move. She tossed her head backward and looked at the rest of us again, then finally bent down over Danny, her breasts slightly elongated. She grasped Danny's shorts and pulled them up, but as she did his penis caught on the elastic band. To free it, she gripped the glans with her fingertips; then, as she tucked it into the pouch of his shorts, she ran her fingers lightly down the length of his thickening shaft. When she let go of the elastic band, his penis bulged against the white cotton. I felt the stirring in my own groin.

Dovie turned toward Killer, wrinkled her nose playfully, then waved her fingers, the ones that had touched Danny, as she brought them to her mouth and kissed them. Killer sputtered pitifully.

Dovie put her blouse back on, and buttoned it. She scrutinized us onlookers, as if daring us to criticize her, as if she knew the men were all in love with her. I held my breath, watching her pleated skirt, the bobby socks, the oxfords. She reached out to put her arms around the other girls as if nothing had happened, and they walked away.

Killer and Harley skulked across Mrs. Farragut's yard to the back alley. The loafers padded back into the domino parlor to begin spinning their yarns, fabricating the legends that would grow from this event on Main Street. Danny was still flat on his back.

"They're horrible, not human," I said, kneeling beside him.

His eyes gleamed like a blue-green fire, and I was afraid, afraid of my own weakness, but more afraid of something else.

"I thought they'd go after me," I covered. "They usually want some weak punk." My admission made things worse.

We both stood up, and I was off balance when Danny shoved me. When I fell, rocks and sand went up the back of my pants.

I ran home, hurting with the pain from Killer's punch, in pain even more from Danny's shove. When I burst into the house, my mother called from where she had been taking her midday nap.

"Sonny, what happened?" I turned and lay my head near her, feeling the divan's scratchy fabric on my cheek.

"There, there," she said, when I didn't answer, "it can't be that bad, I know it can't be all that bad."

She stroked my hair while I cried. I cried for many reasons. Mostly, I cried out of jealousy, that feeling of empty, helpless rage over someone else's privilege. I would have gladly given myself over in Danny's place. I would have given anything to have been touched by Dovie Lasher the way she had touched Danny.

"You're a special boy," my mother said, "a very special boy. God gave us a sign, Sonny. I don't know why you're crying, but just be faithful to Jesus, and he'll be true to you."

I did what seemed natural. I slipped my hand between the buttons of her dress, crawling under her bra where my hand had been when it was small, her nipple dragging on my palm, the tips of my fingers kneading her breast, a touch she had graciously accepted from before the time I could remember. Nothing short of this touch could have comforted me.

"Dear God, you've called my son into your service, protect and keep him so he can win souls into your kingdom," she prayed, as she patted me. And we lay together for a long time.

CHAPTER 5

I soar in the wind like a hawk, lounge in the light sky as an angel hiding in my own transparency, watch what happens in the town, feel the somnolent waiting, how the time drags. We all wait for something to happen, for Jesus to come, for football season, for glory. I have a New Testament open to the Book of Matthew. I spend my time waiting, memorizing Scriptures, but I see those who do not wait. My father, for one, walks blithely along under his hat in midday until he comes to the alley where he turns to some destination he travels often. He enters the back of Mrs. Shuler's dress shop. If you are a hawk you will lose interest. If you are an angel you must not watch what they do. There is another man who does not wait, either. The barns he has built gleam in the sunlight, for he has put on tin roofs to reflect the sun and keep his animals cool. The ones who work for him, the hired man and the boy, make straight rows when they plant, because the man knows when the rows aren't straight, although he cannot see. The man crumbles a piece of dirt, and smells it. A hawk knows his farm is lush with game. An angel knows he has a divine gift.

• • •

My friendship with Danny had returned to normal when I, with my father, covered a Farm Bureau awards dinner for the *Times-Democrat*. Danny's father was slated to receive the state's most prestigious farm conservation award, named for a governor of our state, the Sage of Tishomingo, Alfalfa Bill Murray, who had been born to humble folks in Toadsuck, Texas. It seemed appropriate that the award was named for Murray, because Arved, like Murray, was eccentric. At least his neighbors thought so.

Arved had been blinded in an elevator explosion that was so devastating it had made the *New York Times*. A dozen men had been killed. It had been a miracle that Arved survived. The glass from his truck window, which blew out when the grain dust ignited, had spiked his face, puncturing the corneas of both eyes with hundreds of glass splinters. But Arved's blindness was not the reason his accomplishments were remarkable.

Before he was blind, he had advocated planting windbreaks and digging ponds in order to increase the amount of rainfall. He maintained that the trees cut down the wind, reduced evaporation from the ground, and, in conjunction with the ponds, raised the humidity, thereby increasing the likelihood of rain. It's common scientific sense, he insisted. It's the way nature works. But we all have to do it, or it won't work. Planting trees and digging ponds was costly. The neighbors were skeptical, some thought he might be crazy.

About the same time, Arved purchased used surveying equipment, laid out lines on the contour, and constructed terraces on some hilly, worn-out land he had purchased. Again, his neighbors were skeptical, and laughed at the way Arved spent his money. But when they saw his crops, they asked him to build terraces for them on their hilly land. They'd pay him with money from future harvests, they promised. The best he could do, he told them, was lend them the surveying equipment. None of them developed the precise skill needed for the work, and the rainwater collected in low places, broke over their new terraces, and washed away their topsoil, leaving their fields more scarred with ditches than they had been before.

Lengthy Corcoran, the Boones' nearest neighbor, appealed to the government for help. The government told Lengthy that Mr. Boone had built his own terraces, and if Boone could do it, so could the others. Bad feelings festered.

Arved made things worse. In the mid-forties, as the war was winding down, the jackrabbits had multiplied so rapidly they ate the gardens, the wheat, then even ate buffalo grass so that the cattle starved. The bravest rabbits came into town. The dogs and cats got some of them, but it was not uncommon to wake up in the morning and see fifty jackrabbits in your back yard, even if you lived on Main Street. The state-wide population of rabbits was in the tens of millions. The state legislature passed a bounty, fifty cents per pair of jackrabbit ears, to help save the farmers. People banded together and went on rabbit drives, beating on buckets and tin cans, driving the skittish rabbits into huge wire mesh pens where the hunters stabbed them with pitchforks, cut off their ears, then piled up the carcasses in tall, maggot-filled mounds. The state paid out millions of dollars in bounty money. Administration of the program was a nightmare. There was no systematic way to destroy the rabbit ears, and many of them found their way back into the hands of the hunters, who turned them in again.

Arved drove to the State Capitol, appeared before the legislature, and argued that the rabbit drives were senseless and that the rabbits had multiplied because of the ten-dollar bounty on coyotes. The government had been paying people to kill coyotes for years, so the population had declined. With the coyotes greatly diminished, the rabbits had no natural enemy. God's balance in nature had been upset. The occasional weak calf killed by coyotes was a small price for keeping the rabbits under control and for maintaining God's natural order. The state can save millions by letting nature take its course, Arved argued. The legislature agreed. They voted in a new law to protect the coyotes, and revoked the bounty on rabbits.

Herb Miller, Killer's father, was the first person arrested for killing coyotes. Sheriff Ordway fined him a hundred dollars for running down coyotes with his greyhounds. Miller mumbled around town that Arved had deprived him of his sport. Those who had benefited from the bounty on rabbits agreed. Arved had gone too far. Bad feelings about him reemerged.

After Arved lost his sight in the explosion, it took him months to overcome his depression. But the prairie had been an effective teacher. Above all, he had learned how to be patient.

First, he trained Kirk Schroeder, Thelma's brother, to help him farm. That was an accomplishment in itself, because Kirk was a wild man. He had been a star player for the Dustdevils, but had been seriously injured his senior year. His leg, which had been broken in four places, never healed properly, and he limped. The injury had kept him out of the war, but made him a fighter, and he frequently dragged himself back to the Boones' farm drunk and beaten after a night in town. Yet he was loyal to Arved, and he limped back to the fields to keep up the farm work.

Then, Arved accomplished what finally won the Murray Award for him. Although his neighbors had failed to obtain government assistance for erosion control, Arved convinced the government to finance a model irrigation project on his land, despite an official government report done in the thirties that had warned that irrigation on the plains was futile. The underground water sources were too deep, the supply was too uncertain.

The county agent announced the funding for Arved's project at the annual Farm Bureau box supper. Arved bid the highest price of the evening for Alta Mae Corcoran's box, so he, along with others, lounged within earshot while Mrs. Corcoran, a former Miss

Panhandle broom corn queen, berated Lengthy.

"You've talked for years about an irrigation well, then you sat there on your skinny duff while that crazy Boone got the government to do it for him, and now you durn sure better know he's gonna eat your food and crow," she told Lengthy, shaking her head so violently that her coarse hair, almost the color of broom corn, frizzed out over her sunken eyes.

The irrigation project was completed on schedule. Farmers from neighboring states drove hundreds of miles to see it work. An article my father wrote for the *Times-Democrat* brought Arved to the attention of the state senators and that's how he won the Murray Award.

Danny and Arved stepped forward. Danny accepted the trophy, about a foot high and two feet long, a man following a team of horses and a plow. The master of ceremonies, Senator Lienhart, held out the envelope with a thousand dollar check in it, more money than it had cost Arved to purchase the worn-out land he had terraced and irrigated. As Arved accepted the check, I stepped forward and snapped the picture with my father's camera, then turned to look at my father for his approval. He seemed not to notice I had taken the picture. He seemed to be staring at Mrs. Corcoran, the broom corn queen.

After the neighbors had tromped by and shaken Arved's hand, we stepped outside. A light flickered near the Boones' car, a flame dangerously near. Danny ran to the fire, stomped it out. It was only a paper bag burning. By the time I had guided Arved to the car, only small wisps of smoke and a bad odor remained. Danny stared at his boots. They were smeared with shit.

When I heard the laughter, I whirled to see Killer Miller and Harley Pugh slink away into the darkness.

CHAPTER 6

I felt afraid as I had after Jimmy Lee Watson's burial. That spring, there seemed to be something evil running rampant through the countryside.

First, voracious greenbugs no bigger than pissants hatched in the fencerows, then moved out into the fields, ravaging the green carpet of young wheat. Most of the farmers stood by and watched their wheat plants vanish, then chiseled their land to keep their topsoil from blowing away.

Crop dusters from downstate flew out in World War II planes. Those who paid them to spray with DDT harvested no more grain than those that didn't. Some farmers tried doubling the dosage. The deadly mist drifted into the ponds and their cattle drank the poisoned water and died. The bugs, in the meantime, seemed to thrive, immune to man's interference.

The greenbug infestation was followed by grasshoppers. They ate what wheat the greenbugs had missed, then tree leaves, Johnson grass, thistles, sunflowers, and finally the buffalo grass. They departed suddenly, leaving the countryside practically denuded of all greenery.

The economy died. Ads in the *Times-Democrat* were down forty percent. The Boones were about the only ones who prospered, and the reasons were simple. Arved said it was simple scientific sense. He had made Kirk keep his fencerows clean so the greenbugs had no place to hatch. Anticipating a bad year, smelling it on the wind, he said, Arved had not grazed his wheat land, so the plants were strong and healthy, and, at the first sign of hopper infestation, he had sprayed every few days with a tractor-driven sprayer he and Kirk had built themselves. It sprayed the poison mere inches from the ground so it didn't drift away in the wind.

I went home with Danny on the weekends, and when I looked at Arved's fields rank with heavy heads of grain, then saw the sparsity of his neighbors' crops, I was amazed, and afraid. I dreaded nighttime, afraid of the unknown, and the unknowable.

Danny pranced through his days, whistling, poised, fearless, looking forward to and training for the football season. Killer's attack on him, which had left me full of remorse and self-doubt, had left him with no visible bad effects.

Meanwhile, our minister warned us. The farm plagues of insects had been sent from God to show us the end was near. This belief was widespread and triggered a revival that clamped Cimarron in its fervent grip.

The revival started when the Pentecostals erected a green and white striped tent, scattered sawdust, set up folding chairs, and preached the imminent advent of the Rapture. "There'll be a carload of teenagers dragging Main Street. Suddenly, the driver will be gone, and the car will veer to the side and crash through a fence. Imagine it, when the unrighteous see the Rapture, neighbors carried away to the bosom of Jesus."

The meeting, scheduled for two weeks, lasted three months. The revival converted many prominent people to the Pentecostal way including Danny's Uncle Kirk, and James R. James, one of the bankers, who said goodbye to his obese wife and whining children, and took to the road preaching the gospel of Rapture, tongues, and foot washing in the one gray banker's suit his wife let him keep. Kirk abandoned his devil-may-care lifestyle, helped Arved during the week, and preached on Sundays. Kirk now directed all his spare energy into his ministry, and into the training of Danny's football skills. He taught Danny hip movements, worked on his passing, and preached to Danny about the glories of the sport, and the power of Jesus.

The town lived in a sense of urgency. An early-morning stream of sunlight or late-night flash of lightning might signal the end, "In a moment, in the twinkling of an eye, when ye least expect it, the last trumpet will sound." All the pastors in town, infected by the Pentecostal urgency, reminded their flocks of the signs. The bomb had devastated Hiroshima and Nagasaki; the Russians had it, too. The Jews had returned to Israel, formed a new state, fulfilling what the Prophets had written of the "new Israel" emerging just before the end. Soon, God planned to destroy the world in the fiery chain reaction envisioned by the biblical writers. "Fire will come down from God out of heaven, and the land will shake, mountains will collapse, and every kind of terror," the preachers warned. "The destructor will march from the north to the valley of Megiddo, staging the last great battle, blood flowing to the bridles of horses— Armageddon." The Russians, the Bible meant by those from the north, chosen by God to execute his plan, an incendiary, atomic demise. In my sportive moments, I saw the fun God might be having as he implemented his plan.

In an attempt to conquer my fears, I memorized Scripture and volunteered for everything our church planned, as did my mother. We knocked on doors and my innocent face opened Cimarron's homes for our church's soul-winning campaign. How could anyone refuse entrance to the editor's son? I saw myself through the eyes of my mother, a soul-winner, a savior, a messiah. Late spring, my exalted view came crashing down.

That spring, our Baptist churches in Oklahoma, Texas, and

Kansas staged a crusade for Christ. The idea was promoted by Elberta Munion, my mother's best friend. "We can't let those Pentecostals show us up," she told our minister. Elberta's nephew was
a well-known evangelist, Joe Don Jones, who lived in Iowa where
Elberta originally came from. "He'll be especially effective with
our young people," Elberta told Pastor Toon. Although Joe Don
said he seldom held meetings in such remote areas, he'd preach
this one because his beloved aunt wanted him to.

A rancher from far west of Cimarron donated a rugged parcel of
land that was centrally located between the three states to be used
for the crusade. On this land loomed a mesa with crumbling cliffs
that rose a hundred and seventy-five feet above the prairie.

The crowd clogged a makeshift road that had been cut through
sagebrush and buffalo grass. Vehicles parked randomly at the foot
of the mesa, glinting in the sun like jeweled altars. Most people
walked up the crude road, but volunteers driving old army jeeps
transported those who could not manage the climb, making small
dustdevils as they ascended.

Danny and I walked up together leaving my parents and some
others from our church behind. As we climbed, our view expanded.
Meadowlarks whistled coyly to one another. They seemed to be
God's sentinels, telling him we were on our way. The mesa was
abloom with strangleweed, devil's hair, endless varieties of cacti,
prickle poppies, thistles, and locoweed, which had been unaffected
by the marauding insects.

On the top, it was so clear we could see sixty miles in any direction, the monotonous blue-gray sky blending into the soft flesh
tones of the prairie. To the east, near the flat, breastless horizon, I
saw a small brown spot, like a pigmented nevus. I pointed. "Yes,
that's it," Danny said, "it's Cimarron." And the radiance of God
filled us and his holy spirit beat down upon us with a hundred thud-
ding, whitewashed wings.

When we came near the tent, I scanned the crowd. Many of the mothers and daughters had reworn their Easter outfits. The gaiety of their dresses magnified the seriousness of the business at hand. "Gog and Magog are cast into the burning lake."

The flags snapped in the wind from the center pole, the red, white, and blue of the U.S. flag flying over the purple and white of the Christian flag. A musician lifted his trumpet to call us into the tent. He played:

> Stand up, stand up for Jesus,
> Ye soldiers of the cross.
> Lift high His royal banner,
> It must not suffer loss.

Inside there was a banner stretched across the front:

JOE DON JONES,
EVANGELIST AND COMMUNIST FIGHTER
HEADQUARTERS—OTTUMWA, IOWA

Danny and I sat down a few rows from the front. The hymns were sung. Some men took up the collection. Now the mesa was quiet except for a lark's trill. The evangelist walked to the pulpit, his head bowed. He tended to be obese like his aunt Elberta. Then he lifted up his gleaming eyes and encompassed the multitude, his face enraptured.

"God works miracles. We have climbed this precipice to be closer to our God, and we are witnesses to his son, Jesus Christ, crucified by the Jews, and now we are witnesses to the power of the holy spirit."

Then Joe Don preached. "Communism will enslave us, take over the land of the free and the home of the brave, unless we are vigilant and dedicated. The Communists love to see sexual promiscuity and drunkenness. We as Christians must stand against such evil, even though we must sometimes stand alone." He offered the invitation:

> "All to Jesus I surrender,
> All to Him I freely give."

Those who stepped out did so in small clumps. The trained volunteers, white ribbons pinned discreetly to their shoulders, moved up the aisle, paving the way for sin-blackened souls to end their struggle and come under the cleansing blood.

> "Trust Him, Jesus, trust Him now.
> I surrender all, I surrender all.
> All to Jesus I surrender, I surrender all."

"God is not satisfied," Joe Don whispered, his eyes closed, his face to heaven. "This is not a man speaking, this is not J.D. Jones, this is God, God's words for the young people."

I held my breath. Was this the call?

"Jesus calls some of you, the gifted ones, to dedicate your lives, every moment of every day, to do his work. Don't you dare deny the voice of Christ calling you, step forward and dedicate yourselves to full-time Christian service; as missionaries to foreign lands; as evangelists to travel the world preaching the good news, as local pastors. Only with your help can Christ subdue evil. God is so real here today, listen to him. Step forward now and take that stand, young man, young woman, as we sing the last verse one more time."

The call came, an internal pressure building beyond tolerance. I looked at Danny. He appeared to be in severe anguish. I had never seen him look that way, but the spirit's power was overwhelming. This was my chance to link myself with Danny. We'd become partners in the Lord's work. "God is calling us," I shouted above the singing, "I know he is." When Danny turned to go forward, he went quickly, and I stumbled, falling facedown toward the aisle.

As I fell, I saw coming up the aisle from behind us a beautiful young girl about my own age, so slender, her face so pale and promising, so sweet and virginal, it seemed she was a vision from God. I hit the soft turf and rolled over. In a flurry of crinolines, the girl stepped over me. As she did, I saw with flawless, protracted vision, like time stood still, the full length of her legs, starting from her white anklets, up her slender calves to her knees and thighs. Her skin was pure white, so smooth and accessible I could feel my lips on it. She wore silk panties, like a slender pink ribbon, which did not disguise the mons that protruded slightly toward me, and a gentle fold curled through the ribbon's length. Then she was gone.

Joe Don's workers come up the aisle. They bend over me. They've seen it before, sinners under the power. They take hold of me, stand me up, and point me toward Jesus. Behold the power. But I break free, sprint out of the tent. My mother sees me and is bewildered and heartbroken. I perceive a text in a split second.

"Immediately there met him out of the tombs a man with an unclean spirit . . . and no man could bind him, no, not with chains. . . . And always, night and day, he was in the mountains, and in the tombs, crying, and cutting himself with stones. But when he saw Jesus afar off . . . he cried with a loud voice, and said, What have I to do with thee, Jesus, thou Son of the most high God? . . . And he asked him, What is thy name? And he answered, saying, My name is Legion: for we are many. . . . Now there was there nigh unto the mountains a great herd of swine feeding. And all the devils besought him, saying, Send us into the swine, that we may enter into them.

"And forthwith Jesus gave them leave. And the unclean spirits went out, and entered into the swine: and the herd ran violently down a steep place into the sea . . . and were choked."

I sprint to the edge of the mesa, I choke, hurtle downward. I wake up, and retch, a hundred feet down the side of the embankment, half buried in a landslide. The vomit makes mud down the front of my shirt. The doxology wafts from the tent, "Praise God from whom all blessings flow . . ." I pull my hair and scream in my unmerciful torment. I have been called, and have rejected the call. I do not know the sign God gave my mother when I was born. I look up and see Elberta Munion's heavy legs. She has climbed down the mesa to help me up.

C H A P T E R 7

I know the Scriptures, but I am not an angel. The girl is sensuous like a hawk. She is not a virgin, thoughts of her threaten my sanity. There's a Bible in my desk, I should speak to my classmates about their souls, that's why the Bible is there. In my pants is a penis. It pokes hard against the boxer shorts my mother buys for me. I am afraid I will be called forward, and my sin will be known by the bulge in my britches. I am smart, this is a curse, I know how to conceal a mirror so I can watch Earldeana who sits behind me. She brushes her hair, her breasts point, I want to bite them. I close the mirror in a book, knock it on the floor beneath my desk, reach down, position the mirror. She opens her legs, her panties are stained, chills ripple through me. I remember the mesa, the call, and the virgin. My shirt sticks to my back from sweat. I am about to discover a secret. I lay my head on the desk, but I cannot rest. I am like my father, Jesus will come back, I'll go to hell. Do I hate my mother? But I love her so fiercely. I must try harder to be a better Christian, but my penis is still hard.

I had taken everything for granted until Mother shut me out of the bathroom door. I became curious, desperate. I watched her through

the keyhole. I listened to the sounds with my little ear to the door.
I was astounded when I glimpsed the bright blood she took out of
her panties. There was no question I could ask, no inquiry I could
formulate to probe the secret, solve the riddle. What sign had God
given her, told her, shown her when I was born? Was it the blood?
You must come under the blood. God gave us a sign, Sonny, a sign.
But the riddle was so solemn I did not dare solve it. My knowing
would debase its meaning.

One Sunday morning, soon after the mesa crusade, a family walked
up the aisle when the invitation was sung to join our church. The
father was so odd I became fixated. The man stood over six feet
tall, but must have weighed less than a hundred and twenty pounds.
A massive head was balanced precariously on a thin neck, a large
Adam's apple protruding. His eyes were deep-sunken beneath eyebrows that connected over a sharp nose. A shiver crept along my
spine. He looked like a crossbreed, half man, half vulture.

"The Tendal family have come this morning surrendering their
lives to Jesus," the pastor crooned. "They have a wonderful family
and want to be part of the family of God. They were Catholic, but
want to be immersed in the New Testament way, born of the water and the blood."

The minister reached forward and took the hands of the man
and his wife. Mrs. Tendal was also thin, but her shoulders sagged,
giving her a frail, beaten look. She wore an unstarched print dress
with no jewelry, nothing to detract from her plainness. Then, I noticed the girl.

The girl was extremely straight and slender like her father, but
in her, his features were chiseled down into soft curves. Her dress
was tight across the top, making her small breasts prominent. A
red sash accentuated her narrow waist. She was so unusual-look-
ing, so beautiful, and so familiar. Then I remembered the vision.

This was the girl from the mesa. My heart beat like the heart of a frightened bird.

The pastor held the girl's hand as if it were gossamer. "Anne, do you believe that Jesus Christ is the Son of God and do you accept him as your personal savior?" The pastor's hand brushed back and forth over hers as she answered.

He led them up the stairs to the baptistery, where they prepared for the baptisms. One by one, he took them into the water and buried them. When he baptized the girl, her hair hung down near her waist. I saw the faint lines of her underwear beneath the white robe. If Jesus had not already been born, God surely would have chosen this young woman to bear his child. The pastor lifted her out of the water, pure as a lily, her long, wet lashes glistening. The aura around her, innocent as a dove, hushed the church so that there was not even a single small sound. I loved her torridly, the way the wet robe clung to her. I prayed desperately that God would let me live long enough to repent.

That evening, Elberta Munion, our youth leader, hugged Anne to her powdered bosom, and welcomed her to Christian Endeavor. "We call ourselves Christ's soldiers! Now tell us something about yourself," Elberta said to her.

Anne's voice cooed with a soft lisp as if she had been touched, just lightly, by a speech defect, but she spoke with intelligence and charm. Around her hung a veil of shyness like a lace curtain, and beyond the veil lived a person of unblemished sweetness, and behind that there existed a mystery, a pall of something tragic. I wanted to touch her, take care of her, to be part of her.

But Elberta and the others matched her with Danny. Thelma, Danny's mother, betrayed me and helped, too. Thelma invited Anne to the Boone farm for Sunday afternoons. The church twittered over their romance.

"Mary was only fourteen when she married Joseph," I heard Elberta say. No one reminded her that Joseph was probably thirty and had an established carpentry business. And no one knew, or cared, about my pain.

In my nights, an angel emerged, her body pure and near in my bed. Invariably, I succumbed to my own arousal, then hurled naked entreaties into the blackness, begging for forgiveness.

CHAPTER 8

A few days before school ended that spring, the assistant coach barged into study hall and walked up to Danny. Although Cannonball was a dwarf, a freak, to his credit, he always acted normal. Thirty-three years old, he had spent his life overcoming his freakishness, and, as a result, he was an unsurpassed strategist.

"Coach wants to see you," he said to Danny. "You come, too, Schultz." We walked out to the bus barn where the coaches' offices were. The ruddiness of Coach Lipscomb's face appeared to be faded in the fluorescent light. He had been a highly decorated World War II hero, had gone to the University of Oklahoma on the GI Bill, and came to Cimarron highly recommended by the coaching staff at the university, although he had never played in a football game himself.

He leaned back in his swivel chair, his hands clasped behind his head. He had been talking to Doc McGrath, who was sitting on a folding chair. For a few moments Coach just looked at us. "You know Doc McGrath." He nodded toward Doc and grinned.

Both Danny and I had known Doc all our lives. My mother held him in very high esteem, although he had officiated at my birth, which had been difficult for her. Danny had been born at home, his birth attended by a midwife, but Doc knew Danny well because Danny had suffered a severe illness when he was around ten. He had contracted rheumatic fever, then had developed complications. Arved and Thelma attributed Danny's recovery to Doc McGrath's attention, although Doc admitted he had done very little.

Doc stood up. His white coat, the only indication of his profession, reflected the light's purple haze. A brown stetson covered a mop of gray hair, and he wore jeans and boots like most Cimarron men. His skin was tan, but thin like parchment; long hours indoors exposed to ether and alcohol had made his skin less leathery than other men his age. The grin wrinkles, his trademark, wreathed his face, but his eyes bore lines of hardship from seeing too many people die. In winter the wind froze his patients, and in summer it dehydrated them before Doc could reach them.

"Danny, Doc's here to give you a physical. Hang your clothes over there. We just want to make sure there's nothing that should be looked at before the season begins," Coach said.

"Take them boots off," Doc said. "This may get rough and we don't want no blood on them." Doc's rugged geniality was perfectly natural to anyone in Cimarron. He began the examination from the top, felt Danny's neck, rubbed circles under his arms, thumped his chest, and poked his belly. Finally, he reached Danny's genitals.

"Cough," Doc said. Danny coughed and Doc moved quickly to the other testicle and Danny coughed again. Doc pulled open the urethra. "Well, no signs of the clap," Doc said, then laughed at his joke. "Good to see you're circumcised, though. Those Hebrews have some good ideas, know as much about medicine as banking. I know your mom's side of the family was Mennonite." Doc never paused, just kept babbling. "The Mennonites believe a lot of things the Hebrews do. Whoever clipped you did a damn neat job, too. I've seen a couple of kids who look like some veterinarian did it with pinking shears." He reached for a tongue depressor. He'd forgotten to look down Danny's throat. "I don't know why more parents don't circumcise their sons. There's more reasons than hygiene." He took out the tongue depressor and punched Danny's shoulder. "And I'm sure, with your looks, you'll be finding that out, if you ain't already.

"That's it," he said, then closed up his bag and turned toward Lipscomb. "Hell, Coach, you ought to send some of these town boys out to Danny's father. Maybe he could build some shoulders on them, too."

Doc swatted Danny on the rear when he walked by. "You've got good muscles, developed for your age, you shouldn't have many injuries. Give it your best." Then he went out the door.

After Doc left, Coach pulled up two chairs near his desk. "Boys," he began solemnly, "we have one goal, win state. We have more talent than this town has had in years. But Danny, it's up to you. You're young, but you're the quarterback. That's a lot of responsibility. Cannonball says you can be a great passer, you have a quick release. Take this ball home, son. Practice, practice, practice." He removed a brand-new football from a box and gave it to Danny. Then he gave him a playbook, and a new pencil. "Study the plays. If you can think of some new ones, draw them out. This book has to be your Bible for the next three years." Then his face became long, almost glum.

"Danny, this is important. Stay away from girls. Women can ruin a good football player quicker than anything."

His gaze shifted to me. "You'll take care of him, won't you Schultz? The pride of this town rests on his shoulders." He reached out and touched Danny on his arm. Then he walked around his desk and shook my hand, repeating what he had said. "We're counting on you to look after him. Come in with Danny on Tuesdays and Fridays this summer, go through the equipment, get us organized. It would be a big help." He tousled my hair, then added, "I mean it, Schultz, you keep your eye on our quarterback. You guys better go catch your bus."

We headed out. As had been the case since childhood, I was going home with Danny for the weekend. Before we reached our bus, Killer and Dovie walked across the school yard with their arms around each other. When they passed us, Killer gave us the finger.

Danny's eyes began dancing. The pencil Coach had given him cracked from the tightness of his grip.

The bus bounced through the back roads blowing aside the tumbleweeds that had collected on the roadway. The sun had softened from white to orange as it dropped toward billowing clouds that hovered on the horizon. The window glass refracted the light, mingling the images of passengers with the images of sagebrush, soapweed, and fence posts. The syncopated cries of children, like those of caged, wild birds, pierced my melancholy.

The sense of pending disaster that often shadowed me had erupted when I again glimpsed the hatred between Danny and Killer. After settling into the bus seat, I allowed my eyes to droop shut. I drifted through the ocher light into another evening when we were children, an evening much like this one.

We play near the windbreak that Arved had planted around the Boone farmhouse. The sun is going down into some low clouds that threaten the evening's peace. The thunder mumbles.

Restless, I watch some chickens circle the yard. I'm not watching them intently, I observe absentmindedly thinking about my mother, because I often begin missing her when the sun goes down. A rooster scratches up a whole kernel of corn. Several hens waddle toward him, clucking. The rooster dances around, bobbing his head, then he drops the corn. The hens go for it. Dust and feathers fly. One has it, another knocks it loose. They flutter and squawk. A plump hen picks up the corn, darts away, drops it, and before the others get there, pecks and swallows it. The other hens drift back to their search for the day's last morsel.

The rooster flounces toward the lucky hen, who seems immensely proud of what she has done. The rooster's head is poised and his neck feathers ruffled. He circles her, clucking like a hen himself, round and round her, drooping his wings. His motions, which are gaudy and provocative, send an eerie feeling up the back of my neck, upward, upward until my head tingles at the very crown. I don't know exactly what the rooster is doing, but I know it is lewd, and naughty.

Thelma tiptoes around the corner of the chicken house. For a moment, I think she's caught me and knows my mind. She carries a hook made of number nine wire, ten feet long, with a crude handle Arved had crafted to look like the handle on an old rug beater. The hook jiggles unsteadily, but when she lowers it to the ground, it will slide silently and strike with the deadly quickness of a poisonous snake.

Thelma wears a gingham sunbonnet made from the fabric of a chicken feed sack. Its brim, stiffened with homegrown broom corn, shades her eyes from the low-angled sun, which is about to disappear behind the moaning thunderheads. Her yellow hair falls out of the bonnet and flows over her shoulders, which are bare, except for the straps of a sun dress she wears.

"Help me out with this old boy. We'll see if he struts when we're through with him." She hands me a piece of twine. The sun is behind her; her face is black, set deep inside the bonnet.

The wire snakes toward the rooster. The light deepens the luminescent orange of his comb. Thelma hooks him by his leg, drags him near her feet, while he squawks and flutters, jerking her arms like a large fish on a fishing line, beating at her with his wings, bending his neck trying to peck her. I give her the twine and she ties his legs together.

"This one's not much good for eating," Thelma says.

"Then why are you doing this?" I ask her. My voice shakes.

"He's always messing around with the hens," she says. "He fertilizes the eggs, and then the eggs have bloody spots, and town people won't buy them."

With more twine, she ties the bird to the clothesline. He hangs upside down, crying, struggling. She grasps his head, closing her hand tightly, his beak poking through her fist. Then she backs away, stretching the rooster's neck until the tautness changes the pitch of his cries. From her sash, she pulls a gray-black butcher knife she has sharpened on an old crock. She places the knife alongside her knuckles. The blade makes no noise as she slashes his head off. His flapping wings spread a pink mist over his breast.

Thelma pushes the chicken's head toward me. Her hand is chapped and rough. "Get rid of this so the coyotes don't come after it," she says. She opens her fingers and the red combed head with its shallow eyes tumbles onto my feet. Blood oozes over my shoe.

My eyes open. The bus still bounced along, but the children seemed to have closed like four-o'-clocks in the evening light. Then I realized Danny was talking.

"Remember? Hey, wake up," he gouged me in the side. "Do you remember?"

"Uh, what?"

"I said, when I was in the hospital, remember that story?"

There was nothing outside the bus window to obstruct our view of the horizon except the fencerows packed with tumbleweeds and the prairie's scrubby plants. I remembered in vivid detail, as Danny apparently did, when Danny was in the hospital. Danny had come down with a sore throat. Then the pains came into his legs, then his spine. They took him to the hospital. For days, Doc McGrath had covered the seriousness of Danny's illness. Then, one evening when I was visiting, Kirk brought Danny a gift, a football helmet. I sat beside Danny's bed not knowing what to do. Kirk shifted uneasily, foot to foot, glancing at me, as if he hoped I'd do something. "I'll read you a story," I said to Danny. Kirk left. From outside the door, I heard Doc McGrath tell him it was not a good idea to give the boy false hopes about what he could do. I could visualize Kirk's crestfallen face.

Danny had the covers pulled up around his chin. The helmet lay beside him on top of the hospital blanket. If he died, I was afraid they'd give the helmet to me.

I opened the library book I had selected, *Sports Stories for Boys*. "I may as well read the first one," I said to him. It was about football, its title was "The Lonesome End." I winced at the double meaning, at my own insensitivity.

A prep football team played its last game of the season. The team was extremely dispirited, losing a game the boys wanted to win for their coach, who, they had learned a few days earlier, had a terminal illness. This was the last game of his last season.

The team members, romantic, graceful, mannered youth, had been beaten down by the swarthy, bullyish rivals. Yet, with extreme courage, bloody and wounded, the smaller team trailed their foe by only six points.

The defense held again and the brutes prepared to punt from their forty-yard line. The ill coach looked over his squad. Not many players available. He needed one who could catch a pass. The first-string end was injured, broken ankle. But there, the tall, thin boy, frail as a young willow, quiet, too quiet, the coach didn't really know him, hadn't paid much attention, but no time for remorse. Now "Bones," the team's name for him, must catch the punt, must take his place in glory.

"Don't run with it, don't use up any time, just catch it and put one knee down." The coach drew the skinny kid toward him and whispered, "Then here's what you do . . ."

The brutish punter kicked the ball, and it spun high into the air, end over end. Bones rattled around under it, stumbled, caught himself, and the ball dropped into his hands, slender hands more at ease on the piano than gripping a football.

The opposition jeered when he fell down, slapping their knees, doubling over, holding their stomachs. "They have no guts," they jeered. "Hey coward, you're supposed to run and we tackle you. Afraid you'll break your bones?" They hooted at him when he trotted off.

Bones reached the edge of the field, but stayed one yard inside the boundary line like the coach had instructed. His teammates along the sideline had all stood up. From the field it looked as if he were one of many standing in front of the losing bench. The others were off the field. He was on it. Time for only one play. On the other sideline, the boasters began their victory celebration.

The quarterback barked the play before anyone had time to count only ten players in the huddle. The center snapped the ball. The quarterback, bruised, blood on his uniform, faded back, looking to the left flat. The pass receivers drove their tattered bodies out to the left for what the opponents perceived to be the final futile play by a defeated team.

On the opposite side, the stringy substitute rambled downfield unnoticed. His long strides ate up the yards. With a burst of strength, the quarterback turned and fired his pass.

The crowd hushed, breathless, that perilous time when the ball floats in midair, control is lost, the flow man to man, the intricate connection. The ball settled into the stringbean's fingers, those musical fingers closed over it, and the lonesome end loped into the end zone.

The shocked opponents turned on one another, cursing, pointing, blaming their left-side defenders. The fresh kicker kicked the extra point. Time ran out.

The winners lifted the doomed coach onto their shoulders and carried him off the field in glory.

When I looked up from reading, Danny had kicked off his covers, and his head was pulled forward; the dull heat had evaporated from his eyes, and he looked at me eagerly. A dull panic gripped me. I had heard how some people rally momentarily before death.

"Read the end again," he said, "the part where the quarterback throws the pass."

An uncomfortable sense of disaster, a sense of the personal tragedy that seemed inevitable, spread through me. My love for Danny would not die if Danny died, but what might happen if he lived? The possible tragedies seemed to be innumerable, my envy and unhappiness unalterable. Doc McGrath called Danny's recovery a miracle.

CHAPTER 9

T he sun was so low the shadow of our bus stretched into the east pasture. Before us was a long incline, the valley that Danny's father had terraced, fertilized, and watered. A line of silver mist, streaked with pink and orange, sprayed out of the irrigation sprinklers. At a distance, the stuccoed house seemed like a pearl on the green strand of elms around it.

The valley, the windbreak—Arved loved and protected his family. Yet, I had heard Thelma say to Arved, "That boy has his own interests. If you expect to hold him, you'd better meet him where he is."

Then Arved felt his way to the hall closet, took out Danny's football, and suggested we play. When we threw the ball, Arved couldn't catch, and when he tried to throw, the ball tumbled end over end.

"How was that one?" Arved asked.

"It's coming along great, Dad. Soon they'll be calling you Slinging Sammy Baugh." Arved laughed, but without mirth.

Finally, the bus squealed to a stop, and we stepped off the running board onto the caliche road. It had been ripped into ruts by farm machinery. We entered the house, pulled up to the kitchen table, and Danny opened the playbook Coach had given him. "Hey, look at this," Danny said. The words were handwritten across the top of the page. "The quarterback must be a true leader or the team has no one to follow." Same handwriting, next page: "The coach is the commanding officer, the quarterback is the field general. They bring victory and glory to their team and their town."

Danny closed the book, went to his room, and opened a dresser drawer filled with old clothes. He removed some faded jeans. He pulled out a bright blue envelope from the bottom of the drawer. "I'm keeping the playbook here. Guess I'll get rid of this." He showed me an envelope, and glanced at me with a sly look. I recognized the handwriting. "Do you want to read it before I throw it away?" I stuck out my hand.

> Dear Danny,
>   I watch you and dream of how handsome you are. I'll always remember our good times together. I want to cover your whole body with kisses, every inch of it. I'll always love you. With dearest fond love,
>
>   Earldeana

I fought the nauseous feeling in my stomach. It sounded like Danny might have had sex with Earldeana. Danny wadded up the letter and put it in the trash.

"You look funny," he said.

My mind skipped. I thought of something to say. "What did Doc McGrath mean when he said he was glad you were circumcised?"

"I'm not sure. It was weird, the way he said it." We stood there, and I waited. "My mother wanted me to be circumcised. It's the way Mennonites believe, like the Old Testament."

"How old were you?"

"Around eight or nine."

"Eight? Or nine?" I was surprised. We were friends by then. He hadn't told me about it.

"My mother took me to a Mennonite doctor in Liberal. I didn't know why we were going to the doctor, they didn't warn me. Then, I heard the word 'circumcise,' and I knew what that meant, because, you know, David killed the Philistines and brought their foreskins to King Saul so he could marry Saul's daughter." Danny laughed. We both remembered the day of that lesson, our Sunday school teacher's embarrassment, and then mine, when I asked my innocent question, "What's a foreskin?"

I laughed also, a short, nervous laugh. "Did it hurt?" I asked.

"How could it, they were dead." He teased me.

I laughed again, a high-pitched giggle. "No, not the Philistines, I mean did it hurt you?"

"What do you think?" When he saw my face, he answered, "Yes, of course it hurt. You had it done, didn't it hurt you?"

"I guess I was too young. I don't remember it." The palms of my hands were so sweaty I couldn't have gripped a pumice stone. "What did Doc mean when he said there were other reasons besides hygiene?"

"I don't know."

I didn't believe him.

"It's hard to explain," he said, "it has to do with when you do it to a girl." He stepped out the door away from me. I knew the truth. They had done it, he and Earldeana had done it. I am his best friend, you'd think he would have told me, bragged a little, something.

Fresh cow plops steamed in the evening light as we slipped between the bottom rails of the corral, a shortcut to the barn door. Clusters of insects buzzed over the dark pools. The warm, dry weather had left the floor of the corral dusty, and reduced its stench, odors like stale tobacco, pleasant once you got used to them. I

poured warm water over the "good as milk" powder while Danny
stirred. The powdered milk substitute was more nutritious than
cows' milk, the ad on the bag claimed. But the calves we fed it to
had distended bellies, and their ribs showed through their skin. I
knew they needed their mothers. It was cruel, ripping calves away
from their mothers so we can have the milk. Cats, a dozen or more,
rubbed against my ankles as we worked.

We had our usual places for supper, Arved and Thelma across
from each other at the ends of the table and Danny and I on one
side across from Kirk. "Brother Kirk, will you express our thanks?"
There was a lightness, a humor in Arved's voice, and his eyes jig-
gled, the eyes of a blind man laughing.

Kirk's prayers were long, rambling memoirs of what he had to
be thankful for. While he prayed, my eyes drifted open. In my plate,
a molded, shimmering Jell-O fruit salad began to foment with a
rousing game of fruit basket upset, a game our church youth group
played at "linger longer," hoping, hoping not, to sit thigh to thigh
with her—or maybe an accidental bump on the way to a new chair.
"Apples change seats with the pears. Cherries change seats with the
peaches. Apricots please change with the oranges." The changes
entranced us all. Who will sit next to me? Will it be Evie Lou, who,
at birth, had a set of male genitalia above her vagina that Doc Mc-
Grath had surgically removed, then saved in formaldehyde? Will
it be Martha Lee, who had pubic hair at age ten, as reported by re-
liable eyewitnesses from the rafters of the town pool dressing room?
My heart races. "Fruit basket upset!" Everyone scrambles for a new
seat. I stand up in my reverie, ready to scramble myself. Kirk says
"Amen."

"Where are you going, Sonny?" Thelma asked.

I sat down. I looked around the room, embarrassed. On the wall
above Arved's head hung an embroidered cloth framed with shellacked elm tree branches split in half. I had noticed it before but
had not paid that much attention. A Scripture, Isaiah 14:27, was

embroidered on it, with small cherubim in the corners.

"That's a beautiful wall hanging, Thelma, did you make it?"

"No, Danny's grandmother made it a long time ago, long before he was born," Thelma answered. There was still silence. "It was one of the few things saved when Arved's parents were lost at the river crossing. The writing's so fancy, it's difficult to read. Arved knows what it says."

" 'For the Lord of hosts hath purposed, and who shall disannul it? And his hand is stretched out, and who shall turn it back?' " Arved quoted.

"It's so beautiful I always love hearing it," Thelma said, "but I don't even know what it means."

"Ask our Bible scholars," Arved replied.

"I'm not that much of a student of the Old Testament, yet," Kirk said. "Maybe the boys know."

Danny shook his head. I had an idea. "I think it means God will make certain things happen, and no one can do anything about it," I said. "It's one of those places in the Bible that people quote who believe in predestination." Everyone was eating, clinking, chewing. No one said anything. What I had said seemed to make everyone sad. Mother would have the dishes washed by now. She would be starting her evening Bible study. We finished eating. Danny and I played checkers and went to bed.

At breakfast the next morning, Arved said, "We have to do something about those cats. There are too many." I had thought the same thing myself when I was feeding the calves. The cats had an easy life around the farm, catching rodents until there were no more rodents to catch. The coyotes could have depleted the cat population, but the cats had learned to stay near the farm buildings because the coyotes did not come in close, although one year they had when the snow lay deep and frozen. Three of them prowled the farm. Danny and I had watched them one night through frosty window panes, the moonlight glistening on crystal snow, the drifts sculpted like dunes. We found blood on the snow several times, and the number of cats diminished.

Now the cats had nothing to hunt and nothing to fear. I often fed them myself, so they received their dole, peacefully copulated and gave birth.

"I want you boys to take care of the problem," Arved said.

"What shall we do, give all the tomcats rubbers?" Danny asked.

Arved smiled. "Get rid of the kittens," he said. "If we need to shoot some grown ones, Kirk can do that later."

"I can't do it," I admitted.

"It has to be done. It's for their own good, it's only going to get worse. Gather the kittens in a gunnysack and bring them to me."

We trailed mother cats to find their hiding places, stalking, reaching under them, their nipples erect from nursing, and we snatched away their kittens. The burlap sack filled up with wads of mewing fur, tiny paws, half-opened eyes. Between us, we carried the sack to Arved.

"Okay, the hard part's over," Arved said. "Finish the job."

"I thought you were going to do this," Danny said.

"You can do it. Face it, it has to be done."

Danny tied a knot in the sack. He picked up two pieces of two-by-four, and handed one to me. Taking turns, we smashed the gunnysack. The faint squeaks continued for only two or three swings, dark spots appeared on the rough burlap.

"May as well feed them to the fish," Arved said. With the sack held between us, we ran down the hill and flung it into the pond.

I pull the yarn knots of the comforter through my fingers to bring sleep. Had we killed all the kittens before we dumped them into the pond? I have trouble breathing. I hear, somewhere in the darkness, the snarls, mournful wailing, I know what it means, a tomcat on the back of another female, the scruff of her neck held between his teeth as he impregnates her, and she howls. I run from the sound, Killer stalks me with a gunnysack.

. . .

On the last day of school, the teachers bustled around, busy with tests, makeup work, and summer plans. Cannonball Conner caught Danny in the hall.

"Coach wants to remind you to be ready on Tuesday. Junior will pick you up at eight-thirty."

Two days before, Danny had worked out a plan.

"Dad says he'll pay you ten dollars a day," he told me. "We can spend the whole summer together."

"I'll ask my father," I said.

When I asked him, my father combed his fingers through his hair. "Well, I have some work for you, but maybe you can do it on weekends. We can just reverse it, you spend the weekdays with Danny on the farm, and the weekends with us. I certainly can't match the pay. What do you think, Emma?"

She had been gazing out the kitchen window. When he spoke to her, she turned, very slowly. "It would be fine," she said.

When I packed my work clothes, I reached into the back of my drawer and took out my soldier, the lonely one, the sentinel. That whole summer he traveled back and forth with me from town to country and back to town again. No matter where I slept, he kept guard from the lamp stand near my bed.

CHAPTER 10

By late June, the wheat fields were almost ready for harvest. "I want to check that field across the road," Arved told Danny.

I knew the story of Arved's family and of the field. Arved's father and mother, along with three uncles and their families, had stepped off the train at Liberal, Kansas, shortly before Oklahoma became a state in 1907. They had heard of land, free for the taking because the buffalo had all been skinned, the Comanches killed, and the Kiowa resettled. The Boones, who lived in Illinois, had suffered from poverty in this country just as they had in their native Kent. They sold their few possessions, ignored their debts, and skipped to Oklahoma territory.

In Liberal, they bargained for a light buckboard, horses, and supplies, then headed south on the Plummer Trail. Arved's parents did not make it. The Cimarron River, swollen out of its bed by the spring rains, swept their buckboard off the ford into deep water. Arved, age six, air pockets in his mackinaw, floated a mile downstream before he was picked up wet but unharmed by an uncle on horseback. The brothers searched until dark, but never found Arved's parents.

By morning, the river was again hardly more than a trickle. Arved's uncles, anxious to find their land, moved on. They took Arved with them. Beyond the river there were no trees casting shadows and taking up space, no privacy, nothing but the sky, the grass, and the wind.

They settled only fifteen miles from the river. Each uncle staked out his rightful quarter section, and one for Arved in his father's name. It took Arved a long time to accept the harsh truth. He hated the pelting rain, the relentless wind that had buried his parents. On the prairie, death was not even an inconvenience.

Then, Arved's aunts and cousins all died in the soddy dugout that still serves as the root cellar for the Boone house. Maybe it was consumption from the cold in the winter and the dust in the summer, or maybe they died from fright—the prairie wolves and coyotes in the winter—the electrical storms that crackled, and the rattlers that crawled through the sod walls into their straw tick beds in the summer.

The men, unable to live alone, died from the unrelieved monotony of wind and work until the fourth and last brother blew himself away, his wind-chapped lips over the barrel of a single-shot four-ten. It was an old plains maxim, save one bullet for yourself.

Arved, age fifteen, was left alone with the barren land and the debt. It took him almost twenty years driving freight to save the money. During the intervening years, the land passed from bankers to another owner and back to the bankers again.

"You're sure, Mr. Boone, you want to purchase all six hundred and forty acres? There are a lot of gullies, you know, in some parts."

Arved insisted he wanted the whole farm, just like his uncles had laid it out, all four quarters, including his own, which they had mortgaged with theirs. Arved placed the money in fifty dollar piles on the bankers' table, an enormous sum in the middle of the Great Depression. Then he started to work in the field that was most eroded.

Danny and I walked beside Arved through what had been the field of gullies across the road from the dugout. He had worked here first with the H Farmall and the rusty tumblebug he purchased with a new loan from the bankers. He filled in the gullies and built up the terraces. The hate he held for this violent land that took away his parents had been transformed; his romance with Mother Nature had begun.

The verdant wheat we walked through reached nearly to my armpits. Arved pulled a head from its stalk, smashed it in the palm of his hand, picked out the kernels and put them in his mouth, biting them with his front teeth.

"Three, four more days at the most, and this will be ready to cut," he said. He spread out his hands to feel the heads as they undulated in the wind. He continued walking, his face bathed in the light.

He turned toward Danny, his head pitched forward, as if he were trying to see through the mist, or the haze, or whatever it was that he saw in his blind eyes.

"What does it look like?" he asked.

Squinting against the sun, Danny swept the whole field with his eyes; then, as if to capture the panorama in a still picture, he closed them.

"It's all moving. It's yellow." He stopped, he could say nothing more. I could see many more details. There was a cast of green if you looked below the heads, and when the wind blew and the wheat moved, the field changed colors as if clouds were passing over.

"The wheat is thinner on the terrace tops. Where they drain, the wheat is still green," Danny added.

I kept looking. Beyond the field was a canyon worn out of a bluff by the ageless forces of erosion. Clay and sand showed through its banks in layers of soft purple and brown. Beyond the canyon was a table of grassland set with a cloth of grass in numberless shades of the softest green and yellow. The beauty is not glaring as is the beauty of the mountains, or bald as is the beauty of the desert, or sheer as is the beauty of high cliffs; the beauty of the plains can be seen only through eyes grown accustomed to the pain.

Danny was trying not to cry, but tears made dust-rimmed tracks down his cheeks. The two of them faced each other. At that moment, I understood. Without Danny to continue what he had begun, Arved's struggle was for nothing. He was a man who was already old, who had, at most, only a few more years of life to test his wits against the erratic force of Mother Nature.

Danny was facing the wall when I came back from the bathroom. I switched off the light, but lay awake. As I floated in the wasteland between us, I heard him.

"Don't. Let me out. Let me out." His voice was crisp, and I could see him in the moonlight; his covers were on the floor and he threw his head side to side.

"Danny, are you all right?"

"Let me out!" he repeated. Then he sat bolt upright, and the moonlight from the window caught him. His eyes were open, and his face was blanketed with terror. "Let me out!"

"Danny, wake up. Wake up!" I said it louder. His shoulders slumped, his chin touched his chest. I sat on the edge of my bed.

"Sonny, is that you?"

"Yes, it's me."

"I was dreaming. I wasn't sure what was the dream and what wasn't." He took several deep breaths. "Would you mind turning on a light for a little while?"

I reached for the lamp beside my bed, and knocked over my soldier. I turned on the light, picked up the soldier, and placed him in position again.

"Did I wake you up?" Danny asked.

"You were shouting 'Let me out.' " I glanced at the soldier again. I straightened him so he was facing me.

Danny exhaled a long breath, "That was the worst dream I ever had."

"What was it about?"

"I was in the truck, and there was a fire, up front, under the hood, like some straw had packed there and finally caught fire, and my dad had a pitchfork, and every time I opened the door to get out, he came after me with the pitchfork. I'd go to the other door, and he'd be there. The fire was getting closer, and hotter. He could see. He could see."

As Danny talked, his chest expanded, perspiration beaded on his tight muscles, large veins stood out in his neck. When he stopped talking, he wilted, as if all the strength had left him, and he started sobbing.

"I think he wants to get rid of me," he choked.

"Who do you mean, you mean your father?" Danny didn't say anything. "You mean you think this, for real?"

"I think I caused him to lose his eyesight."

"That's silly," I said. "You're not dreaming now. You know how it happened, there was a dust explosion. It happens. You couldn't have caused it. It just happens."

"I think I may have." There was a hardness to his voice now, as if he might be changing his grief into anger.

"Why do you think that?"

He lay back on his bed and put his head on the pillow. I couldn't see his face. We had never talked about his father's accident.

"I was playing in the dirt, and he called me to go with him to take some wheat to the elevator. Mother was there. We all got in the truck. Dad was driving out of the field. I was learning about trucks. I asked him what gear. 'Compound,' he said. Something about the word made me laugh. Mother asked him to say it again. 'Compound,' he said, in a low, low voice, and we all laughed. Then he let her out and she walked back to the house. We got to the elevator and he locked me in the truck."

"Farmers do that all the time."

"I know, but I was scared. I got onto the floor of the truck. That's what saved me from the explosion, but I got there because I was mad and wanted to hurt him. Then he opened the door, and everything blew up, and it seemed like I did it."

He began to cry again, low, mournful weeping. I turned out the light. The soldier kept guard. I went to Danny, who moved over, giving me room on his bed. He lay his head on my shoulder, his breath warm on my skin. His weeping subsided, and he began patting me as if I were a child in need of comfort.

"It's okay," he said. "Everything's okay." I drifted into sleep. I awakened in Danny's bed. He was up and out.

When he wasn't working, Danny threw the football through the tire. He'd fade back, set himself, and zip the ball with that quick, behind-the-ear snap Cannonball had noticed first. I'd chase the ball and throw it back to him.

It was a relief to avoid bumping into Killer that whole summer, although I could not rid my mind of what he and Harley Pugh had done to Danny.

The second week of August, I baptized my first converts, the Delmar Dumas family. They had been prospects for membership in our church for a few months. They had not made a commitment about which church to join, but went church to church, looking for the right one. Pastor Toon had taken me along to call on them a few times because they had young children, and the pastor thought I might make a favorable impression, as well as entertain the children while he talked to the parents about their souls. Delmar was out of work. The various churches they attended gave them assistance, but what Delmar needed was a job.

The farm work was caught up, and we began spending some time in town. I begged Danny to go with me along Main Street and ask people if they had a job for Delmar, but he said he couldn't, so I did it alone. Duffy Duncan at the Western Auto finally said he could use a man to do maintenance on his building and repairs on small equipment. I sent Delmar down, and it was a match. The Dumases were very grateful, and a week later, they came forward at the end of the Sunday service to accept Christ and to be baptized into the First Baptist Church.

Pastor Toon explained to the congregation what I had done. He told them I was old enough to baptize people. It was a warm day, so we took them to the river. Ever since my mother's baptism, the pastor had baptized people in the river if the weather permitted. In a waist-deep hole in the shallow creek, I buried the Dumases under the water, then raised them to a new life, cleansed by the water and the blood. I had never felt so blessed, so holy, so lucky, so confident. Among the witnesses were the Tendals. Perhaps I had finally done something that might make Anne love me.

Coach scheduled football practice to begin two Mondays before school opened. Danny and I showed up for the final Friday meeting with Lipscomb, and faced two strangers. Harley Pugh, Killer's friend, was also there. He sat next to Coach. Harley was big and a year older than his class because he had failed third grade. He had earned all-conference recognition as a sophomore on last year's team. He played football like he rode his motorcycle, wild and reckless. Harley was counted on by everyone for stardom. R.D. Smyley, a classmate of ours, sat next to Harley. One of the strangers, a small man with a bald head, sat beside R.D.

Coach stood up. "Hey, Danny, glad you're here. I want you to meet Melvin Hibbs. Mr. Hibbs is a sportswriter for the *Daily Oklahoman*. He's here to find out what kind of team we're gonna have this year. He's very anxious to meet you." The bald man shook Danny's hand, and led him toward the cameraman.

When Hibbs finished his pictures of Danny, I was standing nearby. The photographer pointed at me and called to Coach Lipscomb, "Should I get a picture of this one?"

"No," Coach laughed, "he's the water boy."

"Heck," Hibbs said, "this must be some team if it can afford to make a kid this size into a water boy."

On Sunday, we sat in church with Danny's parents. There was a change in people, so many smiling faces and glances.

The minister shook Danny's hand as we went out the door. "Well, you are quite a celebrity." He didn't sound totally pleased when he said it.

We excused ourselves, and ran the three blocks downtown to P.O.'s drugstore. Danny picked up a copy of the paper and took out fifteen cents to pay the clerk. P.O. ran out from the back.

"Hey, Danny, what an article. Dottie, don't you take that money, and give Danny some extra copies, too. He's gonna need some to autograph for the ladies." He added, as we went out the door, "LaFaye wants you to stop in and see him, and Old Man Goggin wants to talk to you. Go see them this week, and don't forget."

Outside, Danny unfolded a newspaper. From the front page of the sports section, Danny's handsome, angular face jumped out at us, his eyes squinting slightly, and his jaw set in that determined way he had. His face was sliced by the shadow of the single-bar face guard on his Dustdevil helmet.

SOPH QB TO LEAD DUSTDEVILS
IN QUEST FOR STATE TITLE

The good feelings from a summer of hard work and from my first baptisms came crashing down, falling around my feet in a pile of jealous rubble. I was nobody compared to the quarterback.

CHAPTER 11

On the day of the first football game, I packed the medicine kit, shoved it, the spare pads and water bucket into the town ambulance, then went to the *Times-Democrat*. There were back issues of the *Daily Oklahoman* on my father's desk. I leafed through the issue that contained Danny's picture and came across a story near the bottom of an inside page.

LOVELAND HS SOPHOMORE DEAD

Promising sophomore lineman Oliver Trammel died Friday while participating in football practice at the Loveland High School field. He was pronounced dead at the site by a local physician, Dr. Emmet Farley. Trammel, who was slated to start in the Tigers' first game next week, had tackled a teammate as part of routine practice and never got up. "Either his heart gave out, or it was a blow to the head," Dr. Farley explained. Funeral arrangements were not completed in time to be included in this edition.

Here was the tragic answer to a question that had bothered me. Can a boy die playing football? I had sensed it was possible. How could it not happen when the organs that control life are pushed to their limits? Yet, I had never heard anyone, coaches, parents, or fans, mention this possibility. Not even my mother had said anything about football leading to death.

I remembered what the day had been like last week when the Trammel boy had died. The temperature during afternoon practice had been a hundred and ten degrees in Cimarron. I had brought extra water to the field, but Coach had refused to allow anyone except me and the coaches to drink it. "Suck it up," was his response to a player who looked longingly at the water bucket.

Loveland lay three hundred miles southeast of Cimarron in the low altitudes near the Red River. I had once been there with my father to cover a rattlesnake hunt for the paper. It was hot as hell. Heat must have been a factor in Trammel's death. I shivered.

I glanced at my watch. It was time, so I scooted across the street to the drugstore where I had arranged to meet Danny. My mouth felt dry. I sat down on a stool and ordered a large cherry Coke. Butterflies swirled in my stomach. I couldn't get it out of my mind, a boy my age, dead on the pale grass of a football field. Hot as hell. Hot as hell. Is this what football is about? Death. Risking it? Is that why football players are heroes? Is that why football is thought of as war? The excitement of seeing someone risk injury or death, sending your own sons to war, then watching them fight. That must be the thrill of it.

I glanced at my watch again. It was still three hours before game time, and I, of course, was not playing. Why was I so nervous? There was little at stake for me in this game, at least not much I could identify. The stake was to stay alive, not take unnecessary risks. But maybe there's more to it. Perhaps football is about something else, too.

I was still sitting at the counter when Danny swaggered in. His head almost brushed the top of the door. He was whistling "Mock-ing-Bird Hill." P.O., the owner, appeared out of the back room. Danny waved to him, then walked to the magazine rack, which was a few feet away from where I sat. He picked up a copy of a sports magazine. Paul Hornung grimaced from the cover in what would become his Heisman pose. We knew Hornung was proba-bly a Catholic because he attended Notre Dame, nevertheless the coaches held him up as someone they hoped the boys would em-ulate. Hornung was tough, played defense and offense. Those qual-ities were more important to the coaches than his religion.

Danny went to the counter to pay for the magazine. P.O. waved him away. "You don't need money, Danny. Just go out and win that game tonight. We'll take care of these little things." Then he added, "And remember, go see LaFaye and Old Man Goggin like I told you before."

Danny motioned for me to follow him. I slid off the stool and started out. "That's fifteen cents, young man," the counter girl called after me. I walked back, sucked up the remaining Coke, dumped the ice onto the scarred marble counter, and flipped a quar-ter into the syrupy water. The coin on the wet counter made me feel good for a moment. Outside on the street, the false front of the hardware store had cast a shadow across the sidewalk. I blinked when we came out of it into the light.

"Let's go see what the others want," Danny said. We passed the vacant lot where I had played with Jimmy Lee Watson, then came to Goggin's store. The screen door swung on decorative iron hinges, one of the few doors in Cimarron that had survived the windstorms of the thirties. The door slapped shut behind us, pulled closed by a twanging spring. Danny began looking at a stack of shirts and did not glance up until Old Man Goggin popped out from behind a pile of overalls. Goggin, the original haberdasher in Cimarron Ter-ritory, had arrived long before statehood. He prided himself on keeping a neat store, on being vigorous for his age, and on driving the snazziest car in town. That year, he drove a black Oldsmobile Ninety-Eight with automatic shift and fender skirts.

The old man bustled forward. He was skinny and limber from years of stretching to reach high shelves. Wide suspenders held up his black cuffed pants, which fit loosely around his thin waist. "Like those shirts, Danny? Pick one out, any one you want." He beamed at Danny, then reached out with blue-veined hands, grabbed Danny's sleeve, and pulled him close. "And I wanted to tell you, if you ever need a car for a Saturday night date, take ours. We don't use it much on Saturday nights." He glanced over his shoulder, as if his wife were there and might hear him, then whispered into Danny's ear, his words whistling through broken teeth. "And the best part about this car is the nice room in its back seat." With jerky movements, he jabbed Danny in the back.

We ambled out the door and let it slam. I carried the shirt Mr. Goggin had put in a white paper bag. Danny shook his head, laughing almost silently, as we headed up Main Street. "I can use our car," he said. "If you ever want a car of your own, let me know and I'll borrow Old Man's for you."

"The Old Man shouldn't say things like that," I said, "it doesn't look good."

"They're his shirts, he can do what he wants to with them," Danny said.

"No, not that, I mean about the back seat. He's a member of the Methodist church; it could be taken the wrong way, you know what I mean."

"He's not a deacon or anything."

"He used to be." We were in front of the boot shop door and went in.

LaFaye Jett didn't stand up, he pointed toward some green and black boots in the dusty, rain-streaked window, and shouted over the noise of the electric boot polisher. "Acme's just come out with a new alligator boot. Win the conference championship and I'll give you some." He paused, then pointed his finger, bent and gnarled from years of tooling leather. "Now I mean it, Danny, you win, then stop in here and I'll fit you up with a pair just like them over there once that trophy's ours."

What did he mean, "He's not a deacon?" The pastor says the same rules apply to everyone, and the Bible says do not commit fornication, which was just what Old Man was suggesting Danny might want to do in the back seat of his car.

I picked up one of the boots. The bottoms were black, with elaborate stitches in the mottled leather, and the tops were soft green with light stitching in leaflike patterns. I no longer felt amused at what was happening, nor was I merely dismayed. Rage spiraled from a place I couldn't touch.

We stepped back out onto the street. "I didn't know quarterback was such an interesting and highly paid job," I said.

Danny laughed. "Don't worry, I'll cut you in," he said, patting me on the rear as if I had just made an outstanding play. Another door slammed. Across the street, Herb Miller, Killer's father, a huge man with a belly bigger than his son's, stepped out of the Western Auto. Behind him, Duffy Duncan hung up his CLOSED sign, and turned out the lights.

"Guess we won't see Duffy," Danny said, "he's closing up."

"Must have made a good sale," I said, "he's probably heading to the domino parlor to lose it. But look who's coming." Herb Miller crossed the street toward us. He carried a new Remington 30.06, the sales tag still dangling from the polished brown stock. We were standing near his truck. When he reached his pickup, he stopped, cocked the gun, aimed it at Danny's foot, and pulled the trigger. The pin clicked on the empty chamber. He drove away without even giving us a glance.

The fear that had stalked me since Jimmy Lee's death flitted in, hovered, settled. As we walked home I kept glancing over my shoulder. Neither of us said anything until we came within sight of my house.

"What's the first play you're going to call?" I asked him.

"A dive play to R.D.," he answered.

"No," I replied, "that's wrong. Go for a touchdown on the first play."

"Coach told me to start the game with simple plays, get used to handling the ball in a game."

"That's what you'd expect a coach to say. That's what the other coach would do and what he will expect you to do. No one will expect a new quarterback to try a long pass on his first play. Take a chance." We stepped into my mother's kitchen. I exhaled a long, sighing breath.

"I might," he said.

The kitchen looked like a painting Norman Rockwell might have done called A *Bride's Dream*. It was furnished with items Mother had bought from the bank at the liquidation sale of her father's possessions. A porcelain rooster, statuesque and full-breasted, maybe a leghorn, stood proudly on his shelf, not one chip in his white feathers, his deep orange comb dusted and shiny, his lid intact. The slaw graters hung in order from the coarse to the fine cut. Everything was polished and in its place. Mother was staring out the kitchen window. She seemed to be trapped in time, like her kitchen, on the verge of a "spell," my father called her deep, hypnotic daydreams. Finally, she stopped staring.

"Sorry," she said, "here's the catsup for your burgers." She lifted the bottle from its place inside the refrigerator.

"You haven't cooked them yet," I reminded her.

"Oh, how silly of me. I'll do it now."

She turned on the burner and withdrew again. I knew she was not worried about Danny, the pressure of his first game. Her concerns were for her "Sonny boy." If only someone could have com-

forted her, "Don't worry about Sonny, all he has to do is get the
equipment out. He won't get hurt. What he's doing is not a sin,
it's just a game, wholesome clean fun for boys." But she stood alone
with no one to help her. She gripped the edge of her scoured white
sink entertaining the idea that her husband might have been right.
I, her Sonny, might have been better off if she had shamed me for
stabbing the football and had sent me back outside to endure more
sandburrs, bleed more blood, swallow more snot. I felt her ache—
a vacuum between her womb and her heart—how it hurt her to
see me and Danny together. Danny admired, respected, and cod-
dled by the community; her son ignored, transparent, disposable
cellophane. She hated the male mind, which adhered to the Old
Testament's manly idea of "an eye for an eye" and paid only lip service to the New Testament's more gentle "turn the other cheek."
Now her son, the water boy, was about to leave her kitchen for a
game. Game! Some game, where boys in the bloom of youth can
be injured, maimed, killed; the excitement, it's life itself. Afterward, what will there be for the Danny Boones, those who can walk
without limps, those whose brains are not scrambled?

We walked out into the evening light. They owed my mother a
compliment. "Your son is the best durn water boy this town's ever
had." No one said nice things about the water boy. Just the sound,
"water boy," it was derisive. The fans had reasons for being in their
seats—too old—out of school—flunking—retarded. But the water
boy has no excuse; he has a reason, he's scared. He lives the danger and excitement vicariously. Maybe some of the glory will rub
off on him.

CHAPTER 12

"Good luck." I forced a smile. Danny smiled back, tousled my hair, and we stepped inside the dressing room. The heat of late summer lingered inside the high walls of the Quonset building. It had once been a bus barn, but was now the football dressing room. I had done my job earlier, so there was little for me to do.

"Come here, Danny, let's get your ankles taped," Cannonball called. Danny had shaved off the hair below the calves of his legs. Cannonball tore strips of white adhesive tape from a large roll and wrapped them around Danny's ankles to make a castlike support. The room shimmered from my shame of being an outsider. I'd never have a reason to shave my legs, but it was not too late. I could still do it, I didn't have to count Band-Aids. Then I remembered the sandburrs, impossible to remove once they penetrated, and I remembered my mother. I must not be distracted by temporal glory. Yet, all the preaching I did to myself did not diminish my self-deprecation.

The rest of the team drifted in. Harley Pugh stomped to his locker without speaking. There's something wrong. He should not share the spotlight with Danny. He's a braggart, foul-mouthed, coarse.

Danny's clean, wholesome. But Danny had worked with Harley as if he had no memory of the attempted humiliation on Main Street or the fire at the Farm Bureau dinner. It was Harley who acted sullen toward Danny.

Cannonball ran the last strip of tape up Danny's leg into the unshaven hair. "My motivation tape," Cannonball said. "If we win, I jerk this tape off with one yank, a little burning, but virtually painless. If we lose, I pull it off hair by hair. Hurts even more than a linebacker." Cannonball punched Danny playfully.

"Shit! Quarterbacks are sissies," Harley hissed. It could have been part of a good-natured challenge, a teammate trying to motivate another, daring him to perform better than expected, but the words sizzled with such hate everyone froze. The last sunlight streamed through the high windows. Odors of whirlpool chemicals and analgesic balm filtered through the orange, smokeless air.

Danny's football pants were partially unlaced, a faint line of hair ran downward from his navel and disappeared beneath the elastic band of his jockstrap. He ambled toward Harley, who squared to face him. I thought there was going to be a fight. Danny stopped about two feet away, and, as he spoke, he reached forward and tapped Harley's bare chest with his fingers, as if he played a chord on a piano.

"Hibbs called you all-state material. Ends only catch passes that are thrown to them. Only ends who catch passes make all-state teams. Be ready. The ball's coming at you. I'm not letting you get in the way of winning this game."

They stared at each other while the rest of us waited.

"Everyone get dressed," Coach ordered gruffly. "Let's get this season going." I suppressed another wave of loneliness and shame. Admiration for Danny swelled up in my chest. He had handled Harley's challenge, had risen to face it. His courage, that's what I lacked.

"Schultz, walk around and help anyone who needs it," Coach

shouted at me. Soon they were dressed. They milled around in their white, black, and gold, patting one another's rumps.

"Stick it to 'em, big guy." They all looked into one another's eyes. "We can do it," they kept repeating.

"Let's go, but no noise," the coach ordered.

I had stashed the equipment in back of the ambulance where the injured or dead usually rode. Cannonball let me drive while he sat on the passenger side. I flipped on the flashing light, which reached with sharp red fingers into the shadows of late evening. We crept ahead of the players, their cleats crunching on the gravel road. I began to feel better, as if I were a vital part of the event. We passed between the concrete pillars of the stadium. The emptiness vanished. I kept the ambulance on the sideline while the team charged out onto the field. The stands were not yet full, but the cheering swelled. I stepped out of the ambulance. I had never been on the field when people were in the stadium. It had been built just after the war, seating capacity twice the population of the town. By game time, all the seats would be filled by people driving in from the countryside, and latecomers would be forced to sit on the aisle steps. I felt transformed into someone worthy of admiration. I was no longer anonymous.

The Shattuck Savages dashed onto the field. Their fans cheered, waving their red pom-poms, building energy for the fray. They huddled close to one another, evident to them they were in hostile territory.

Lipscomb signaled, the team divided. Each unit knew its place. The offense ran plays. The defense blocked lightly, pounded one another's shoulders, clenched fists clacking on hard pads, staccato notes against the murmuring of stadium noise.

I scanned the crowd. I hoped Killer had stayed at A&M and would not be at the game. The Main Street merchants huddled near me on the lower steps just back of the equipment. They'd heard the coach brag and they'd watched the practices. But tonight was Danny's real test.

"You gotta admit he looks good warmin' up," LaFaye said. "He's a natural. But you don't really know until you see what he can do under pressure. It's like Duffy Duncan," he said, jabbing Junior Goggin in the ribs, "always talkin' about women. But if one ever points her tits at 'im, he hightails it like a scairt coyote." He punctuated his point by spitting tobacco, which landed on the grass not five feet from where I stood.

The first few rows of seats had already filled. Pay Day Ottinger, "the whittler," his name a legacy from his mule-skinning father, tapped by, using a cane he had carved and bent from hickory. He was on his way to a seat near the cheering section. Blinded by cataracts, and older even than Old Man Goggin, he came to the game for the company and the cheering. His wife had died young so he had been alone fifty years. At games, he rose with the throng, bleating out the chants, "Give me a D—D, Give me a U—U, Give me an S—S, Give me a T—T," his voice sounding like the sheep he had fought to drive out in the range wars.

Other local celebrities were scattered through the stands. Everyone was there. The Parker triplets, born in a chicken coop, sat on the bottom row near the bathrooms. Bud and Ruthie were cleaning out chicken manure when the pain hit. At least it was fresh straw the baby came out on. Bud tied the cord, put the girl in a hen's nest, and a boy landed. Bud got him in a cubby, how would they support twins? And the other girl popped out.

Up top of the stadium, Alfred sat with his mom. People put coats on empty seats when they walk by. One time my father refused to behave that way, and they sat beside him and Mother. Mother complained. "I don't mind the drooling. But they smell." "They have to sit near someone," my father explained. So Mother stays at home.

But there, they just arrived and sat down, what I was afraid of, behind the Main Street merchants, they are the ones to watch. They are the ones who wreak havoc. The girl pokes her right arm inside her lover's shirt. The other fans can see this. She doesn't care. She appears distracted, as if she's thinking. She's looking at the tall young quarterback who warms up less than thirty feet from where she sits. She sees, not the perfect spirals, the gold jersey with the number ten, or the padded shoulders. She sees him, as I did, on Mrs. Farragut's lawn, slender, smooth, helpless, aroused.

At seven-forty, Coach called the team off the field. Danny walked with our star linebacker, Joe Lee, behind the coach, while the other players trudged after them. I held the locker door open. I smelled their sour breaths as they walked by. I handed towels to those who wanted them, and draped a parka over Danny's shoulders to keep him warm. Everyone got quiet.

"We're a young team," Coach said. "We have to stick together. One team member in trouble, on or off the field, means the whole team's in trouble. Every member of this team is a friend. Don't leave a friend to fight alone. I'm talking to you all, from the water boy to the quarterback." His gaze drifted to Harley. Harley glared back. Coach snapped his clenched fist into the palm of his hand. "Hit hard. Remember, it's collision football that's winning football. You have to hit those fuckin' Indians harder than they've ever been hit. Get out there, kick their butts."

They grabbed their helmets, regrouped on the runway, and on signal from Coach, burst onto the field. I ran with the team. It felt like we were a pack of wild animals. My feet hardly touched the ground. In the stands, frenetic euphoria, waving arms, jumping bodies, billowing skirts. The Savages won the coin toss but chose to kick off.

"Cannonball said they'd test me, they think they can get me rattled," Danny said. "I better do what Coach said, call simple plays at first."

"No!" I moved my mouth close to the hole in his helmet's ear-
piece. "Use opposite end, Z out, flare left. They'll never expect it."
    We sang the National Anthem, a preacher said a prayer, and the
team huddled together and said the Lord's Prayer, and then took
the field. I rested my knee on the medicine chest. R.D. took the
kickoff on the fifteen, slipped at the twenty-five, and went down
at the twenty-eight. Not great field position, but it wouldn't matter. Buried far beneath the excitement, was a wish that he might
fall on his butt so hard he'd never get up.
    Their hands clapped in unison and the team trotted to the ball.
Danny read the defense, a standard six, three, two. The ball snapped
into his fingers, he faked a handoff to the halfback as if it were the
dive play everyone expected, then pivoted, flaring toward our bench,
hiding the ball on his hip. Coach looked stupefied. I felt immense
satisfaction, a sense of power. I could manipulate men from the
sidelines of a football field as if they were toy soldiers.
    Harley loped downfield, speeded up, angled left, in line with
Danny. Danny planted his foot, and, with a move so quick we
hardly knew it happened, he threw the ball. It spiraled like a bullet. Harley spread his fingers, the ball arrived. It took him only four
or five seconds to lumber into the end zone after the catch. For
those seconds and a few more, an eerie silence lingered over the
stadium. The speed of the play had shocked the spectators, then
the spark built up force traveling fan to fan until the hometown
folks burst with frenzy unknown since the end of World War II.
The fans fused to one another and to the team, but most of all to
the quarterback who had thrown a football farther and more accurately than they had ever seen, and made it look easy, a beautiful boy to inspire them. No failures, no dangers, no dreads could
cut off the dynamic power created by the event. Four thousand
people in the Cimarron stadium linked with their sons, victorious,
glory to all.

Hibbs reported the win in the Sunday *Daily Oklahoman.*

DEVILS' SOPHOMORE QB TOMAHAWKS SAVAGES

Displaying the courage of his pioneer name-
sake, Daniel Boone, sophomore quarterback for
the Cimarron Dustdevils, shocked the hometown
crowd by throwing a long pass on the opening play
of the season for a seventy-two-yard TD. The pass,
caught by all-state candidate end Harley Pugh, was
brilliantly conceived by the coaches and flawlessly
executed by the young star. . . .

I could read no further.

As I lay in bed sleepless that night, I remembered those years I
had spent with Mother in her room. I heard her soft moans, and
my father's snores from his room, and then my mother's moaning
became sobs, and I began to cry with her, until my exhausted mind
slipped away into a field of white tombstones, Jimmy Lee's mother
whispering—why didn't you tell us? Danny running toward the re-
volving purple darkness.

FAIR GAME

PART II

C H A P T E R 1 3

Glorious hysteria fanned out from Cimarron into the countryside. Danny was no longer the mere son of a farmer, nor was I any longer just the friend of a handsome, mysterious boy that nobody knew. I was the friend of the Dustdevils' quarterback. People stopped me on the street to ask about Danny, invited me into their homes and shops offering Dr Peppers and bologna sandwiches. I drank in the admiration flowing from young boys who looked first at Danny, then at me, their eyes wide with wonder that they, of all boys, should be near the quarterback and his friend, and if they could not speak to Danny because they were too shy, they could speak to me, and they did.

But it was not just children who were awed. LaFaye summed things up for the Main Street merchants when he brought in his weekly ad on Saturday after the second game. He told my father, "That boy's a wonder, he's increased my business twenty, maybe thirty percent. They come in to talk about the game, and while they talk, I fit 'em with a pair of boots they might never've bought otherwise."

"It's not just Danny, it's the whole team," I said.

"Oh, I know Danny can't do it without the others, Sonny, but he's the one they talk about." And LaFaye was right. The downstate press wrote about Danny, the frontier quarterback with the pioneer name and the rifle arm. He had captured their imaginations, not shy, but so unassuming; not embarrassed about the attention, but unimpressed by it.

Hibbs, the reporter who had started everything, explained it to Lipscomb when they were talking in Coach's office. "You begin with the way he looks, so wholesome, even the way he talks," the reporter said, "that drawl like a bull rider; then, when he takes the ball and glides along on air, and suddenly cuts, you wonder, 'What the hell, why's he doing that?' Then there's a hole that only he saw, and he's through it like Moses parting the Red Sea. It's instinctive."

"The teaching's paid off," Lipscomb said.

"I don't know, Gus," Hibbs replied. "That kind of thing I don't think can be taught."

"You're right in one way," Coach replied. "We aren't dealing with your regular kid. This is a once-in-a-lifetime kid. If we can keep him healthy, years from now people will say to me: 'I remember you, you coached that kid who played quarterback for the Dustdevils back in the fifties.' Coaches work their whole lives, and most of them will never coach a boy with this kind of talent. He's a career-maker. I might get a university job." Then he begged Hibbs not to print what he'd said.

Hibbs said he'd print what he wanted to, and that Lipscomb had known he was on the record.

I had been cleaning out the whirlpool bath. "Do you want me to fill it now?" I asked the coach. He ignored me, but Hibbs looked over.

"When are you converting the water boy into a halfback? He looks like he can run, to me."

"Oh, he can run fine, he runs after the Lord Jesus, don't you Sonny? Now print that, you bastard."

Only the bad feelings between Danny and Harley Pugh diminished the good feelings surrounding the team. Harley had caught four touchdown passes in the first two games, but he remained aloof and hostile toward Danny. It wasn't a public feud, the coach forbade it, and no one on the team, not even Danny and Harley, dared disobey Coach. He had his own brand of authority, and he was backed up with the complete support of the whole town. There seemed to be little danger of actual fights, but the team could feel the tension between them, and the townspeople knew about it and they worried. Harley was still hanging around with Killer, who often cut football practice at A&M and came back to town to see Dovie. It was rumored he was hanging on to his scholarship by the skin of his teeth. His visits kept Harley riled up against Danny.

I had mixed feelings about Harley. I hated how Harley exuded violence, how there always seemed to be trouble when he was around. However, I was sympathetic to Harley because he was devoted to his mother. I often saw him shopping with her, helping her choose items from the shelf they needed, carefully figuring for her what they could spend because they lived on a limited income from Mrs. Pugh's job at Tice's laundry.

Harley's mother, like mine, was not entirely stable. She was an insomniac who prowled the streets at night, poking through people's trash cans, making dogs bark. Sheriff Ordway had escorted her home more than once after someone had called him reporting prowlers in the alley.

The whereabouts of Harley's father was unknown. Harley often bragged that his father was in South Texas working in the oil fields and was making a lot of money, that his father had purchased the Harley-Davidson that Harley rode and had given it to him as a present and that his father was so rich he was going to retire soon and come to Cimarron to live with him and his mother.

The Wednesday after our second victory, I walked with Danny toward Charlie's garage. Danny had driven the Boone family sedan in for repairs, and we were on our way to pick it up. Ahead of us, three blocks from school, Harley and a biker acquaintance who had quit school last year were hazing Cletus Goodner into a vacant lot. Cletus was almost a year too young for our sophomore class, and was maturing slowly, but he was smart, so Egbert, our superintendent, had let his parents push him ahead. With some fancy bike riding, Harley and his friend cornered Cletus, flipped down their kickstands, and caught him. Cletus did not put up much of a fight. The lot, overgrown with muletails and some ragweed, was in full view of Main Street.

"They're taking his pants off, same dumb trick," I said. Danny loped with easy strides to Harley's bike. The black finish of the Harley-Davidson gleamed in the evening light. New leather saddlebags, which Harley claimed his father had sent him, were strapped behind the seat. Danny dug out his pocket knife.

They had Cletus undressed, boxer shorts with baggy elastic down to his knees. Cletus's pubic hair was just beginning to grow in, and clung to his groin in two stringy clumps like eyebrows over a floppy little nose. They had not yet seen us when they stood him up to push him into Main Street. A pickup truck rolled by, Duffy Duncan's International, Duffy craning his neck to see what was going on.

Danny pressed the point of his knife blade against the new leather saddlebag on Harley's machine. "Let the kid go," Danny called. They still had not seen us, and were startled, but they continued to hold Cletus up, his bare bottom in full view of the street. No one spoke for a few seconds.

"What did you say?" Harley asked.

Danny moved his knife away from the saddlebag and held it in front of his face so they could see the blade, then pushed its point back against the leather.

"I said, let the kid go." His voice was cold, determined. A couple of cars slowed down, more drivers rubbernecking.

"We're just having a little fun," Harley said.

"Nothing wrong with a little fun," Danny answered. "Ask Cletus if he thinks it's fun."

Harley glared at us, then kept looking around as if the answer to his dilemma about how to save both his ass and his face was somewhere out there, if only he could locate it. There'd be hell to pay if the quarterback got hurt in a fight. There was no good solution, so they finally let go, and Cletus scampered away, pulling up his pants and running at the same time.

Danny stood up also, faced them, folded the knife blade into its slot, and said to Harley, "We're not saying anything about this, you don't have to either. See you tomorrow in practice."

We walked away. "Don't look back," Danny told me. It took all my willpower. We had walked a full block before we heard their engines. The noise became louder, quickly, and for a moment I thought they would run us down, but Danny didn't stop. They pulled in front of us, dust swirling up from around their bikes as their wheels skidded. The exhausts belched when they cut their motors. Harley swung his leg over the seat, kicked down the stand, and planted his big boots about ten feet away. I tried to stay even with Danny, but my muscles were so taut it was difficult to move. I knew I had to fight this time. There were no other options. Danny stopped within an arm's length of Harley, then waited for Harley to make the first move.

"I always felt bad about that time last spring," Harley said in a high-pitched voice, "and about the brown bag fire."

"It's okay," Danny said. "We're even."

Harley's face relaxed, and he grinned. "Okay, we're even," Harley said. "Where you goin'?"

"Charlie's."

"Get on, we'll take you."

And, of course, becoming friends off the field helped Danny and

Harley connect on the field. Hibbs claimed they were the best passing combination the state had ever seen. Certainly, no one around Cimarron disagreed.

The team now seemed to be invincible. Every time Danny retreated to pass, we all felt only by the grace of God could anyone fling that stitched leather ball with so much speed and accuracy. When he ran with it, his reverses and deceptions created a kind of uncanny mass hypnotism. And they all found out what I had known since we were kids, Danny was what coaches call "a hitter." He never gave a tackler a clear shot, never waited for anyone to hit him. He hit first, like a steel coil exploding, destroying their timing, and, as often as not, knocked down the tackler instead of falling down himself. When he hit an opponent, he set off a crack like a buffalo gun and left them stunned by his force. The fans learned to imitate the sound with their mouths and with their hands. After each hit, the imitations echoed through the stands and climaxed in spontaneous applause. By game's end, the fans of our opponents left the stadium shaking their heads, saying, "We didn't think he would be quite that good."

Even the weather on game nights was unusual that fall, voluptuous sunsets, the dusty air laden with unbridled energy. The team and cheerleaders rode the bus to the stadium, while I drove the ambulance with Cannonball beside me. The bus pulled up near the arch of the stadium entrance, then the cheerleaders scampered out, gliding into the blue transparency of the stadium passageways, becoming, first, black nymphs of darkness, then winged, golden fairies as they flowed into the light of the field. The crowds cheered them; pretty girls uniting fans and team in the creation of glorious fame.

The farmers with sunburned faces, as well as the merchants, surged into the yellow light of the stadium where they drank in the courage and hope ladled out by a slender, tough farm kid, a big burly end, and a whole team of boys that followed them.

Someone, certainly a minister, some man of God, should have

spoken up, should have warned us that the game had become too important, that it was wrong for all spirit and hope to ride on the simple fact of whether or not the team won its weekly football game. Some pastor should have stepped out to be the prophet of the age, warn us it was not the end of the world if the Dustdevils lost a game. Life would go on as it always had. But the whole town seemed to believe life simply wouldn't be worth living without a Dustdevil victory, and the ministers all came to the game and pronounced majestic prayers over the loudspeaker, prayers for the safety of the players, prayers for victory as if our nation were at war and God was being asked to be on our side.

CHAPTER 14

Then, the team ran into difficulty. The Boise City Bearcats always played brutal football, and, it seemed, had always been a nemesis of the Dustdevils. It was not a home game. The team faced a four-hour ride from Cimarron to Boise City. The road was rough. The bus the team used jostled its passengers, mile after mile. The team was exhausted when we arrived.

The Bearcats were fired up over how the press had said the Dustdevils had a great team and would defeat them this year with hardly a growl heard. From the first play, the hitting was savage along the line of scrimmage. Their defense tackled Danny viciously, even after he handed the ball off to a running back. In the third quarter, they dinged him so badly Harley had to call plays and tell him what to do. I complained to Lipscomb, so Coach pulled Danny out for a few minutes. Doc McGrath, who had driven to the game with LaFaye, P.O., and Junior, came down to the field and looked in Danny's eyes. Doc said there was nothing to do, it was only a temporary loss of memory, it can happen when they're hitting as hard as they were hitting Danny.

Our defense also took a beating. The Bearcats ran their two-hundred-ten-pound fullback up the gut of our defense. Joe Lee, our best linebacker, and co-captain, couldn't stop him. By the third quarter, Joe had started to retreat when the ball was snapped. Coach tried everything, yelled at Joe Lee from the sidelines, pulled him and chewed him out; Cannonball talked to him, quietly, reasonably. They put in an extra linebacker. Nothing helped. I couldn't tell if the other team was that good, or if Joe Lee was having a very bad game. Twice, Harley prevented touchdowns when he tackled the Bearcat quarterback and stripped him of the football only a few yards outside our goal. With the game almost over, we were fortunate to be trailing by only six points. With thirty seconds left, the Bearcat center hiked the ball ten feet over the head of their punter, and Harley recovered it in the end zone for our only touchdown. Our kicker kicked the extra point. We came out with a miraculous seven to six victory, although physically whipped by a team we had been favored to beat easily. Despite the victory, nobody felt like celebrating.

The townsfolk started to grumble. Some said the Board of Education had to do something about that bus. Others said the coaches had let the team peak too early. Two weeks from playoff time, and the Dustdevils were faltering. The town was scared and angry.

Monday, Tuesday, and Wednesday practices stretched long into the dim, cold evenings. The morale of the team sagged, and dived again on Wednesday, when we read Melvin Hibbs's analysis of coming games. "I rate Cimarron's game with the Hardesty Bulldogs for the Panhandle conference championship a toss-up," he wrote. "Last Friday, the Dustdevils' opponents found weaknesses in the young Cimarron team that had not yet been exposed. You can bet the Bulldog scouts watched and learned." Although still undefeated, we fell from third to eleventh in the state rankings.

Thursday, there was no dawn, a thick overcast with drizzle lasted all morning. The rain stopped by afternoon, but the gray ceiling threatened to let go again. The team tramped into the bus barn to dress. Lipscomb, who always had the team practice without pads

GARY   REISWIG

on Thursday, avoiding contact so the wounds could heal, was huddled in the corner with Cannonball. That Thursday, black Thursday, the team named it, Lipscomb changed his tactics.

"Put those pads on, boys, we're gonna rock 'em and sock 'em today," he ordered. The lethargy had to be shaken.

Joe Lee and Harley called out the warm-ups, but their voices had
no ring of authority and leadership. Chatter, encouraged by the
coaches, sounded like the senseless barking of skittish prairie dogs.
They completed their exercises.

"Come over here," Coach called to the team. "Sit down and get
your helmets off. I want to see all your smiling faces." He paced
back and forth, hands behind his back, a father advising his sons.
He droned out his well-worn themes: loyalty, hustle, dedication.
When he finished, he kneeled down on one knee, his face at the
players' level.

"I've watched football players for years. They tend to do three
things while they're in school. They play football. They study to
keep up their grades so they can play football. And they chase girls.
Nothing wrong with that. You've got to have your diversions. But
sometimes there's a guy who's so bad at woman chasing he lets one
of them catch him."

He shot up onto his feet, startling us, one hand across his midriff,
the other pointed at the players. He bent his knees like a gunfighter
ready for a showdown. His voice, no longer modulated and fatherly,
rumbled from deep inside his throat like thunder that precedes a
hailstorm.

"Don't get serious about any fuckin' girl if you want to win football games!" With his trigger finger, he pointed at Joe Lee, who
had been unable to stop the Bearcats, and who, last week, had given
his class ring to Karen Lynn Handly.

Coach lined them up, offense against the defense. Coach assigned Harley to the offensive side, and he assigned the other players, who played both offense and defense.

"Last game, our linebackers got blocked. We're gonna correct that fault." His eyes sought out Joe Lee. He turned his back to the goal. The players stood waiting, their legs apart, hands on hips. "Our blocking in the backfield stunk. Our quarterback spent more time on his ass than on his feet. We're here to correct that fault. The two most fundamental techniques in football, blocking and tackling. That's what we're here to learn because last Friday night we forgot how."

The corners of Coach's mouth cracked, more a smirk than a smile. "This little drill I picked up from the coaches down at OU. They call this drill 'hamburger.' It separates the serious men from the pussies." He walked past the boys like a drill sergeant peering into the eyes of his players.

Joe Lee had positioned himself last in the defensive line. Coach stopped when he reached him and looked first in his eyes, then up and down his whole body. Joe stood, resting on one leg, with the other foot tipped up like a pony at rest after a frolic around the pasture. Coach shuffled back to the gap. He used his football shoe to tamp down a soft ridge pushed up by a grubbing mole. When he looked up, his eyes were tired, teary.

"I see some of you will not make it to the end of the season," he said, "and probably will not make anything of your lives, either. I've failed you. That makes me sad, real sad." Then his face hardened. He knew his job. A coach must turn boys into men, not cater to some kid who forgot what was important, some boy who fell in love and became a coward.

"You blockers, when I hit you on the butt, you tear out and knock those linebackers on their asses. You linebackers, watch out, these bastards are after your balls." Coach had set up the drill in the worst patch of sandburrs he could find. The one who got beat and fell down would face picking out a lot of stickers. He grinned at them, walked along the line of crouched blockers and paused by Harley, then slapped the big end on the rear. Harley, running with his shoulders low as he had been taught, closed the gap between himself and Donnie Boggit, always eager, reserve linebacker. Their pads clacked when they met—the linebacker's forearm caught Harley's upper chest. Dirt and grass kicked up from their cleats. The stand-off was momentary, then Donnie toppled and landed in the sand-burr patch. He got up as if he didn't mind. Coach looked pleased.

The line moved quickly and reached Joe Lee. Joe stepped up to the goal and took his linebacking stance. Coach slapped the next blocker on the butt, and the two met. As they each struggled to gain an advantage, Coach sent the next blocker. Then blocker after blocker attacked Joe. As soon as he got up from one hit, the next one hit him. He fell easier each time, and got up slower. His legs and arms oozed blood. Dirt and grass clung to his wounds. His practice jersey was pinned to his skin by the sandburrs. This went on for about ten minutes, until Coach slapped Harley's butt, and Harley, the only blocker with any fierceness left, hit Joe Lee mid-chest with a vicious forearm shiver. Joe Lee went down flat on his back. When he didn't get up, Lipscomb bent over him. "Get up, or you're off the team," Lipscomb said in a flat voice. Joe Lee did not move.

There was a hollow ring in the metal-ribbed building while the team undressed. The showers hissed and cleats scraped on the concrete floor, but there was no banter, no teasing, no gibes.

Joe Lee had finally dragged himself in and sat fully suited in front of his locker. "Go help him get his pads off," Danny told me. "It looks like he can't face all the burrs."

"I'll help you with your shirt," I said to the beaten linebacker. When he raised his arms, the shirt pulled on the sandburrs, and he cried out with the pain. Danny helped me peel Joe's clothes off, and we led him into the shower. The hot water stung him. When he was dry, we found tweezers and began pulling out the barbed spikes. Each tug brought blood to the surface of his skin. I dabbed him with cotton balls dipped in alcohol. Tears spilled out his eyes, mingled with the alcohol, and disappeared into the cotton. He whimpered, but never said a word.

I glanced back when we went out the door. Joe Lee sat on the bench, still not dressed, a faded towel draped over his groin. He did not attend school on Friday. When the team dressed for the Hardesty game, his locker door stood open, empty.

The dressing room was naked and quiet, all talk stunned out of us. Coach made the team walk to the field. The night cloaked us in cold darkness. Each breath sent a wispy white plume into the air where it disappeared in time to be replaced by another.

Beside me in the ambulance, Cannonball chirped like a happy sparrow.

"I don't see why you're so cheerful. We won't win this game. Everybody's so low."

He didn't respond to me, just whistled an unrecognizable tune, and smiled his crooked grin.

"Why do you think Coach drove Joe Lee off the team?" I asked him. "He had a bad game, but he was our best linebacker."

"He did it because I told him to," Cannonball said. He laughed, a high cackle. "You're a smart kid, Sonny, but not that smart in some ways. Watch and learn something."

Lipscomb gave no speech in the locker room after the warm-up. We sat in silence. Game time arrived unceremoniously. Coach stood, and said, offhandedly, "Boggit, you'll start at center linebacker in place of Joe Lee. You all know what you have to do." His arrogance was unbearable. I thought of quitting right then so I would not be a party to the breakdown of a spirited, winning team. But it was not the Dustdevils who broke down.

The Hardesty Bulldogs suffered concussions, broken bones, sprained knees and ankles, and blood by the pint on their uniforms and on the field. Every scrawny third- and fourth-string Dustdevil had a chance to play and to lay a few hard licks on the unfortunate dogs. Cimarron, sixty-three, Hardesty, zero.

P.O. came through and shook each player's hand, right down to the fourth-stringers. "Come in for a milk shake on me," he told them. He shook Coach's hand. "I've never seen a team so fired up. It was wonderful to see them beat up on someone like that, especially after last week. Does my old heart good." P.O. hit himself on the chest, chuckling with deep satisfaction.

Melvin Hibbs reported the victory and now called last week's game one of those unaccountable letdowns on the part of a vastly superior team.

The Main Street merchants argued over which of them had remained loyal to the coach. "You gotta hand it to him, he knew what he was doing." LaFaye punctuated his point with tobacco juice, spotting the sidewalk in front of the Elite Cafe.

"Just goes to show you, no one player makes or breaks a team, you gotta bite the bullet and weed out the chaff," Junior said.

"Well, maybe," P.O. added. "But pray nothing happens to the quarterback. 'Cause we ain't got a prayer without him."

CHAPTER 15

Before I got out of bed on Saturday morning, my foreboding, temporarily interrupted by the pleasure of the win, returned. Primarily, my misgivings were about Joe Lee. Although he had never been a close friend of mine, his fate was not pleasant to contemplate. Having been humiliated, he would now be blackballed, looked down on for the rest of his life if he chose to stay in Cimarron where people would always remember that he didn't have the character it took to be a football player. If he moved to some other town, he would be forced to lie about where he was from. If he told anyone he was from Cimarron, then that person would someday meet someone else from Cimarron and mention Joe Lee. The humiliation would be repeated.

Joe Lee's situation left me with a queasy feeling. His fate, I realized, was not dissimilar to mine. I would always be remembered as the water boy. If I moved to another town and let it be known I was from Cimarron, then people would say, "Oh, you must have played on those great football teams that always came out of Cimarron." And I would say, "No, I was the water boy." The nod, the tilting head of understanding, the pity in the eyes, the smile dimpling the edges of the mouth.

But there was something else that bothered me, the extent of damage the Dustdevils had inflicted on the Hardesty Bulldogs. The carnage unleashed from boys who were my contemporaries made what Coach had done seem to be larger than winning one game, humiliating one boy.

I spent Saturday helping my father. Late afternoon, I finished sweeping out the press room. Dad had his feet on his desk. "Anything else you want me to do?"

He appeared to be distracted, involved in his work as usual. He was looking out the window into the street. He always made sure the windows were clean. Someone was passing by, Alfred and his mother. They had a little wagon Alfred was pulling.

"What did you think of the game?" my father asked.

"It was a great game," I said, my voice pitched with enthusiasm, father and son having a sports chat, happens in America a million times a day. My father, however, leaned back in his chair and looked out the window again. He seemed to be on the verge of tears.

"You seem different," I said.

He put his hands to his eyes and rubbed them as if he were very tired. "I'm just wondering, that's all, about those Hardesty boys getting hurt. I didn't think anything about it while the game was being played. I enjoyed it, tremendously. But I've been wondering how I might have felt if you had been out there with Danny and the others popping those guys. Or worse, if you had been on the other side, getting popped."

I sat down on a folding chair. "What was it like when you were my age?" He was still looking out the window.

"I don't remember much," he said, "but it's interesting that you ask because I was just then thinking about a kid in the orphanage. He wasn't any bigger than any of the rest of us, but he could fight like hell. He had everybody looking up to him, bringing him candy and presents. If anybody got out of line, they got popped. The headmaster loved him. He got the award for best citizen. Twice he got it. Two years after he was out of the orphanage, they hanged him in Arkansas for murdering a family, husband, wife, and three little kids. He even killed the dog. He popped them just like he'd popped us, except they died."

He kept staring out the window, then he seemed to gather his thoughts. "Well, I can't sit here all day with my feet on my desk. Your mother called. She wants some groceries from the Ideal. Here's the list and some money."

That evening, Danny drove into town and came by our house to pick me up. We drove by Harley's house, a shack with a rusting tin roof situated near the edge of town where the sandy land sloped toward the river. It was still light enough we could see the thread of riverwater, then the cottonwoods and the sand hills on the other side. Danny honked the horn, and Harley came bounding out, then we headed to the drugstore to collect the milk shakes P.O. had promised to give us after the game.

We parked in front and got out. Killer and Dovie were sitting on a bench sharing a bottle of Dr Pepper. It seemed to me Killer had put on some weight. The Aggie sweatshirt he wore was tight across his belly. The girl's basketball team had begun practice last week, and Dovie was in excellent condition. Her slender shapeliness made Killer appear bloated. She wore jeans with a bright yellow scarf tied around her waist, a white Western style shirt with pearl snaps, and her hair bobbed in tight ringlets. They had only one bottle of pop and two straws, so they took turns sipping, and when Dovie sipped, she kissed Killer on the cheek as she pulled her mouth away from the straw.

Harley called out, "Hey, Killer, didn't the Aggies play today? How'd you get home so fast?"

"I quit," Killer said. "You hanging out with the queers?"

Harley stopped dead in his tracks.

"We have to go," Dovie insisted. She stood up and turned her back toward us. She got Killer into his pickup and they drove away.

The half-consumed Dr Pepper was on the bench. Harley seemed numbed, confused by Killer's snub. He stood staring long after they had disappeared up Main Street.

I felt strangely pleased by the encounter, as if progress toward some unspoken goal had been made. "Your friend doesn't like the company you keep," I said to Harley.

I opened the door to the drugstore. No sense keeping Harley in the dark. "Killer doesn't like you because he knows Dovie's in love with Danny, and Danny's going to have her and he can't stand the thought of that, nor the thought of you hanging around with us." I was surprised at what I said. It was not anything I had thought about in advance.

Danny was waiting for us inside. "It's coming anyhow. I should have punched him, finished it," he said.

"You could get hurt," I reminded him. "You have too much riding on you to risk it."

On our way to the soda fountain booths, we passed a woman who was bent over looking in the cosmetics case. Her skirt was tight and smooth across her rear end, no lines of a girdle, and as she straightened up, she ran her hand down over her trim rear. I recognized her by the cut of her clothes before she turned around. Beverly Shuler, owner of the only local dress shop, the wife of Walter Shuler, owner of Shuler Abstract Company and indisputably the richest people in Cimarron. Mrs. Shuler had been elected to be head of the church deaconesses at our church last Sunday. The debate about her election to such an influential position had gone on for weeks, because many members of the congregation were suspicious that she was too rich and too beautiful to be a committed Christian. It was one of the few times I had ever seen my father angry about anything in church. In private, my father had uttered a few choice descriptions of those who had spoken against Mrs. Shuler's election. "Hypocrites, pharisees, whited sepulchers, that's what they are," he muttered.

"William," my mother replied when she overheard, "what a surprise, you've been studying your Bible." My father snorted. He did not appreciate her sarcasm any more than he appreciated the others' hypocrisy.

"My, you guys get bigger every time I see you. Congratulations on the game last night." She was wearing a light brown silk blouse tucked into her skirt. The blouse was loose, and hung elegantly over her shoulders. I had the urge to reach out and touch the fabric, feel its tight sheen between my fingers, which were more used to handling the soft weave of cotton. I wondered if my father had ever touched that blouse.

"Thank you," Danny replied. "Congratulations to you on your new position with the deaconesses," he added.

Mrs. Shuler smiled. She brushed back her hair, which had a slight reddish tint, as if it had been washed lightly in a rinse. The diamond on her finger was the largest one in Cimarron, but she had the elegance of carriage to support its size and glitter. "Thank you, Danny. May I call on you for help when I need some?" She reached out and touched his arm, moving her hand upward to his bicep. Her fingers tightened.

"Yes, please do," Danny replied.

Mrs. Shuler smiled again, arching her eyebrows, then let her hand slide down his arm until she took hold of his hand and squeezed. "I'll remember your promise," she said. There was a light, flashes of dark obsidian in her eyes. She turned to me. "Please greet your mother, Sonny. Is she feeling well?" I felt something inside me turn over. I took a step backward.

"Yes, fine," I told her, "I'll tell Mother we saw you." I struggled to identify what had unsettled me.

Danny slid into a booth. I slid in beside him, but Harley stood watching Mrs. Shuler as she turned toward the door. When the door closed, Harley whistled. "Jesus Christ, I've never seen her up close, she's beautiful. I should've been a quarterback. She's hot for

121

you, Danny boy. The shame of it is you won't even take advantage of it." Harley shook his head back and forth, amazement scrawled across his broad face. "I would," he said, "you can bet I would." He seemed to have forgotten the confrontation with Killer.

Danny seemed angry, or maybe embarrassed. Perhaps, I was the angry one. I didn't know where the rage came from, but it stuck in my throat like a hot brick.

"Did you see how she looked at you?" Harley pointed two fingers at Danny's face. "Right at you with those black eyes of hers. Women don't look that way unless they're asking for it."

"She belongs to our church, that's all," Danny said with a lightness to his voice. Harley smirked.

Jagged images, sparkling Communion tray—diamonds, Mrs. Shuler, silk blouse—church deaconess—sometimes has tea with my mother—the alley behind the dress shop. The expression on her face when she looked at Danny beamed through everything. I felt a childish kind of fright, the unalterable truth draped on the back of fear's strange lucidity. I shook my head to clear it, but it was already clear. Harley was right. I had seen it in her eyes, almost a leer if a woman can leer. Mrs. Shuler desired what our pastor referred to as "carnal knowledge" of Danny, a boy young enough to be her son.

The feeling that came next was graphic and unequivocal. It was the same feeling I had that day on Main Street when Dovie Lasher had defied all social convention, stripped herself bare to the waist, and bent over to touch Danny. I wanted nothing more than to have Mrs. Shuler want me more than she wanted Danny.

Reggie Riccio, P.O.'s counter boy, an out-of-towner from Faith, the Catholic community a few miles northwest, came to take our order. P.O. had hired him because his school had a work-study program for seniors, and P.O. needed the help by one o'clock. Junior and LaFaye had warned P.O. about going soft on Catholicism, he could lose business by not hiring a local boy. P.O. said bullshit, he'd do what he wanted to.

"What ya want?" Riccio asked.

"Strawberry milk shakes," Danny said.

"And lots of fruit and ice cream." Harley tilted his chin upward, making it an order.

I felt rattled. Over Killer, and Mrs. Shuler. And we were in for free milk shakes and Harley acted like they owed it to us. The presumptuousness made me uneasy. It was the kind of behavior toward the local businesses my father hated, and often railed against, people taking advantage of the proprietor's goodwill. And Harley was lost, bound for hell, and I couldn't speak to him about it, my soul as black as his. There was something wrong with the way I was living. And I could find no way out.

I watched Riccio as he worked behind the counter. His hair clung to his head in tight curls. He wore a white smock one size too small. It showed how muscular he was. He delivered milk shakes to Harley and Danny.

"Where's the other one?" Harley asked.

"He's a water boy. P.O. said give them to the players." Up close, Riccio's neck boiled with white-headed pimples.

"He's part of our team," Harley said.

"Not according to my orders," Riccio said. His thick, hairy arms stuck out from beneath the white shirt.

Harley grabbed Riccio's wrist, enunciated clearly, softly. "He wants a milk shake, lots of berries, extra thick." The veins on Harley's hand popped out, his knuckles white where he squeezed.

I became alarmed. "No, forget it, it's all right. I don't want anything. Like he says, I don't play."

Harley ignored me. "He's part of our team." Harley's high-pitched voice sounded almost comical. "He patches up my boo-boos," Harley said. I laughed, a nervous rattle. Danny sat observing. Riccio wrenched his arm but could not pull it away. "And remember, extra berries and extra, extra thick." On "thick," Harley let go. Riccio staggered, striking a display case. A tinkle of glass, the smell of perfume. Riccio's face turned whiter.

Harley stood up, gestured toward the soda fountain with his middle finger, glaring at Riccio like a madman. The smell of perfume filled the store. Riccio mixed the shake, and slammed it down on the scarred table in front of me. I saw some lumps, it had not been mixed properly, but I wanted no more trouble.

Riccio cleaned up the broken perfume bottle as best he could, then hid behind the counter while we finished. Harley glared at him one more time, then we flowed out of the fluorescent light into the dim street. Killer and Dovie were not in sight. The domino parlor lights were on. I knew Duffy and a few others were already in there, and LaFaye would be in later. Across the street, the light of LaFaye's sewing machine flickered against his dirty window. He worked late because he always got a late start.

We crossed the river driving north, past the sand hills. From the road we could see the dune where Coach had attacked Killer. It almost gleamed in the moonlight. We were just riding and talking. There was not much to do. No one to spy on at Lovers' Roost, a couple of hours too early. The milk shakes and the trouble had taken so little time. The looseness, no plan, vines of tingling nerves. Somehow, I felt responsible for the trouble we'd had at the drugstore.

"I'll buy us all a hamburger," I said.

"Drive this boy around, and he'll eventually come up with a good idea," Harley said.

"Let's go to the Elite Cafe," I suggested.

CHAPTER 16

T he lights had been turned out in the drugstore. It was closed. Danny parked in front of the Elite Cafe, owned by Eton, the only Frenchman in town. Everyone around town called it the EEE-light. This mispronunciation didn't matter much, because Eton leased space for his cafe from Slim Hall, who owned the motel, and Slim couldn't spell. I had been in the office the day he bounced in with the first ad. My father said to Slim, "The 'Blue Peecock'? That's an unusual name, but you don't spell 'peacock' that way." Slim bristled. "Whatdaya mean you don't spell it that way? You spell pee, p-e-e, and you spell cock, c-o-c-k. The sign's already made and that's how I'm spellin' it. You want this ad, or not?"

The whole place had a vibration that probably started before the building was even erected. Slim had built the motel and cafe on land he had inherited from his daddy, Spade Hall, a gambler who had won the land from another shyster in a card game in Taos, New Mexico. It was only natural that the cafe was a gathering place for gossip, business negotiations, and weather reports, and for the planning of many different kinds of skulduggery.

Eton, a friend of my father, was working behind the counter and spoke when we entered. "Hey, young Mr. Schultz, welcome to the

Elite." He pointed toward a booth for us. We sat down before we
noticed Reggie Riccio was sitting with his family a few tables away.
I should have expected some kind of hassle. After all, this was the
Elite Cafe. You don't come in here if you aren't looking for trouble.

Harley started, "Why don't assholes eat in their own towns?"

"There are no restaurants in Faith," I reminded him. "His name's
Reggie," I added. Harley grunted.

Mr. Riccio had a dark, trimmed mustache. Mrs. Riccio, who faced
us, wore her hair tied up in a bun. Reggie's sister sat beside him.
She appeared to be at least a year younger than Reggie, more the
age of Danny and me. Her expression was flat and reserved, eyes
turned down toward her plate. Her face was long, with nice pro-
portions, what my mother might call "high class." Her left hand
lay clenched in the vee of her plaid skirt.

"Catch that babe," Harley said to us.

"Read the menu," I said, "or can you read?"

"Hey, listen to our friend, the one who gets strawberry milk shakes
because we stick up for him around assholes who don't know up
from down." Reggie glanced at us. Harley ranted on.

"Look at her hair! Boy, I'd like to get my hands in it."

The girl's hair, raven black, bushed out wildly. She reached up
and patted the black, wavy mass to make it lie closer to her head.
Her hands were slender with long white fingers and red nails. It
was pretty obvious she was aware of our interest.

"I'll bet her pussy's hairy, too," Harley said. I cringed at the crude-
ness of his remark. Both the girl and her brother glanced toward
us. She placed her fork on her plate and used both hands to press
her hair close to her scalp, then ran her hands down the nappy mass
until she divided it in half, bringing it forward over each shoulder.
Mr. and Mrs. Riccio seemed oblivious of us.

We ordered. I managed to get Harley to talk about a motorcycle
trip he was planning for the summer. This diverted him, but every
few minutes he would glance back at the girl and make some ob-

scene gesture that he thought only Danny and I could see. Eton arrived with our hamburgers. He noticed we were watching the Riccios.

"Watch out for the brother," Eton whispered. "I hear he's a tough customer."

Harley shook his head, but didn't take his eyes off the girl. "He's easy," he whispered.

We finished. I was anxious to leave before Harley made real trouble. On the way out, he detoured by the Riccio table, and made it obvious he had noticed the girl. We watched from the car as they came out the door.

Danny waited until the Riccios disappeared. He started the car, made one circle up Main Street and down, then drove south and turned at the football stadium, heading west on county road twenty-three. The stadium loomed dark and ill-omened against the backdrop of the town's lights. No one talked, no one said anything about where we were going, what the plan was. It took us ten minutes to reach Dove Creek. We crossed the plank bridge, the car bucking gently over loose boards rumbling beneath us. A ride, that's what it was, nothing more, I assured myself. Just being with friends. Out my window I saw the willows along the creek, fluffy silhouettes against the sky's dim light. I felt a vague prickling inside my gut. The journey held some unmined vein of importance.

"Shall we go back?" Danny asked.

"Since we're out this far, why don't we go on over to Faith. What is it, another five or six miles? Maybe we'll run into our ugly friend, and his lovely sister," Harley answered.

"Okay, you call the plays tonight. You need the practice for when I get dinged again," Danny said. We laughed, it was funny now, although it wasn't so funny when he was on the football field and could barely remember what his name was.

I thought it was unlikely we'd see Riccio, and if we did, he'd stay out of our way. I also thought of Anne Tendal, who lived near Faith.

I wished for a way to tell her I was nearby, for a way to say I was in love with her. I wondered how girls like boys to communicate their feelings. Not like Harley did, I hoped. I doubted it, he hadn't had much luck with girls so far. Not that I was much better off. How did Danny do it? How did he let them know he was interested in them—Anne, Dovie, Earldeana, Mrs. Shuler? Or did he? Did the women take initiative? Were we supposed to wait? I didn't know for sure.

"Would I like to dick her," Harley said, striking the back of the seat with a clenched fist, "mostly just to show up that bastard of a brother." For a moment, Anne was so much in my mind I thought he meant her, then I realized he meant the Riccio girl.

"I don't think you have much of a chance she'd say yes," I replied. "She didn't seem too impressed with your manners back in the cafe."

"Shit, if I got the chance, I wouldn't even ask her." What was I doing in the same car with a person like Harley? I seemed to always feel bad when I was around him. It took us ten minutes to reach Faith.

The Roman Catholic church with a ten-foot-high lighted cross dominated the town's one street. It was the only community in the Panhandle where the majority of citizens were Catholic. The town had been one of the main targets of the Ku Klux Klan in the thirties. But once the war broke out, and the men who went and weren't killed got back, the Klan disappeared. I checked my watch. It was ten minutes to ten. There was no one in Faith, no stores open, no gas station open, just a dozen dark buildings, hardware, grocery, post office, elevator.

A yellow dog barked at an animal he apparently had treed, maybe a cat, perhaps even a coon. Danny drove the length of the street, a quarter mile, then turned around. We made a second turn, one more pass. The dog had given up, and was no longer in sight.

"There he is, the son of a bitch!" Harley exclaimed. The customized pickup with dual mirrors, radio antennas, and wide tires came at us and passed. Riccio must have expected us, and had come out to see if we would show up.

"Make another turn," Harley told Danny. "It's about time we teach this Faith fucker a lesson." Harley rolled down his window and when we met Riccio he extended his middle finger, and gestured vigorously up and down.

"Let's go back and see if he knows his Italian hand signals," Harley said, his voice squeaking with pleasure.

"If he wanted to make anything of it, he'd be on our tail by now. We're going on home," Danny said. "We'll take the north route, come back into town from the other side. We won't have to cross the Dove Creek bridge again."

Harley spat out the open window, then rolled it up as we gained speed. We left Faith behind. As its lights receded, I began to relax.

"I need to piss," Harley said. "Would you mind stopping up ahead? If I'd thought of it, I'd have pissed in the middle of their damned street."

"We're not going back now," Danny said. He let the car coast until it stopped. Harley sprang out and moved toward the trapped tumbleweeds caught in the barbed wire fence.

"For someone who was about to pee on Main Street, he needs a lot of privacy," I told Danny. He had started to laugh when our heads snapped back. I looked behind us. The cab lights went on when Riccio got out of his truck.

"He followed us with his lights out, and bumped the car," I said. By that time, Riccio was standing outside Danny's door.

"Get out," he said. He glanced into the back seat. "I said get out!" He drew a billy club from his hip pocket, held it high in the air to make sure we saw it, then smashed the window Harley had leaned out of to give him the finger. "Which one of you was in the back seat before?"

I realized Riccio had lost track, didn't know for sure how many of us there were, and hadn't seen Harley head toward the fencerow. "Where's the big guy who was in the cafe?" he asked. "He owes me ten bucks for the perfume. Then, I want to hear an apology for my sister."

Danny and I got out. I had no plan, but I wanted to stand with Danny. My feet crunched in the gravel. Darkness pushed in from one side, and the headlights of the Buick blinded me from the other. When I passed the second light, I tripped and lurched forward.

I could smell the perfume lingering on Riccio's clothing as he struck me with the club. I went down. It was dark for a moment, then I rolled over. Through the haze I saw Danny step in close to Riccio and grab the club. Their feet shuffled in the loose gravel alongside the road. Riccio yanked the club loose to strike Danny, who dodged, and the club clanked against the car's hood, denting it, cracking the paint. I found I could sit up. Danny reached for Riccio's throat, his thumb crushed Riccio's lips, Riccio's mouth opened and Danny's thumb slipped in. Riccio bit. Danny screamed.

Harley burst out of the darkness, drove his shoulder into Riccio's side, and they both disappeared into the night. I turned to Danny. He was bent over, hands between his legs.

"I'm all right," the words hissed through clenched teeth. I stepped closer, pulling on his hand so I could see it. Danny turned on me like a trapped animal. "Leave me alone!" I backed away, then turned toward the fight.

There were no longer any sounds of a struggle, just low, rhythmic thuds, bone against bone. I moved toward the sound, and my eyes adjusted. Riccio was flat on his back. Harley sat astride him, flailing away, striking a foe who appeared to be unconscious.

"Stop it! You'll kill him," I shouted. Harley hit him a few more times. Riccio's head rolled limply with each blow. Finally Harley stopped swinging, brought his hand forward, dropped three fingers and the thumb, leaving his middle finger, bony and erect. "Here's my apology." Turning toward me, he said, "Let's get out of here."

"We can't leave him," I said, "he may be badly hurt."

Harley wiped blood on Riccio's shirt, called me a dirty name, and told me to get in the car. Danny, who was already in the driver's seat, started the engine. He spun the wheels and we were away.

We didn't say anything for a few miles, then Harley started to laugh, short bursts, then deep, releasing laughter. "I can't believe I gave him the finger," he said between laughs, "he couldn't even see it. For all I know he was dead."

For a moment, I thought I saw the humor, and I laughed also. But the impulsive flow of laughter touched something deeper inside me and suddenly, with no warning, I began to cry. I stifled the noise, but couldn't stop the tears, and I couldn't figure out exactly why I was crying.

Finally, the car crested the long hill north of town, and there were the sand dunes by the river, the dark fringe of cottonwoods along the banks, and beyond the river blinked the lights of Cimarron.

Danny drove to Lipscomb's house and we told him what had happened. Coach called Sheriff Ordway, who left for Faith.

Coach called my father. "Please don't be alarmed, Mr. Schultz, there was an accident and your son got a little bruise, nothing serious at all. I've patched him up."

He paused while my father asked a question.

"The boys were in my basement playing pool and there was a scuffle, and he fell against the edge of the pool table. The table's fine, no damage," he said with a laugh. "I'll bring him home shortly."

Coach called Charlie Farrell. He came to the coach's house and exchanged a three-year-old Ford for the Buick. He'd repair the windows and hood that had been damaged by the club. Meanwhile, Danny could use the Ford and tell his parents whatever he wanted.

Finally, Coach noticed Danny. "Why are you holding your hand that way, son?"

We had all forgotten what happened during the fight. He lifted his hand, his throwing hand. "He bit me," Danny said. His thumb was green and black around the knuckle, swollen twice its normal size, and the swelling had spread over the back of his hand.

"Jesus Christ, that's it," the coach said, "the season's finished." Coach bent over his dining room table, and wept.

Hibbs wrote the epitaph in a brief newspaper article.

STAR QB INJURED AND OUT

A thumb injury suffered by Dustdevils' quarterback Danny Boone ended his season and probably the season of the Cimarron Dustdevils, who face a stout Watonga team in the first round of the state playoffs.

The Dustdevils lost seventeen to zero. Surgeons in Oklahoma City removed several bone chips from Danny's thumb. The cast extended to his elbow to hold the thumb and wrist rigid, insuring perfect alignment. They prescribed rehabilitation exercises to strengthen Danny's grip when the cast was removed.

Sheriff Ordway informed Coach that Reggie Riccio had been taken to Wichita where he was hospitalized with several broken ribs, a ruptured spleen, and six missing teeth. My father wrote the story after speaking with Reggie's parents, who got their version from Reggie. Reggie's story was verified by Sheriff Ordway, or perhaps concocted by him in the first place.

BASKETBALL STAR INJURED IN FREAK ACCIDENT

Reggie Riccio, star forward of the Faith basketball team, may miss his senior year of eligibility because of a freak accident suffered this past weekend. Riccio reported that he stopped his customized

1947 Ford pickup to relieve himself along a lonely stretch of county road thirty, did not realize he stopped on a hill, and was run over by his own truck.

The youth was discovered by Cimarron County Sheriff Orville Ordway, who found the injured youth while making a routine patrol of the isolated area. Ordway took Riccio to Seward County Memorial Hospital in Liberal, Kansas. From there, he was transferred to Wichita for treatment of multiple injuries.

My vision, my purpose, my faith receded, casting me adrift in a sea of grass. I no longer wanted to be a minister, I no longer wished to save the lost. I was lost myself. Rage boiled inside me, rage born of loss and deception. I wanted to feel like the others, that I owned the world, that every dream imaginable was being fulfilled on those Friday nights when the lights of the stadium came on, and the stands filled with cheering fans. I wanted to play football, I wanted to knock someone's head off and experience the conviction that I was rock-hard, and unafraid.

CHAPTER 17

The townspeople moped around, and argued. "You can't blame him," P.O. said from his stool at the Elite Cafe counter, "he done his best."

"Heck he did," LaFaye replied. "I should never've given him those boots after we won the conference. He stayed healthy just long enough to earn 'em. But I said I'd give 'em and I'm a man of my word." He spat, missing the spittoon. Eton tossed him a rag from behind the counter, pointing his finger at the bubbly pool. P.O. looked disgusted, but didn't reply. LaFaye added, "He may have hurt hisself on purpose, like old Verl Nelson, shot his own damned foot so he wouldn't have to shoot geeks." LaFaye pushed the rag around with the toe of his boot, waiting to see if anyone was going to agree with him.

"You mean gooks," P.O. corrected.

"Geeks, gooks, they're the same to me," LaFaye sputtered. He bent, picked up the rag, and tossed it back to Eton.

"All I know is he's young, and it was an accident, yet maybe not an accident, if you know what I mean, like he might have been scairt, at that," Junior added. "I can't remember no play when it could have happened."

"You're crazy," P.O. said, "that boy ain't afraid. It could have happened on any play and he just didn't notice it and the swelling came later."

None of them said anything about their doubts within Danny's earshot. They didn't avoid Danny, but they didn't go out of their way to do things for him either.

Coach Lipscomb overcame his grief and tried to make the most of the situation. For him, there was one good thing about the injury. It gave him time to set up weekly meetings with Danny. They drew up new plays, and planned strategies. Coach made Danny run laps around the gym, using the stairs to strengthen his legs, build up stamina. I watched him run one evening as girls' basketball practice was ending.

Danny had avoided Dale's barbershop since the week of his injury and his long hair stuck to his head, matted and dark with sweat. Signatures of well-wishers had colored his cast a smeared blue-black, and its weight made his arm swing awkwardly across his chest when he ran.

The basketball boys stood on the sidelines with their sweat clothes off. It was easy to tell which ones did not go out for football. Their bodies were pale and their arms thin and frail next to the muscular football boys.

The girls' team had fifteen minutes of practice time left. Under Cannonball's coaching, the girls had become the winter pride of the Panhandle. Their winning record, coupled with the coach's circus antics, brought out the crowds.

I stood beside Cannonball while the girls finished practice. I liked standing with a man who was shorter than my armpit. Cannonball tossed the ball to Dovie Lasher, one-on-one drills. Dovie dribbled the ball slowly toward the goal, its rhythm strong like that of a healthy heartbeat. Vesta Goode, the team's best guard, tried to steal the ball from her, but Dovie held her away with her elbow, then spun around her. The taller guard recovered and prepared to block the lay-up she expected, but Dovie veered away and popped the net with a jump shot, a shot no girl had even attempted until Cannonball suggested to Dovie that girls can shoot jump shots like boys.

Graceful as a ballerina, muscular development that rivaled some boys, Dovie's body was perfectly balanced, athletic, yet feminine. There was an open sensuality about her, the way she moved, the way she touched people, and, of course, nobody forgot about the day she had exposed her breasts on Main Street. No one in school had asked her for a date. She was Killer's girl. Not that a guy away at college is immune from competition, but Killer had that way, an air he carried that made it seem he could not be challenged. Yet, I had told Harley I thought Dovie was in love with Danny. Dovie emitted signals when she came near Danny. I couldn't explain what they were, but I could hear them, could feel the pull, the irresistible lure of her call to him.

Dovie's total concentration on the basketball court added to her attractiveness. Nothing could divert her attention. To have that attention must be remarkable, I thought. That's what Cannonball loved about her. That's what worried him today, and it concerned me, too.

While we watched her, she watched Danny, who was running his laps around the gymnasium bleachers. She sank another jump shot and turned to look at Danny, who, by then, had finished his laps and was resting on the pine seats where spectators sat.

I moved closer to Danny. He was sweaty. His cotton T-shirt clung to his chest. When he moved his arm, the muscles bulged and rippled across his shoulders. He bent over to rub the calves of his legs.

I thought of what the other girls had said about Dovie. Three years ago, she showed her teammates how she could pee standing up. The other girls were amazed, and wasted no time spreading the news. She had practiced it since age three, she claimed, lifting the toilet seat, thrusting her hips forward, pulling upward with her fin-

gers on each side of her vulva, hitting the water, forcefully, accurately. I wondered if it hissed, that girlish sound I'd heard in the
bathroom with my mother, then through the bathroom door when
she shut me out, then at the town swimming pool where the boys
took turns pressing their ears to the thin walls that separated our
dressing room from that of the girls; the sound that sometimes
poked into my consciousness at the oddest moments.

Dovie finished her free throws. Practice was over. While her
teammates scrambled toward the girls' locker, she walked the other
way, slicing through the boys who sprinted out dribbling balls. Her
hips swung gently, her thigh muscles rippled, strands of hair clung
to her neck where the curls had gone straight. I smelled her perfume and her sweat when she walked by. She glided onto the bench
next to Danny, relaxing her bare leg against his.

"How's your hand feeling?" She leaned on him, placing her arm
on the bench behind his shoulders, pushing her breast against him.
Danny patted his cast and smiled.

"I don't have a date for the junior-senior banquet. Will you go
with me?" Her directness made it easy. He accepted without hesitation.

An electric smile lit her face. She kissed him on the cheek as
she had kissed Killer when we saw them drinking the Dr Pepper.
"That's wonderful, simply great. We'll make the final plans in a
few days. We'll have a party and dance all night."

She loped across the floor and disappeared into the dressing
room. Goose bumps erupted on my arms. I realized there was no
use reminding Danny that our pastor did not encourage dancing.

The town buzzed with the news. A senior girl had asked a sophomore boy to escort her to the junior-senior banquet. Some people
thought it was a lark, not to be taken seriously. But others thought
it was a sign the moral fabric of the community was breaking down
and the churches were too lax. A girl with the reputation of Dovie
Lasher, the sexual signals she gave off, should not be allowed to as-

sociate with a younger boy whose morals could be damaged. Worse than that was the fear the two of them, because of their popularity, would influence others, even younger, to experiment; not only with reverse-age dating, but with other even more dangerous practices. People worried about where it would end, but no one seemed to know how to stop it.

When Killer came home from college that weekend after the news hit town, the sheriff picked him up dead drunk where his truck had run into the bar ditch south of town and he spent the night and the next day in jail. A woman came to see him, his girl from college, some said, and she must have sneaked in some liquor, because Killer stayed drunk the whole day, and the sheriff wouldn't let him out until he was sober.

My hope soared. I was in love with Anne Tendal, and had been since the day I first saw her on the mesa. Up to now she had had a clear preference for Danny. But if Danny dated Dovie Lasher . . .

I clung to my fantasy through the next few weeks. On Monday, after Danny had gone with Dovie to the banquet, I stood near my locker before the first bell.

"Hey, how was the banquet?" R.D. asked Danny.

"Fine, I had a good time."

"That's it? Can you give us a few more details?"

I stood by to hear answers to questions I dared not ask for fear of self-betrayal.

"I liked being with her," Danny said.

R.D. stepped back, books in his left hand, his right hand on his hip. "Look, don't be dumb. It's over. She ain't gonna give up Killer for you. He's already in college. Besides, he'll be after your ass if he isn't already."

"I said I just like being with her, it's no more than that. And don't call me dumb." He left us standing, burned by the heat in his voice.

I was pleased. I wanted Danny to date Dovie again. It was my only chance to have Anne develop some interest in me.

On Wednesday, Danny stayed in town with me. At five o'clock, Dovie called, and then picked him up a few minutes later. He wasn't back until eleven P.M.

I knew how it was with Dovie. I knew from the day she touched him on Main Street. She wore simple bras, no wires or pads, no tricks, no hands resisting, no whispered "don'ts" or "not theres," no minister's words ringing in her ears. She helped him with her blouse and jeans. She lived outside ordinary morals, because she was extraordinary, and so was Danny.

The long winter nights started to shorten. Danny's cast was taken off. The girls' team made it to the third round of the state playoffs before they lost. The winter melted into a busy spring. I was making no progress with Anne. One Sunday, Thelma invited both Anne and me to spend the afternoon after church with Danny at the Boone farm.

Anne picked up the baby kittens from the nests in the hay loft. Rushing noises filled my head when she touched their tiny noses to her face, a caring, loving light shining from her eyes. I thought of the kittens Danny and I had killed. What would she think if she knew? We roamed the gullies and pastures where Danny and I had played as children. We stood at the edge of the pasture where an arroyo swerved east away from the house, the light from the afternoon sun shading the creek bed.

"When I was a real little kid, I played Rin Tin Tin. This was the wilderness," Danny told Anne.

"What about the dog, who played the part of the dog? Was it Sonny?" she teased.

"I once defeated a whole tribe of Indians on this very spot," he said, smiling at her.

She knitted her brow, placing her finger on her upper lip as if pondering what he'd said. She shoved him, ran, and he chased her. He could have caught her easily, but she darted like a barn swallow, while he allowed her to stay just out of his grasp. She ran back beside me, excited, breathless, and faced him.

"How could you have killed a whole tribe of Indians if you can't even catch one little white girl?" I wanted to grab her, pull her down on top of me. They sensed my pain, grabbed me, and dragged me down between them onto the buffalo grass, and we lay looking up at the changing shapes of the clouds racing through the sky and I would have died for the love of either of them.

Then there followed a feeling of something nameless, unidentified, nonetheless filling and real. Love merging from two parallel lines into one spirit of free love, me between the two of them; their beauty one with me, an eternal love that would exist always but never be consummated; and what I felt was the resulting unmitigated sorrow.

Thelma called us in for the Sunday dinner, which was served midafternoon and replaced both dinner and supper. After dinner, I momentarily closed my eyes. I was asleep longer than it seemed. When I awoke, Danny and Anne were gone.

I grabbed Danny's binoculars off his dresser, then bolted out to find them. We had talked earlier about walking to a box canyon that was at the far end of the east pasture. I supposed they were there. It was one of those extraordinary, still spring days, when important events seem destined to happen. I took a shortcut, sprinting through the wheat stubble that Arved had left from last year to keep the soil from eroding. From the peaks of the terraces, I saw the gash where the canyon cut into the bluff almost a mile away. The stubble crackled and broke beneath my feet. I jogged, and a sense of my own daring rose with the puffs of dust. Running did not diminish my stamina. I did not know for sure where they were, but deep within myself I must have known, and I sought them with a vehemence that was feeding on my own loneliness.

I intercepted the creek bed and used it for a path. In some places, its banks were higher than my head. I watched for signs of them in the whimsical patterns of soil washed in by past rains. Finally, I

saw where they had slid down the creek bank. I followed their foot-
prints. I walked briskly, deep breathing increased my sense of exhilaration.

The creek bed wound toward the canyon with its high bluff, now
only a quarter mile ahead. At first I couldn't see them, but I knew
they were there, somewhere. I looked through the binoculars, scanning the sand plum thickets and the bluff until I found them,
halfway up. There must be something about growing up on the
plains that makes people fascinated with climbing embankments.
Danny's feet were lodged on a layer of sandstone, and he reached
back down the slope to grasp Anne's hand to help her up behind
him. The dirty white layers of stone were eight or ten feet apart.
Multicolored clay and gravel had washed down the slope, the layers of sandstone and the loose clay and sand making a streaked hillside that looked like Mother's English trifle melting on a warm day.

With Danny's help, Anne struggled up the loose shale onto the
stone ledge. Below them, a few cattle stood knee deep in the pond
Danny's father had dug at the head of the gulch. I jogged ahead,
leisurely. The glasses bumped against my chest. I felt a calmness,
the calm of a person who has guessed his fate and is coming to
terms with it.

The lay of the draw prevented me from seeing them again until I was close, only a hundred feet from where the creek ended and
the layered canyon wall slanted upward. It was so quiet I could hear
the cattle as they shifted their weight in the mud and water. I slid
out of the arroyo into the plum thickets. I was well hidden by the
dense twigs that were bursting with bright green buds, yet I had
perfect vision of Danny and Anne as they reached the highest ledge.
I had not consciously intended to spy on them, but now I had arrived without them knowing I was there. With the canyon wall in
front of them, and the stillness, I could hear everything, including
their breathing. It was as if they were performing in a small, acousti-
cally perfect, theater.

Anne was still below Danny. The last layer of sandstone protruded out of the hillside just above his head. He reached up with his hand, then swung his leg up and over so he lay, half on, and half off the ledge. He reached back for her and she scrambled up, breathing hard from the effort, resting her cheek against his lower thigh.

I saw the snake before they did, like a prop placed there for the sake of the drama. The snake must have left hibernation only recently, and it lay on the rock sunning itself, Danny's arm only inches away. The binoculars brought the snake so close to me I could almost hear it slither into a slow, amorous coil, its head rising more than a foot above the rock, a silver luster surrounding the gray and black markings around its eyes. It rocked side to side, in a lethargic, drunken way, its thin ribbon tongue flicking in and out, tail erect, as it started to coil faster. And I watched. Danger, the thrill of it, Danny was in danger, and so was I, another kind of danger, but no less life-threatening.

Anne poked her head over the ledge, saw the coiled snake, screamed, and fell backward down the hillside. The snake tightened its coil, buzzing. Danny turned, saw it, and froze, his face only inches from the snake's head. They must never, not in a million years, know I lay there and watched.

I put the glasses down to see the complete picture. Anne lay dazed about twenty feet below. The fall had forced her blouse up. I brought the binoculars up to my eyes. There were smudges of red-orange dirt above her navel. She appeared to have had the breath knocked out of her.

I looked back at Danny. Danny had not flinched in the face of his danger. Then, the snake uncoiled and flowed through a crack in the ledge and was gone. The playwright did not have a flair for climaxes.

Danny slipped off the ledge. Anne had propped herself up on one elbow. "The snake's gone. Are you all right?" he called.

Anne's face was as white as her baptismal robe. Danny helped

142

her stand up, then they held hands to run down the slope. Small rocks rolled ahead of them down the hillside into the thicket that sheltered me. They stopped where the loose silt met the sand, where the gulch began its twisting descent through the grassy pasture, and near me. A few perilous feet away.

She pulled him close. "Dear Danny, my dear Danny, God saved you, he must have. I've never been so scared—or did he put the snake there—I'm so mixed up."

"If he had struck me, we'd have cut the bite to make it bleed," he told her.

"And I would have sucked out the poison." She kissed his face, and down his neck, violent noisy kisses, biting him and sucking the skin on his neck. They fell down in the silt. Her hands slipped under his shirt, stroking his stomach. Danny lay on his back, his eyes closed against the sunlight. She wrapped herself around him, writhing, entwining him with force stronger than I had ever thought possible for a girl so slight. She did not relent and he did not stop her. Her clothes peeled off like the petals of a lily. She wore the same shade of pink panties I had seen on the mesa. She pulled down his Levi's to mid-thigh. A feathery wisp of dark hair was all I saw when she straddled him, her buttocks and back toward me, the whitest of white.

I knew little about making love, but I knew from the way she moved Anne Tendal was no virgin. And I knew what they did had a name. I'd seen it in a book R.D. showed me. He'd found it in his parents' dresser drawer. They called it "inverse missionary position." When I thought of the word "missionary" denoting "one who is sent to spread the Christian faith," that became what I focused on. "Missionary, missionary, missionary," I couldn't get the image out of my mind, "missionary," a slender, pale girl riding.

She could never repent and be forgiven. Her life, unlike Mary Magdalene's, was lost forever. Her sin was so vile there was no hope.

I was afraid they would follow the arroyo home and see my tracks.

But they walked across the pasture, the most direct route back to the house. I jogged back through the creek, and came to the house, walking the last hundred yards to control my breathing. I exulted with a lucid, dispassionate power, potent with my secret, knowing the truth about the virginal Anne, knowing I had been able to sit by calmly to watch Danny die.

"Where have you been?" he asked when I walked in the house.

"Out looking for you two. Where have you been?"

That evening, Pastor Toon read from Revelation 6:7-17, the New Testament version called *Good News for Modern Man*. He called his sermon "Hiding from the Wrath of the Lamb."

"'Then the Lamb broke open the fourth seal . . . and there was a pale colored horse. Its rider was named Death. . . . They were given authority over a fourth of the earth, to kill with war, famine, and disease, and with the wild animals of earth.'" The prophetic sense of death I had lived with since Jimmy Lee Watson died now seemed imminent, more horrible than ever. The choices on death's menu were extensive, the ways to die as innumerable as the sands of the sea.

"'Then the Lamb broke open the fifth seal. I saw underneath the altar the souls of those who had been killed because they had proclaimed God's word and had been faithful in their witnessing.'" There was one death I'd never die, a privilege I now knew I'd never be worthy of, I could never die a martyr's death, I would never be a missionary. I would die young, anonymous, alone.

"'And I saw the Lamb break open the sixth seal. There was a violent earthquake, and the sun became black, like coarse black cloth, and the moon turned completely red, like blood. . . . Then the kings of the earth . . . hid themselves in the rocks and the mountains. They called out to the mountains and to the rocks, fall on us and hide us from the eyes of the one who sits on the throne, and from the wrath of the Lamb. The great day of their wrath is here and who can stand up against it?'" The power of my secrets had worn off. I was burdened with shame, alone, devastated. I had even hoped Danny might die, had not called out to warn him. I could never forget that. Now I knew something, something that had been bothering me for a long time. I could have saved Jimmy Lee if I had wanted to.

I needed a visit from Jesus, the Jesus who had appeared beside my bathtub, who had given my mother a sign at my birth. I had to make another effort to find him. When the invitation to come forward at the end of the sermon was sung, I darted to the front just like I had when I was small. The minister was surprised, but quickly composed himself.

"I don't need to tell you of the dedication of this young man," he said. "He's about the best-known face in this congregation. But Sonny has come forward this evening to reaffirm his deep faith and commitment to the service of our Lord," the minister explained. "What a fine example this young soul-winner has set for the rest of us. Let each of us pray for this young man and for ourselves that we may remain ever faithful to Jesus Christ."

Through the blur of my tears, I watched Mother come forward to stand beside me. The pastor put his arms around both of us while I buried my face in her bosom.

CHAPTER 18

S ometimes it is impossible to see things from the ground. To
understand, we must look through the eyes of a hawk, perceive with the intuition of an angel riding on thunderheads.
People in Cimarron don't talk openly, so we must be clever.

I loved Danny. Yet, I watched while the snake coiled and did not
warn him. It is not unequivocal adoration that makes parting with
loved ones so difficult, it is this very ambiguity, the two-edged love,
love that is angry and loving and guilty and adoring. If Danny had
died because of a snake bite, I would have felt responsible for his
death, as if my hate alone had killed him. But he lived, I loved him,
and somehow I also resented him. Perhaps this is an irreconcilable
contradiction.

School let out before I felt the languor of spring. I went back to
work on the farm with Danny, suffering daily with what I had seen.
That summer, my days were torturously long as I waited for night
to fold over me. At night I fell into the black pits of slithering vipers,
or rode the pale, galloping horse in Pastor Toon's sermon.

Because everyone was so busy, the church suspended its evangelistic efforts and I had no opportunity to test my renewed dedi-

cation to saving souls. The farm work was all I had to pull me
through the bright days and the dark nights. I walked into the sunlight and plowed the soil, turning over the earth so what was on
top was then underneath. I walked around Arved's farm, felt its
bulk and assurance. It grounded me. I knew what Grandfather
Raleigh had meant when he said "a man's not much good without
land." I wondered if my father believed what Granddad had said
and that was why he had sent me to the farm, to come under the
tutelage of Arved Boone, who knew the value of land.

I seldom saw my mother that summer. She attended many church
meetings, not just meetings at our Baptist church, but meetings
held by the Pentecostals, the Church of Christ, and any other religious meeting that was announced in the paper.

All that summer, Danny went out with Dovie when she could
slip away from Killer, then Danny saw Anne on the weekends. She
went out to the farm with him on Sundays while I stayed in town
with my parents. I imagined them together in the hay loft, in the
canyon, and even in Danny's room where I stayed Monday through
Friday.

When I arrived back at the farm with Danny after Sunday night
church, I could smell her in his room, the musty, steamy fragrance
of spiced wild game simmering in some unseen kettle.

Early in August, when Lipscomb was away on vacation, I took a
Saturday afternoon and found Cannonball. I had decided to approach Cannonball rather than Lipscomb about my desire to play
football for a number of reasons. Mainly, I identified with Cannonball's disadvantages. The fact he was a freak and had to be better at what he did in order to succeed made me feel he would
understand my situation in ways Lipscomb would not. I found him
at LaFaye's boot shop. He and LaFaye spent time together because
Cannonball rented a small apartment in back of the shop from
LaFaye. I pulled him aside. "I want to go out for the team. You'll
have to get another team manager," I told him.

His eyes bulged behind his thick glasses. He reached up with his meaty hand to pat me on the shoulder. There was, momentarily, a softness to his aging face, a slight shimmer in his eyes. No school would ever hire him as a head football coach. He was quite lucky someone like Lipscomb had befriended him, had seen his brilliance, and had hired him to be the assistant.

"Sonny, you're so far behind, the other guys will kill you. Besides, you're more valuable at what you do, you keep us organized. Stay with what you're good at."

"No, I've decided. I'm going out for the team. It's too humiliating to be on the sidelines."

Now his eyes narrowed and he squinted at me, as if he thought I had said something about him, about the humiliation he felt.

"Come out here with me," he said, and he waved his stubby arm and went out LaFaye's back door into the alley. The wind was blowing acrid smoke out the rusty barrel LaFaye used to burn his leather scraps. Something blew in my eye. I stopped to rub it.

"Stand right here," he said.

"Wait, I have something in my eye."

"You think your opponent on the football field is going to wait while you rub your eye?" My eye was tearing, but I took my hand away. Behind me were some weeds that were going to seed, a couple of large thistle plants and a few sunflowers. "Are you ready?" he asked.

"For what?"

His head struck me with incredible force just above my navel. I shot backward, landing on my back in the weeds. I couldn't get my breath, it wouldn't come, no matter how hard I tried. I'd seen the coaches run onto the football field many times to grab a writhing player by the belt and pump air back into his lungs. But Cannonball offered me no help. I thought I was about to die when some air found a small opening. I smelled dust from the weeds as I was becoming lucid. My eye still burned, and I rubbed it some more.

I got to my feet, my voice wouldn't work. I finally managed to croak out, "You son of a bitch."

"Now it's your turn," he said. "You do it to me."

I sucked in breaths of the hot August air. It was dry and the dust burned my throat so I had to cough. My eye was finally clearing up. I wanted to hit him, to kill him. I wanted to knock him down so he'd never get up.

"What's the matter?" he asked. "I know what's the matter. You don't like hitting, do you? Or is it just that I'm short, and you can't hit a guy shorter than you? I may be short, but I'm strong, as you know. Come on—let's see what you've got. I'm two feet away, I don't know when you're coming. You can knock me down if you want to. I can't possibly dodge. You have the advantage over me just as I did over you."

I gauged him, crouched slightly. He circled until his back was to the weeds. I sprang. What I wanted was to smash him, but as I reached the apex of my spring, something, some kind of limitation held me back for only that last half inch. I couldn't quite put every ounce of my strength into my drive. What if I really hurt him? That hesitation, however slight, gave Cannonball time to dodge. My shoulder only grazed him. I landed facedown in the weeds, dust and seeds flying, thistle spines sticking in my skin. He waited until I sat up.

"You don't have it, Sonny. Even if you can take a hit and get up like you did. In football, you have to hit the other guy harder than you get hit. You have to intimidate him, hurt him, because if you don't, he's gonna keep hurting you until you can't take it anymore."

Cannonball's glasses magnified the intense look in his eyes. My own rage, my violence had been short-circuited years ago. I could imagine violence, I could participate vicariously, but when it came down to the hitting, I mean hitting the way good football players have to compress every ounce of strength, then let it explode into each violent play, to harm, to fracture—I couldn't do it. That's why I was the water boy.

Danny organized informal practice two weeks before it was legal for the coaches to begin official practice. His hand had healed. The ball zipped. The coaches watched him from a distance since they could not be near the practice field without violating athletic association rules. I came around the corner of the bus barn on my way to the field with a bag of footballs I had inflated. Cannonball was peering through the high chicken wire fence that separated the school yard from the practice area, his stubby fingers enmeshed in the wire. Lipscomb was resting one foot on a bucket he had turned upside down. He wore a purple baseball cap, he had several like it, and always kept one on his head.

"Shall we do anything about these girls?" Lipscomb asked. He took off his cap and rubbed the top of his head.

"I haven't decided," the dwarf answered. "If there's not a problem now, there could be soon." Cannonball must have sensed I was behind them. He looked over his shoulder. I looked away, too late.

"No doubt about it," he said to Lipscomb, "there's a problem. Of all possible difficulties, this was the one least likely. That's what I thought, anyhow, with the religion. Who'd have thought he'd turn out to be such a stud?"

Lipscomb said, "Religion never did much to control the sex drive. Look at the preachers. And look at those guys in the Bible. I'll talk to Danny, but I think we wait to see if he can handle it before we do anything more drastic. Things can change with kids this age."

"I don't know, I don't think I'd wait, but you're the boss," Cannonball replied. "What would you do, Schultz?" He turned around to look at me.

At first, I only stared back, but he wasn't joking. He wanted to know what I thought. In public, I was the water boy. Privately, I had

Cannonball's respect. "Someone better do something," I answered. All the team members received a telegram.

REPORT FOR PRACTICE. STOP. 6:00 A.M. AUGUST 21.
STOP. TWO PRACTICES A DAY. STOP. PREPARE
TO WIN. STOP. LIPSCOMB AND CANNONBALL.

By six-fifteen, the men from town were already there. I was distributing equipment, the players were trying on pads, pants, and practice shirts. Coach poured coffee for the men. Cannonball was missing.

"Two sugars for me," ordered Doc McGrath.

"Make mine like Doc's," Sheriff Ordway said. "I'd like to be as ornery as that old cuss."

"I'd like mine with brandy. But I know Coach, he don't have none, so make it black." Junior Goggin's eyes watered like a pink-eyed Duroc hog when he said it.

"Where's the dwarf?" Slim inquired. "Eton needs me to help out with breakfast at the cafe. Let's get on with this."

"Eton needs for you to stay out of his way, is what Eton needs," P.O. said.

At six-thirty, Melvin Hibbs and his photographer arrived. They took a few shots of the players, had a short interview with Danny, and then snapped a picture of him gripping the ball, showing the healed hand. That was all for now. The heat was already oppressive. It would be a hot day for practice. Outside, a horn sounded, throaty, like a heavy truck.

"Let's go outside, boys," Coach ordered, "we're goin' up to the dunes to get in shape."

Outside, a luxury travel bus rolled around the yard. Cannonball drove from the high, padded seat. There was no wind, and dust rose like smoke and hung in the air behind the bus. I stood beside

Harley watching Cannonball park. "Look at that. How the hell can he drive that thing, the little bastard?" Harley asked me.

"You'd be surprised what Cannonball can do when he sets his mind to it," I told him. Danny joined us.

The bus gleamed, black and gold. Someone had painted our school symbol, the prairie dustdevil, on the bus's side.

Cannonball stepped out. He wore long blue pants, a uniform jacket, and new black shoes. The shoes looked too large, and Cannonball, suddenly, seemed almost normal, his legs longer. We crowded around. "Sorry I'm late, boys. I had to practice with these." He stuck out one leg and pulled up his pants. Strapped to his stubby legs were carved stilts; feet shaped like real feet with no toes had been forced into the shoes.

"Pay Day the whittler made them," he said proudly. He strutted around with amazing agility. "With these, I can drive this monster," and he jerked his thumb toward the bus.

Lipscomb stepped forward and spoke to the team. "I can tell by your faces we have surprised you. Now I want to call on Junior Goggin."

"Make it short, Junior," Slim said.

"Well," Junior began, "I don't have much to say. It's just that a few of us said we'd split the cost of a new bus with the Board of Education if they'd allow us to find one and buy it." Now his face was beet red. "Actually, this isn't a new one. It's a rebuilt Trailways. But now, there won't be no excuses about how you're tired from riding to those out-of-town games. You just lean back and relax. This bus runs so smooth you'll think you're ridin' in a new Olds."

He paused and then he kicked the ground a few times. "We're proud of you guys, we wanted to encourage you after what happened last year. We're really looking forward to this year." He looked up at Danny with his piggy eyes.

"Everyone in," Coach said. "Cannonball will drive us up to the dunes so we can get in shape." Cannonball hopped into the driver's seat. Lipscomb sat down in the first seat behind him. The rest of us trooped in. There was an insular feeling inside the bus, not even the sound of the idling diesel motor. Lipscomb hooked Danny by his jersey when he walked by.

"Boone, you ride with me." I sat down in the seat behind them. Cannonball drove the bus down Main Street.

"How was your summer?" Coach asked Danny.

"Fine, I'm ready to go," he answered.

"Good, glad to hear it, 'cause we're all depending on you. Hand feel okay?"

"Good as new."

"Good."

Coach looked out the window while the bus gathered speed.

"I know you already know this, but I'll remind you. I'm here, you ever need me, I'm here. You're the most important person in this town. With our talent, we have a chance to win state championships the next two years. That would be unheard of." He stopped talking and Cannonball shifted gears.

"Come to think of it, I don't have much to say." Coach sniffed in, cleared his throat and swallowed a hawker. "I'll make it short. There are some things you're doing I don't like. I'm talking off the field. Right now, I'm letting it go, but I'm watching. If you let this town down again, all these fine people that support you, you're gonna wish you'd listened to your preacher and left that peeled pecker in your pants." Danny's ears turned redder than Junior Goggin's.

That week, my father wrote an editorial that came to be widely acclaimed, framed, and hung in the windows of some shops.

KEEPING OUR PRIORITIES STRAIGHT

I hope you are all aware of the wonderful contribution that our football coaches make to our community. Their dedication, their willingness to help our young boys grow up to be men, is without comparison. They, along with our churches, help families turn out boys we can all be proud of.

Although the town has recently purchased a good-looking and quite comfortable bus for the boys to use for traveling to out-of-town games, it is not enough. The coaches and the team deserve our total support. Traditionally, there is always good attendance at home games. This year, I'm suggesting that we make an effort to attend away games also. We drive hundreds of miles for all kinds of reasons. What better reason than to support our football team? We can make a car train and travel together so if anyone has trouble, there's help right behind.

Some of you may have other ideas about ways to support our boys. I will be happy to publish them. Regardless, I urge you to consider the importance of our support. The future of our young men and of our town depends on our interest today.

After the editorial appeared, the board of our church purchased another of the used Trailways with funds from the missionary rally, and called it the "Joy Bus." The preacher invited people from any denomination, saved or unsaved, to ride free to out-of-town games, on a first-come, first-seated basis. On the way to the game, they sang gospel songs and prayed for the team. On the way home, the preacher led devotionals about our Baptist doctrines, and prayed for the boys who were injured and asked God for their speedy recovery.

Business boomed on Main Street. My father had to add extra pages to the format of the *Times-Democrat* to accommodate all the advertisers. The Chamber of Commerce designed a business promotion. Each store sponsored some players. The merchants displayed the players' pictures in their windows. A free picture of a player was given to each customer who spent ten dollars or more. When they had spent a total of two hundred dollars, the chamber gave them a free frame for all their pictures. It wasn't just the first team's pictures people wanted to collect, they wanted all the boys who had football suits, down to the third- and fourth-stringers. If you were a football player, if you could stick out the punishment, take the heat of practice, and the hitting, and the psychological abuse of being called a "pussy" when you made a mistake; if a boy could endure that, then it was possible to feel that wonderful dreams were coming true. No one would ever be able to take that recognition away, nothing would ever replace that feeling of being special. Without those boys, this team, life around Cimarron would hardly be worth living.

As the two-a-day practices continued, the coaches became more relaxed about Danny. It helped when Dovie Lasher took a job in an insurance office in Liberal, Kansas. She often stayed overnight with an aunt because it was an eighty-mile drive round-trip. But she still managed to pick Danny up every week or two when he stayed in town with me, and he returned late.

No one told Killer about Danny and Dovie. Usually, someone would kid a man, or drop some hint when he was being cuckolded. Because it was Danny and Dovie, no one said anything. But Killer must have known there was something amiss. After school started, he came home from college every weekend, as if he were doing his best to keep his eye on Dovie.

The smoking pit and the pale horse interrupted my sleep. The warnings from Pastor Toon echoed in the darkness. The voice of Jimmy Lee Watson called me from his grave, "Come play, come play, come play." My father knew my grades were suffering. He never asked me what was wrong, but he called me into his office one Saturday, asked me to stand while he sat behind his desk. He reminded me nothing was easy, he'd had to work for everything, and I should get down to work myself. When he had finished speaking, he bent to wipe the dust off his shoes. Then he went out and left me in charge for the rest of the day.

The Dustdevils won their first seven games. Danny played well, no one could fault him. The team won easily. Between Danny, Harley, and R.D., we could make a touchdown whenever we needed it. But missing were those unbelievable plays from last year that left us shaking our heads in wonder.

The eighth week of the season arrived, time to pay back the Boise City Bearcats, who nearly beat us last year. This time, they'd be in Cimarron stadium. This time, the Dustdevils would blow them off the field.

CHAPTER 19

Coach made it clear in his Monday talk he did not expect last year's Bearcat debacle to repeat itself. In practice, he kept the pace brisk and regimented. The mood was spirited, optimistic. The townsfolk talked confidently. The first distraction appeared on Tuesday.

As practice began, two well-dressed men seated themselves in the bleachers the school had erected for the townspeople who liked to come out to the practice field and watch. The men were young, dressed up like Mormon missionaries. Coach ignored them through drills and warm-ups, then walked over and introduced himself. They told Coach they were from Southern Methodist University, and had heard about a couple of his kids and wanted to watch them practice, if that was okay. Coach asked for their identification, checked it, said he didn't mind if they stayed so long as they didn't talk to anyone without his permission.

The SMU recruiters and those who followed transformed the Blue Peecock and Elite Cafe into the headquarters for a campaign that has never been repeated in Cimarron. From the simulated leather stools and the Formica counter spread the rumors that quickened dull lives and revived sluggish businesses.

Slim spread the word, the news traveling through town. There were recruiters staying at the Blue Peecock! "I listened in on one phone conversation," Slim told LaFaye. "They're interested mainly in the Pugh kid now because he's a senior, but will make Danny their number one target next year. They want one of their graduates from some place downstate to start making friends with Danny's family."

That week, folks poked Danny on the shoulder, "Hey, I hear they're after you. Now you be careful and don't take the first offer they throw out."

Thursday, Coach practiced the team without contact, and he called it off early. "All you have to do is play like you've practiced," he told the team. "This is the best week of work I can ever remember."

We walked out of the bus barn with plenty of light available, and energy in the air. It was my idea to go hunting, but the others were all for it. I can't say why I suggested hunting because I had never killed anything larger than a cockroach except for the kittens Arved had forced Danny and me to smash. Although my father was a gun enthusiast and had taught me to shoot at the local skeet range, he never went hunting, either. He never had the time it took to hunt real game, so we shot clay pigeons.

Danny and I met Harley and R.D. at the Hogendorn Ranch sign at four-thirty. We all brought our shotguns. I experienced a deep excitement, anticipating a kill. I wanted to shoot a bird, a bird with blood and feathers, with flesh I could cook and eat.

We hunted in a wide circle around two sections of Hogendorn Ranch land. We tramped silently through tall bluestem grass, sagebrush, and sand plum thickets. Each time we approached the clumps of sand plum bushes, we sensed the pheasants were in there. Any moment, the whir of wings would bring our guns up and the air would smell of burnt powder and warm blood. There was time as we walked to think and remember, and for some reason my thoughts came around to Killer, when he first became jealous after Danny tackled him, when Dovie took her blouse off and made him look foolish, when he and Dovie were drinking the Dr Pepper and I thought Danny would fight him. I thought of other fights, fights between my parents, although they had not had a real fight in years. Between them existed a wide demilitarized zone.

Exhausted after trekking about five miles, we stopped at a windbreak, a double line of tamaracks and elms that protected a salt lick. Our shoe soles were glossy where they had been polished by the long tramp. I leaned back against the hedgerow next to Danny, settling into the darkening shadows, disappointed. Having never shot at anything except tin cans and clay pigeons, I longed to kill something swift and alive and beautiful.

Our guns leaned against the low branches of the tamaracks. There were roots exposed where some ringnecks had recently scratched up the soil beneath the trees. The birds had then used the dirt for dusting their feathers, dropping a few iridescent bronze plumes. I picked up one of the feathers, drawing its edges through my fingers. Its silkiness reminded me of the yarn knots on the comforter my mother used on my bed when I was a child. Our prey seemed to mock us, probably scant feet away, while we lay down to rest where they had scratched.

Through spiny leaves, the sky narrowed as the sun went down. Soft wind nudged the heads of ripe grass. R.D. and Harley talked of football scouts and girls, and of victories. I fell victim to an old childish habit as the sun went down. I began to miss my mother.

A fluttering whistle startled me. A dove, slender and blue-gray, with white tips on her wings and tail, darted and dipped, then alighted on the top branch of the tamarack where Danny and I rested. The waning light brightened the pinkish wash of her breast. Her tail twitched as she preened herself. The others paid no attention. I saw my chance. My fingers wrapped around the gun stock, which leaned against a tree, with its butt resting in the soft soil, my thumb eased onto the trigger, I released the safety, it might have been a stalk breaking, her only warning. The blast sprayed a puff of dust where the gun butt kicked the ground, the shot tore through branches and leaves. The dove seemed to leap upward at the sound of the shot, her wings folded, then she tumbled, branch to branch through the tree, landing near Danny and me. It had been a remarkable shot because I had not sighted down the barrel. Everyone was alert.

"Bird flies over here, she's fair game," I said. They didn't reply. "She shouldn't have flown down here if she didn't want to get shot." I walked to the dove to cover the panic creeping in. She lay in the grass, her eyes open, one wing askew. I picked her up. She was warm and limber. I closed my hand, leaving her head out as if she were wrapped in a thick comforter.

"Take her while I get this shell out of the chamber," I said to Danny. He backed up, turned away.

I felt a strange mixture of surprise, pleasure, remorse, and amazement. Surprise at Danny's sentimentality, pleasure at having killed the bird, remorse over the waste of one dove's life, and I was amazed to find out I was not the only one stifling tenderness.

"What shall I do with her?" No one answered, so I flipped her away. I spat as she tumbled, her wings opened, so when she landed, the tall grass supported her like a bier.

Danny walked to the dove, bent down, crouched like a tracker. He cupped the dove in his hands and carried her nearby to a flat patch of buffalo grass, little bell seed pods hanging down. "If she had any young ones, at least they're grown up by now," he said. He pulled his knife from his jeans, the same knife he had used against Harley on Main Street. Near a staunch cactus, he sliced through grass roots, making a hole with steep, smooth sides. We crowded in around him, but I felt detached from the judgment being pronounced. Danny put the dove in her grave.

With his brawny hand, Harley touched Danny's wrist to stop

him from filling in the hole, then he plucked some soft grass and lined the crypt. R.D. found a piece of bark, softened by weather, a pillow for her small head. Danny tucked in the broken wing and the dove lay beneath the narrow sky until he closed the grave with a flat sandstone.

None of them looked at me while we walked and it was dark when we reached the fence. I held the guns for them, barrels pointed upward as my father had taught me, while the others climbed through the barbed wire. I handed each gun over the high wire, one by one. I looked back, the tamaracks lost in the darkness.

Our headlights shot narrow bright beams into the emptiness that stretched toward the horizon's final light. It was totally dark when Danny and I reached home.

"Did you get anything?" my mother asked when we walked in. She stood with water running over dishes she had already washed.

I waited for Danny to answer. When he didn't say anything, I finally told her. "Nope, never saw a single bird." I tossed Danny an oiled chamois. He wiped the dust off his boots, then slipped out to see Dovie. I dreaded the game that was less than twenty-four hours away. I knew something had been shattered when I shot the dove.

Egbert dismissed school early and staged the pep rally on the front lawn, same kind of burrs that grew on the practice field. The shopkeepers all hung up their signs, GONE TO PEP RALLY, BE BACK 4:00 P.M. Ranchers arrived in their pickups, chaps wrapped around saddles in the back. The cheerleaders passed out yellow chrysanthemums, donation, one dollar. We burned an effigy of a Boise City Bearcat. Everything had been done that could be done.

Game time arrived, clear and crisp. I heard the comments from the Main Street merchants. "He don't look sharp tonight," Junior said.

"Ah, he's okay, he's just warming up," P.O. assured them.

Behind Junior, P.O., and the others, on the first row above the

161

far end of our bench, Dovie Lasher sat with Killer. One of her former teammates, married and expecting, stopped by. They talked secretively, giggling.

The men near Dovie stared at her. She wore a pink, loose-fitting man's shirt tucked in the denim pants she had tapered to fit her hips and legs. In a striking feminine touch, she had cut the sleeves of the shirt, then gathered them up near her wrists so they puffed out. Over her shoulder she carried a royal blue sweater to put on when it became colder. The women dug their elbows into their men's sides to make them stop watching her. A young girl skipped by her, pigtails bobbing. You could see the longing to be like Dovie, so sure of herself, the young girl's wish to make rainbows with a basketball that swished through silken nets while the crowd stamped in unison on the hardwood floor.

Killer put his arm around her and pulled her over against him. I could sense how it felt to have been a hero, then to recede into the crowd and become anonymous, how much this made Dovie mean to him. She was friend, lover, and symbol of past glory.

The game began. It was the worst game of Danny's career. He completed no passes. He called the wrong plays. He could not execute anything more difficult than a handoff. He lacked confidence, seemed timid, like he dreaded the hitting. Was it something about the Bearcats? Was there truth to those mysterious nemesis theories? Or was it merely coincidence that the Dustdevils played poorly when they faced them? Or had the death of a mourning dove taken away Danny's power?

As the Bearcats punted with four minutes left, I was standing beside Cannonball. "We've got to do something," he said, "the season's going to be over if we can't pull this game out." I went down on one knee. I looked for Danny, he was putting his helmet on. He appeared to be dazed, disoriented. If we lost the game, the repercussions would be severe. If we won the game, there would be something to look forward to. I thought of Harley, how he, a year ago, had beaten Reggie Riccio within an inch of his life. I thought of his raging strength.

"Harley is our only hope," I said to Cannonball. "Give him a speech, make him mad, move him to fullback and see if he can run over them."

Cannonball spoke to Lipscomb, who called time out, brought Harley over, got in his face, then moved him to fullback. He instructed Danny to give Harley the ball, and he ran off tackle, play after play. No deceptions, just strength and size, running low, plowing over the Bearcats. They tried everything to stop him. They beat on him, they kicked him in the pileup, they poked at his eyes, they bloodied his nose. It only made Harley angrier, and he hit them harder. When the referees caught the infractions, they called penalties and it all helped. Harley scored with less than a minute left. Final score, seven to zero.

The fans, who seemed to have caught Danny's timidity and had spent the game quietly fearing the worst, ran onto the field and carried Harley on their shoulders. When they put him down, Killer came up beside him, put his heavy arm around Harley's neck, and they walked off the field together.

Danny slouched off a few paces behind them. The death of the dove had worked on Danny like a solvent, fraying his strength and dissolving his sense of purpose. What worried me was something else, my sense of how I had betrayed him.

We had won the game because I suggested Coach move Harley, but once again there had been a scene like the one at the canyon when Danny narrowly avoided the snake bite, a stage designed so cleverly he would not know I had stood on the sideline to watch him fail.

C H A P T E R   2 0

A fter the game, Coach barred all outsiders from the locker room. Although we had won, there was no sense of triumph, the mood was subdued, gelded. The players examined their bruises, cuts, and broken fingers, but there were no jovial comparisons of bloody jerseys and helmets, the usual macabre speculations about which opponent the blood came from. Lipscomb sat on a low stool, hands folded in his hair. His voice quavered when he spoke.

He thanked the defense for holding the Bearcats scoreless, thanked Cannonball for his idea about moving Harley, and thanked Harley for how he had won the game.

I looked for Cannonball. He was helping Harley get his pants off. I half expected Cannonball to stand up on a chair and announce it was I who had thought of moving Harley to fullback. Then I realized how desperate Cannonball must be to have a little of his own glory. It was one thing to respect me when we were alone, quite another to hand over an idea, something he might have thought of himself, and give credit for it to the water boy.

Finally, Coach continued. "I have nothing else to say, next week . . . we correct our problems, or if . . ." He couldn't finish. He appeared weakened, humbled, a man who had given up hope, then had been rescued from the brink of disaster.

I felt sad for Danny, for myself, but mostly for the dove. I remembered how she had flown into the tamarack, free, her wings whistling. I thought of the instant before I pulled the trigger, death staring at her down the barrel of a gun, but before she could fly, her life had been blasted away. I remembered how I felt when I pitched over the side of the mesa, free flight, then extinction, but in my case only temporary unconsciousness.

As the team members left, they walked by to touch Harley. He, R.D., Danny and I were the last ones to leave. Coach watched us from his stool while we walked out.

Outside, Harley puffed up. "My dad said he was coming to this game. Bet he liked it."

I crossed my eyes. Harley's father was like a childhood imaginary friend, at least that's what I thought. "Well, it was nice to meet him when he came around to congratulate you," I said. Harley didn't say anything, and the others shifted from foot to foot. There was a chill in the air.

"We'd better relax tonight," R.D. said, "Coach will have plans for us next week." Although a fast runner, and lean and muscular, R.D. was lazy, and hated practice more than any player on the team. He had faked injury so many times to get out of practice the coaches no longer paid any attention if he got hurt. And when R.D. grinned, one side of his mouth spread farther than the other. It made him look apathetic, dull, and he was grinning now, and I wanted to pop him in the mouth.

"I messed things up for all of us," Danny said. His voice quavered like Coach's. His face was drawn-looking, drained of all color, his shoulders slouched. He slammed the heel of his palm against the car fender. I remembered the hand injury last year after the Bearcat game. I grabbed his hand. I could hear Coach's words when practice had started in August, "If you let all these fine folks down again . . ."

"You're only human," I said. "You can't play like Superman every game." I had started something when I shot the dove, then told Cannonball to move Harley. I had caused more attention, more of the critical spotlight to be turned on Danny.

I decided to get the focus off him. "But you don't have to worry, big man," I said to Harley. "You're the hero." The gravel crunched beneath our feet as we opened the doors of Danny's car, the same one Riccio had damaged with the club. "This is your night, your chance."

"Yeah, Schultzy's right," R.D. said. "You saved the whole fuckin' season." R.D. slapped Harley on the butt. We got in the car.

"But knowing you, Harley, all you want is a piece of ass." I heard the words, not my words, but they came from my mouth and I didn't stop them. They were words from somewhere, I heard them echo through the deep, sharp draws of my mind. Harley and I both had been unsuccessful with girls, although for very different reasons. I was afraid to approach even Earldeana, restrained by some powerful, all-righteous chains, but Harley was so crude he'd driven off the most brazen of the bold girls. But there was one girl, Tina Rexrood, Harley had not yet offended. We had found out Harley was interested in her, so we advised him. We had listened to his report from their first date, how he had, as he had been instructed, stroked her hair, touched her cheek, then kissed her firmly, but not roughly.

We all knew Tina's parents had gone to a funeral in Enid. She was home, alone, with her younger sister. "This is the night you can get in Tina's pants," I said. "Take her a gift. With a gift on top of your being a hero, she can't turn you down."

Harley suddenly seemed to be shy. "I don't have a gift."

"P.O.'s open late after games, we'll go down and buy her a bottle of perfume. I'll loan you the money."

We drove to Main Street and I helped Harley select a cheap, but ornate, bottle of perfume, and paid for it. I told him he could take his time paying me back. It was pretty much understood I'd never see the money. We drove Harley back to where his bike was.

"You ride out to see her. We'll meet you in the Dove Creek willow grove at twelve-thirty. If things go right, you'll be in such bad shape we'll have to bring you back to town in a coffin."

"Wish me luck." Harley bounced around on his heels with jovial, clownlike movements.

"You don't need luck," I said. "Remember, you are a genuine Friday night hero."

He threw his leg over the motorcycle. "Wait," I called. I pounced and grabbed hold of him. "Let's see your jacket, stud." Harley had snapped the large silver grippers on his coat but he was one snap off. I yanked the coat open, then snapped each one slowly, and as I did, I looked at him. I realized how little he had in life, just football, his friends, and a crazy mother. I kept jerking the jacket to make it fit better. This had started as a joke to get the attention diverted away from Danny; yet, I found myself on Harley's side. I wanted him to seduce Tina, I wanted him to fuck her, for her to lie submissively beneath his massive frame, for him to moan in bliss, and come back to us as a jubilant man.

I finished snapping his coat, then gave him a little shove. Contempt, the other side of my mixed feelings about Harley, started in my stomach, then expanded into my chest. No, not contempt for Harley, but for myself, and a town that held Harley in such high esteem on a Friday night, a kid who had failed one grade and still barely passed, a kid whose primary joy in life was to get in a fight, a kid who couldn't snap his own coat. I had made him into a hero, and the town had crowned him as a king.

"We'll meet you at the grove, be there," I ordered. "Do you have the perfume?" He tapped his jacket pocket. We let him leave. The bike roared away beneath the dull street lights toward the intersection of county road twenty-three. Harley, then we, would travel the same route we had taken that night almost a year ago when we headed out for Faith and met Riccio. In the past, Harley had fallen into the wrong crowd. But now he was one of us. We'd take care of him. We watched until his taillight was swallowed by the darkness.

"You're a schemer, almost on Cannonball's level," R.D. said to me. "Too bad Harley's a dumb big asshole and will screw it up somehow." R.D.'s hairline was already receding in front. I started to say something about it, but Danny was already in the car.

We pulled out of the parking place in front of P.O.'s, and as we did, the sheriff, who had been parked across the street, motioned for Danny to stop. The sheriff's belt buckle was a replica of the U.S. Cavalry buckle worn by the army when they fought the Plains Indians. The buckle had been polished and it glinted in the street lights.

"Let's see your license, son." It took Danny a few minutes to locate his license. His hand shook when he handed it to Sheriff Ordway.

"Oh, I'll be darned, it's Danny Boone," the sheriff said. "I'm just kiddin' you," he added. "It was like you were a different person tonight, no one could recognize you. What was wrong out there, Danny?"

Danny's feet shuffled on the floorboard. His knuckles were white where he gripped the steering wheel. He grimaced. This was the very thing I resented. Wasn't it just a game? Yes, if pressed, they'd admit it was, but why did they behave as if it were so much more?

"I don't know. I feel fine, I'm trying not to worry. Coach says I'm better off if I don't think about it too much."

"Well, better luck next week," Ordway said. "And listen, you got a headlight out, better get it fixed." Danny got out and walked around front to check it. It was the left one.

"I don't think it's such a big problem," he said, when he got back in. "I can still see to drive."

"Stupid bastard," I said, when we pulled away. "Let him get out there and play if he thinks it's so damned easy." I continued to cuss, and to amaze myself.

We drove around, none of us said much. We stopped at the VFW Hall where teen town was held. "You Ain't Nothin' but a Hound Dog" was playing on the phonograph when we went in. The activities consisted mainly of chatting, checkers, and shuffleboard. But it was where the parents and ministers insisted their good kids go, and it was where the kids all made plans for whatever else was going to happen after the sponsors went home and the kids were free to get back into their cars.

When it was time to meet Harley, we headed west on route twenty-three, past the football stadium, now a gray mass against the lights of town, accelerating into darkness toward Dove Creek and the willow grove where we were meeting Harley. The asphalt, black as a Bible's cover, stretched in front of us, then ended abruptly five miles from town. The car swerved, gravel pinged beneath the fenders. Light from the west. It came closer, separated, and the driver dimmed them. Danny pulled over to the right and the vehicle hurtled by. Stones stung the side of the car. A cloud of dust fell over us.

"Lenny Williams's pickup," R.D. said, "his wife's probably kicked him out again." We rode in silence. The four tracks in the gravel road merged into three, less traffic out this far. R.D. tried the radio, but it was the wrong side of town to pick up signals. There was nothing but static and a late-night preacher. I assumed a mood of amused indifference; my inner control surprised and pleased me. In the blackness of the night we seemed to be the only people alive. Then the lights of another vehicle popped up in front of us.

"If Harley doesn't make it in tonight, maybe we ought to take him to Liberal for his birthday. My cousin knows a colored girl up there who's really nice and is only ten dollars for school guys," R.D. said. I looked at R.D. The lazy man's approach, I thought. I couldn't believe how bald R.D. was getting. He was very self-conscious about it. He needed to be taken down a notch or two.

The light ahead disappeared into the Dove Creek valley. We were only a mile or two from the meeting place. A white glow hung on the dust left by Lenny's pickup. We rode on in silence, then the light ahead came out of the valley. Still one light, farther away than I thought. In my mind, Dovie in her pink shirt with the ruffled sleeves, sitting with Killer at the game. How Danny might have felt if he saw them. Perhaps that's why he played poorly, perhaps it had nothing to do with a dead bird.

"I don't think Harley should go to a whore," Danny said to R.D. His voice sounded deep, vibrant, as if he were exerting enormous pressure to control it. "You wouldn't want Harley to go through his life knowing he'd had to pay to get it his first time."

"That's easy for you to say, you've got Killer's second-hand piece anytime you want it," R.D. taunted. I looked at R.D.'s balding head. It was too late to bring it up.

Danny clamped his mouth shut. In five seconds, he was angrier than I'd ever seen him. He struck the dash with his hand, shattering the glass on the clock.

"You don't know that," he shouted. "You're only guessing." He lifted his foot off the accelerator, the car started coasting. The light from the other vehicle shimmered, very bright for the distance. "You don't know when to leave well enough alone," Danny screamed.

Ear-splitting shot. Metal against metal. Spinning.

"Sonny, can you hear me?"

Fog clearing, it was R.D., "Yes, I hear you," then I remembered. I called out for Danny. No answer. "Can you see Danny? . . . Is he okay?"

"Fuckin' pitch black, can't see anything."

"Did you see him?" I asked.

"Fuckin' no, I told you, I can't see a thing."

"No, I mean Harley."

"Harley?"

"On his bike. I saw him for an instant."

"It can't be. He went to the grove."

The spinning . . . out of control again . . . R.D. was right. But the image returned, Harley, shoulders forward, body coiled, knees up, the same way he had ground down the Bearcats, unaware of the disaster a split second away.

"Fuckin' roof's smashed in on us," R.D. said, and he kicked the metal.

I guessed where the door was and kicked, but pain shot through my head. I began to wake up, really wake up, terribly frightened. One friend inches away; two others, somewhere, no fire, the possibility. I attacked the metal . . . and the pain came.

I'm home. I'm in mother's room. I hear voices. My parents don't like noise late at night. I don't want anyone to know I sometimes sleep in my mother's room. Too late, someone's there, many voices and many lights. Flat-brimmed hat behind the light.

"Take it easy in there, we're trying to get you out."

The metal, bending, screeching, creaking. My friends are pulling the crowbar, breaking in so they can get me out. My mother is already awake, baking biscuits, scones. They're taking me away. I don't want to go. There are large hands reaching under my arms. Usually I get out of bed myself. Doc McGrath bends over me. The doctor says he's not worried about this one. It's the other one, the quarterback, that's injured.

"Danny?" I asked.

"Already on his way to the hospital. Was thrown clear, alongside the road when Tuffy Smith came by."

I wanted to know the worst. "Is he alive?"

"Yes."

I closed my eyes. Doc's hands probed, pain everywhere.

"Harley, what about Harley?"

"That I can't say. The bike, what's left of it, is a hundred yards down the road. Sheriff sent for some bloodhounds. They can't start until daylight, and maybe he'll show up by then."

"Has anyone told my parents?"

"Not yet. You've got to lay back until I can examine you better, make sure there ain't injuries we can't see."

It was easy to close my eyes, but when I did, I saw Harley again. I shuddered with a terrible cold chill.

My father published the State Police report.

ONE KILLED, THREE INJURED IN ACCIDENT

At approximately 12:20 A.M. Sunday, October 28, on County Road 23, nine miles west of Cimarron, a 1955 Buick four-door sedan driven by Daniel Boone, age seventeen, traveling westbound at an estimated speed of forty-five to fifty miles per hour, was struck by an eastbound motorcycle, evidently traveling at a high rate of speed, ridden by Harley Pugh, age nineteen. The cycle rider was killed.

The driver of the auto was thrown out when he lost control of the vehicle. At the time of this report, the driver remains unconscious in the Mc-Grath Hospital. Two passengers in the auto, R.D. Smyley and William Schultz, Jr., both age sixteen, were hospitalized. Both suffered numerous cuts and abrasions, but no serious injuries were reported. Smyley and Schultz were released at noon on Sunday.

Using bloodhounds, police found the motorcycle rider approximately one and one-fourth miles from the site of the accident. Attending physician Dr. McGrath estimated that Pugh died between

172

5:30 and 6:30 A.M. Among other injuries suffered
by the youth, both legs had compound fractures.
It is believed he was crawling toward a yard light
at the Artie Elston farm that was visible from the
accident site, not realizing the light was several
miles away.

The prairie had fooled everyone, like the glitter of fool's gold had
caused prospectors to spend years sifting and hoarding, only to have
the assayer tell them they had found something not real, something else. They became madmen, laughing, only fool's gold, it was
only fool's gold. The clear sparkle of light in the prairie blackness
had deceived us, then had lured Harley away from rescue, away
from the warmth of human help. The prairie had created another
illusion and now laughed at us in scurrilous silence.

I had suggested the hunt, shot the dove, distracted Danny; I had
sent Harley off on an unholy pilgrimage. In the past when I had
found myself in the depths of crisis, I had gone forward at church,
uttered words of repentance, vowing never again to forsake the
sanctuaries of pure thought and holy words. This time, I stayed detached, as if I were merely an observer flying over it all, as if the
events had been beyond my control, under no control, not God's,
or fate, or any power, merely events outside all forces of constraint
and order. My only role in the aftermath of the accident was to observe, stay calm, keep the powers of my mind focused on being
alive.

CHAPTER 21

Danny remained in a coma. Doc McGrath said there was nothing to do, just wait and see.

They held Harley's funeral at our church. I went with my parents. R.D., on crutches, attended with his parents. His hip was so sore Doc was afraid of blood clots.

Harley's mother sat alone, bent and dry; a hat with a veil covered her face, her black gloves were spangled with dingy lint balls. Her employers at the laundry, Mr. and Mrs. Tice, sat one row behind her. Everyone else sat near the back of the sanctuary. The laundry, along with most businesses, closed for the day. Harley's father, if he existed, did not show up. Dovie attended with Killer. Both of them, along with many kids from school, cried.

While everyone waited to get in their cars, Doc said to P.O., "What a waste, but it's just as well he went once it happened. He had nothing to look forward to, he'd have had trouble walking good, much less ever catching another pass."

"Another season out the window," P.O. said. "It's very discouraging. God knows I've been a supporter of that boy, but I just wonder if Danny has a curse on him. It'd be just our luck to get mixed up somehow with the devil. You know what I mean? With his dad being blinded in that accident the way he was? You just don't know what might be causing all this bad luck."

"I think it's just bad luck." After a pause, Doc added, "Or maybe you're right, it's someone bigger than all of us trying to tell us something."

The following Sunday, Anne stayed in town after church to be with Danny. He was still unconscious. I sat with her in Danny's room. Doc had been talking about shifting him to Oklahoma City to be under the care of a specialist. Arved and Thelma, who had sat dazed in his room all afternoon, left for home to do chores. I was staring at Anne. Her hair was stringy, unwashed. She wore a full skirt gathered around her small waist. Her blouse was a bright pink with elaborate embroidered patterns, and it gave her a cheap look, a look of poverty I hadn't noticed before. She seemed so waif-like, her thin body like a small child's. I remembered how she looked in the "inverse missionary position," nubile, but seasoned. She was sitting in a Naugahyde chair. The room gave off a pungent odor, disinfectant over dry, aging plaster. It was the same faded blue-green color I remembered from when Danny was hospitalized as a child. It seemed no time at all had elapsed since I was there with him then. I looked out the window. Sunlight angled through, the window had been recently cleaned. I looked back at Anne. She was so slender and straight, with such soft rounded lines, skin smooth like a polished stone. Danny lay beyond her, silent, motionless. Tears came to my eyes, not tears of sadness, or even loss, a feeling of awe as if I had seen something wonderful.

I felt myself slide into a mist, and through the mist I walked across the worn tile floor to where Anne sat near Danny. Danny's eyes were slightly open. I touched Anne's shoulders. Her blouse was coarse, unstarched. There was a slight tremor beneath the fabric along the surface of her skin. She touched my arm, a gentle, brushing stroke. I felt something odd about her gesture, an impulse, heat, although she seemed to be looking at Danny. Then my hands flowed over the slopes of her shoulders, down her arms, and as I bent down near her, her hair smelled toasty, of her father's tobacco. I bent so low my chin was on her shoulder. My hands touched the backs of hers, blue veins running through their slender whiteness where they lay in her lap. She turned her palms upward, slipped her hands, which were very warm, over the backs of mine and pressed them first against her legs, then pulled them upward to her stomach. Her rib cage was hard, and the softness below it, and her shape where her waist narrowed and her hips curved out. My hands crept behind her belt, over the shallow indentation of her navel, under the elastic strip of her panties. Her skin was soft like a baby kitten's, her panties silky against the backs of my hands, her pubic hair downy on the tips of my probing fingers. I felt her breath, then her mouth was on my ear and I expected bayonet-sharp pain as she bit me to stop my intrusion. Instead, I felt the wet, warm flick of her tongue in my ear, and my fingers were inside her, more slippery than warm plowshare grease. For a moment, I thought I might faint. Then the light changed.

The door to the room, which had been open only six inches, swung silently on its heavy hinges. I stood up and backed away, terrified at what I had done. The light blinded me, then I saw Dovie. She had let her hair grow, her tangled mane hung down to her shoulders, eyes the same blue as the faded shirt she had tucked into her tight jeans. She mouthed a soft hello through her full lips. She looked at Danny, then back at me, then faced Anne, wary like a cat who has cornered an animal larger than itself. My thoughts ricocheted round the room.

"Who are you?" Dovie asked her.

"Anne Tendal, I'm a friend of Danny's. And who are you?"

"Dovie Lasher, I'm a friend of Danny's, too." They scrutinized each other. Anne's blouse was puffy at the waist where my hands had been. Dovie stood waiting. Then Danny began to move slightly in his bed. First his head turned, then his legs moved. He moaned.

The three of us froze, none of us seemed to breathe as we watched him.

"I'm thirsty," he called, quietly. My heart sank, while my desire collided full force with my relief. Anne moved to the door to bring the nurse. I collapsed in Anne's chair. I could still feel her warmth radiating from its Naugahyde cover.

No one asked difficult questions at the coroner's inquest conducted on Harley's death. They had talked to Danny in the hospital. I don't know what he said. I told them how the light on Harley's bike appeared to be another car a distance away. The sheriff said nothing about our missing headlight. They didn't ask why we were meeting at the willow grove, or why Harley might have changed his mind about staying there until we arrived.

Harley's mother stared straight ahead through dark glasses and waited until everyone left the room before she hobbled out. The next day, she shot herself at the laundry, and fell down between two Maytag washers that continued to agitate until the soap overflowed, and her blood ran down the laundry drain with the blue, soapy water.

The county paid for her burial beside her son. The Tices were the only ones from town who attended.

The Dustdevils lost their last three games.

THE LONESOME END

PART III

CHAPTER 22

After the accident, clouds moved in from the northwest. The temperature stabilized in the mid-thirties; too warm for winter, too cold for comfort. Mornings, blue rain fell, drenching the countryside. The unpaved roads became quagmires, the half-frozen muck rolled up, packing automobile fenders with cold, impenetrable mud. The clouds hovered low and merged into the landscape, it was difficult to know up from down. The prairie lost its yellows, pale greens, and sage blues. Nothing but sodden gray. In the evening, when the sun dipped near the horizon and poked through, the clouds turned the color of bloody phlegm. At night, the temperature dropped, sleet fell, stinging like whips.

The townspeople draped themselves in hats and scarves, their grief hung limp and somber, their handshakes went slack, they had lost all hope. When they spoke, they were gruff and impatient.

Old Man Goggin stood in his window hour after hour, watching the empty street. He had tightened his suspenders, the inseam of his pants was hiked up so high it exposed his socks and garters. LaFaye hunched over his sewing machine making holsters and chaps, although he couldn't even sell what he had in stock. P.O. stayed in the back of his drugstore, letting Dottie, his tottery cashier, handle customer relations. His business diminished to a trickle.

Up and down the street, the spirit of fellowship and cooperation, so prevalent when the football season was going well, evaporated. The Nazarene preacher caught some kids betting on a checker game, and forbade his young people to attend teen town. The other ministers, fed up with the bickering, canceled the whole thing. The Methodists petitioned their bishop to reassign their pastor. The Church of Christ fired theirs, and blackballed him with other congregations. The Ku Klux Klan, unheard of for years, planned a rally for Christmas eve in the American Legion Hall. The featured speaker was rumored to be a Mississippi Nazi. The sheriff issued dozens of traffic tickets, handing them out like he thought they were Christmas cards.

Danny had been discharged from the hospital a week after he woke up. At home, he stayed in his room, his face shrouded with pain. R.D. and I went out to visit. We helped him open a stack of cards. There were funny ones, religious ones, and one I tried to hide.

"What is it?" Danny asked.

"Nothing." I casually tossed the unsigned card aside.

Danny picked it up. The words were written with an unsharpened pencil. "You conceited bastard, you murdered my friend."

Danny's mood worsened. He refused to go anywhere and did not return to school, doing assigned schoolwork at home in a slipshod fashion. I worried Egbert might fail him, and he'd lose his football eligibility. If that happened, he might never recover.

I felt fine and functioned well in the daylight, when I was fully conscious. Cannonball had been right about me. I did not have the instincts of a blocker, a tackler, the kind of killer it takes to be a football player. But what about the intuition of a killer? I would not risk injury to my body and brain on a football field in order to hurt an opponent and obtain the applause and admiration of my town. The desire to inflict pain, the proclivity for violence did not appeal to me. However, I had killed, not with my bare hands or a vicious tackle, but with subtle suggestions, gentle misdirections, finely honed gibes. It was a kind of power I found appealing. I exulted in it during the daytime, but at night my fragile shell cracked, I dueled with ghosts, imprisoned with them in the vast, colorless landscape. Screams and whispers haunted me, the way I had cursed and jeered, then sent Harley off to his death, the sounds of the accident, how I felt when I couldn't find Danny. These images alternated with scenes from our childhood.

We were nine, or maybe ten. I was staying with Danny on the farm, and Arved had taken Danny to guide the truck while he scattered hay for the cattle. I think Arved didn't want me to distract Danny, so they left without me.

I was angry. I ran to the house, but the house was empty. Thelma was out somewhere. I started to cry. When I went back outside, Kirk was mounting up on the pinto horse. He saw me crying, said he'd take me to them because he was going to the pasture to bring in a fresh cow.

It had rained during the night, then the air had suddenly become colder than the ground, and fog rose up in little wisps. Kirk plunked me down on the horse's rump, a puff of dust from the heavy winter coat rose up around me. The saddle creaked when Kirk mounted. I gripped the leather side strap with one hand and the seat with the other. The horse cantered along the buffalo trail the cattle now used. I slipped on the broad rump, to the left side, to the right. Dust swirled around us, stinging my eyes. After what seemed to be an interminable, fearful ride, Kirk put me into the truck as it crept, geared down in compound, Danny steering while Arved kicked off the hay.

After Harley's death, I dreamed repeatedly of this incident, but in my dream, Kirk and I don't find the truck. Instead we come to a barbed wire fence. "Arved must have put it up," Kirk says, "it wasn't here before. You stay on the horse, I'll open the gate." The

reins hang loose, the pinto has been trained that way. Kirk leans
into the gate, but it is well made and tight. "Praise the Lord," he
says, "praise the Lord for life's trials." He stoops lower to align his
shoulder with the gate post, and finally lifts the looped wire latch.
The cow pony feels taller. His ears point and he swings his bald
face over his left shoulder, his translucent eye fixes on me, no hands
on the reins. His ears lay back, the ever-lurking fear invades, and I
freeze. Kirk holds the gate post. Its bark hangs in strips, smelling
of creosote. Then it's not Kirk, it's Harley. The horse leaps over the
gate. The horse is saving me from Harley. With choppy strides, he
rumbles over the trail. The ground blurs below me. From behind
I hear fiendish laughter, Danny with Harley, pleasure in my plight;
then Lucifer and the fallen angels all laughing while I am engulfed
in red-orange fire. The thin leather reins fly loose in the wind, they
wrap around me, and I am tied to the galloping pinto, hurtling into
the burning moon. There's a fork in the trail. I lean with the horse,
but am wrong and he veers the other way. Cruel terror flaps down
on me, the pinto whinnies shrilly, I fall, pulling the horse with me
through the amber smoke that veils the brink of hell.

The fifth or sixth time I had this dream, I awoke from falling
with my mother opening the curtains to a fiery dawn. Finally, there
was sunshine. "Enough of that moaning," she said, "praise the Lord,
it's a beautiful day. How about breakfast with me at the Elite Cafe?"

It was Wednesday after Christmas. We sat near the front window. I remembered the time Danny and I had come here with
Harley, when they pursued the fight with Riccio. It seemed like
that had been aeons ago. Oddly, I felt flattered by my mother's invitation to have breakfast. She had been unusually lucid since the
accident, as if the terrible thing she feared had finally happened, I
had survived, and now she could stop her worrying. She sat against
the window, smiling, with the sunlight behind her. People moved
past the window with more energy now that the sun had burst
through the clouds.

When our food arrived, my mother said grace. I kept my eyes open as she prayed, noticed she had applied a light dusting of makeup and had darkened her lips with lipstick. She wore a small pearl necklace that had been her mother's, and her dress was low enough to expose the cleft between her breasts. She appeared to have dressed for a fancy dinner.

As she finished her prayer, the cafe door opened, Cannonball walked in with Elberta Munion. It seemed like a circus had arrived in town, and the fat woman and the midget had come in for breakfast. They waved when they walked by us and sat down in the back of the cafe.

"What in the world is Elberta doing with the coach? They make quite a pair, don't they?" I snorted when I said it, and from my mother rolled deep laughter, then we both laughed, compulsively, unable to stop. "I can't imagine what they're talking about," I said between snickers. "I hardly imagine they have much in common."

"More than you think," Mother said, controlling herself. "They're talking about Danny. There's a plan to help him. Elberta has talked to your father about it."

"Elberta, and my father?" We both began laughing again at the thought of those two—my father so carefully dressed and groomed, Elberta frumpy, and obese.

"We shouldn't laugh at her," Mother said, "she's my best friend." We stopped laughing.

"Whose plan is this?"

"It started with the coaches. They talked to Elberta and then to the pastor. That's all I know." She paid the bill and we left.

On Sunday, we rose to sing the doxology. Danny and his parents were sitting across the aisle from my parents and me. Thelma flicked her hand, waving at me, but Danny ignored me, nor did he sing. Other people seemed less apathetic. The balm of Gilead had been applied, time had begun to heal.

After the doxology, Elberta came up the aisle. She leaned past

Arved, her stomach lapping over the pew, hiking up her dress and exposing her legs. She had rolled her hose down above her knees. Her thighs were much too large for a garter belt. She gripped Danny's arm above the elbow. In a hoarse whisper, she spoke, "Danny, this is for you." She shook him. I could not yet understand what was happening, and what Elberta had to do with it.

Two church elders walked forward on the outside aisles. They reached the stage, stretched on their toes, and untied ropes I had not noticed. A banner unfurled from the sanctuary's vaulted ceiling. It was the same banner from the revival on the mesa, but along the bottom were new words, more recently painted in red and blue.

JOE DON JONES,
EVANGELIST AND COMMUNIST
FIGHTER
HEADQUARTERS—OTTUMWA, IOWA
Healing   Prophecy   Laying on Hands

Elberta had persuaded her nephew to come save Danny. The service floated by, the evangelist stepped to the pulpit. He had aged since we saw him on the mesa. His hair had receded, and there were other signs of his lifestyle—paunchiness in the middle, pouches beneath cold, brown eyes. Danny sat erect, his eyes were round. He appeared to have been startled.

At first, Joe Don talked to us as if he sat in our living room. "Jesus chose twelve disciples, and one of them was a devil because it was Judas Iscariot who betrayed him, and that left eleven. Eleven is the same number of men it takes to make a football team. Had that thought ever occurred to you? Praise Jesus, it has to me.

"That thought occurred to me a few months ago when I boarded an airplane in Oklahoma City. I sat beside a man who looked familiar. I leaned toward him and introduced myself. 'Yes,' he said,

'I've heard of your work. My name is Colonel Blaik. Most people call me Red.' 'Oh, yes,' I said, 'I've heard of your work. What is the coach from Army doing in Oklahoma?'

" 'Well,' he said, 'no place grows better football players than Oklahoma, and no place grows better soldiers than Oklahoma. To me, they're one and the same. I was down here trying to convince some of these rowdy boys they should play football, and become career officers at the United States Military Academy.'

" 'Tell me, Colonel Blaik,' I said to him, 'when you're scouting players, what qualities do you look for? I don't mean the physical attributes; given those, what are the intangibles?'

" 'There are four I look at,' he told me. 'The first is commitment. If a player will not give up other pleasures to play football, he can't succeed in a major college program. The second is courage. He must be able to face opponents, to intimidate and not be intimidated. The third is durability. His body must take collisions without serious injury, and he must be able to play even when hurt. The fourth is obedience. There's no room on my football team or in the army for a kid who won't follow orders.'

"I have thought a great deal about what Colonel Blaik said. *If Jesus was a football coach*, what kind of men would he recruit for his team?

"You see, the game the Lord's team plays is not confined to one stadium seating sixty thousand fans in some university town, nor are the stakes Big Ten or Ivy League titles. No sir, no ma'am, the contest is worldwide, the stakes—everlasting life or eternal damnation for every human being on the face of the earth."

Joe Don began preaching in earnest. His eyes were more open and sparkling, he swung his hips like a dancer, he swept his arms in wide arcs. He no longer appeared pudgy, out-of-shape.

"First, Jesus needs people who are committed to his team. As Coach Blaik said, the goals of the team require sacrifice. When Jesus called Peter and Andrew, the Bible says, 'And he saith unto them, follow me and I will make you fishers of men. And they straightway left their nets, and followed him.'

"Straightway. That word means immediately. They didn't say, my friends want to throw me a goodbye party, I'll be there soon. They forsook their nets, and followed him. Christ calls us to his team in the same way. Praise Jesus."

The evangelist rocked side to side with the lyric flow of words, thrusting his hips, beckoning with open arms, moving discreetly between sensuality and grace.

"Jesus recruits courageous people for his team. The great coach cannot use the fainthearted. Friends, do not be afraid. Christ is with you. Reach out to the lost. Go down to the hell hole. Yes, it's frightening, but Jesus is with you. If you're a Christian, you're under the blood. Nothing can harm you.

"When you have accepted the Lord, no danger can touch you, the Lord is near. It doesn't matter what happened, how bleak things look. 'Be not afraid, it is I,' Jesus says to his team."

While Joe Don spoke, I sensed something unnatural was happening. My heart pounded blood upward until my neck swelled and my Adam's apple pressed against my tie. I felt a fullness, a hopefulness, leaping joy. I felt the holy spirit violate me. Joe Don finished his second point. My mother put her arm around me, and pulled me close against her breast. I felt the old closeness, the old love.

"Jesus recruits players for his team who will endure. Like Coach Blaik said, we must take the bumps and bruises of the game and not collapse. Jesus cannot use us if we let life's trials beat us. We must be durable. We must be steadfast. We must play even if we're hurt. It's a problem of conditioning. We stay in condition by training, just like any team. We train by attending church and Bible study, keeping ourselves in the fellowship of the saints, and by prayer. 'Pray without ceasing,' the Apostle Paul urged. If you feel yourself weakening, giving in to your problems, you have broken training, you've neglected your prayer life.

"Do you believe Jesus can answer prayer?" Joe Don paused. "Do you believe Jesus can answer prayer? Say, 'Yes he can.' "

"Yes he can," my mother and a few others said.

"Can Jesus answer prayer?"

"Yes he can," I shouted aloud, too.

"Can Jesus save the alcoholic if we ask him to?"

"Yes he can!"

"Can Jesus save the perverts?"

"Yes he can."

"Can Jesus save a whore?"

"Yes he can!"

"Can Jesus save the mentally ill?"

"Yes he can!"

"Can Jesus save the depressed and discouraged?"

"Yes he can!"

Joe Don let the noise subside. There had settled over me a confidence, a blessed calmness—a sense of power and assurance I had not felt for a long time. Someone else lived inside me. Jesus had returned as real as he had been the day he came to me beside my bathtub.

"Finally, Jesus seeks team members who will obey. When the coach sends in the play, the good team runs it. And that is what Jesus expects. When Jesus calls you, he expects you to come. And if you don't listen, if you resist his call, if you ignore your coach, you'll be off the team, gone, damned. How could a loving Jesus do that? How could he send anyone to burn in hell? Because he gave his blood. He took on human nature so we might take on the divine nature. He was born in a manger so we might live in a mansion. He became mortal so we can become immortal. Because of his blood, he expects you to obey."

Joe Don finished, and glided away from the pulpit. He rested his hand on the carved wooden Communion table. He continued, pleading.

189

"That day on the plane, I asked the great coach of the Cadets one more question. I took hold of his arm so he could feel the urgency of my question. I could feel how well conditioned he was although he's not a large man. 'You've told me the qualities you seek in all players,' I said, 'but what about the quarterback. What do you look for in a quarterback?'

"There was a glint, like a lust, in his eyes. 'That's always my dream,' he said, 'to find a great quarterback. Every coach looks for that one player who can do it all. Not only must the quarterback have all the qualities of the other players, he must be gifted far beyond them. There have only been a few, the Sammy Baughs, the Johnny Lujacks, the Otto Grahams. These are the men who have been given special gifts.' " Joe Don paused again.

"My friends, I am here this morning on a divine mission. This week, I had a visit from Coach Jesus. Do you doubt it?" Joe Don stood absolutely still, waiting, only his eyes moved as he engaged us in his dare.

"Do you doubt it?" he shouted.

"No," we shouted back. My mother pulled me closer.

"The Lord leads me to say this. These are God's words, and God speaks the truth. There is a young man in this church who has been gifted by God. He has that personality, what we call today charisma. His physical talents, his God-given gifts, make him a leader, a boy with wondrous responsibility before God. We look at him and we envy him, 'Oh, he's lucky,' we say. If we could only throw touchdown passes like he can, make those darting, daring dashes for the end zone like he can, how we would use our talents to the glory of God. Oh, yes, we envy him.

"But special gifts may mean extraordinary tests. Our young man is graceful, a born athlete. Women look on his countenance, we don't like to admit these things, and they desire him. Nothing is more dangerous to the servant of God than that pretty young woman who beckons, 'Come lie with me,' she says, like Potiphar's wife said to Joseph. The devil himself disguised in the form of a woman has tricked this young man and betrayed Jesus."

The bald shock of his accusation jolted me. I looked back at Anne. She sat, terror-stricken.

"But God has sent his servant to help. God is calling this young man with a voice so loud if he fails to hear, he will have no place to turn. He will be alone, outside the grace and mercy of God. Let me assure you, this young man is not a bad man, but maybe he has become a little conceited, too reliant on himself. He's not a totally flawed sinner, but the sins of the flesh have appeared more desirable than the true ways of God.

"You may be one short step from hell," he shouted, and it seemed he was pointing at all of us, not just Danny.

"But God is patient, praise him, he has given us another chance. We're going to stand . . . and sing the invitation hymn.

"All to Jesus I surrender;
All to him I freely give.

"Don't sing it unless you mean it. Don't utter a single note if you're not doing what this song says. Remember, Coach Jesus wants you on his team."

The words of the first stanza began in a slow, rising sweep as the voices caught up with the organ. Danny stumbled one step out, then forward, and knifed down the aisle, falling into Joe Don's arms. The rest of us stood in miraculous suspension. Joe Don lifted one hand to heaven and cradled Danny with the other, holding him upright.

"I know Danny Boone needs no introduction to any of you. I don't have to tell you of his success, or his sadness. But I am happy to tell you of the great work of Jesus who saves lost souls. Jesus moved me to come to Cimarron today. I canceled another engagement because Jesus told me to. Jesus has led me here, and Danny has answered his call. Danny will join my Southern crusade, which begins tomorrow in Macon, Georgia. The fields are ripe unto harvest. Souls need the redemption of Jesus. He is our coach, he sends in the plays. What joy Danny's decision this morning brings to the heavenly host."

He paused to let his words sink in.

"There are others who need the forgiveness, others who need the baptism of the holy spirit to fire up your witnessing. Come forward as we sing the next verse. For Jesus, I will lay my hands on you and God will work. For Jesus, praise Jesus, holy Jesus."

The organ played louder, then, above the music, I heard a rhythmic, mournful voice, rah-ma-ta-ma-ta-ma-ta-rah-ma-ta-ma-ta-ma-ta, a hollow sound as if words were being spoken in a barrel, close yet far away at the same time. I looked around to see where it came from. My mother was reaching up, only the whites of her eyes were visible, her face was twisted while her mouth twitched with the odd cadence of the words. Then I heard other sounds, and I looked around the room. Pomp Reed and Elberta Munion danced in the aisle, and from them came similar sounds. They and others had been baptized in the Holy Ghost.

I turned to go down the aisle, to take my place beside Danny. Anne, bent and weeping, brushed by me as she had that day on the mesa. I followed and she knelt at Joe Don's feet, her face down near his polished black wingtips. Her wailing filled the sanctuary, while the tongues beat out a pulsing rhythm. I waited behind her, remembering despite everything when I had touched her. Joe Don reached out to lay his hands on her. She swooned, then sprawled unconscious on the aisle carpet. He lifted her, sliding his hand beneath her buttocks. Her long legs dangled, he held her triumphantly, and as he lifted her before us, her skirt shifted up her thighs. Then he put her on the church pew.

I ran, as I had on the mesa, but this time I ran to my father, even as Mother, having finished her fit of echolalia, scuttled down the aisle to join the others.

Elberta rushed forward to help, fanning Anne with an open hymnal. Behind her, the multitude of people lined up; my mother, the Tendals, Arved and Thelma, and the rest, all weeping and shuffling forward. Joe Don pressed their foreheads with his hands while he prayed for those under the blood to receive the baptism of the Holy Ghost. My father and I were the only ones left in our seats. My father shifted from foot to foot. He took out his handkerchief and bent to wipe the dust off his shoes.

"I don't think God cares if your feet are dirty," I said.

He straightened up and really looked at me as if he were aware for the first time I was there, beside him, and we were the only two who were not down front. He puffed up a size or two. It didn't matter if we talked out loud, the others were paying no attention. "You think you have a right to criticize me? After the way you've sided with her all these years?" He nodded toward my mother, who was dancing with Pomp Reed.

So that's what he thought, he thought it was a conspiracy, that I'd chosen to be her sidekick. He didn't understand I felt he had abandoned me to her; he didn't understand the soldiers I had played with under the covers, and how the sentinel, down on one knee, had been helpless to do anything but watch.

"You're just like her," he added. "Why aren't you down there with the rest of them?"

"You married her," I said. "I didn't have a choice. I didn't ask for her to be my mother, and I didn't ask for you either. It all just happened."

He sized me up, considered what I had said. He began to deflate. "When I first knew your mother, and the newspaper was brand-new and I owned it, the first thing I ever owned in my life, that seemed like all I'd ever want because I'd had so little in my life. Then you were born. I thought that was going to be the greatest day of my life. But your arrival did something to your mother. She couldn't get enough of you. It wasn't a matter of giving, it was what she could get. Whatever she wanted, I couldn't give. She wanted it from you. She thought you were special, that God had given you to her, alone, because she had suffered the pain when you were born. I know I should have been stronger, but I couldn't fight her. I'm sorry."

There was a commotion in the front of the sanctuary. Anne had recovered from her fainting spell. She and Danny were standing next to each other, stiff as strangers. The others were all praying for them, some kneeling, some with arms spread to heaven. When I turned toward my father, to say that I loved him, and that he should not feel bad, he was gone.

Within hours, the evangelistic team departed. Danny drove the Cadillac, Joe Don lounged in the back seat. Danny had his schoolbooks with assignments prepared by the coaches and teachers.

I stood a block away and watched them leave. I couldn't believe Danny was gone, that he had left me behind. I was left with a hollow noise, like a hum inside an empty barrel. At night, I tossed from the torture of the hum. I piled up my pillows and blankets to cover my ears, and I whimpered, pleading for help from a God whose voice I could not hear through the din. Jesus had visited me for the last time. I returned to another source of comfort.

From my drawer, I lifted my toy soldiers. I arranged them on the top of my dresser, the sentinel safely to one side, the battle lines carefully drawn so neither side had the advantage.

CHAPTER 23

A few weeks after Danny's departure, I sat at breakfast, spooning Mother's overcooked oatmeal into my mouth the way I had since I was three and first learned to feed myself, and, at the same time, I read a newspaper that I had folded in the special way my father had taught me. The Holy Ghost baptism had made my mother happy. She moved around her kitchen with energetic steps, anticipating my needs, smiling to herself, and humming church songs. I hid from her behind the newspaper. I had lost a bond, a connection that had been important to me for a long time. I found a small article in the paper that alarmed me.

STATE CASEWORKER MISSING

A welfare caseworker, John Freeman, has been reported missing to the State Police. Freeman, thirty-seven, from Elk City, was sent early this week by the State Welfare Department to visit a family in Faith, a small community in the Panhandle. The Welfare Department, after filing the missing-person form on behalf of the department and Mrs. Freeman, is providing no further information.

Freeman's wife, Angela, reached Wednesday, said she knew very little except her husband told her the case involved possible neglect and mistreatment of an adolescent female. She claimed their marriage was stable and her husband had no history of disappearances.

The Tendal family did not attend church Sunday morning. I asked Elberta if she had heard from them. She said no, but looked away when she answered my questions.

My imagination was becoming too lurid, the whole thing I was building up, the work of a warped mind. But the image of having seen Elberta with Cannonball, their combined aptitude for chicanery, came clearly into focus, and persisted.

I was the first one outside after the service. A blustery wind hit me, and as I wrapped myself in my coat two men got out of a black Ford and charged by me. The pastor left with them, not waiting to shake hands with the congregation. The people filed out, looked around, mystified. No one could recall ever walking out the church without shaking the preacher's hand.

At the service that night, Pastor Toon had reappeared but his face was ashen. His announcement was simple: the Tendal family had disappeared. The police were looking for them.

I didn't know what to do because I did not yet know what had happened. Or I knew, but I couldn't grieve.

The brown sugar melted and spread out in little rivulets over the gray mass. The spoon I held never reached my bowl. This time, the story was front page, a moderately sized headline.

• • •

BODY OF CASEWORKER FOUND IN STOCKTANK

The body of State Welfare Department caseworker John Freeman, missing for nearly a week,
was found yesterday three miles north of Faith, a
small community in the center of the Panhandle.
Freeman disappeared after he was sent by the Welfare Department to investigate charges of incest
and child abuse in the Arthur Tendal family. Tendal was a hired man on the Harper Ranch, one of
the largest ranches in the state.

Freeman's body was discovered Sunday in a ranch
stocktank. He had been killed by a shotgun blast
at close range. His body was then stuffed through
a watering hole below three inches of ice on the
tank. It was not found until the weather broke. A
team of State Police detectives is investigating.

The Harper Ranch owner, Orville Harper III,
reached at his residence in Wichita, Kansas, said
he did not know where the Tendal family was, and
Mr. Tendal had not notified him that he was leaving his employment.

The Welfare Department has confirmed the
Tendal family was part of its caseload when they
resided in Durant, southeast of Oklahoma City
near the Texas border. A spokesman for the department told reporters, "We lost track of the family three years ago, and had no idea where they
were until someone from Senator Lienhart's office
called, asking us to investigate."

State police said all indications are that the Tendals departed Faith quickly. "Most of the house-
hold furnishings appear to be in place," the State

197

Police spokesman said. The Tendal family auto, a 1951 maroon Studebaker, and Freeman's 1955 two-tone blue Ford Fairlane are both missing. Any information regarding Freeman's death or the whereabouts of the Tendal family should be given to the State Police.

The article wiped out my fear of the night. All my dreaming, the phantoms and delusions, ended abruptly. My mind became unsullied, my vision barren, without expectation, without mirage. I knew now why Anne had seemed so precocious, yet so childlike, purity and holiness of a wronged innocent. I guessed more or less accurately what had caused the Tendals to disappear. Someone, with connections to power, with fears for Danny's performance this coming football season, with no confidence in the power of the holy spirit, by careful study and research, had discovered the tragedy of the Tendal family, and had found a way to get rid of them, and to get Anne away from Danny. I doubt they had expected to trigger a murder.

I slept the leaden sleep of the dead and I moved through my days intent upon reaching the nighttime. Death was now so irrefutable, so graphic, that it grew remote, irrelevant. Extinction was so irreversible it no longer felt more important than any other event. Salvation was meaningless. I had lost a major life force, I had lost my fear of death. Without illusion there was no fear.

To pass the time, I read. Everything except what was assigned. Why read *Macbeth*? And why *Hamlet* and *Romeo and Juliet*? Why did they always assign those plays? I knew there was a reason, and I knew it was not a good one, so I read other plays of Shakespeare, *King Richard III*. I found a bitter, depraved man, cheated by God, a villain who believed himself to be exempt from the laws of God and man. He committed incest, murder, no law had meaning to him. I despised him, hated his weakness, for, in the end, he capitulated: "O coward conscience, how dost thou afflict me!"

In my mother's bookshelves, I found a novel published the year I was born, *The Private Life of Helen of Troy*. She had read it during the time she was recovering from my birth. It had contributed, she claimed, to her depression.

For two days, I read and reread Helen's story, and I gloried in her beauty and power that made her exempt from the Trojans' wrath, exempt from the death sentence that should have been hers, for her unfaithfulness, for her treachery. When Troy had fallen and Menelaus entered her room with his sword drawn, she bared her breast so he might know where to strike her. But when he saw her, his anger became impotent and he dropped his sword. He was under her spell again. I hated him for his weakness. I loved her madly, her beauty, her guile. I did not return to church, and sometimes played hooky from school.

Three weeks after Anne disappeared, my mother left the house to take my father his lunch. I had stayed home from school complaining of a headache.

"I'm going calling this afternoon, I won't be back until late," Mother informed me.

A few minutes later, the front door opened. Someone was calling, "Sonny, I want to talk to you. Sonny. Sonny." My mother's friend, Elberta Munion, burst through my bedroom door. She paused beside my bed where I cowered. She wore dark red lipstick, and had fluffed her hair so it perched on her head like an upside-down nest.

"I got a letter from Danny," she said. "He's fine. Now, I'm worried about you. I know what you need," she said, "all that pain and suffering, I'm here to give willingly. Mary Magdalene gave to Jesus, and I'll give to you."

She peeled down the front of her dress, exposing her shoulders, releasing her breasts. I pulled the covers over my head. She pulled all the blankets off, tossing them onto the floor. I lay exposed in only my underwear. Her breasts swayed over me until she reached to support them, gripping them underneath so her flesh oozed around her fingers, and her nipples lengthened. I squirmed sideways, away from her. She hiked up her skirt, and vaulted onto the bed with extraordinary quickness, pinning my legs between her thighs.

"Suck me," she said, "suck me." I thrashed around, she slapped me on the cheek. "Suck me!"

I was frightened, then I grew angry. She pinned my arms to the bed. Her breasts nuzzled my lips. "Just do it, Sonny."

Her areolas were no larger than half dollars, her nipples both bumpy and velvety. "Relax, that's a good boy, just relax," she said quietly, her eyes only half open.

I was still struggling, but weakly. Suddenly, in the midst of the anger, everything felt familiar. I opened my mouth. "Yes, good," she said. She closed her eyes and started to moan while moving her crotch against my legs, which were still pinned beneath her. "Rougher," she ordered. "I mean it, harder . . . even harder." She let go of one arm, reached down, and began to massage me, her movements varied, slow, then faster. She began using both her hands, which were elastic, rubbery, gripping me so lightly I could not help but buck toward them, bringing my knees upward against her heavy buttocks. She breathed out with little grunts. "Now do it, bite me," she hissed. "No, no, too easy . . . I mean bite me, hard." I bit into her spongy flesh, clamping her nipple to the roof of my mouth. "Tighter, tighter," she whispered, still stroking. She leaned more toward me, giving me slack. "Yes, yes," she squealed and pulled back. I stiffened, holding on, biting, feeling the anger flow out, screaming, as if my rage were demons that had to be exorcised. She pulled, her head thrown back, making unheard-of noises, her face twisted with the mixture of pleasure and pain. I opened my mouth and let go so she fell backward; at the same time, my semen shot upward and landed in globules on my chest.

My breath came back, rasping. When Elberta recovered, she pulled up her dress, tucked in her breasts, and sat down on the side of my bed, which sank, causing me to roll against her massive buttocks. She reached back to touch the side of my face where, moments ago, she had slapped me. My own smells were now fresh on her hand.

"Remember this, you're a virgin, Sonny," she said. "You're a pure sweet boy Jesus loves. Let all your anger go." She patted me, gentle little pats. "Now listen, your momma knows I came to help you, don't you ever tell her how." She stood up, walked to the door and turned around, shaking her head sadly. "You're the best boy I've ever known, if you had only been my boy . . ." Tears rolled down through her rouge, then she waddled out.

I got up and dressed. When my mother came home, I had prepared tea.

201

CHAPTER 24

Danny's letter arrived the next day.

Dear Sonny,

Sorry I have not written sooner, but here I am and I'm feeling fine, praise the Lord.

It was the most wonderful thing for me to join up with J.D.'s crusade. It has given me a new lease on life and God has lifted me from the miry clay. Praise Jesus.

When we arrive in a town, the first thing we do is set up the tent. I drive the stakes in with the sledgehammer. It's good football training. We lay out the canvas, get all the ropes stretched out from the center, and when the poles are ready, we all pull, and it's up. It's like a miracle. There's nothing, then, suddenly, it's this big room, a sanctuary for many.

We always open the service with "Onward Christian Soldiers," it's a theme song for us. J.D.

says this hymn is our marching order. J.D. leads
the opening prayer, because the object is to get
the congregation saying "amen," and "hallelu-
jah," bring them into the feeling of fellowship.
Sometimes I give a testimony. I've never
preached the whole sermon, but sometimes the
Spirit has led me to speak for fifteen minutes.

Then J.D. preaches. You ought to see the people being saved. J.D. says they are mostly drunk-
ards and harlots, and the Bible says that God's
mercy extends to all. We feel it's a poor night if
fewer than thirty come forward. Think of it. In
our church if someone comes forward once a
month, we think it's good. The souls being saved
here—I feel wonderful. It sends me into fits of
praise.

And the healings, I can't even begin to tell
you about the miracles. I've seen people walk
who've been crippled all their lives, a deaf man
who could hear for the first time. You'll believe
it, too, when you see it. The power of God, it's
wonderful, praise Him. Someday J.D. will raise
people from the dead, because the Bible says
death is the last enemy to be conquered. J.D.
says he's just waiting for God to tell him to do it.

The service closes with a "prove God" offering. J.D. challenges the people to give in such a
way they prove God's promise to bless them ten-
fold. It's such a wonderful thing, to be able to
actually prove God exists by giving. I can't believe how He is blessing me, praise His holy
name.

The coaches sent a workout program. I run

about three miles a day, do push-ups, chin-ups,
sit-ups, and the like. Then, the tire gets hung
out at each location, and I throw the football
through it. Sometimes J.D. mentions this to the
audience, and people come around to watch in
the afternoon. Usually, one of them chases the
ball for me like you used to. J.D. says it helps the
Lord's work if people know our team members
do other things besides just preaching and
singing. And it helps me try harder if I know
people are watching and may be led to Jesus.

Evangelism will definitely be my life's work
after high school. J.D. says God wants me to
play football and use that to His glory. Maybe
the Lord has a plan for the two of us to work together. Think about this seriously.

Please say hello to Anne for me. I've written
to her, but, of course, have not heard, since
we're always on the move. I hope to see you
soon, depending on how the crowds hold out as
we reach summer.

Your friend in the name of Christ,
Danny

My sense of wonder and illusion returned. The dreams that had
forsaken me came back. But I no longer saw life in black-and-white.
There was good in evil, and evil in good. The variations of themes
seemed endless, the shades of color in the beams of a rainbow could
not be counted. I kept remembering an incident from childhood.

Danny and I were eight. Danny was wearing his blue-checked
mackinaw and a brown furry hat with the flaps tied under his chin.

I had thrown a fit so Thelma gave me the matching gloves, while Danny had to wear a mixed pair of mittens. We stood outside the corral at the Boone farm.

Arved, Kirk, and a neighbor were working some calves, separating them from their mothers. The calves darted toward us, struggling desperately, but the men always caught them. Arved cradled a knife in his hand. It fit there, reeking of pain.

"Okay, he's ready," Kirk shouted. Arved dipped the knife in a bucket of disinfectant, took a cloth, and walked to the calf. He found the calf despite his blindness by listening to the sounds of struggle. With the cloth, Arved washed the small sack between the calf's hind legs. Moving as swiftly as a sighted man, he ripped open the small rubbery pouch. The calf bawled, while its mother went wild, throwing her head, blowing out her nostrils. With short slashes, Arved removed the little bull's testicles.

The neighbor, tobacco dripping from the side of his mouth, tossed them out of the corral where two hawks hovered, floated on the wind, then dived for them. Suddenly, a testicle landed at our feet. Hawk wings flapped. I looked up, the hawk was above us, talons spread, beak open, crying. "That one's for you boys," tobacco chin called. "Here, you eat it like this." He took one of the testicles, put it in his mouth, ground his teeth in exaggerated motion, and swallowed it; at least I thought he swallowed it, he gave us the illusion. "I'll give you a dollar for each one you eat." He pulled a silver dollar out of his pocket and held it up. Arved and Kirk grinned.

We squatted near the tear-shaped testicle. It was encased in a white film, streaked with tiny purple veins. Danny took off his mitten. His pink fingers touched the white, fibrous coating. "It's warm," he said.

I boxed the air while I ran, the only way I could beat away the hawks. The door to the house wouldn't open, the hawks had another chance.

In the dream, I am carried off, out over the great smoking abyss, and I fall, fall endlessly, until I awake.

That day, when she finally heard me, Thelma said, "Did those mean men scare you?" And she laughed. She wiped the flecks of dried manure off my wet, streaked face. I whimpered my blubbering sobs. She didn't hug and kiss and hold me like my own mother would have.

Danny came in with the men at noon. He showed me his silver dollar. "Eat one," Danny said in his superior way, "and you'll get your dollar."

The men watched and laughed. "I'll save you a nice plump one from the afternoon's batch," tobacco chin said.

The evangelistic team pulled into Cimarron on Sunday morning, second week of June, just as morning church let out. Danny drove the Cadillac while Joe Don slept in the back seat.

The congregation had made plans to welcome them with a potluck dinner. Pastor Toon always joked at these affairs, "No one can accuse this church of believing in a 'pie in the sky' religion. We have more pies on earth than will be needed in heaven."

Danny shook my hand as if I were a potential convert. His face seemed thinner, older. But the fire was back in his eyes.

Arved shook his hand. "Son, you're as tall as I am." He touched Danny with his gnarled fingers. "You have to show me the wheat. Your mother says it's the best we've ever grown, all that moisture last winter."

Elberta hovered around him, ruffled like a setting hen. Finally, Danny asked me, "Where's Anne?"

Elberta jumped forward to answer. "They moved away."

"Why? What happened?"

"We don't know, there was some trouble, they left and haven't been heard of."

Pomp Reed, who had continued to speak in tongues during ser-

206

vices, tugged on Danny's sleeve to get his attention. "Welcome back, boy," he said, "I hope you'll get Sonny involved in your work. The two of you will make a fine team for the Lord." He beamed, shaking our hands, then hugged us enthusiastically.

Monday, Danny stopped by my house, driving their new car. He asked me to go with him to see Coach. Coach sat with his feet on his desk. He didn't know who we were until we were ten feet from him. "Danny!" He sprang to his feet. "We didn't expect you back so soon. Tell me, how are you, and how was your trip?" He made it sound like Danny had been on a vacation to the Grand Canyon.

"There must be something to this religion thing. You look fantastic, bigger. Hey, I have some news for you. There's a new end coming to school here, from Lubbock. Last year made all-region, heart of Texas. They've given his father a job out at the gas plant. Some people around town pitched in and helped them make a down payment on their house. That helped them make up their minds to relocate. Most wonderful people around here, don't you think?

"Anyhow, Danny, wait until you see this kid. Tall, I mean real tall, and can jump like a jackrabbit. Real nice kid. I know the two of you will hit it off."

He turned to me. "Schultz, where have you been? I thought you might be around to start through the equipment."

"I don't think I'm coming back this year." I did not look at Danny.

"I don't want to hear that. I'll tell you what, I'll make the first inventory so we can order, then you report mid-August for getting things organized. And listen, you won't say anything to anyone else about how we got this new player, will you? This isn't something we'd want any newspaper to get hold of." He smiled, pumping my hand, which I allowed to be limp inside his.

Two days later, I went to the farm to help with the harvest. It hardly seemed Danny had been away, although he prayed more. A new vocabulary of religious jargon, "sweet Jesus," "God's will," hung on the tip of his tongue, reminders of his close call.

"You'll stay with the team, won't you?" he asked me one evening.

"Do you want me to?" I asked him.

"Yes."

"Okay," I answered.

My mother insisted that my father write a front-page article about Danny's work in the Southern crusade for the July Fourth edition of the *Times-Democrat*. Joe Don Jones supplied the information. "More than two thousand people saved from the fires of hell. Almost six hundred thousand dollars raised for the work of Jesus, worldwide. The country strengthened, Communism held at bay, by the renewal of Christian values. The Cimarron community should be proud that one of our own sons has helped in this great crusade." That was what my father wrote.

A record of a crusade service, including a version of the sermon *If Jesus Was a Football Coach*, with Danny singing and testifying, sold briskly in several Cimarron stores.

First of August, Danny and I went to town. Coach wanted to meet with Danny. We walked up Main Street an hour before the ten o'clock appointment. A new silver Bel Air pulled up beside us, a brief toot.

"Can I show you my new car?" Dovie Lasher was still around Cimarron. No one had found a way to run her out of town. We slipped into the car's red interior, there was an oppressive new-car smell. She shifted the transmission like a man.

"My dad gave me the down payment with some oil lease money, I'm making the monthlies." We laughed. "I've rented Mrs. Hewitt's house, the stucco one on G Street. I hope you guys will come visit me."

It was difficult not to stare. Her hair was longer, and the worried lines of a woman, so familiar to me, had appeared around her eyes. She was wearing lipstick. She was more beautiful than I remembered. We rode in silence. Finally, she reached out and touched Danny's hand.

"I'm just so glad to see you're okay." Her hand slipped, briefly, onto the inside of his thigh.

A little before ten, she dropped us back on Main Street in front of the boot shop. On the inside of the dusty window, LaFaye had hung a homemade display rack for his knife holsters that fit inside a man's boot. Behind the holsters, I saw the dwarf fade back into the dark store.

At the bus barn dressing room, Coach introduced us to the new end. "Danny, this is Rodney Strong, recently of Lubbock, now of Cimarron. Schultz, our equipment man," Coach pointed at me. I put out my hand, hardened by farm work, and it felt like a child's hand inside new Harley's. Rodney Strong was several inches taller than both Danny and me. His face had a relaxed, indolent look that was too studied to be natural. There was no doubt the coach had found a physical specimen who would make everyone forget about Harley Pugh.

"Tomorrow, I want you guys to start getting together, show Rod the pass patterns, Danny. The important thing is, get a feel for each other. If you need me, come to my house, but you know I can't be on the practice field until the official date because the state watches the teams they think will be contenders for the title."

So it began, senior football. Rodney Strong was everything Coach wanted. He could jump, and those hands, which he kept soft and pliable by wearing oiled gloves to bed, caught any ball thrown close. When real practice began, the Main Street merchants came out to watch, but they were subdued. My father, with uncharacteristic restraint, wrote short, factual articles about the progress of the team. Melvin Hibbs wrote only one small piece for the Sunday edition of the *Daily Oklahoman*. No one said anything about taking it all this year. Nobody wanted to be part of any jinx.

C H A P T E R   2 5

The team finished practice about six o'clock on Friday before school opened. Rick, our right halfback; Rod, the new end; and R.D., the other halfback and survivor of the accident that killed Harley, had been hanging around with Danny and me since football practice began ten days ago. I was standing near them tossing a football in the air and catching it while they dressed. Cannonball wobbled over. "You boys better get in your partying, 'cause next week, we start serious workouts," he said. "You'll be too worn out in the evenings for any fun."

"Great idea," R.D. said. "You having us at your place?" Cannonball's place, the small room made out of a lean-to in back of LaFaye's boot shop, was barely large enough for his appliances, with ceilings so low a normal person had to hunch over.

"You don't need a place," Cannonball snorted. "You have the whole fuckin' prairie, and you have your cars." He threw his stubby arms up in the air. "Sonny knows what I mean."

They all looked at me. Within seconds, I had a plan formulated. We'd have a sock hop, use cars for lights and music, and steal watermelons for refreshment. It was a simple plan, a plan laced with danger.

I snared Donnie Boggit, the linebacker who had replaced Joe Lee, and who had been hanging around us hoping to be included in our circle. I told him, "Tell everyone to meet at the Hogendorn Ranch intersection."

I asked Rick to borrow his parents' car for the evening. They drove a new Pontiac four-door sedan, and we needed a car that was large and ran quietly.

Rod said, "At a sock hop, you take your shoes off, don't you? Well, it's a start."

Cannonball punched him on both shoulders. "Just what we need, a horny son-of-a-bitchin' end. Wait until next week, we'll take it out of you."

"Horny football players are good," I said. "That way we take it out on the other teams."

"Listen to this 'we' stuff from the water boy," Cannonball chuckled. They all laughed, and Cannonball shook his head, wobbling back toward Coach's office. It was obvious Cannonball and the others regarded me in the same old way, but there was a difference, a change inside they could not see. I no longer assumed God received some kind of vicarious satisfaction from the way I lived my life. I no longer saw my heavenly father waiting above me, ready to say "good boy, bad boy." I was in control of my own life.

By the time it was dark, Rick had backed the Pontiac into a shelter beside the road. We were hidden among some old hedge apple trees so the lights from other vehicles would not bounce off the car and expose us. I explained we were waiting for the watermelon truck I knew came in from Colorado every Friday night, then I told them the plan.

Danny, Rod, and R.D. would ride on the hood of the car. We'd chase down the truck. Danny would get onto the truck, Rod would catch the melons when Danny threw them off, and R.D. would hand them to me while Rick drove. We'd pull back before the railroad tracks. There was a stop sign at the crossing. When the truck stopped at the tracks, Danny would jump off and we'd pick him up. They agreed, it was a grand scheme, the best they'd ever heard. They all agreed, that is, except Danny.

His face was tense. I knew what he was thinking. Every year, our pastor preached a sermon on each of the Ten Commandments. These were dramatic events, staged with great handmade charts and illustrations. The sermon Pastor Toon preached on "Thou shalt not steal" was one of his favorites, second only to "Thou shalt not commit adultery." The person, he claimed, who stole a nickel was just as guilty of breaking the Fourth Commandment as the man who stole a million dollars.

"Surely we have enough money between us to buy watermelons," Danny said.

"Of course, that's not the point," I answered. The others agreed with me.

Outside the church doors in Cimarron exists another code. This code is not in the Scriptures or any written text, but in the lore of the community, the telling and retelling of exploits performed by spunky youth, feats that measure the mettle of boys and predict what kind of men they will be. That code is as powerful and as real as the written word of God. Despite what Pastor Toon said, that code went against Danny and forced him to conform to our plan for stealing, not buying watermelons.

From the west, a light. "This might be it," I said. Rick started the car. Less than a minute passed before the headlights separated, and we could make out the orange cab lights on top of the semi-truck cab. Fear fluttered in on the dancing light beams. Out of the night raced Harley, the image of him hunched over on his bike, only one headlight, deceived not so much by the distance and space, but by the unlikelihood of death, by youth's sense of immortality. Dread shuddered out of my stomach and hardened into a familiar brick in my throat.

This time, my plan was not for Harley, or Danny, this plan was for me, to get something for me, a plan even more dangerous than the one that had killed Harley. I had reserved the most dangerous part for myself. In order to take the melons from R.D., I'd have to ride with the car door open, hanging out over the road, with one foot holding the car door, the other wedged on the narrow ledge where the car door fits when closed. But there were risks beyond the physical danger, there was the gamble with Danny's friendship, the uncertainty about giving up all my usual alibis. I fought through my fear; too late to turn back.

"Get in your spots," I said to them. They slipped into the darkness, Danny and Rod on the front fenders, their feet on the bumper, R.D. lying down across the hood.

"There will be a tarp," I called to Danny. "Use your knife to cut the ropes."

The truck seemed to shiver as it slowed down for the curve. We could see the shape of the melons beneath the tarp. The road turned unbanked, and the driver crept around it to keep his load from shifting, then headed south.

The new Pontiac caught up quickly. The red glow of the truck's taillights provided more light than we needed. Rick drove to the right, out of range of the driver's rear-view mirror, driving up so the hood ornament was only a few feet from the tailgate of the lumbering truck. Fumes from the exhaust made our eyes tear. Danny stood up, leaned forward, and grasped hold of the top of the tailgate, his feet on the bumper of the car. He paused hanging between the two vehicles, gauging how much strength it would take for the leap. Then, he uncoiled and swung himself over the tailgate as if it were a task no more difficult than stepping over a crack in the sidewalk.

The marvelous control, the magnificence of his grace and strength, the danger I had placed him in, our whole history as friends flashed before me. I loved him more at that moment than ever before, more than when Killer stripped him on Main Street, more than when I saw him make love with Anne, more than when I tried to protect him by sending Harley off into the darkness.

Danny opened his knife and slashed. "He cut the tarp," I said to Rick, "one more thing to deal with if we're caught."

We had no more time to talk. I opened the door and leaned out. The wind whipped me. The tires thumped on the road and I saw the weeds in the bar ditch whip by in the reflection of light. Recently, I had decided I did not want to be buried in a casket or a grave. I wanted my body to be burned and my ashes to be scattered somewhere, over a place that had meaning, someplace important to me. I had not yet decided where. I needed time and experience before I chose. I was not sure I'd have the time. I had never been in such a precarious position, one slight slip, I'd hit the pavement and be dead. R.D. handed me a melon. My fear subsided as I worked.

The plan operated so smoothly it might have been plotted by a commando instead of a water boy. Then a hitch developed, the driver didn't stop at the railroad tracks. Rick had to speed nearly a hundred miles per hour to catch the truck before it got to town. When we passed the truck I yelled to Danny, telling him we'd be hiding at the stockyards. We could only hope the driver hadn't heard, too.

We turned at the Shamrock station. Cattle trucks had ground the road that led to the stockyards into white caliche dust that spewed out behind us. Rick stopped beside a stack of straw bales and we waited, the dusty haze settling over us. There was a strong odor of moldy hay and fresh cow manure.

We waited. Five minutes passed. Something might be wrong. My father, how he'd struggle with the right wording for his article he'd have to print. His son, arrested, stealing and destruction of property. Young Baptist evangelist caught red-handed with stolen property. How could I bear the guilt of having placed Danny in such a delicate situation? My mother, she'd be the one who really suffered. These pranks only worked if you didn't get caught.

Running feet, on gravel. Rick pulled on the parking lights so Danny could see us. He was muddy. He'd fallen when he crossed the small creek where the Shamrock dumped its dirty oil. His face was scratched. He was breathing so hard he couldn't talk, but he was smiling, exhilarated. He'd caught the spirit of the event.

"We got . . . to move. They're on their way . . ."

Rick shifted into drive. "Don't," I said, and I squeezed his arm. It was an order. We stayed where we were. Through the open windows we heard the siren, then saw the flashing light of the sheriff's car as it emerged from among the buildings on Main Street. It slowed briefly at the intersection near the Shamrock. If he turned toward us, we'd dump the melons and move, then hope the sheriff couldn't find them. But the sheriff's car sped north, across the river bridge, the direction the truck came from.

"It doesn't make sense. But we better not sit here. Let's get out before he returns. But leave your lights off until we get to the main road," I instructed Rick.

I sighed, a sense of relief. I had planned a whole scheme that had worked. I was sure it was one of the riskiest, and most clever, pranks ever pulled by any set of boys in the long history of Cimarron stunts. I felt enormous satisfaction. I anticipated how it would feel to be congratulated, to live with a sense of my own daring.

When we neared the street to the Shamrock, Rick turned on the lights, and there stood the sheriff in the middle of the road, legs apart, holding his gun a few inches above his holster as if he were a lawman in the old West. Rick stopped the car ten feet from him.

The sheriff walked to the driver's side. He had run from the highway and was breathing hard. He had on the U.S. Cavalry belt buckle he had worn the night he stopped Danny before Harley was killed. He shifted the gun to his left hand with a nifty toss, then reached down and opened the car door. "Step out," he wiggled the gun barrel, "all of you, and put your hands on top of your heads. Don't make any quick moves.

"Well, well, look what we have here, some heroes. Hey you, water boy, come here, but keep your hands up. Now don't be nervous. There ain't no bounty on water boy ears. Open up that car door, and you bring out two of those melons, two of the biggest ones. Put 'em in that ditch right over there," and he pointed with the barrel of his gun. "Hurry up, the truck driver'll be back with my car. Put those tumbleweeds over 'em," the sheriff ordered.

"Okay, you guys get back in that car and get the hell out of here, and remember, think twice before you mess with the sheriff of Cimarron." We heard him laughing as we drove away.

I couldn't figure out if being caught by the sheriff, then having him join us in our crime, had spoiled my moment of glory, or if it had enhanced the magic of what we'd accomplished. "Remind me to send the sheriff a thank-you card," I said. "Now we need ice. We don't want to eat warm melons. I'll get ice from the Ideal. Get your tire iron," I told Rick.

Rick eased the car into the back alley behind the Ideal grocery. A pole light brightened the yard where trucks delivered produce. The area was littered with wooden crates and old tires.

I started to get out of the car. Danny got out with me. "I'll help you," he said.

"No, it's not necessary, you've already done enough. I'll have to break in. I don't want to get you in trouble."

"Come on," he said, "if one of us is in trouble, we're all in trouble. We better get the ice and get out of here before the sheriff figures things out." He jammed the flat end of the tire iron in the crack near the door's latch. We both yanked and the door popped open. I handed him a set of ice tongs, and we loaded up four fifty-pound blocks.

CHAPTER 26

We drove out of town. The car seemed to float. At that moment I felt as if I could get away with anything I wanted to. Kill a dove, steal a watermelon, commit fornication. No rule or commandment applied to me.

Around fifty others were already at the intersection near the Hogendorn Ranch when we arrived. Four of the cars, including Dovie's new Bel Air, had their parking lights on and their radios blaring. A bonfire had been started in the middle of the intersection. The hard clay was red and shiny where the trucks that used this route to the oil fields had packed it down.

We carried our melons into the circle of light. The rock and roll music wailed around us, beating the air like a thousand black wings and I could feel why our ministers railed against it, because it corrupted the minds of Cimarron's children.

I sensed something was wrong. Things were too set, organized, not the way I had expected. "You did a great job getting people here, and where did you get the firewood?" I asked Donnie Boggit.

"Cannonball."

"What else has Cannonball done?"

"He helped with everything. He left only ten minutes ago."

Outside our circle, the prairie was lighted by a moon that seemed almost supernatural. I could see the windbreak on the Hogendorn land where the dove's grave was. I felt the futility of resisting whatever it was that propelled me.

"Where did you-all get the watermelons?" Earldeana asked with her Texas way of making two syllables from one. So the story unfolded, how I stood up with the door open, and the sheriff made me hide the melons, then we got ice from behind the Ideal.

I had risked my life for something, or nothing. It was immensely pleasurable. I danced my first dance with Earldeana, who pressed close against me. I vowed I would never back away from anything daring.

I watched while Danny danced with Dovie. She wore a long dress with crinolines that stood out when she jitterbugged, her curves illuminated by the light. The radio station broke for a commercial. When the music started again it was slower, love songs. Earldeana pulled me into the intersection. She had a bottle of vodka in her purse, and she offered me a sip. It burned my throat, its heat adding to my intoxication. The voices from the radios crooned the lyrics of "The Tennessee Waltz."

All of us were lifted out of Cimarron to a place where no one of us had ever been. The mood was uninhibited and dangerous. Boys could dance with boys, girls with girls, and we all danced with one another. No one felt odd or offbeat. The possibilities seemed infinite.

"Lights," someone called, "coming from the direction of town." Most of the dancers stopped, but not Danny and Dovie. They danced close, her hips were pressed against him and she appeared to be making small thrusts. His face was forward in her hair. They seemed to have melded into one person. The mood was lost, and I felt a moment of loneliness, then sadness for Anne, how much I missed her, was afraid of what had happened and of what I did not know, afraid I would forget and never feel sad again. Danny and

Dovie, moving, dancing. Maybe a man can love two women at once, or maybe he can love a woman and a man. I wasn't sure.

The lights coming toward us might be the sheriff about the ice. No one knew exactly what to do. Soon, I should step forward and take charge. That responsibility had fallen to me because of what Cannonball had said. As of yet, I did not have a plan. The vehicle had cab lights, and it slowed down before it reached us. Someone had known where we were and had come to the party.

Dovie stepped away from Danny. With her hand she shaded her eyes from the headlights. When the lights went out, the cab was backlighted by the brake lights.

"It's his truck, but Brice isn't driving," Dovie said. "I don't know who it is."

"I'm afraid I do," I replied. There was that same sense I'd had earlier that something was wrong. I was in control of nothing.

Killer opened the passenger door and got out. The light of the truck's cab illuminated the dwarf sitting up on something, a crate or a sack of chicken feed. He must have been wearing his stilts to drive. Killer was in no hurry. Danny was leaning against one of the cars. His stance was casual, but alert. The rest of us waited.

Killer walked into the light. "Like I heard, whores do make it clear out here." He slurred the words, he'd been drinking.

"Brice, go home. You weren't invited," Dovie pleaded.

"Shut up. I came to see the fuckin' little smartass preacher."

By now, Dovie was close to Killer and she took his arm.

"Come on, I'll go with you."

He jerked his arm away and shoved her, but she did not fall. He shook with rage and hate. The time had come as if it were a day ordained when Danny must fight Brice Miller, settle things between them once and for all. Cannonball had set it up. But why? Why did he want to risk injury to Danny before the season even started? I couldn't make sense of the situation.

"Let him alone, it's an open party." Danny's voice, though soft, rang as if he offered the invitation at church, as if he called "come forward, accept the Lord, be saved." He walked toward the tub where the watermelons were cooling. Turning his back to Killer, he picked up the knife. It was an old gray kitchen knife someone had provided; then, to my relief, Danny used it to cut open one of the melons. It was so quiet we could hear the crackle of the melon breaking as Danny sliced into its ripe heart. He cut a piece of the melon, thick and shaped like a half moon, then jabbed the knife's point into one of the melons left in the tub. He stepped toward Killer holding the glistening fruit out in front of him.

"Hey, big man, why don't you join the party and have a piece of our watermelon?" Some might have thought Danny's gesture was conciliatory.

A low growl began somewhere deep inside Killer's big belly. His face twisted until he appeared to be demented. He clenched his fists, cocked his arm, and swung to knock the melon out of Danny's hand, but Danny jerked it back so Killer missed, and the momentum of his punch carried him forward, stumbling. Now it was obvious Killer was very drunk. Just before Killer regained his balance, Danny mashed the ripe melon into his puffy face. Surprise momentarily erased all Killer's rage. Pink cold juice ran down and dripped off his chin. Earldeana laughed, a warbling, shrill giggle.

Killer twisted and charged, bellowing, sputtering. Danny stepped aside, tripped him, and Killer sprawled, stones flying, dust from the roadside drifting into the darkness.

Dazed, Killer sat up. Danny waited, totally relaxed, no sign of concern or indecision. When Killer charged again, Danny did what he had done as a skinny freshman when he had tackled the big fullback. He dropped sideways, protecting his own ribs with his left arm, and caught Killer below the knees. Killer flipped into the air, and his out-of-condition body absorbed the full shock of his fall as he landed on the road.

Killer lay stunned for a moment, then slowly sat up, struggling

220

to regain his feet, staggering as he did. His face was bloated and his eyes were now fearful. Danny attacked, hit him below the rib cage, driving out his breath. Killer seemed surprisingly soft and started to topple forward. Reaching as high as he could, Danny locked his hands together, then smashed down on Killer's neck. The sound was like an ax striking a dry post. Killer dropped in a heap near the bumper of Dovie's car. I was afraid the blow had killed him.

"Earldeana, your bottle," Danny said. I was surprised he knew about the liquor. I didn't know he had seen us drinking. Earldeana gave the bottle to him.

I thought he planned to use it to revive Killer. But Danny forced his toe under Killer's shoulder and lifted until his body flipped over. Killer's mouth lolled open. He was alive, but I worried he'd choke if Danny poured the liquor in.

Danny pulled his knife from his pocket, the same one he had used to cut the tarp, the one he had used to bury the dove, and the one he had used against Harley on Main Street. He disinfected the blade with the liquor, as we had seen his father do when we were young. His eyes reflected light more intense than the lights of the cars. He crouched beside Killer and unfastened Killer's belt, one of LaFaye's, then ripped open the bronze buttons along the crotch. A tug on the boxer shorts and Killer lay exposed in the parking lights of Dovie's car. Danny poured the remaining alcohol over Killer's genitals. He started to wake up.

If I had stepped forward at that moment, speaking quietly to Danny, breaking the stifling inertia that had encapsulated those of us watching him, if I had deterred him at that moment, then, perhaps, the matter would have been settled. But we all remained frozen with wonder and horror over what Danny was doing. We thought he intended to castrate Killer. It certainly would not have been the first time a guy around Cimarron had picked a fight with a rival lover and ended up losing his testicles. The community lore

221

was full of those stories. It was the horror of that thought that stopped the rest of us.

But Danny intended only to mark him. He took hold of the wrinkled foreskin on Killer's penis, then pulled upward, stretching the skin until it was thin and taut. The lights of Dovie's car were behind them. He made a quick slash with his knife, cut off the foreskin, and dropped it on Killer's belly. Killer screamed and writhed, still only half conscious, his penis flopping back and forth. The glans, large as a good-sized apricot, emerged through the shortened foreskin. Instinctively, before he was fully conscious, Killer brought his hands down to cover himself.

Everything was quiet except for the beat of music behind us and the groaning of the mutilated man. A trickle of blood mingled with the mass of hair on his lower abdomen. Dovie went to him, bent over him, and pulled Killer's hands away so she could press a scarf on his penis to stop the bleeding. Killer's hands were bloody from holding himself. She wiped them.

Danny asked Donnie Boggit to drive him home. Dovie got Killer into her car. Cannonball, driving Killer's pickup, pulled out behind her. Earldeana and two other girls got in with Rick, R.D., Rod, and me. I sat next to Earldeana, and we held hands. We rode around for hours. No one said much. None of us could figure out what kind of trouble Danny or the rest of us might be in. We knew Killer wouldn't die. It didn't seem, in one way, to be any worse than the cut Killer had made on Danny's ear that day on Main Street. But there was a feeling about what had happened, it left us unsettled, convinced that the future was dangerous and uncertain.

Three days later, the Methodist minister married Killer and Dovie. They held a small ceremony in the parsonage garden. When the word spread, Lipscomb gave a loud shout, picked up Cannonball, and they did a dance on the bus barn floor. Cannonball's stubby legs stuck out like a child's when Lipscomb whirled him around.

"I told you she'd fall for it," Cannonball croaked. "She loves damaged men."

"You're a smart little son of a bitch," Lipscomb said. "I don't know what I'd do without you."

The newlyweds must have spent their first week of married life celibate while Killer healed. They returned to Cimarron after a short wedding trip in the Rockies, and the town shivareed them. They brought a wheelbarrow and made Killer push Dovie down Main Street in the middle of a procession of fifty or sixty needlers singing bawdy songs. There were many jokes made about eating peeled apricots. They sprinkled their bed with sugar.

Killer did not go back to school. Dovie kept her job at the insurance office in Liberal, and was, apparently, their only means of income.

I indulged in an old game. Every night I arranged my soldiers, changing the battlefield, prolonging the stalemate, making sure something was always different, and something was always the same.

Danny entered his senior-year season with no distractions.

CHAPTER 27

The town chomped at the bit, waiting for the football season to open. There were practices twice a day, so the townsfolk came to watch before opening their stores, sharing thermoses of coffee, then returned in the evening to see if the coaches had made any changes.

Rodney Strong, the new end whose family the merchants had helped bring to Cimarron, was better than anyone had dared to hope, better than Harley Pugh, the best Cimarron ever had. Danny was his old self, smart, focused, bold, unstoppable.

The season opened with a win over the state-contending Shattuck Savages. Hibbs's article on Danny in the *Daily Oklahoman* was picked up by the national press services, and Danny became the first player from western Oklahoma to be touted for the national high school all-American team.

Scouts and tourists poured into Cimarron for home game weekends. Slim moved in a couple of trailers to accommodate additional guests at the Blue Peecock, and Eton at the Elite Cafe gave Slim, his landlord, free meals because the additional rooms meant more business for the cafe.

The merchants welcomed the tourists, selling pet tarantulas, rattlesnake tails, and shellacked souvenir cow chips. The merchants gave out free pictures of the football players with a ten dollar purchase, then punched their cash registers and smiled. People spent money because it made them part of the extraordinary events that surrounded the team.

Dovie Miller stayed away from Danny, but she watched him from a distance as she had before she had invited him to the junior-senior prom.

The others watched Danny also, to see what he did and how he did it. If he stood, absentmindedly, and piled up gravel with his boot, they piled up gravel with their boots. If they didn't have boots, they went out and got some at LaFaye's, ones as near like Danny's as LaFaye could supply.

At the clinic, Doc McGrath recommended circumcision for all the young boys. He told their parents it would prevent problems in the future. What kind of problems he never said, but many families followed Doc's recommendation. He gave part of the credit to Danny.

"That boy's helped me clean up this town," Doc said at the Elite Cafe. "Did two more little tykes yesterday. He's done more for hygiene than all the years of health class put together. Done the next generation of Cimarron girls a favor, too."

No one made any more fuss than that over Danny's mutilation of Killer. Killer, although no longer in college, kept out of sight, and spent long stretches of time out of town. Sheriff Ordway kept close track of him when he came and went in case Killer planned any revenge.

Around town, the prime topic of conversation, moving ahead of the weather and the Communist threat, was where Danny would go to college. I listened to everything that was said. But Danny seemed to be above all the attention, more aloof and unreachable than he had been before the accident. He seemed to be handling the enormous adulation with grace and humility.

The day of the third home game, a white Cadillac pulled up Main Street and parked in front of Dale's barber shop, which was directly across the street from the *Times-Democrat*. My father called me out from the back where I had been putting away paper stock. Our relationship had been unaffected by the church service when we had tried to clear some of the bad feelings between us.

"What would you think a car from New York would be doing in Cimarron on a Friday?"

"He's going in for a haircut, I can find out."

"Okay, you need a haircut anyhow, here's a dollar. Dale won't let him out of there without giving him the third degree. New York isn't exactly next door. There's got to be a story."

I walked across the street and into the barber shop. A tall man stood waiting. He was quite handsome, his smooth, tanned skin stretched across a lively, expressive face. He ran his hand through a mop of wavy, graying hair. Dale had swept up a pile of clippings, probably the whole day's work because it covered a dozen of the white and black floor tiles. There was a gust of wind as I walked in that scattered the hair. Dale didn't notice because he was watching the stranger, then he introduced himself to the man. "Hello, I'm Dale Borden." The man shook Dale's hand but didn't say his own name.

Arnie Ritterbush and Elvin Leeds, who dug graves and did other odd jobs when they were not in the domino parlor or the barbershop, sat in the mahogany game chairs Dale used for his customers. They were arguing, as they always did when they were together, about some sports event that happened years ago. The stranger eyed them, especially Arnie's baseball hat. On their silver anniversary, Arnie's wife, a seamstress who supported them, had embroidered a New York Yankee insignia on the front of his cap.

"Never mind them," Dale told the man who was still looking at Arnie, "they're not waiting for anything but their wives to figure out where they're at. You're next. Take that first chair by the window. I'll be finished in a minute." He turned back to his sweeping, and noticed his pile had scattered, so he put the broom away. He looked at me. "Hey Sonny, mind waiting? Or can you come back in half an hour?"

"I'll just wait."

Dale wrapped a white and blue striped cloth around the stranger, tucking it into his collar. "I never cut a man's hair without knowing his name," Dale said.

"I'm Clay Moray. You have a nice shop." His voice was deep, polished, the crispness of a trained speaker.

"You must be here to see our boy play football," Dale said. He stood with the scissors in one hand and the clippers in the other, glancing at himself and his customer in the mirror. "Where do you come from?"

"Back east." Arnie and Elvin quit arguing. No one spoke while Dale shaved the man's neck with the electric clippers.

"Back east, huh! That don't tell us much, does it boys?" Dale winked at Arnie and Elvin. "Could be Missouri, Arkansas, any of those," he said.

"You have me on the spot interrogating me with the scissors in your hand," the stranger replied. I doubted Arnie and Elvin knew what the word meant. "I thought the Southwest was supposed to be friendly. This feels like the streets of New York or maybe Philly."

The three of them laughed, the funniest joke they'd heard in months. Then Dale walked to the window. "New York plates, that's quite a drive. Half the people in this town think it's only a city, don't know it's a state. What school are you from?"

"The Academy," he said, "the United States Military Academy at West Point. Colonel Blaik sent me."

"Jeeez Us Chrrrist," Dale said. He made a few snips with the scissors. "You're dreaming if you think our boy's gonna leave home and go that far away. That's leaving the planet."

"I doubt your quarterback is as good as his press releases, anyhow. I'll probably only take a fast look, depending."

Dale snorted, but didn't reply. Snippets of wiry salt-and-pepper hair accumulated on the cloth. "Depending on what?"

"Lots of things. Performance on the field, mostly. But off the field, too."

"Off the field?"

The stranger paused, as if he were considering whether or not it was a good idea to go any further. He shrugged. "For example, does he have an important girlfriend? A serious girl is the biggest barrier to recruiting for Army. A guy can't have a girl visit him, and he can't get away during the year to see her at home. I have to know if a prospect is in love."

"He ain't no more, is he boys?" The three of them laughed again. Dale glanced at me, and the room got silent. Dale finally changed the subject. "You know, you're sitting in his chair," Dale said. "He comes in before games, and I trim him. We've never lost a game after he sat in this chair." He winked at Arnie and Elvin.

I sat opposite the two of them, lined up with Moray in the mirrors, the big plaster of paris framed one behind me and the wall mirror that Dale used on the opposite side of the room. I couldn't get what Moray had said out of my mind. He needs to know if a prospect is "in love." "In love." The phrase kept clicking in my mind like a cracked record. The churches forbade sex before marriage and preached against violence except in war, but to fight in a war made men into heroes, which made heroes of football players because football was like war. Their violent behavior seemed to make football players more sexually attractive, even gave them permission to be "in love." The rest of us lived under a stricter code. Moray had his finger on the pulse of something that lived below the surface of Cimarron's moral and religious convictions. Clay Moray knew a good football player was going to be sexually involved because some girl or some woman was going to offer herself to him with the tacit approval of the community. I thought of the time I had sent Harley off to his death by convincing him he could seduce Tina Rexrood because he was a football hero. He had taken his body, made it into a lethal weapon, had beaten the Bearcats. It seemed, then, he had a right to Tina's body, or someone's. The community of people who had vicariously benefited from his sacrifice owed him something. Where had I gotten that idea? I looked at Clay Moray with growing wariness.

Moray was the antithesis of the first two scouts, young with Texas twangs, who stopped through last year, the game before Harley was killed. Our images, Moray's and mine, with Dale moving in and out, stretched on within the mirrors, alternating front and back where each mirror reflected the next image, then the next and the next.

A scout from Army had come all the way to Cimarron, the wonder of it, and the mirrors; there came over me a feeling of awe, a feeling I was part of something larger, a participant in events more wondrous than anyone would expect to happen in Cimarron.

When I found out that Moray was a minister, a chaplain in the U.S. Army, I knew he had seen those same possibilities in the mirrors. He knew what to say to Danny.

The day of the seventh game, I left school and entered the Elite Cafe through the doors of the Blue Peecock, checking the registry. Full. People from seven states. Scouts. Recruiters. And those who were merely curious.

Clay Moray, known well by then as the "reverend recruiter," sat in the cafe near the men from town. I sat down in the booth Mother and I had used when she took me out to breakfast almost a year ago and we had seen Elberta and Cannonball together. The customers today were much different, the situation had changed drastically over the past ten months. I stared out the picture window past the rusty car bodies in back of the Texaco, beyond them up

Main Street as far as the movie theater. Outside, Sputnik circled over our prairie. I felt spied upon by an unscrupulous enemy. I watched the Reverend Moray until he glanced up and saw me.

The town had adopted Clay. They liked his genial manner, and LaFaye happily rented him the small apartment above the leather shop that he had decided to lease after he saw Danny play the first time. For Moray, it was the ideal location for him to stay when he was in town, on Main Street, near the restaurant where information was disseminated, a close neighbor of Cannonball. He made trips out to other towns in the Oklahoma and Texas Panhandles to scout. But his main objective was to recruit Danny. No other scout located so permanently, yet he conducted his business with complete discretion.

The townspeople thought he was wasting his time. No kid of theirs would ever leave Cimarron and go east. It was beyond comprehension. I looked up at Moray again, who seemed to be looking back at me.

My father thought the Academy was the ideal place for Danny. Not so large he'd get lost, close to influential Eastern newspapers, a regimented, disciplined life, a respect for religion within the school, a useful career when he graduated. He'd like his son to go to the Academy, and he stated this openly.

Clay Moray seemed to be optimistic about his chances. He believed Danny Boone would follow a line of glamorous Army backs, Doc Blanchard, Glenn Davis, Rip Rowan, men who went on to glory, influencing politics and presidents. Danny fit the mystique perfectly, clean-cut and naive, absolutely dedicated, and unaffected by it all.

Clay Moray was the only recruiter who understood that the usual inducements wealthy colleges offered talented football players would not attract Danny. Other universities pitched money, cars. But Danny was above all that. A chance to be faithful to Jesus Christ and to serve his country by playing football, and to establish a reputation that would enhance his evangelistic career, that's what Clay Moray offered. That's how he'd put it when the time came. That's why he'd been sent. He might succeed, because Danny was not "in love" with anyone he'd have to leave behind.

I half listened to the banter that drifted over to me from the cafe counter. "I'm for the underdog," the sheriff admitted. "I was glad when Podres kicked the Yankees' butts and I hope Danny'll go to Stillwater and play for the Aggies. Besides," the sheriff added, as if he had thought of something no one else had, "he'll have to study something, probably be agriculture. He's helped his dad on that farm all these years."

"It's money," LaFaye argued. "Those Baptist Bible thumpers from Texas, pardon my reference, have the bucks and they're not afraid to use them. Don't be surprised come spring if our boy is trottin' around in an orange Longhorn jacket and about anything else he can think of to ask for from the state of Texas."

P.O. disagreed, and he stomped on LaFaye's toe, marring the finish on his alligator boot. "I'm sorry, didn't mean to do that," he apologized, "but I've watched that boy in the store since he was a tyke. He's just not that kind of kid. He'll do what's right regardless of the offers. He'll be at home, the good old University of Oklahoma. You wait and see. Or if not, Clay here'll get him."

The others laughed and Junior leaned over and slapped Moray on the back. His coffee, halfway to his mouth, splashed on the linoleum countertop. Eton reached out and wiped up the spill, then filled Clay's cup again.

Around the room there were two other recruiters having an early supper. Some of them worried that the competition was not first-class like it would have been had Danny played in a more populated region. But the sophisticated schools had ways of assessing talent. A scout from Ohio had said Danny was the Bob Feller of football. No question about his ability to play major college ball, just a matter of helping him adapt to social situations. Smart football programs know how to do that.

I calculated the expenditure. By the end of the season, probably fifty schools would have sent from one to three different people, each spending an average of three to five days, some flying in private planes that landed at the Cimarron airport, if you could call it that. It was just an open pasture with a wind sock. Schools were spending hundreds of hours of personnel time and hundreds of thousands of dollars to get a kid to choose their school because of his ability to take an inflated piece of pig leather and push it down the throats of other boys who had been recruited with the same expenditure of time and money.

But in Danny's case that wasn't all. There were the Bible colleges that train preachers and evangelists but don't have football teams. Their representatives came into town, stayed with Elberta, who had opened up a Christian guest house, and told Danny his first loyalty was to Jesus Christ, "the way, the truth, and the life." They wanted him to attend their colleges and they wanted to train him for evangelism because he was already famous, he'd bring in contributions, and other recruits.

I was handing Danny his equipment, and, in that way, promoting all this. But I rationalized. Better to be alongside him, to be part of the possibilities. But there was a nagging voice telling me I was there because I liked the spotlight, even if it was only the light that bounced off Danny.

Then, the Reverend Moray shuffled across the cafe floor. When I looked up, he was standing beside my booth. He was impeccably dressed in a blue suit, white shirt, and tie. He had been watching me even as I had been watching him. He reached into his suit coat. "Sonny, with your principal's help and with the sponsorship of Senator Lienhart, I sent your records to the admissions office at Army. I have been authorized to offer you admission to the United States

Military Academy." He handed me two envelopes; one had my name on it.

"Oh," he exclaimed, "that one I need to mail," and he took back one of the envelopes. I saw the address: Joe Don Jones, Evangelist, Box 233, Ottumwa, Iowa. He walked away before I could say anything.

The envelope that I held in my hand had the Academy's return address printed in shiny black ink. It felt weightless. It seemed to exist outside the constraints of time, space, volume, or any scientific or moral law.

C H A P T E R   2 8

C oach Lipscomb fumed over the distractions. He resented the well-dressed men from the universities who, in their attempts to befriend Danny and not get caught in violation of recruiting rules, walked up to him on the street and pretended it was an accidental meeting, then requested a private meeting with Danny and his parents.

Cannonball suggested someone from the team accompany Danny at all times, and I was assigned to be with him that Friday when Moray handed me my envelope. I had skipped out for a break to the Elite Cafe where Moray found me.

In some odd way, I believed my admission to the Academy was an honor I had earned. I basked in this honor, because someone, finally, had recognized my worth.

The Dustdevils won games eight and nine. Coach let the second and third teams play to avoid running up a high score. Meanwhile, a team downstate, the Tahlequah Hornedtoads, a team with lean, swift Indians in the backfield and rawboned Irish linemen, beat their opponents into the ground. Hibbs wrote about the dream battle, the western plains against the eastern hills.

The Dustdevils reached the first round of the state playoffs and won again. Coach ordered Danny to hold down the score. He threw only five passes, completing four of them to Rod, two for touchdowns. The final score was twenty-one to seven. It counted in the win column, but was distinctly unimpressive. The strategy, the process of psyching the opponents into thinking that the Dustdevils were not so good as everyone thought, had the distinct earmarks of Cannonball's scheming. The Hornedtoads hopped over us to number one in the state rankings. It was exactly what the coaches wanted; they wanted the Dustdevils to be underdogs.

The Main Street merchants winced at the news and they griped. They thought Lipscomb was losing his nerve, breaking the team's momentum, and hurting Danny's chances to be all-American.

We won the second round of the playoffs against an unranked team. Again, Coach substituted liberally, keeping the score down. Cannonball grinned when people wondered and complained.

The competition stiffened for the third round. Pawhuska, a perennial state playoff team, won the coin toss. The Dustdevils would face a strong, experienced team on their home field, a team who always ran at their opponents, gave no mercy, and asked none. The odds-makers made the Dustdevils favorites by only three points. The Pawhuska team appeared to be confident they could win at home.

Lipscomb worried. Only one game away from the championship. We all wondered if the team could recapture the dominance needed at this level of competition.

Coach leaned back in his chair after the Thursday workout, dug out his pipe, and while he cleaned and scraped, I walked over. He tamped in fresh tobacco, and when he finished I struck a match and held it for him. For a moment, he looked at me, then he accepted my gesture and inhaled, drawing the flame down to the crinkled tobacco.

"You must be wondering if you've listened to Cannonball one time too many," I said to him. Surprise registered on his face, then he composed himself. "I think he knows his stuff," I said.

"You're a smart son of a bitch," Coach said. "You'd make a good coach if you were tough enough. Don't you worry, I know a thing or two about psychology and strategy."

I walked out of the bus barn door thrilled by what he had said about my being a good coach, but burdened by a new uneasiness. I was ashamed I had not quit last year after I found out the coaches had sent Danny away with Joe Don Jones because they were afraid he might miss his senior year of football eligibility. I had allowed Danny to be used by men who had ambitions to achieve ends I did not fully understand. I remembered the day I had taken my mother's scissors and stabbed my football. I should have told Danny then I would not be his friend if he continued to play the sport.

Then, my mind flipped. My imagination had turned comical. Finally, I was demented. Tens of thousands of boys across America play football, and are coached by thousands of men who come from good families and attend churches, and who say the same things to motivate their team that Lipscomb and Cannonball say to Danny and the others. How could I, one half-grown, insecure kid face such an overwhelming outcry of voices? It is irrational and bigheaded of me to think I know something that the hundreds of thousands who participate in the sport and the millions of fans who support it do not understand. What right do I have to be their judge? I must have misunderstood something, there is something I had missed, something beautiful, an intimacy among men I cannot fathom because I had listened to the wrong voices, had chosen the wrong paths.

Coach sent the team onto the field to warm up earlier than usual. The stands at Pawhuska were close to the sidelines, and steep. The players would hear everything shouted at them. The game could get raw. Ten minutes before game time, Lipscomb pulled the team back into the locker, something he had not done since the first game of Danny's sophomore year.

"Hard work and dedication to our task, that's been the key to our success this year. We still have one goal to accomplish. Things have gone our way this year, making up for some bad breaks we've gotten in the past. But we cannot depend on luck. God helps those who help themselves. Reach down, deep down inside and push out that extra effort. Don't be whipped. Be a man."

I felt ashamed and bewildered by my doubts. I wished Danny and the team well. I wanted them to smash Pawhuska, go on to the state, take it all this year. The glory would be ours, it would belong to the whole town.

Coach delivered his pregame litany, "Get out there and kick some butts." The team rose as one, shouting and pounding. Danny moved to the front of the line. I opened the door and held it. Coach caught Danny by the sleeve, and told Rick to lead the team out. They slipped away to the battle, their cleats scraping on the floor, except Danny, who waited for the coach while I stood half concealed behind the door.

They faced each other in the dank, concrete room. A bare bulb provided weak pink light. Coach appeared almost shrunken next to the power of Danny's physique.

"Danny, that day, almost three years ago, when I first talked to you about this job, I had many questions. You seemed very remote. But I made up my mind to let you do things in your own way, be yourself." The coach's eyes moistened. "My wife and I cannot have children. I will never have a son. I consider your father the luckiest man in the world, but I think of you as my son, too. I love you."

The sharp blue eyes peered back at Coach over the single-bar face guard, that same, faraway look Coach alluded to, the look that mystified me, the look I loved and admired and was determined to know. Deep within him there was the fire. Then, sparks scattered from the metal cleats as he sprinted up the concrete alley.

"Well, just like Cannonball says, answers aren't so hard to find if you just put yourself in his shoes," Coach said to himself. When

I stepped out from behind the door, the look on his face told me he had not wanted me to be there.

The Huskers won the toss. We kicked off. Their return man disappeared under a wave of black and gold tacklers on their own thirty-six-yard line. They called three off-tackle plays, alternating left, right, left, and gained six yards. The Husker punter booted a high, spiraling kick that R.D. failed to catch. It slid off his shoulder pads, hit the field, and bounced crazily out of bounds. The collective sighs of relief mixing with the whines of disappointment made a wheezing noise like the first winds of a night storm.

Danny called the first play, Z out, flanker right. The Huskers were ready for the play as if they had called it themselves. "Eat it, take what you can get!" Lipscomb shouted at Danny, but Danny saw an opening. It was as if the whole field lay under a magnifying glass, every detail, every angle and distance, was in exact focus for Danny. His pass threaded a breach between defenders as if a seamstress had threaded a needle, the spinning ball drilled softly into Rick's hands. The defender chased Rick and caught him near the goal, but the momentum of the hit carried him over.

The touchdown began what Melvin Hibbs called the greatest individual performance in the history of the state football playoffs. The final score, fifty-four to seven, devastated the hometown folks around Pawhuska, and insured Danny's place on the all-American team. By the time the game ended, there was hardly a Pawhuska fan left in the stadium. One by one, then by the tens, then fifties, they had slunk away.

After the game, Lipscomb leaned back against the cool concrete, almost satisfied. A few regrets sullied his pleasure. The media crunch on Danny would be fierce for the next two weeks. And he knew if he had fooled the Tahlequah Hornedtoads by the point-cutting performances, this game had awakened them. Their scouts would carry this game back play by play.

Cannonball came in from outside. "Here's their score." Lipscomb looked at the slip of paper, dirty from Cannonball's hands. Tahlequah thirty-five, Vici twenty. "They can be scored on," Cannonball said. "I can just hear what they're saying about our score," he added, his bugged eyes gleaming as he chuckled. "We have them right where we want them."

Perhaps I should take Coach's comment about being a good coach seriously. If you're good at something, perhaps that's your calling. Perhaps God was speaking to me through the most unlikely of sources. After all, God spoke to Balaam through an ass. Perhaps I had been looking for the word of God in the wrong places, from the wrong people. Perhaps the evangelists, the preachers, the Sunday school teachers were not God's messengers to me, nor were the churches the tabernacles of his speech. That's why I kept missing his call. Perhaps he spoke to me through someone else, someone who looked so unlike a messenger from God it would take a genius to figure it out. Perhaps that is the way God works, why he had to strike down Saul of Tarsus and make him blind, why Jonah wound up in the belly of a whale. Could God be speaking to me through Cannonball in the vast concrete tabernacles of the football stadiums? He was the one I was most like, he was the one I learned from. All along, he had been my mentor, had taught me to watch and learn.

I had to stop worrying, ignore all this internal combat. Just do my job. Two weeks to prepare, the coaches were glad for that, then to Norman for the state championship.

On Monday, the team had to pick its way through writers, photographers, and television crews; all of them grasping for a few feet of film, a new pose, an idea to shoot about the wonder team from the small Panhandle town, the team that the wind swept up from the hard clay, swirling it into the limelight of football mania. Mostly, they fought one another for Danny's time. The first all-American from the western half of Oklahoma.

The writers wrote of the Dustdevils as lighter, quicker, the team of finesse and strategy. The Tahlequah Hornedtoads, with their massive line, and Blackie Beavers, their two-hundred-thirty-pound fullback, were physically superior, they said. They searched and sifted for angles, but unanimously they wrote that the Dustdevils' quarterback must have a super day if our smaller team expected to win.

Wednesday, Lipscomb put his foot down and excluded all media people from the field and surrounding area. They moved to town and stalked the Main Street merchants and the recruiters who were holed up in the Blue Peecock. The recruiters who believed their schools to be in contention for Danny Boone's services spoke guardedly and mainly stuck to their hobbies, stealing messages from their rivals and spying to see if some relative, friend, or teacher was being aligned to a competitor.

No one knew about the envelope from West Point tucked safely in my drawer at home, nor the envelope that Clay Moray had sent to Joe Don Jones. My imagination told me the rough form of that letter's contents. It promised Joe Don Jones something he wanted, perhaps a new tent for his meetings, perhaps some real estate that an alumnus no longer had need of but would be perfect for a religious retreat, if only Joe Don would help persuade Danny to attend West Point. None of the other recruiters knew the recruiting war was already over.

Lipscomb obtained a photograph of the Tahlequah team from the file at the *Daily Oklahoman*. He hired a photographer in the city to blow up to life size the face of each first-string Hornedtoad. He pasted these photographs to plywood and assigned freshmen to carry them around in practice.

"I want you men to know these faces," he said. "You'll see them all night a week from Friday. They're human like the rest of us. They put their pants on one leg at a time, and they want your women, your balls, and your championship."

The team was so intense in practice, Coach eased up on Thursday, dismissing practice early. After Danny had dressed and stepped out of the bus barn, a tow-headed boy who lived near the practice field ducked shyly as he handed Danny an envelope, telling him it was from a lady.

There was no writing on the outside of the envelope. The handwriting on the note inside was not particularly feminine, the letters were tall and plain. "Dear Danny, I want to see you. Please. Dovie."

"Danny, she's married," I reasoned.

One block from my house, the Bel Air crouched in the alley like a silver cat. I took hold of his arm, pleading. He broke away. I followed him. He opened the passenger door, and she drove away. I ran faster than I had ever run, driven by my uselessness, until I came near her house.

I sat down on the wheel of an old John Deere drill that had been parked for decades in a vacant lot, and I watched the flowery curtains flutter in her windows, which were all open. There was a tree with most of its leaves off between me and the house. I felt like a child who had been sent outside to play while something secret and wonderful happened.

Dovie's house was the last one on the street. Beyond it there was only a barbed wire fence, buffalo grass, soapweed, and sagebrush that stretched to the river. Beyond the river, I could see the first of the cottonwoods that rimmed the sand hills until deep night folded over us like purple velvet, and I flew like a hawk upward, then fell in free flight until I became transparent, floating through the open window into her house. Her underwear lay trampled on the floor near the high iron bed that was hers.

I hover over her, our bodies entwining on the rumpled bed, the one she shares with Killer, and Danny, and now me. She is still well conditioned. My blood is hot, my hands are sticky with it, and they touch first her, then Danny, and we both make love to her, and I love them both for what they dare to be.

I huddled, chilled, ill with the tension, until Danny came out. He headed toward Main Street, and my house. I needed a plan— go to LaFaye's and pick up my shoes he had repaired, claim that's where I'd been so Danny wouldn't know. I'd get LaFaye out of the domino parlor if I had to. I got to Main Street just as Brice Miller turned off it. He hadn't been home in more than two weeks. He'd missed Danny by less than two minutes.

I was torn. Killer could not be that dumb. He'd know Danny had been there, he'd smell it. He might kill Dovie. I turned, retracing my steps, running. When I came near the house, I heard her. Screams, groans. I was too late. He was already beating her, marring her face, flattening her beautiful nose, only a few blows until death. As I dashed by the window, I caught a glimpse of them. It was the same window I had peeked in before. She was on top of Killer, her blouse was ripped half off her shoulder and he was squeezing her breasts with his massive hands. Her head tilted back, veins stuck out of her neck as she groaned.

I turn to run. I trip, fall with the same sensation as when I pitched over the side of the mesa. I wonder about the nature of my birth, the sign that made me special. The thoughts flicker in my mind so much longer than the instant it takes my head to strike the rock. When I awake, it is quiet and dark. My head aches, but it is not sticky with blood. I long for someone to comfort me, for some arms, soft and assuring, to wrap around my shivering body to tell me everything will be fine. I no longer need an explanation. All I want is a feeling the small world around me makes some sense.

More times that week and the next, Danny slipped away to see Dovie even though Killer was still in town. I understood now why Danny took the risks. I knew from the way I had felt when I woke up outside her house. I wanted her arms around me, I wanted her to take me wherever she took Danny.

Wednesday, two days before the game, a television crew from Denver set up cameras and lights in Goggin's store to interview the territory's oldest haberdasher and football fan. The interviewer, hair slicked back with hair tonic, stuck the microphone out: "Mr. Goggin, what do you think about Danny Boone's chances of bringing a championship to your town?"

Old Man Goggin hooked his thumbs in his suspenders, pulling the inseam of his pants tighter. Before he could answer, he fell over dead beside a pile of overalls.

I went with my father to the funeral home. "What a shame he had to go before the game," my father told Junior.

"Yes, he would have gotten a big kick out of being on television, too," Junior added.

I heard Doc tell Dale and P.O., "I think the Old Man shortened his suspenders too much and cut off circulation. His heart couldn't get enough blood pumped through." They put their heads together and laughed quietly.

P.O. said, "I hope this ain't the beginning of things going wrong. I can't imagine the death of our oldest citizen bodes well for the game." They became somber as grave robbers.

Junior and Mrs. Goggin held the funeral in the Methodist church at noon on Friday and the coffin was scheduled for burial at one P.M., plenty of time for family and friends to join the caravan to Norman.

The pallbearers, waiting for the family to leave the church for graveside, planned an appreciation day for Danny Boone. "Win or lose, what that boy has done for this town should not be forgotten," P.O. said. "He's put us on the map. People all over the country now know about Cimarron."

LaFaye cut in. "He's brought business to town, money in our pockets, that's what I'm grateful for."

Dale shook his head as if ashamed, and P.O. glared at LaFaye.

The camera crews who had been staying in town folded up their equipment. Among those working was a tall young man, a cameraman and technician. Skinny, black, he had stayed at the Blue

Peecock with the Denver television crew. So far as anyone knew, he was the first black man who had ever been allowed to stay overnight in Cimarron.

Mrs. Farragut, in pink curlers that bound her hair close to her blue-skinned head, who had once watched while Killer and Harley had wrestled with Danny, and Dovie had bared her breasts, glared from her window on Main Street and watched the young black man load up the TV equipment. She and others did not share the view of the men at the funeral, and believed the hullabaloo over Danny Boone had done irreparable damage to the way of life in Cimarron.

CHAPTER 29

I n his funeral prayer, the Methodist preacher pleaded for mercy for the dead, repentance for the living, and safety for the travelers. The mourners prayed by Old Man's grave, then hurried back to watch the team leave town.

The coaches had checked every supply bag to make sure nothing was left off the bus, which was parked around back of the bus barn for loading. I assured Lipscomb everything was packed, but he wanted to make sure. I went back in, checked the cabinets, Coach's office, and was halfway down the row of lockers when I heard a vehicle pull up and skid to a stop. Kirk came running in the front door. His face was haggard under three-day-old whiskers.

"Where's Danny? Look!" He handed me a piece of brown corrugated cardboard. It was slit in the middle, with what looked like dried blood on it. His breath rasped in and out between words, "This was stuck in a dead calf . . . Didn't tell Arved, one of his registered Herefords. He'll wonder what happened to me. Hurry, we have to warn Danny."

On the cardboard was a message scrawled with a blunt pencil: "QB, don't go on the field or you're dead."

My first impulse was the same as Kirk's, run and warn Danny.

Just then, Lipscomb came charging through the back door. "Schultz, what the hell's taking you so long?" I handed him the bloody note.

"Kirk found this on a dead calf. We have to tell Danny his life's in danger." Coach's eyes bulged as he read the warning.

"Take this to Sheriff Ordway," Coach told Kirk. "I'll take care of it with Danny." Kirk ran out the front. "Schultz, finish checking those lockers," Coach ordered. He ran out the back toward the bus.

I followed Coach's orders. Who could have killed a calf, then stuck him with a knife? First thought of course, Killer. But why? Plenty of reasons. Probably knows about Danny and Dovie. Danny used a knife on him. Everyone has been expecting Killer to exact some kind of revenge.

There was no time to squander. I heard Cannonball hit the starter, then the bus's tires crunching on the gravel. Still six lockers to go. I decided to forget it. But by the time I was outside, the bus was easing onto the highway. The fans were whistling through their fingers out open car windows and honking their horns as they escorted the bus on its way out of town. The polished paint and chrome of the bus sparkled in the winter sun hanging low in the sky. I looked around for someone to chase down the bus for me. There was only the dust of Kirk's hasty departure and of the other vehicles that had followed the bus.

"Son of a bitch, they left me." I kicked the ground. At first, I couldn't believe it. I expected to hear the bus whine as Cannonball backed it up, Coach calling out the window for me to hurry. I stood waiting. I couldn't decide if Coach had done it on purpose, or if the pressure had gotten to him and it was accidental. My mind raced.

That must be it, Coach doesn't want me around. Images appeared in dazzling, random flashes; the dead calf, its mother stretching her white face, licking her calf's reddish brown coat, sniffing the carcass that, by now, would be cold and only faintly remind her of the baby she once had; Arved, how his blank eyes smolder with the fear they hide as he finds out his only son is in danger; Anne, who disappeared from our lives without even saying goodbye as if these little deaths when people leave don't matter; Harley, dragging himself through the darkness of the starlit night toward a light he would never reach; then, an image I had not seen in a long time, Jimmy Lee Watson, bound up in baling wire, staring from his coffin. I knew Coach had no intention of saying anything to Danny.

Danny is in no danger yet, I thought. Sheriff Ordway will know what to do. I ran the half mile to my father's office. I was telling him what had happened, how they left me, there was a dead calf, and Kirk had shown me the warning, when the sheriff sauntered in. He was wearing his usual half grin beneath the wide brim of his hat.

"Hey Sonny, looks like they left you." He saw the worry on my face. "Don't worry about Danny, I've taken care of it. There'll be more state police than ants crawling over that stadium."

"You've warned him?"

"No, no. No sense disturbing Danny, he'll want to play anyhow. And you don't want to put added pressure on him." What he said seemed almost right, I wanted to believe he was right.

My father asked him who he thought killed the calf.

Ordway tipped his hat back. "My best guess is, it's somebody bettin' on the game, and wants to weigh the odds in his own favor," Ordway answered. "And in this case, we have somebody with a grudge against Danny. No sense beatin' around the bush. We all know about the feud between those two boys. And Killer's always been the kind who wants things the easy way. And it looks like Danny's pokin' his wife again. And if Killer suspects anything, that'll rile up a guy. Now let me get out of here and get with the motorcade. See you all down there."

It would be hard to prove Killer had written the warning note. I doubted the sheriff would even investigate. The sheriff was probably right. Killer was trying to make a lot of money gambling against the Dustdevils, not the first Cimarron citizen to try that shortcut. And to get even with Danny at the same time. What could be better from his point of view? The sheriff knows about Danny and Dovie. Nothing surprising about that, that's his job, keep his eyes open, know what's going on around his town. That's also trouble. The football season is almost over. Not such a need to protect Danny once it ends. One of these evenings in the domino parlor, everyone in town will know the whole thing's started up again. People will be bored and someone will start tormenting Killer about Danny and Dovie. I couldn't think of any way things might work out well.

The worst thing about being left off the bus was traveling to the game with my parents. Only this morning, my mother had decided to accompany my father to the game. He had tried to discourage her. But she had been adamant. She had not attended a game since Danny and I were freshmen.

I tried to tell myself I was better off riding with my father. At least he was not a half-blind midget driver who had to wear stilts so he was tall enough to reach the foot pedals. But Danny, he was on the bus, and in danger. Nothing to do about it, I had to be calm.

Half an hour later, the church began loading the Joy Bus we had purchased to transport people to the games. All the seats were filled by advance reservations. When the door was opened, Alfred and his mother trooped onto the bus as if they had season tickets. Fortunately, Pastor Toon had not reserved the back seat because it rode too rough, and because he used it to store hymnals. He moved the songbooks to the floorboard in front, making room for the rumpled, drooling, unexpected guests.

Pomp Reed also arrived early to claim his reserved seats, which were only one row in front of the back. When he saw Alfred and his mom sitting back there, he objected to the preacher. He said his brother-in-law had been turned away, that the preacher had told him the seats were all reserved. If anyone should get the back seat, it should be his sister and brother-in-law. But the preacher looked Pomp in the eye and quoted the words of Christ, " 'In as much as ye have done it unto the least of these, my brethren, ye have done it unto me.' "

"According to that Scripture," the preacher added, his nose barely six inches from Pomp's face, "that's Jesus himself in that back seat. You make those people get off and you'll be the only deacon in history ever to kick Jesus off a bus. We're not doing anything that could cause us to lose this game."

The motorcade formed behind the Joy Bus. The sheriff's car, then other vehicles with signs and slogans stretched down Main Street from Goggin's department store with its black, draped windows, past the leather shop, the barbershop, the drugstore, beyond the Blue Peecock and the Elite Cafe.

At two o'clock, Pastor Toon stood up, raised his arms, then dropped them, making jerky triangles, six-eight time, and all the passengers started singing as the bus pulled away.

"Come we that love the Lord, and let our joys be known.
Join in a song with sweet accord,
Join in a song with sweet accord.
And thus surround the throne, and thus surround the throne.
We're marching to Zion, beautiful city of Zion,
We're marching upward to Zion, Zion,
The beautiful city of God."

Flags whipped from the fenders, American on one, Christian on the other. Confident banners streamed from the bus's sides: THE LORD JESUS CHRIST IS COMING SOON, ARE YOU READY? And: THE CIMARRON DUSTDEVILS, OKLAHOMA STATE CHAMPS.

Three hundred and fourteen vehicles, twelve hundred and fifty souls, pulled out of town.

My father planned to leave later, at two-thirty. He was setting up the presses so he'd be ready to print the story when he returned, win or lose. He had refused when I had attempted to persuade him to travel with the caravan.

Dovie Miller stepped onto Main Street five minutes after the caravan left. A small, reddish mutt named Chigger bounced at Dovie's feet. The dog belonged to no one, lived in the vacant buildings around town, and begged food from people who walked by. He wagged his tail, jumping and yipping beside her.

She was the only person on the street. The town had never been that deserted. Dovie wore a full print skirt that hung just below her knees, and a matching jacket. The skirt fluttered and shimmered as she walked south with long strides, the muscles rippling in the calves of her legs, past Mrs. Farragut's gate. I watched her until she was out of sight.

We picked up Mother and pulled out of town only five minutes later than Dad had promised. The way Dad drove, we'd catch the caravan before it was halfway to Norman. I leaned back to relax. I tried not to think about the game, and Danny, or the warning. The station wagon picked up some speed as we neared the edge of town, although my father seemed to be driving more cautiously than usual.

Sensing our location, I closed my eyes, but not quickly enough; I had glimpsed the stadium and beyond it route twenty-three, and I thought for a moment I had seen a man on a motorbike. But when I opened my eyes to confirm it, there was only the road, narrow and black, as it disappeared into the western horizon before its skull turned gravelly. The surrounding landscape swept neatly into the sky, but as it stretched out, the black ribbon of road broke when it entered the willow grove near the Dove Creek bridge. A clamor of weeping arose. A few pale, dry leaves hung lifeless on trees stark in their winter nakedness. The meek trees with little to do were bent down in grief over the loss of one mourning dove. The whine of the mud-grip tires diminished, the car was losing speed.

"Bill, that's the Lasher girl, the one that married the Miller boy at the end of the summer. I wonder what she's doing? Girls shouldn't hitchhike like that," my mother said. I sat up as we passed by. Dovie had her thumb out. The dog was on his haunches beside her. My father stopped about a hundred feet beyond her.

A fuel transport truck powered past us, big red letters. Dovie staggered when the swirling air hit her. It bowled the dog over, but Dovie caught herself with her right hand and kept her feet, her skirt curling between her legs as she ran toward us. The dog righted himself and stayed at her heels.

Dovie came to the passenger side. "Hi, I was hoping for a ride to the game." She was looking at my mother as if it were up to her. Then she saw me. "Hi Sonny. I thought you went on the bus."

"Get in," my father said.

She bent to pat the dog, then opened the door. My eyes were drying and Dovie sat beside me, more in the middle than on her side. My father could see her in the mirror, and she smiled at him. I wondered if she thought he was handsome.

It was odd that Dovie had been on the road hoping for a ride after the caravan left. Was she expecting to take a ride from a stranger who happened to be going to Norman?

"Didn't your husband want to attend the game?" my mother asked. The car picked up speed. I looked out my own window.

"He's away for a few days," Dovie said.

"Away?"

"Yes, working on some kind of job in Colorado. He was sorry to miss the game, but he had to leave early this morning. He wants us to move there."

I snorted quietly. She didn't seem to notice. I doubted Killer was in Colorado. I wondered if he'd sneak into the game to see if his threat worked.

"I never knew what kind of work your husband does," my mother said.

"Well, a lot of different things. You may find this strange, but I'm not real sure, myself. That's the neat thing about us, we each have our own areas. He makes good money, and with the money I make, we're saving up to buy a place. We want to start a family and we need to plan ahead."

Through her window, the light in the darkness, Danny leaving, Killer arriving. Her charm and directness. My hand, only inches from hers on the car seat, moved and touched her, a brief, brushing touch, might have been accidental, but she turned and leaned toward me, an unmistakable warmth within her eyes.

"If you're starting a family," my mother said, turning in her seat so she faced us, "you should be thinking about what the Lord Jesus Christ means to you. No one should raise children without the Lord in their lives." Mother lifted her chin.

"Oh, we're Christians," Dovie said, "we belong to the Methodist church."

"I don't mean that," my mother said, her voice becoming soft and cajoling. "I mean letting Jesus rule, being faithful to Jesus, living with him to avoid living in hell."

An expression of alarm appeared, disappeared, reappeared on Dovie's face. Mother's testimony had touched some nerve, some point of vulnerability in Dovie, some tiny seam of guilt.

"Emma, I don't think this is the time," my father interrupted.

"That's just what I mean," Mother clipped her words. "Would Jesus say, 'Oh, this isn't a good time to think about saving our souls'? Hell is real!"

I cringed in my seat. Dovie looked down, composing herself. The whole situation seemed so odd. Dovie in the car beside me only inches away, not even aware her husband had threatened to kill Danny, apparently willing for me to touch her. Is she concerned about hell? Have my presumptions about her been all wrong? What if she knew about Killer's threat, would that make her love Danny more?

In my mind were the images of how Dovie had made love to both Danny and Killer within minutes of each other, and how she had looked on Main Street as I secretly watched her a half hour ago, so free, walking as if she were on some wonderful journey, and longer ago baring her breasts to spare Danny the shame of his own nakedness. Her husband, a lover of this beautiful young woman beside me, had killed an animal and left a blood-soaked note. Now, my mother was talking to her about Jesus and hell while my father drove as if nothing were happening. How many lovers can one woman have?

"Think we have a good chance to win?" my father asked, flinging the question over his shoulder toward Dovie.

Dovie didn't answer for a long time. My mother sat composed and serene, isolated in her own innocent righteousness.

"It doesn't really matter that much," Dovie finally said, answering my father's question, her voice barely above a whisper. "Win or lose, they'll talk about it for years. We all will. It's the hope we all need, hope that life doesn't just go on and on staying the same forever. It's hope we can't all find in the same way, Mrs. Schultz."

This was a part of Dovie I had never seen, a person who suffered and struggled as I did to keep life from losing its grace and meaning. I wanted her. In my heart, I wanted her. I cared about what people thought of me. I could not disdain public approval, but around Dovie existed a transcendent freedom that elevated her above that kind of caring. I had been right about her. Whatever fear had possessed her earlier had disappeared.

We caught the caravan at Watonga. Additional travelers had joined along the route so the line was longer. A police escort led us out of El Reno, radioed ahead, and they blocked side traffic at all major intersections. Men on tractors waved from the fields. Women with their hair tied up in bandannas stood on their porches to watch us stream by.

Like an invading army, the motorcade overran Norman, captured the parking lots and the steak houses and pancake parlors. The town talked about that journey for years. "Nothing like it, not even close, until finally we travel that last highway to heaven," Pastor Toon said.

I strolled into the dressing room at six o'clock. Before I was three feet inside the door, a large man accosted me. Coach yelled, "It's okay, he's our water boy." The police security were doing their job. I was both shaken and comforted. Coach caught me before I got to Danny.

"Sorry we left you back there. I forgot you were inside, and we were almost to Woodward before we figured it out."

"Well, I made it anyhow," I said. "Did you tell Danny about the threat?"

"No, he has enough on his mind. It wouldn't change things. I've told the boys the security people are normal for a big game."

The team languished in the locker room, which smelled of stale sweat and reviving salts. They sat on the cool gray-green concrete, waiting for game time like soldiers who wait before a battle that will surely destroy many of them and decide who wins the war.

At six-thirty, Coach ordered everyone to dress. Cannonball taped ankles but worked quickly and used little tape. "Nothing to save you for now," he told Rick, "so we'll leave it a little loose, for good movement."

Danny put his foot on the wooden bench so Cannonball could tape him. We both scanned the room while Cannonball worked. Danny appeared to be relaxed and confident. We both saw the man wearing the leather jacket. He stood with his back to us, as devil-may-care as he had always been. A mind trick; in fact, this was not the first time I had imagined seeing Harley. But this time, there are his wide, rounded shoulders, the hint of a fat roll just above the belt, the extremely narrow hips and the tight jeans around heavily muscled thighs. Even the black motorcycle jacket with the silver grippers appears to be undamaged. My heart flutters, so happy he's there, terrified it's true. I am swallowed into a white sack of insanity. I see the room through eyes that are like tiny, hard cranberries, a gambler playing my last hand. Danny moves. "Hey, I'm not finished with that ankle," Cannonball says. The guy in the motorcycle jacket turns around. He was a member of security, gun bulging beneath his coat. I sat down, resting my face in my hands, poking my fingers in my ears to bring on the ringing, narrow silence.

Cannonball stuck on the last piece of tape, ran it up two inches into the hair of Danny's leg. "One more time for luck," he said.

"For luck," Danny said, and he smiled.

The dwarf pinched the calf of Danny's leg. "If anyone can do it for us, you can."

Danny led the team around the white-lined field. The Hornedtoads entered from the opposite end, charging through their cheering supporters. Cannonball studied the Hornedtoads' lineup, comparing their numbers, scratching with a pencil.

"Their weights are different," he said. "What they listed the last few games has been changed. If this is right, they outweigh us twenty-five pounds a man. That coach has done this on purpose."

"We can't tell the boys," Lipscomb said, his voice quavering with rage.

"We have to tell them," Cannonball said. "Better they know it than to wonder 'what the hell?' "

"It's the same-sized field, same striped shirts on the referees, grass a little more tended to, players a little bigger, but everything else is the same. It's just another game," Coach told the team. "The waiting is over, a piece of our lives is ending, in this place, in three hours, that will be it, winner take all. If you want it, you can have it." He looked around, man to man.

"I want the seven defensive linemen to go with Cannonball. I'll talk to the rest of you."

In a dark corner, Cannonball arms his warrior linemen. He cuts rectangular pieces of quarter-inch foam rubber. Out of a satchel, he pulls pieces of aluminum irrigation pipe, split down the seams and partially opened, four-inch and five-inch pipe, like the pipe at the Boone farm, pipe for brawny arms. With a rubber mallet, he bends these pieces of pipe over their forearms, then wraps a piece of the thin foam rubber over the outside and tapes it down. With finger pressure, it feels like a padded arm. With the speed and force behind a forearm shiver, it will scramble an opposing player's brains. "Now, one more thing." Cannonball leans toward them, his voice, though softer, is meaner. "Coach has a nice-sized fund the businessmen put together. There's fifty bucks for anyone who can take out an opposing player. If you feel you've earned it, report to me to make sure I know. We'll settle up next week." I am standing where I can hear this, and I say nothing, to anyone, ever, until now.

Lipscomb was still talking when Cannonball let the linemen rejoin the others. "You'll have to sacrifice," Coach said. "Reach down and call up everything you've got. This is the only opportunity like this you will ever have. This game is the most important event of your life. You'll pull out pictures and newspaper clippings and tell your children and they'll tell their children. Forget the pain, you inflict pain. Forty-eight minutes of game time, three minutes of actual physical exertion, each play six seconds long on the average. Give your very best, your all, every ounce of strength and courage on every play and you'll win, and the glory will be yours."

Coach turned to Cannonball, who leaned over a round plastic cake box, the kind women buy at Tupperware parties. The lid was perforated with holes the size of dimes.

"Be headhunters! You hear me?" Coach shouted. "Be headhunters! You hear me? Be headhunters!" There was fury on his face, he was chopping the air.

Cannonball pried off the lid from the container, then lifted out a common horned toad, its head the size of a good-sized thumb. Spikes decked its head and its broad flat body. With his webbed fingers, the dwarf held up the toad. Its black eyes shimmered like dots of liquid coal. Its tiny feet hung down.

Lipscomb spoke again, quietly, fatherly. "Take off their fucking heads. Beat the Tahlequah Hornedtoads."

His eyes, then our eyes shifted to Cannonball. The dwarf stuffed the horned toad half into his mouth, his yellow teeth closed slowly on the spiked head. The lizard's back legs clawed the air. Its neck bones cracked. The dwarf flailed his hair when he severed the toad's head from its body. The horns made white spots on Cannonball's pocked cheek. He held up the toad, headless, its legs still twitching, blood dripping off the tip of his thumb onto the concrete floor. He turned and shuffled out.

CHAPTER 30

The Hornedtoads won the toss and deferred their choice until the second half. Lipscomb was happy to go on offense first. Then he questioned what the opposing coach had done.

"Damnedest strategy I ever heard of," he exclaimed. "You'd think they'd have wanted to receive and keep the ball out of Danny's hands."

"They're up to something," Cannonball said.

I stepped on the edge of the field. It felt placid, almost soft. I looked for Dovie and my parents in the special boxes reserved for the press. Uniformed policemen ringed the stadium, and there were many others in plainclothes. If Killer was there, he would avoid the area where the Cimarron fans sat, and the press box where my parents and Dovie were.

The kickoff fell end over end. Someone in the first row had a radio and I heard it described, into and out of R.D.'s arms, out of bounds on the fifteen. The team was nervous.

There was a swelling of noise when Danny ran onto the field. The radio blared from the front-row seats, "High school all-American Daniel Boone takes the field for the Dustdevils. With him behind center, the Devils can score from anywhere on the field as they've proved this whole year."

Danny called the first play. He looked down the defensive line. I knew them all from the pictures we'd carried around for two weeks. Donovan, Goetz, Krupinski, O'Neill. No, that isn't O'Neill, not nearly as large, not number seventy, number forty-three. Hightower, program lists him, a reserve linebacker.

Before I could tell Cannonball about their change, the ball snapped into Danny's hands. He faked the handoff to Rick, boot-legged back to his left; Rod moved downfield, relaxed and ready. He cut inside as Danny flipped the ball, number forty-three in late. Rod did not even have to jump; perfect, twelve-yard gain. Yellow flags floated onto the green grass. Danny did not get up.

I ran out with Lipscomb. Danny's nose was askew and bloody. Coach held his hand up in front of Danny's face. "How many fingers?" Coach asked.

"Four," Danny said. He was conscious enough to count fingers.

"You're gonna have to come out while we stop the bleeding."

"First down at the forty-two," the referee screamed as we stood Danny up. He wobbled as we helped him off the field.

Rick moved to quarterback, ran two dive plays and a quarterback sneak. And we punted.

The Hornedtoads ran dive plays and one sweep, the latter a seven-yard gain by Blackie Beavers called back, illegal motion. Our defense, solid. Their center already out, loss of memory, forgot the snap count. Our nose guard on the five-three defense had knocked him cuckoo with one blow of his forearm to the chin. The punt-receiving team went in.

Our ball on our own forty-one. Danny jogged on to the field. Doc McGrath had pushed his nose back in shape the best he could, and padded it with gauze taped and trimmed so it wouldn't obscure his vision or disturb his breathing. O'Neill was in. Number forty-three, Hightower, the kid who had broken Danny's nose, had moved from the right side to the left side replacing Donovan. I screamed out to Danny, "Watch forty-three on the left." But he had already called the play, quarterback option, to the left side of their defense. Number forty-three charged across the line into his path.

Perfect, make him come to you, commit himself, that's what Danny had been taught. Just before contact, he flipped the ball to R.D., the trailing halfback. The ball tumbled perfectly into R.D.'s gut, and he cut up the field, big hole, good yardage, while Hightower hit Danny, and O'Neill came in from the other side. As Danny went down, a fist came at his face. This time Danny was prepared; he twisted, and the blow rocked his helmet. No flags, the refs had seen nothing, they had followed the ball. R.D. was knocked out of bounds on their forty. A nineteen-yard gain.

Danny was bleeding again, from not enough time, from the exertion, and from the shock of the second clout across the head. He came out and Rick ran dive plays.

I bounced on the springy turf, which bore up my feet as if I were preparing to enter the game and could not wait until the coach called my number. I wanted to be on the field, armed, deadly. I lusted for blood. I wanted to see fear on the face of someone who had glanced, unwittingly, into my eyes, hear the crack of my bones against the glass of his chin, hear him retch as he puked on the grass, whimpering, begging to be taken out so he could sit humbled in safety along the sidelines. The expansiveness of my rage then contracted and became a black hole. I had failed the whole town by being the water boy.

Danny went back in, cotton in his nose, third and six. Fake right, sprint option left. The ball snapped into Danny's hands. One step right, the ball secure in his belly. Exaggerated hand fake, the linebackers froze. Danny planted his foot, pivoted left. Our blockers cut down the defense like ripe stalks. A linebacker escaped the scythe, but one defender is no match for an all-American. Danny moved his head and shoulders outside, and at the same time shifted his feet and cut inside. The defender's instincts betrayed him. With perfect grace, Danny moved by him.

The crowd was on its feet in a split second. Danny ran toward the goal with both teams in pursuit. The opposite-side defensive back had an angle and caught Danny at the ten-yard line. Danny twisted, trying to make it into the end zone, going down, arms pinned, over backward, face up. When the cheap shot came, it came over the top after he was already down, number forty-three trailing the play, Hightower, slender reserve linebacker.

Instinctively, Danny turned his face away from the painful nose, and the clenched fist with one knuckle extended caught him just below the eye.

They assessed the penalty, half the distance to the goal, and threw Hightower out of the game. They put Danny on a stretcher, and loaded him into the back of an ambulance. Dovie ran down from the stands, and we crawled together into the cramped space beside Danny. He kept his eyes closed against the pain. Dovie and I held hands. I wondered if Killer had seen her.

"Schultz, stay here," Cannonball yelled, "we may need you." I ignored him. The attendant stepped in on the other side of Danny, the driver closed the door, and we drove toward the gate.

It was dark inside the ambulance, narrow shafts of light flickered through the small side windows. Dovie and I both watched Danny. The attendant bent over him, holding a large patch of gauze on the injured eye. Dovie edged closer to me.

"I'm afraid. Hold me, Sonny, please hold me," Dovie whispered, her mouth so near my ear I could feel her breath. "Has anyone ever died in a football game?" She flattened herself against me as if she wanted to disappear.

I felt dizzy, so near to Danny I could hear his breathing, Dovie pressing against me so eagerly, and the thought of death quivering through me.

"Not often," I answered, "he won't die."

"Don't you just love him so terribly you could die?"

"Yes, I do."

"Hold me closer," she said. "Closer."

My eyes had adjusted to the darkness. I watched Danny's chest rise and fall as he breathed. I pulled Dovie's head gently forward until her cheek was against mine and I could whisper so Danny couldn't hear. "Can I come see you in Cimarron?"

"Yes, oh, yes, yes. Please. Please. Hold me, hold me."

Ninety minutes later, we arrived back at the stadium. Rick had been unable to push the team over even from the one-yard line, so our kicker had kicked a field goal from the spot Danny had been driven out of bounds, giving the Dustdevils a three to zero lead at the half. Midway through the third quarter, Rick had fumbled the snap. The Hornedtoads recovered on their twenty-two. Six plays later, Blackie Beavers plowed over from the one. R.D., from his outside position, knifed through and blocked the kick, and the Hornedtoads led six to three. That's the way it was when I pushed Danny's wheelchair back onto the sidelines with five minutes left.

It was an incredibly long game. Coach had used every trick in the book to string out the time, hoping Danny might get back.

Danny's eye was covered with a white bandage. Patches of dried blood obliterated the grass stains on his white pants. I had run from the room to throw up while Dovie stayed with Danny, who took twenty-two stitches with no anesthesia.

The game had become a trench battle between two teams with no offensive punch; one missing its quarterback, the other operating with a decimated line.

Cannonball wobbled over. "How are you?" he asked Danny.

"Fine," Danny said.

I made my points that I had carefully rehearsed with the doctors before we left the hospital. "Doctors say the injury is very dangerous, a probable concussion, and a fracture of the orbital cavity.

The muscles have prolapsed into the fracture; any hard bump may cause permanent loss of sight. He must not walk in unlighted places where he might stumble, he cannot blow his nose, and above all, must not play football until the fracture heals, meaning months from now." By the time I finished, I had bent over so my face was inches from Cannonball's.

He turned away from me, toward Danny. "Can you go back in?"

I moved swiftly so I was in front of the dwarf. "Doctor said he can't play for months," I screamed, bending even closer to Cannonball's currish face.

"Schultz, did I speak to you? Danny, I want to hear it from you. Can you go back in?"

"Yes," he said.

I sprang at Cannonball. All the hatred I'd stored up for the conniving little half man, all the underhanded ridicule I had endured and only joked about, all the fear I harbored about being like Cannonball burst out of me, and my hands were around his scaly throat squeezing with all the strength I had. Harley's death had been an accident, and Jimmy Lee's, too. This time, I would have killed a man on purpose, but Lipscomb and some of the substitute players pulled me off and held me down until I quit struggling.

They helped Danny with his pads. I lay on the grass and watched. His T-shirt was bloody like his pants, and I heard the radio, its professional voices drifting down to me from the front row. "Quarterback Boone may be on his way back into the game. He's getting his uniform on. Apparently, he's not as seriously injured as we thought."

I looked up at the press box. I knew the writers like Hibbs were already writing in their pads about the brilliant strategy of the Tahlequah coach; sacrificed a second-string linebacker, got him kicked out of the game and branded him forever, the Indian kid who took out the all-American quarterback with a protruding knuckle punch.

I sat up so I could see the action on the field. The Hornedtoads made another first down. Maybe Danny wouldn't have to go back in. They could run out the clock and win. Now, it didn't matter. They ran two plays, and the Dustdevils called time out with one minute and forty seconds left. It was third and four.

Danny was dressed, his helmet was on, the chin strap dangled ready to be fastened. "Are you okay?" he asked me.

"Yes." I was brusque.

The Hornedtoads ran a play and lost two yards. They'd have to punt. The Dustdevils would have time for one or two plays.

"Any ideas for me when I go out there?"

"Yes, don't go."

I thought of him when I first began to love him, when the illusion first was made, the boy who, if he chose to, could crush me to ashes with that violent streak that ran in his blood and hardened him into a machine of muscle and bone.

"I can't let people down again. I have to try," he said.

"Run the 'lonesome end,' " I said.

He looked away from me, toward the field, the clock, and then at the coaches.

"You remember? The play in the book I read to you a long time ago." I looked at my hands. My nails were trimmed and smooth. I thought of the pianist in the story, how he had been sent into the game with his clean uniform to hide along the sideline and then to catch the only pass and win the only glory of his football career. I was that boy. I wanted to go in.

"I remember," Danny said, and he gazed off again. "I can't think of anything better."

"The coaches won't go for a play they haven't practiced. They won't believe we can do anything without their help. We don't have time to argue with them. You set it up on the field, I'll keep the coaches out of the way. And Danny, pray, pray now like you've never prayed before." What I think was a loving grin flitted across his bandaged face, as if he realized we were the only ones who knew prayers to win football games were not worth the breath it took to utter them.

The punt floated high like an erratic leaf in the brittle air. Rick and R.D., paralyzed by the fear of what seemed now to be the inevitable loss, let it fall. It hit at the twenty-five, and as if guided by an unseen hand, it bounced for us, back toward midfield. It stopped and was downed on our thirty-three. I was already dragging reserves off the bench, making them stand up with their helmets on so when our pass receiver stood in front he might appear to be another substitute if anyone looked from across the field.

Danny ran gingerly onto the field fastening his chin strap as he ran. Rod limped off, late, apparently injured, according to Danny's instruction.

"Purdin, where's Purdin?" Coach was yelling for Rod's substitute. I dug my hand into the medicine kit, grabbed a towel and smeared it with analgesic balm, then ran toward the coach as he pushed Purdin onto the field.

"Stop." I grabbed Purdin by the jersey. The sticky towel slashed Lipscomb across his eyes, and he fell screaming to the grass, the balm working like mace. I wiped the yellow balm onto my pant leg, its acrid odor stinging my own eyes. I pulled Purdin back off the field.

Rod, still faking a limp, stopped one yard inside the boundary, feet spread, facing the teams on the field like Danny had told him, making little scratch marks with his cleats so he could show the refs later where he was standing. Our reserves stood camouflaging the subterfuge, and Danny had already broken the huddle.

Cannonball, seeing the formation, threw a fit. "Call time. Ref, ref, time! Time!" Waving his stubby arms, he tried to get their attention until I picked up several parkas and smothered him under the weight of the green army slickers.

Neither coach saw what happened. I have great satisfaction neither ever had the real image of what Danny did. Cannonball struggled to get out from under the rain gear, Lipscomb was abandoned by everyone to grope blindly through the commotion of the moment, searching for water so he might wash his eyes and rid them of the searing artificial heat.

Danny rolled out left on the quick snap. He kept the ball tucked into his arm, like he planned some last-minute, superhuman effort to run over everyone.

Because Danny had sent no pass receivers into a recognizable pattern, the Hornedtoads came after him with all eleven men. When he neared the Hornedtoads' bench on the opposite side of the field from us, he planted his foot, whirled, and whipped the ball toward Rod, who ran down our sideline, alone.

Perilous moments while the ball floats free, away from human interference, subject only to the light and the wind, a flight requiring such precision and strength I wonder yet at the skill it took. Rod caught it around the twenty-yard line about five yards inbounds. From where Danny threw it, the ball traveled nearly seventy yards in the air, a feat unprecedented in the annals of high school football. Hibbs claimed he went out with a tape measure and verified it.

The Hornedtoads' coach was outraged, and the referees were flustered. They checked everything, where Rod had stood, how many men were on the field. The Tahlequah coach dogged their steps, shouting and cursing.

Finally, the referee threw a penalty flag, moved to the public address system, and made his announcement. The touchdown was legal. A technical penalty was called on the Tahlequah coach for language unbecoming a sportsman and for leaving his sideline. The score was nine to six. Time ran out. We rocked against one another, dancing.

Cannonball helped Coach flush his eyes adding a solution of boric acid to the water in the water bucket.

In the locker, the players peeled off their suits until they were almost naked, running around in their jockstraps, hugging one another, showing off their injuries. Cannonball made sure the linemen left their rubber pads taped on their arms until the room was cleared of all press.

The reporters interviewed the coaches. Lipscomb's eyes were red and teary, but no one thought anything of it in such an emotional moment. "When had they decided to use the play?" "Had they practiced it in secret?" "Had they ever seen it work before?" The writers were calling the coaches brilliant strategists, students of the great game of football. Then Danny stepped up to Hibbs. With the patch on his eye and the blood on his pants, right in front of the coaches, he pushed in and he told them.

"It was our water boy who called the play, he thought of it. The coaches didn't even know." Then he turned to the whole team and shouted it out loud. "Listen to me, all of you. Sonny won the game for us. He called the play. He's the reason we're state champs."

By the next day, the writers had searched the literature for origins of the play, long before Sammy Baugh, Red Grange, and the Four Horsemen, back to the early years of Eastern football before helmets were used, in the headlines of an Army victory over Navy, "Cadets Baffle Midshipmen with 'A Lonesome End.'"

So the headlines plastered the state. WATER BOY CALLS WINNING PLAY. WATER BOY USURPS COACHES. WATER BOY BECOMES GLORY BOY. No words were spared, every angle was explored. Even the headless horned toad was resurrected from the trash can and photographed and eulogized.

No one, including myself, gave the threat against Danny's life any more thought.

CHAPTER 31

The parade down Main Street became the biggest event in Cimarron's history. My father was afraid there would be no one to watch it because everyone planned to participate. But he needn't have worried; the whole countryside turned out. People from towns fifty and sixty miles away came to help us celebrate. Cars were parked along the highway past the sign that said, THIS IS DEVIL COUNTRY. SUPPORT THE CIMARRON DUSTDEVILS, and past the sign that said, JESUS DIED FOR OUR SINS, HE IS LORD IN CIMARRON. The whole town was ecstatic. LaFaye sold fifty handmade belts with the words CIMARRON IS OK on them. At the Elite Cafe, Eton ran out of calves' liver and substituted hogs' liver, charging the same price. The Blue Peecock turned away guests by the dozen.

I was at the center of the celebration, alongside Danny Boone, riding with the top down in Duffy Duncan's new convertible. The coaches' objections could not squelch the public support for me. They acquiesced to Danny's insistence that I ride in an honored seat.

As the car rolled leisurely down Main Street past Mrs. Farragut's clapboard house, Goggin's store, and the theater, there was a warmth that flooded me from the outpouring of love by the Dustdevils' supporters. Danny hung his arm on my shoulder. The thick gauze patch was still on his eye. Rod, sitting on my other side, cradled the football he had caught for the winning touchdown.

As we neared the Elite Cafe, a swarm of young boys buzzed around the car. They reached up to touch us, the frail ones afraid they'd never be football players, but maybe, if they were lucky, they could be a water boy. As we passed between the rows of false storefronts, the crowd lining the sidewalks cheered and whistled while we waved and smiled. There was one person missing from the jubilant celebration.

In the dawn hours before the parade, Killer had pulled into the Shamrock station and had told Lenval Jenkins, who filled up his gas tank, he was heading back to Colorado. But Verl Nelson said he saw Killer heading east on the road to Enid. "Drivin' like a bat outta hell," Verl said. "It would be some trip to Colorado headin' that way," he added, "clear around the whole damn world."

The sheriff said Killer had lost a lot of money on the game. He was avoiding some serious creditors.

That night, after the parade had dispersed near the river bridge, after the farmers had left to do chores, after the crowds had vanished back to their homes, their farms, their ranches, to rejoice in the glory of the event; after Danny had gone home with his parents, when the dust of the day's traffic lay thick upon the stones, Dovie Miller, wearing a pale yellow shift with nothing beneath it except white cotton panties, opened her back door to accept another lover.

I was almost ill with tension. She, so wise and gracious, stilled my apologies, dispelled my pretenses, permitted no awkwardness— she was forthright and natural. Her hands were directive like Elberta's had been. She touched me and I yielded. All questions flew out of my mind. I seemed to know naturally what I should do.

269

Everything faded that belonged to the past. Memories lost their brilliance. I suffered no guilt, and fear of reprisal seemed to prolong my joy.

I told her everything about me I had never told anyone, silly stuff; how, when I was small, I lay awake at night so I wouldn't wet the bed; how much it frightened me to see my father naked, that I always dreamed of snakes afterward; that I thought women were the same as men except they'd had their penises removed surgically; that I got erections when I saw female farm animals in heat. Dovie listened, smiling, laughing, but without judgment, without mocking, with cool, detached, erudite attention. Then we did it all again before it was time for me to leave.

I falter in the details, not because I was inexperienced, but because I was dazed by the feverishness of those hours, and am, when I think of it, instantly transported to that shadowy night, and I hear her ask as she moves softly against me, "What do you feel?" But I have no answer, I feel only blood, in my head, in my fingers, everywhere. I want to scream. And I grieve, because what I have done with this woman enables me to grieve much less. The emptiness is gone, and I am not accustomed to feeling full. There is no hope our loving will ever work out, and that pain somehow makes life sweeter. No yesterdays. No tomorrows. No heaven. No hell.

The day after the parade, Elberta came to our house for prayer. She and Mother had a list of people who had not yet been baptized in the holy spirit. They finished praying for each person, and Elberta left first. When my mother left later, she was wearing a pair of white summer sandals, a light purse and gloves, and nothing else. She rang Mrs. Shuler's fancy doorbell.

"Emma, don't you think you should be wearing a dress? It's quite brisk this morning."

" 'Girt your loins with truth, having on the breastplate of righteousness and the shield of faith,' " my mother quoted.

"I'll get us some tea, then," Mrs. Shuler replied, heading to the kitchen where she called my father. We took her to Fort Supply. The doctors recommended shock treatments, over a period estimated to be several months. My father drove down to see her twice a week. He did not ask me to go with him, so I stayed home, read, and went to see Dovie when Danny was not in town.

Based on Sheriff Ordway's report, my father had written a short article about the threatening note Kirk had found stuck in Arved's calf.

STATE POLICE PROTECT ALL-AMERICAN QB

State Police from several barracks responded to an emergency appeal from Cimarron sheriff Orville Ordway and attended Friday night's championship game at Owen Field in Norman after a note was found that threatened the life of all-American quarterback Danny Boone.

The note, pinned to a dead calf, was found by Kirk Schroeder, who works at the Boone farm. A butcher knife had been stuck in the calf's side to hold the note in place. The calf, a prized registered Hereford, had been shot at close range by a high-powered rifle.

No additional information has been released by the sheriff's office.

Two weeks after the parade, the doctors in Oklahoma City took the patch off Danny's eye. They found no permanent damage.

The optometrist in Liberal fitted Coach with glasses. The lenses were almost as thick as Cannonball's. Coach blamed me, believing the analgesic balm had caused his loss of eyesight. I stayed out of the way of both coaches.

My mother came home from the hospital for Christmas, but sat in an old corduroy robe, looking out the window. Even simple tasks were too difficult for her. My father took her back to the hospital before New Year's Eve.

Because Killer was gone, Dovie had invited Danny for dinner to celebrate the new year. Their relationship was now well known. After he went home, I slipped over to her house and stayed with her the rest of the night. I didn't even bother to go home before my father awoke.

Late January, Killer came out of hiding. He'd paid his debts, the rumor murmured. Dovie took him back in as if it were the most natural thing in the world. He took a job at the gas-pumping plant southeast of town, was settling down, he said. Some said it wouldn't last, he'd be off again, soon. Others said he'd had a good scare, and that's what it takes, sometimes.

Mother returned home again in early February. She seemed to be herself, except she did not volunteer for the evangelistic teams at church. She had lost all fervor. Elberta came to see her every Monday, and Mrs. Shuler invited her over for tea on Thursday afternoons.

By mid-February, Dovie suffered severe bouts of morning sickness. Since Killer was regularly employed, she quit her job, stayed home, sewing and cleaning, and seldom emerged from her cottage before noon. Even then she appeared wan and drained of her natural spunk.

Every other week Killer went on the graveyard shift. On some of those nights, I sneaked out my bedroom window to see Dovie. Contrary to the warnings of our minister about the dire unhappiness caused by adultery, I found myself possessed by a furious elation. I cheated, I deceived, but life did not capsize. I was never so content as when I lay with Dovie on her bed, holding her, rubbing her stomach. Sometimes we talked about whose baby it might be. Dovie really couldn't say. It could belong to any one of us.

A week before letters of intent could be signed, the universities, based on Danny's favorable medical reports, loaded and sent out their big guns. Representatives, coaches, even presidents of universities, came to speak with Danny and his parents. Along with them came the evangelist Joe Don Jones. The faith healer sat with us in the living room of the Boone farmhouse while Thelma served Sunday dinner. She passed the fried chicken on a blue platter that had belonged to Arved's mother and had been found and saved after the wagon capsized in the Cimarron River. Joe Don ate enough to fill his paunch, wiped his hands, then settled back with a glass of iced tea to talk God's business.

"I had a dream," he said, his voice deep and vibrant. "The Lord spoke to me, and I saw a great wide river, and a new day dawning to the east. There were great expanses of ripe grain fields, more vast and bending with the weight of the grain than any I'd ever seen. The need for laborers in the harvest was so evident, I thought I must go. But when I tried to cross the river, I couldn't. Each time I took a step, the river receded. Then an old man spoke to me. 'Not you, not you. You must send Elisha.' 'But who are you?' I asked him. 'I am Elijah, the Communist fighter,' he said.

"After days of prayer, I believe we're the people in the dream, Danny. I'm the old man, Elijah, and you're Elisha. Where is the need for evangelism greatest today? In the East, across the Mississippi, where the people are. This has been heavy on my heart for years. There's only two million people in the State of Oklahoma, a state six hundred and forty miles long. There are places in the East where there's more people in an area smaller than Cimarron than there are in this whole state. And none of them have the living Jesus and his Holy Ghost alive in their hearts. They're all Catholics and Jews and atheists, along with a few liberal Protestants. They're all lost. Hopelessly, eternally lost; every one of them doomed to hell unless they're washed in the blood.

"Army, Danny, this dream says that God wants you to go to West Point, and from there to open up the great white fields unto the harvest, to serve your country against Godless Communism, and to save souls in the great mission fields of the East." He paused, raised his hands to heaven, then bowed his head in prayer.

The merchants were not surprised when Danny chose Army. "That first day Clay came into the shop, I knew the other schools didn't have a chance," Dale said, from the center stool at the Elite Cafe. "He just had a way about him."

"When he took my apartment for the price I quoted, I knew he was determined to get his man," LaFaye added.

When they noticed I was listening, they gouged me in the ribs. "So what about you, Sonny, what are your plans? Gonna stick around and take over for your dad?" I had not yet told anyone of my secret acceptance to the Academy. Had I told them, they, of course, would have claimed they were not surprised.

Graduation, a time of celebration and regret. I had some of both. Lately, I had been drinking imported beer, imported from across the Kansas state line because Oklahoma, then, was a totally dry state. I was slightly under the influence of Pabst Blue Ribbon while I delivered the valedictorian's address; self-honesty and commitment to humanity, my themes. Afterward, my mother congratulated me and hugged me. "Your breath smells funny," she commented.

Voted most likely to succeed from our class, of course, Danny Boone. I was denoted as the class philosopher. I had until July 1 to accept or turn down my invitation to leave town with Danny. So I, the class sage, argued both roles, Socrates in prison, and Crito, his friend. My friend had made the arrangements for my escape, as had the friends of Socrates, but I wrestled with the same question. Was it *right* to escape?

Should I, like the sage who drank the hemlock, remain in my confinement? Are the laws of Cimarron more unjust than the laws of Athens? Can I abandon a mother gone mad, a father who may soon need my help, a son or a daughter whom I may have sired, a woman who will always be a part of my soul, a town that has shaped and molded me to be the man, the person, I am?

CHAPTER 32

T he middle of June, I went to the Boone farm to help as I had the past three summers. The first night, I broke what I thought was a surprising piece of news to Danny. "I'm going to West Point with you. Clay Moray helped me apply and I was accepted. I told my parents yesterday."

"Reverend Moray told me about it a long time ago. Everything works together for good, it is God's will." We made plans. I'd leave with him a few days early, because he would be going to football practice.

Harvest time came and passed. Kirk talked to Danny and me all through the harvest season, about our careers, offering money when emergencies arose, and he had a plan to drive back east and attend one of Army's games during the coming season. The plans of men were made.

But the God who speaks through the softness of dreams also speaks through the unharnessed power of nature. That Wednesday, the second week of July, the thermometer streaked into the nineties by midmorning. Danny, Kirk, and I were all on tractors plowing the stubble field south of the highway. It was ninety-eight degrees, and still wasn't even time to break for the noon meal. I watched a large dustdevil swirl tumbleweeds across a field a mile or so away. It drifted across the flat land until it gradually disintegrated. White clouds with tinges of dark gray beneath them had arisen in the southwest. Thunder mumbled in the distance. I watched the clouds. The heat was so heavy I shivered as if chilled.

I thought of the storm cellar Thelma had often taken us into when Danny and I were children, and wished we were closer to the house, the smell of soil and roots, water dogs dragging into dark, wet corners when Thelma lit the kerosene lamp.

I smelled rain on the wind, the clouds were above us, but the heat remained stifling. Lightning, parallel to the horizon, illuminated the dark underbelly of the cloud. It grew dark with incredible, swift oppressiveness. The storm burst around us. At first, there was just swirling air, more wind than rain, and then a few marble-sized hailstones, then intermittent torrents of rain. I pulled the hydraulic lever, lifting my disks, shifting into road gear for the race to the house. To the south of us, sunlight streamed through holes in the clouds making silvery streaks in the rain and hail.

The flash was bright yellow, then blue, the clap of thunder like a thousand planks dropping on a concrete floor, then the prickling coppery smell of ozone I remembered from the time lightning struck our crab apple tree. I braked the tractor.

Danny had stopped his tractor too. He was holding his hat on with his hand. Kirk's tractor veered, its front wheels locked in a sharp turn, the forty-horsepower machine circling. Nothing else seemed to be wrong. I couldn't figure out why Kirk had chosen to turn without lifting the disks out of the ground. Kirk sat straight on the high tractor seat as if he had not even seen the lightning or heard the strident clap of thunder. There was only the tractor circling, a machine gone mad, out of control.

Then Kirk leaned slightly, his hands slipped from the steering wheel, and as he toppled he hit the lugged tractor tire, and it rolled him forward and over. The disks covered him with dirt, and the tractor, as if it were a remote-controlled toy, circled and plowed him in again before Danny and I got there.

More horrible to me than the jagged disk wounds and the dirty blood was the burned spot on the back of Kirk's head where his hair had been sizzled away, and his skin was black and blistered. It looked as if a sharpshooter had looked down the barrel of a gun and shot him with a carefully aimed lightning bolt.

Danny held him while I drove the tractor down the long hill toward the house. The rain had not yet reached the valley. I turned into the driveway at full speed, the tractor bouncing dangerously as it crossed the ruts. Arved heard us and came running out of the shop, groping his way through his sightless haze.

"What's wrong?" he called.

"Lightning struck him," I shouted.

Jumping to a conclusion that was his worst fear, he screamed, "Oh, my God, Danny, Danny, my son," clutched his chest and fell down. He woke up in the hospital still thinking Danny had died. Thelma told him it was Kirk.

"Better rest for a few days, that's what you need," Doc said to him. "You're not a spring chicken anymore. It was probably a mild heart attack. You were ready for it, wasn't no one's fault. I'm sorry about Kirk's death," Doc added. "He was a good man. I know you'll miss him."

James R. James, the former banker, conducted Kirk's funeral in the same Pentecostal church where Jimmy Lee Watson's service had been held. It was a eucharistic service of joy, not grief, he said. James called Danny forward to help wash feet, an act Kirk himself had often performed. While Danny went person to person with a small basin and clean towels, dabbing and rubbing the callused feet of the faithful Pentecostals, James read from the Gospel according to John, how Christ washed the feet of his own disciples. The pitch of James's voice rose until his words were unintelligible, yet melodious and seductive, and then others also began speaking in unknown tongues. Again, I felt soaring belief, a rush of unexplained hope reminiscent of the time before Joe Don took Danny away, when my mother was baptized in the Holy Ghost.

It was then Arved walked out, his arms extended, groping, searching. His face was pale. Danny was busy washing the feet of a woman I did not know, so I followed Arved, caught him by the elbow when he neared the doors, helped him through, and sat with him on the small pine bench in the vestibule. The building had not always been a Pentecostal church building. The bench had once provided a place for taking off boots when it had been a schoolhouse. I wondered how Arved could possibly get along on the farm now that Kirk was dead and Danny was leaving.

On a shelf above the coat rack lurked an old set of *The Book of Knowledge*; unopened, I'm sure, in years. I stood up and took down one dusty volume. I supposed it might contain some answers to the questions I hardly knew how to ask. I opened the book to a section of medieval fairy tales, pictures of deep, dense forests where wolves hunted their prey and knights rescued damsels in distress.

The front door of the old schoolhouse was open, and I glanced out, back and forth at the book and at the prairie. I breathed in the air, the soft wind and warm smells, the mustiness of the old book. The prairie receded behind a fence made of cedar posts dipped in creosote and strung with strands of barbed wire. Beyond the fence, the frail colors intensified the flatness of the land, the delicate purple of the sagebrush, the pale green spines of soapweed with their white flowers, and beneath it all the lackluster yellow of the buffalo grass.

"What does it look like out there?" Arved asked. "I've almost forgotten." His voice was soft and hollow and tired.

For a moment I saw the fairy tale picture, of forests, and streams, moss-covered rocks and ferns draping over hollow logs where bees stored honey. Then once again as I looked out the open door I saw the absolute loneliness that drove the weak insane, the vast anonymity

278

so many of our ancestors sought when they entered the madness of no-man's-land. I gave Arved the picture he had seen before the explosion blinded him.

"The space never ends. The land sweeps into the sky as if the two were one, as if you could run forever and never get anywhere. And finally, if you found your way, you'd be so lost, you'd never get back."

He squinted so that deep crow's-feet widened into his cheeks. He mumbled something.

"What did you say?" I asked.

He rocked back and forth, his eyes shimmering in their attempt to see. He spoke toward the prairie. " 'For the Lord of hosts hath purposed, and who shall disannul it? And his hand is stretched out, and who shall turn it back?' "

It was the Scripture from the embroidered picture hanging in the Boone kitchen. He repeated it over and over, and reached out, groping down my arm until he had hold of my hand.

I had known it for a long time, and now it came to him, too. His losses and mine were one, those that had been and those that were yet to be. The prairie had failed, we were not insane; but it had brought us to our knees, left us both with alternatives that differed only in their degrees of futility.

The distracting hum that had buzzed in my head for a long time now became the clanking of gears not meshing. The random pieces of life floating in my mind that formerly had appeared to be parts of a beautiful mosaic waiting to be assembled as soon as I became wise enough, now bore no relationship to one another except in their own uniqueness. So far as I could see, there was no plan, and no God who was concerned about me. I was outside the eternal event.

A week before Danny and I were scheduled to leave, Arved had another heart attack. The pressure of adjusting to Kirk's death and

Danny's departure was more than he could stand. "No doubt he'll recover," Doc McGrath told Thelma and Danny. "It's not that bad, but the man will need rest, and he'll never be able to work like he used to. This was brought on by his stubbornness from before, and he better follow my orders this time. And to make sure he does, I'm keeping him in here for a few days."

The day after Arved was hospitalized, Dovie gave birth to a son. That same evening, I went to the hospital with Danny to see Arved.

We discussed our departure for West Point. Arved explained how he thought things might work after Danny was gone. He had already hired two of the Dumas boys I had baptized. Danny had started to train them in many of the farm routines. Arved reached out toward Danny, who sat near him, and tears came out of his heavy eyelids. It was plain to me he and Thelma were grieving for the loss of their son. Then the door opened and Doc came in.

"Well, you heroes," he said good-naturedly, "visiting hours are over. I want you both to get out of here and let this man get some rest." We stood up. "But there's a young woman down the hall who said she'd like to see you guys. It's after-hours, but a few minutes won't hurt no one."

Dovie answered our knock, softly, "Come in. Well, hello," she said to both of us. It was the first time I had been with Danny and Dovie at the same time since we had accompanied Danny on his ambulance ride during the last game.

"Please come in and see my boy." The baby lay beside her, nestled with its head near her breast. He was small, red, moving his fists in tight, jerky moves.

"Doc says he's very alert for being just a few hours old." We watched him for a while, even as Dovie watched us, then she glanced at the baby, then back and forth.

"Who do you think he looks like?" she asked us. Even through the exhaustion, her smile was sly, impish.

"Gee, babies just look like babies," I said, looking down. "They don't look like anybody for a long time."

"Doc says this is no ordinary baby," she finally said. "I'll show you something." She picked up the baby, carefully supporting his head, and placed him on top of the bedsheets, then leaned slightly forward, turning on her side. Filmy blue milk veins ran through her distended breasts. She unpinned the baby's diaper. The pouch for the baby's testicles was large. I had noticed this about other newborns, but I saw nothing else unusual until she gently squeezed the pinkish glans of his baby penis between her thumb and finger. The baby had no foreskin.

"Doc says it's only the second time he's ever seen this," Dovie said, her voice quiet, reverent. "I think God has given me a very unusual blessing." There was a look on her face, perhaps fear, or more like awe; a look like the one she had the day Mother had warned her about hell, that point where self-reliance falters, where fear and trembling begin, where the need for a faith in some power outside the self overwhelms one's sense of self-control.

Danny stepped to her, buried his face in her breasts and she held him close. She got out of bed, and I went to her. The three of us put our arms around one another. With no words spoken, we knelt down. When Dovie and I stood up, Danny stayed on his knees. "Thy will be done, amen," he said.

It was a startling moment, the force of subliminal awareness pushing out the boundaries of my mind. In that moment, I saw things through Danny's eyes. Something was terribly wrong, it had to be made right. This was a special baby. He could not allow the baby to grow up with Killer as his father. We were enmeshed in a tragedy that would inevitably unfold.

When Danny stood up, there rose in him the same power and presence we had seen on the football field. His face was serene. He stood straight, yet perfectly relaxed. His was a special moral calling, a responsibility, a genius.

"Brice wants to name the baby Brice Junior. I told him his name was fine but not for a first name. Do you have any ideas for a name?" Dovie asked us. I adored her terrifying honesty. I was surprised how much I could love without judging.

Danny looked at me. I waited for him to answer. "I like Sonny," Danny said. He smiled as he put his arm across my shoulders.

"I like it, too," she answered. "I'll name him Sonny Brice."

CHAPTER 33

The Chamber of Commerce planned a celebration to say goodbye to those who were leaving town and to kick off the new football season. The day before the celebration, Danny found another dead calf, a prized Hereford, son of Zato Heir, the Turner Ranch's million-dollar sire. At great effort and expense, Arved had taken one of his best cows to be boarded at the Turner Ranch and bred to the famous herd bull, hoping to produce a new, valuable herd bull of his own. He was grief-stricken, and mystified, over his loss.

The calf, like the other one, had been shot at close range with a high-powered rifle. Then, the killer had sliced off the little bull's testicles and crammed them in its mouth. The sheriff could find no clues, not even the bullet that had entered one side of the calf's head and blown out the other.

Danny picked me up on his way to the celebration. "Do you think Killer did it?" I asked him. "Cutting off the balls must mean something."

"Yes, he did it," Danny answered. He seemed too calm.

"You must be right, but it's little more than a guess. I don't know how we can prove it. Even the sheriff couldn't find anything. He suspects Killer just like you do."

"I'm praying," Danny replied.

The music was live, blue grass and country, no rock and roll, the officials insisted. They were taking no chances. Billy Bob and the Bobcats, the musicians called themselves. Billy Bob, bearded and barrel-chested, played lead and sang, his voice like gravel swirling in a tin can as he warmed up. The Bobcats were skinny, more like jackrabbits than bobcats. Tight buckskin pants hugged their weedy hips. They sang the background, mouthing softly into the microphones, strumming their instruments, boots jiggling on a wooden bench.

It was the last opportunity to let off steam before football season forced everyone into a more disciplined life, and the last chance for everyone to say goodbye to Danny and me. There were some other kids going to college, but to places close, Alva, Goodwell, Weatherford. They'd all be back for home game weekends. For them, and the others around town, going to West Point was no different from dropping off the end of the earth.

This year, there'd be no small circle off by themselves, with trouble brewing. Everyone would be at Lovers' Roost, keeping a watchful eye out. The Chamber of Commerce saw to it.

When Danny and I arrived, Coach called, "Hey Danny, come here." His heavy glasses reflected the last of the natural light. Danny walked over. "Help me string these lights, will you? How's your father?"

Danny had not talked to Coach Lipscomb since the day of the parade. Their relationship had been as close as father and son for over three years. Now Danny must be replaced with a new boy if hopes for another championship were to be kept alive.

"Have you been working out?" Coach asked Danny.

"Yes, doing the regular things."

"When do you leave?"

"Tomorrow, around noon."

I walked away. I popped my first beer from the secret cooler Rod, R.D., and I had stashed earlier in the afternoon. I sucked air through it to speed up its effect.

The last sunlight filtered through thin clouds. The sun had changed from orange to red, and the sagebrush and sand plum thickets were turning purple as the sun set behind the dunes and darkness crept in. In a couple of hours, there'd be a full moon in the east, and there were clouds on the southwest horizon. Didn't matter to me, it could rain all it wanted.

The cottonwoods, those that had not yet been swallowed by the dunes, were decked out in bright, waxy leaves. I wondered if they had feelings, if they were aware of their fate, aware they couldn't run away from the smothering sand that crept up their trunks. I finished another beer.

The officials of the REA had rigged an electrical hookup from its nearest pole. "We here at the Rural Electric Association like to help our communities, especially the state champions," the REA man had said. It was almost dark when the lights came on and the music began. By that time, I had tossed away my fourth beer bottle.

Everyone wanted to dance with Danny. They all wanted to bask in his aura, to touch the football player who had brought such glory and fame to Cimarron. Earldeana hugged him, her auburn hair sparkling in the artificial light.

A pickup truck with three cab lights pulled into the parking area. As Killer got out of his truck and the interior light came on, I could see the gun rack above the seat, and the brown stock of a high-powered rifle. Killer finished the beer he had been drinking, and tossed away the can before he joined the group.

I felt distant, detached, anesthetized. I remembered events without fear or remorse; I seemed to have developed an unexpected clarity of vision. I thought of Earldeana, how I had dropped my book and she had opened her legs for me. I thought of last year when Cannonball drove Killer out to the intersection party. And, I remembered, this year things were different for Killer. For one thing, he was circumcised. He'd never piss in his whole life without remembering what happened that night. And he was married, to Dovie. And I was his wife's secret lover. Now, there's a difference to ponder. I had said my goodbyes to Dovie three nights ago. I presumed it would be a long time before I saw her again, maybe never. She was losing two lovers with one exodus. Would she replace us? Or had she already? Were there even, perhaps, other lovers I didn't know about? Anything was possible.

Everything suddenly felt different. All that had happened was now immutable, everything that was yet to occur seemed unpredictable. The sameness, the safety, knowing what to expect and where you stand, all the good qualities of small-town life in America seemed to have been wiped out. Life was precarious and dangerous, its events random and unreliable.

Sheriff Ordway greeted Killer when he reached the celebration area. "Hey, big man, haven't seen you around my place for a while." Killer grunted, and Ordway laughed. "How's that little drinkin' buddy of yours? I wanna congratulate you, and wish you the very best despite our little run-ins of the past." He pumped Killer's hand.

Killer approached Coach Lipscomb and tried to engage him in a conversation about the team's chances for this season. Coach ignored him. He was talking with Dolleta Dirks, a former cheerleader, now college graduate who had returned to Cimarron recently and had opened a new dress shop, the only competition Mrs. Shuler had. My father had helped Dolleta work out some ads. People said they were too sexy, but her business had been brisk. Old maid, though still very pretty at twenty-five, people said about Dolleta.

The sheriff, who had heard Killer ask Coach about the football season, slapped Killer on the shoulder. "Not ever going to be a team like we had last year," Sheriff said. "A team like that comes only once a lifetime." He slapped Killer's big shoulder again.

"Come on, Sheriff, there ain't nothin' magic about it. It's just gettin' the bodies out there, then it's coachin'."

"Yeah, we'll see, we'll see what a team can do without an all-American quarterback. You just don't know all that boy's done," and the sheriff shuffled off, laughing at his accidental joke. Killer scowled, found someone to dance with, then mixed in with the dancers.

Sure enough, there was a storm coming up. From the west, still a long distance away, I heard the low mutter of thunder. Billy Bob and the Bobcats began another round of music. Those couples in the shadows returned to the light, girls patting down hair that had been rumpled by wild hands. I tossed away another bottle. My empty hand seemed detached, removed from my larger emptiness. I walked outside the circle of light, and opened another beer. A hand reached out of the darkness and took mine. Her hand, strong and insistent, pulled me down on top of her. Earldeana, secretly admired by many, forgiven by a few.

"William," she began, using my formal name with a slight mocking tone, "you've gotten very handsome. Why have you never asked me out?" Her warm breath flowed into my ear. She stroked the back of my head, and I could not find the answer to her question. She'd been drinking, too.

"I wanted to. I'm not sure why I didn't," I finally answered. A text from the Bible I had once memorized echoed through the draws of my mind. "When Judah saw her, he thought her to be a harlot. 'Let me come in unto thee.' And she said, 'What wilt thou give me?' 'I will send thee a kid from the flock.' 'Wilt thou give me a pledge, till thou send it?' 'What pledge shall I give thee?' And she said, 'Thy signet, and thy bracelets, and thy staff that is in thine hand.' And he gave it to her, and came in unto her."

"Would you like to have my Dustdevil letter jacket?" I asked Earldeana. "I can't wear it at the Academy."

She puckered up her face.

"You can't tell what the emblem is unless you get close," I assured her. "The bucket isn't well designed, it could be almost anything."

"Sonny, that's so sweet." She began nibbling my shirt, pinching my nipples with her teeth. "Now unbutton me," she said.

I stroked her silky skin, inhaled her and all the cooling smells of night around us, her perfume mingling with nature's own blossoms, and the danger around us; not just the danger of discovery, another danger not recognizable with normal cognition, but no less real. All my senses were honed, razor-edged as a knife sharpened on the finest whetstone, listening as if I were a thief for any noise I might hear. I heard only her noises, sharp little bursting points of utterance, so unlike the languorous, lazy way of Dovie whose pleasure built slowly and ended the same way.

Afterward, we lay together, she with her head on my chest and hand on my groin, her dampness and mine mingled and cooled. The storm came closer and the lightning illuminated us in glimmering purple light. I was still alert, and I heard something moving through the grass not far from where we lay.

I lifted my upper body, and Earldeana's head slid off my chest onto the leafy ground. My head spun as I looked down at her and she receded into the black earth.

I crouched, straining to see. There was someone moving a short distance away from us. A flash of lightning. I saw Danny about thirty yards away bent over at the waist, skulking toward the dune he had once raced up with Killer, Coach egging them both on.

"Go back," I whispered to Earldeana. "I'll meet you where the others are."

I crawled on all fours through the grass and sagebrush, moving fast to catch up with Danny. I waited for the lightning to help me see, and then, when it flashed, I saw both of them. Danny was stalking Killer about twenty feet behind him.

There was an opening in the brush to my right and I took it. The wind shifted as the front came through. Killer had stopped at the base of Pork Chop Hill. I got so close I could hear him humming the Bobcats' rendition of "You Ain't Nothin' but a Hound Dog," and hear the piss hitting the sand. Danny waited for him to finish. Then he spoke.

"It's time to settle this," Danny said, in a soft, controlled tone.

Killer plunged his hand into his boot, he must have had one of the holsters LaFaye made, and pulled out his knife. The wind was gusty, and I was so near the dune it whipped sand up into my face.

"With knives," Danny said. He reached in his pocket. Danny's knife, the one he had used to circumcise Killer, had a good long blade, but it was still shorter than Killer's knife. I could not see Danny's face, but I imagined the faintest lines of a smile I had seen many times.

In the moonlight, he lifted up his free hand, pointing toward the sky. He prayed. "Oh Lord, stretch out thine hand and smite down thine enemy. Withhold not thy mercy from the faithful." A shiver traveled through me. His voice had the hollow, vibrant ring of an evangelist. "Joe Don will raise the dead," Danny had once said. Now he prayed for the power to kill someone.

Killer began to back up. It was one thing to pray for victory in war, or even victory on a football field. We all had heard those prayers prayed. But I had never heard anyone pray out loud for God's intervention in a private fight between two people who had a grudge to settle. There was something so audacious, so much like Samson who prayed, "Lord, Jehovah, I beg you, give me strength," then, thrusting with all his might, pulled the whole building down on the Philistine rulers. The night felt so supernatural, it was easy to believe it might work, that God was accessible to those who had real faith, that the sky with the storm coming up might open at any moment and rain down fire and brimstone if Danny asked for it. As he backed up, Killer seemed to be totally spooked.

Danny attacked while he had the advantage. He pushed Killer back against a cottonwood tree. They both had hold of the other's wrist. For a while there was a stalemate. But slowly Danny's knife blade began to inch toward Killer's neck. This was a fight to the finish, it would end with one of them dead.

In that instant I saw all the events of Danny's life—his gift for uniting us in spontaneous applause; I saw him stretching out his hand over the fields as he described the wheat crop to Arved. I knew my efforts to protect him in the past had been foolish. He needed no protection. He loved the risk, the danger; he loved playing a game under threat of death. But this was insane. I made up my mind quickly. I had grown in size and weight significantly since I had tried to break up the fight between Danny and Killer on Main Street.

When I drove my body into Danny's shoulder, he fell sideways. "It's me," I shouted. "Stop this, it's crazy."

For a moment, I was on top of him. He rolled me off, and sprang to his feet, poised to fight. I rose to stand beside him. A feeling of intense excitement began rising in me. Killer might attack us both. I could feel the danger, the possibility of dying.

We waited. And waited. When nothing happened I began to relax, and an odd disappointment began creeping in. Killer had fled. Now I felt cheated. But I had done the right thing. Everyone was alive.

Danny still waited, alert, turning, taking no chances. Lightning struck close. The flash blinded us. Thunder was instantaneous. Something flew by us, a crashing noise, breaking of small branches in a bush to my right, behind Danny. He whirled, coiled, knife lowered, blade in front of him. I sensed, more than heard, Killer come up behind him.

I had no time to warn Danny. With movements quick and powerful, the way he had been taught to play football, Killer grabbed Danny, pulled him back against his chest, and slashed across Danny's neck. Then he pulled both arms away from his body, a gesture a football player might use when the referee has blown a whistle, pointing toward an illegal hold. "Me, ref? I did nothing wrong." The knife was still in Killer's hand.

Danny slumped. For a moment I stood beside Killer, stupefied. We both looked down at Danny in the moonlight. It took me a few seconds to know what I certainly had fathomed instantly, that Killer, in one artless sweep of his fist, had cut Danny's throat, that it was irreversible, that Danny was dying.

In the silence between thunder there was the rustling of the cottonwood leaves, and gurgling as Danny's life force thrust his last breath through the hole in his throat. The unbelievable horror of the scene had turned me to stone. I didn't want to see his disappointment, in me, and in God.

"You saw it," Killer said, "it was a fair fight." He dropped his knife, as if to convince me of his innocence, but his hand was bloody with Danny's blood. I staggered backward and fell. My head caromed off the bark of a small cottonwood seedling. I was dazed, shaking my head to recover.

Killer came closer. He was bending over near where I sprawled, held awkwardly off the ground by the spindly branches of the sagebrush. As I reached down for support, my hand touched something smooth, a rock, the rock Killer must have thrown into the bush distracting Danny's attention. I ran my hand over it, a rock not quite the size of a football, and more round with one flat side. I lifted it an inch or two, hefting it, calculating the strength it would take.

"Sonny, you'll tell them the truth, won't you? It was him or me, it was self-defense." Brice's voice had a pleading quality, a vulnerability I had never heard before. "Jesus, I have a son," he said, "I can't go to jail."

I began to see Killer's point of view. Perhaps I had misjudged him, he was not as bad as I thought. Danny had attacked him. What else could he do? But Danny was dead. Danny had intended to kill him, that much I knew. I remembered the hospital when we saw Dovie and the baby. I knew then Danny could not leave a baby he thought was his son to be raised by Brice Miller. Danny felt it was right to kill him, and he would have finished it except I interfered. I had altered the natural course of events. Danny was dead.

I started to get up. Killer bent down closer, still pleading with me. My hand was on the rock. I knew what I had to do. It was not a voice that told me, but an internal swelling, a welling up of conviction I was right. There was one thing to do that might make my life livable now that Danny was dead. Without warning, I slung the rock up toward the vague shape of Killer's head.

There was a sharp crack, like a bat striking a baseball. It was a funny feeling. My hand was empty, the rock was missing, but I knew it hadn't fallen to the ground. It had crushed his skull and now existed as part of him. Killer crumpled and fell.

Around me, there fell the deep silence that exists the moment before the full fury of a storm hits, not even the rustling of the cottonwood leaves.

Two young men, dead. I had killed them both. One with volition, the other without. I float in the air above them.

I can see a great distance. To the east, the moon is shining like cold brass, the terrain is serene, almost eerie. I can see the foothills as they rise gently beside the river, and the dark patches where the cottonwoods dot the landscape, and in the flashes of lightning the entire panorama is streaked with long, strobing shadows cast by the dunes and the trees. And to the west the pale dune recedes from my feet into a labyrinth of darkness.

I know what Danny had planned to do. The evening is perfect for it, dim light, wind to muffle the noise, a storm coming that will move the dune. I swoop down, grab Killer by his boots, and drag him to the base of the great dune.

The storm breaks at last. I look at the sky. The clouds above me boil both dark and light, betraying the winds that had been held in abeyance. Now they vent with all their fury, whipping up sand like shrapnel. It is finished.

I clenched my fists and dropped slowly to my knees near Killer's body, which sprawled arms spread out at the foot of the dune. The high octaves of wind howled through the cottonwood trees. I shouted with all my strength, "Bury him, God damn it, bury him!"

I wept bitterly. When I started to stand up, my legs were already buried in the voracious sand. My prayer was being answered.

I walked back to where Danny lay. I tell this all so calmly because even then I felt as if there were nothing about what happened that I had not understood and prepared for a long time ago. I felt so tired, so absurdly exhausted. I had been right from the very beginning, from the day Jimmy Lee Watson died. Death was bitter. Silent and bitter. I had been enthralled by it, in love with it for a long time.

I lay down beside Danny as I had the night when he dreamed his father was trying to kill him, as if this were our plan to sleep out under the stars tonight. Sleep came almost instantly and I dreamed.

When I awoke, there was a cold drizzle falling, my clothes were drenched. A mist lifted off the warmth of my body in thin wisps. Morning was about to break. I reached over to touch Danny. He was cold. Voices filtered through the light rain, sensuous, slithery. They were searching for us, the sheriff, my father, and the citizens of Cimarron.

The next few days were like a continuous bad dream. I established with the authorities exactly how Killer had killed Danny. I did not omit the part about how I had broken up the fight, and thereby turned it to Killer's advantage. I told them Killer had disappeared in the great dune. They assumed I meant he had run away, and they put out an all-points bulletin and staked out Killer's truck where it was parked in the Lovers' Roost parking area. No one suspected the water boy of murder.

Danny's funeral was held three days after his death. People packed the church, and those who could not get inside stood outside waiting for a glimpse of his casket, and of us who had been with him during those miraculous days. Something had passed, a time, an event. For most people nothing much wonderful happens in their whole lives, but it had for those of us in Cimarron, and the likes of it may never be seen again. The hundreds who came that day to the First Baptist Church of Cimarron came to mourn the passing of the time.

His teammates were the pallbearers. Danny was buried not far from Jimmy Lee Watson's grave, where I first became his friend. The blistering prairie lay beyond a fence that protects the graveyard from grazing cattle. The wind carried away the sorrowful hymns, the words rising to the heavens on shimmering heat waves.

Arved had been discharged from the hospital. He and Thelma endured the funeral stoically, as if they had already grieved when they knew we were leaving for West Point.

Dovie did not attend the funeral. The sheriff had advised against it. He had reason to believe there might be fanatical responses directed against Dovie and the baby people thought was Killer's son. Ordway persuaded the state police to post a watch on Dovie's house in case anyone got funny ideas about how to handle their grief over Danny's death, and in case Killer returned, although no one thought he would.

I did not try to pray again. No matter how much I paraded in misery's somber dress, or screamed as if this were some savage festival, or laughed as if God had merely played a clever practical joke, I always returned to the same place, my thrill at the moment of danger, my fear that part of me wanted Danny to die, my awe of the self-affirmation that erupted in that one violent act when I killed Brice Miller. I had wanted to kill a man for a long time.

Oddly, these soundless, candid admissions kept me from going insane. There was no space now for those dream-remembered times; it was time to finish my business, get out of town, find out what kind of man I'm going to be.

CHAPTER 34

I left home a week after Danny died. My father went to his office early, set up his presses, then returned to the house and helped me load my luggage. Mother was subdued, almost formal, when we said goodbye.

Dad wheeled the station wagon onto Main Street, heading toward the river. We drove past the churches, between the false fronts that lined both sides of the street, past the Western Auto, and then the Blue Peecock, the precise route I had traveled the day of the parade after we won the championship.

P.O. was out in front of the drugstore sweeping his sidewalk. He waved when we drove by. Goggin's window was bare and unwashed, a CLOSED sign dangling from a hook. Junior didn't keep things up like Old Man Goggin had. The light from LaFaye's sewing machine flickered through his rain-streaked window. It was an early start by LaFaye's standards. Dale already had a customer at the barber shop, but he must have left his door locked because Arnie was pushing on it, and Dale was acting as if he didn't know he was there. As we passed, Arnie jerked off his Yankee hat and flung it on the sidewalk.

"One of these days Dale's gonna tease Arnie so much he'll go berserk and kill someone," my father said. "You shouldn't mess around with a person who's not so mentally stable to begin with."

The car tires thudded over the concrete slabs as we came to the river. We crossed the bridge. The station wagon swayed when the wind hit us. We began the swing up from the river bottom. There were the cottonwoods, the splashes of yellow where the dunes bubbled out of the bluestem and the brush. Near the great walking dune, sand had crept two feet up the trunk of another cottonwood tree. In the small parking area, Killer's pickup was stark against the height of the yellow dunes. The sheriff no longer had a stakeout placed to watch it. In a day or two, he'd cross-wire the truck to get it started and drive it down to Dovie. The land seemed so fresh from the ample rain we'd had, the sand hills and the prairie awash in clean beiges and purples and pale greens.

With my eyes I measured the width of the dune's base and tried to calculate how long it might take to walk over Brice Miller's body. At least ten years, probably twenty, I thought. And even when the dune had walked on, there might be enough sand left so he'd never be exposed. My secret was buried for a long time, maybe forever. Time enough to figure things out.

We completed our climb up from the river valley and leveled off onto the shelf of prairie beyond it. The car bounced when we crossed the railroad tracks, where the watermelon truck had failed to stop that time so Danny could jump off. On our right, the grass and brush had overgrown the ruts of the Jones and Plummer trail, wider than a modern freeway, an endless ribbon indented into the landscape by the prodding hooves of longhorns on their way to Abilene, and later Dodge; and by the wagons of the buffalo hunters making the first ruts; and by the freighters bringing in supplies to the ranchers and hauling away the bones, all that was left of five million buffalo that had lived in the Cimarron basin, all that was left of the Kiowa, the Cheyenne, and the Comanche, whose way of life had been destroyed by the white eyes' need for buffalo robes. Then the desperadoes, the last of Quantrill's men, the James boys and the Daltons used the trail to elude authorities who reined up their posses at the border, no lawful jurisdiction in no-man's-land. Law in the Panhandle had been left to the vigilantes.

The last people who traveled the old trail through Cimarron were the family-minded sodbusters who paid a terrible price in hardship to own part of the American dream. Among them, Arved Boone's family, Danny's grandparents who drowned in the flooding river less than a mile from where Danny died.

"It's strange you've never told me what you're thinking of doing as a profession," my father said.

"You've never asked me."

"Well, I'm asking."

"I'm going to be a soldier."

"I know, at least for a while. But just because you're going to West Point doesn't mean you'll always be a soldier. They can qualify you for a long list of jobs."

"I think I might want to be a coach," I said.

He was surprised.

"Do you think coaches have to do things like Lipscomb and Cannonball?"

"I don't know," he answered. "They get results." We rode on for a while through the grasslands. The landscape was pretty much the same until we got near the Kansas border, where some farmland began to appear.

"If you don't like the army, you can always come back home and enroll at Southwestern or some college closer," my father said when we were halfway to Liberal. "You haven't signed your life away, you know. You can learn to be a coach at another school." There was a long pause. "I'm sure you can handle the book work, but the physical training will be tough. Don't for a minute think it won't." The miles of grassland, interrupted here and there with wheat stubble and fields of ripening red maize, rolled by.

I tightened my grip on a small drawstring sack I carried that contained my soldiers. "I'll make it," I said. "I'm tougher than you think. I won't be back."

"I'm glad you're going even without Danny."

"No reason not to."

"No, even your mother seems to have adjusted to the idea now. You'll write to her, won't you? Assure her you're not an infidel?" He laughed. He seemed a little nervous. "She's always had this idea about you."

I knew we were close to something, almost aware where this would lead.

"What I mean is, she felt God planned to use you, sort of like a modern messiah, or maybe more like Moses. I always blamed Doc for getting the idea started in her head. When you were born, he was the one who pointed it out and made a fuss over it. And you know how she is, once she gets something in her mind."

"Pointed what out?"

He was mildly surprised at the question. "That you had no foreskin. She never told you about this? She was always bringing it up to me. She thought it had religious meaning, the son of Abraham, she believed. She thought it was a miracle, that you'd been chosen for some special mission. I tried to tell her it was just a physical thing, like being born with a clubfoot, but she never listened to me, at least on religion."

Terrible grief struck. My response came from the deepest roots of my unconscious, from a burden that was weighing me down.

"Will you take care of Dovie, make sure she's getting along?" A startled expression flickered across my father's face. I now believed for sure Dovie's baby was my son, born without a foreskin as I had been. Doc had pointed it out to Dovie, just like he had pointed it out to my mother, so Doc knew who the father was.

"Yes, of course, I'll take care of her." He paused, reached over and placed his hand on my knee. I did not want to listen, but I had to hear. "Please understand how things have been with your mother all these years . . ."

What I think is unthinkable.

"How did you know about us?" he asked.

My mind had refused to entertain such thoughts, not on the trip to Norman when we picked up Dovie, who was hitchhiking, not during the months I had visited her following the victory parade, not at the times my mother had accused him of being unfaithful. It did not seem to be possible.

The fields undulated by my window, the pale colors of the grassland contrasting to the reddish brown of the maize. There was that deep, vague, rich ache I had felt before, coupled with a sense of exhilaration. I could see my father with Dovie as if I were standing again in the darkness outside her window, his shirt and suit hanging neatly on a hanger over the knob of her bedroom door. She was nothing like the other women of Cimarron where the harsh life beat them down into smooth, flowing compliance. I began to shake as if I had chills.

"How did you know about us?" my father repeated. "I don't think anyone else in town knows, we've been very discreet. I never thought I would have another son," he said.

I still didn't answer his question. He waited.

"I'm the water boy," I finally said.

Outside the car, the sky was immaculate, not a cloud in sight. But I could not stifle the tangled pain. It reached into the very deepest parts of me, my flesh, my bones, every fibrous tissue, every cell. I felt a tremendous urge to unburden, a reservoir spilling over from accumulated storms. I almost told him everything, about what happened to Killer, and Harley, and Riccio, the sheriff, the coaches, Elberta, and the Tendals, everything a water boy knows; that he couldn't be so sure Dovie's baby was his son, the little boy could be his grandson.

Instead, my grip again tightened on the small sack, only twenty-two soldiers in it, the sentinel left on my dresser at home to watch what remained of a life that was slipping away.

"Well, if you come home, things will be the same," he said. "We'll keep your room set up."

Anguish, mixed with some affection, drove back my urge to unburden. He was right, that's all I wanted. If I came back, I wanted everything to be the same.

"You don't have to wait," I told my father at the airport. "You have plenty to do."

"Well, I know your mother would want me to stay and see you off, but there are a couple of things I could catch up on." He shook my hand again, then looked down at his feet. His shoes were dusty. "Let us know if you need anything," he said, and once more he shook my hand. "Say hello to all those soldiers," he said. A smile wreathed his handsome but aging face.

I held up the sack. "You mean these?"

He laughed, and shook his head as if amused, then he walked away. I stood alone in the airport, really just a single runway and a small hangar with an office in one corner, watching him take off his suit coat, and hang it over the back seat. Before he got in, he took his handkerchief out of his pocket and wiped the dust off his shoes.

Gary Reiswig was born in Texas, grew up in Oklahoma, and has lived in South Dakota, Illinois, Indiana, Pennsylvania, and New York. He has been a farmer, preacher, community health worker, day care administrator, university professor, city planner, and innkeeper. He lives in East Hampton, New York, with his wife, Rita, son, Jesse, and dogs, Amos and Ashley. He is at work on two new novels and is host of a radio show, "Speaking of Writers," on station WEHM. *Water Boy* is his first book.